ACCLAIM FOR
A Good Man

"The interplay between love triangle and historical drama, both fraught with uncertainty . . . gives the novel its sense of depth and complexity."   – *National Post*

"*A Good Man* is a rollicking story as large as the prairie is wide. . . . The story unfolds with consistent charm and erudition."
                                                          – *Quill & Quire*

"Guy Vanderhaeghe is a rare combination of good storyteller, vivid historian and skilled writer, and [*A Good Man*] may be his best to date. . . . A splendid story."   – *Calgary Sun*

"Hugely readable, a historical Canadian novel offering a continuation of the sheer enjoyment that came with *The Englishman's Boy*. . . . And to mimic the last words of the novel, it is 'Joy. Nothing but pure joy.'"   – *The Sun Times* (Owen Sound)

"Stunning. . . . In its melding of character, plot, and history, *A Good Man* is an extraordinary novel, unquestionably the trilogy's crowning achievement."   – *Salon.com*

"A sprawling Western, in just the way that some of Cormac McCarthy's novels are Westerns. . . . Sharply observed and rich in period details . . . utterly believable. . . . Entertaining and thoroughly well-written."   – *Kirkus Reviews*

GUY VANDERHAEGHE

A Good Man

EMBLEM
McClelland & Stewart

Cloth edition published 2011
Emblem edition published 2012

Emblem is an imprint of McClelland & Stewart Ltd.
Emblem and colophon are registered trademarks of McClelland & Stewart Ltd.

Library and Archives Canada Cataloguing in Publication

Vanderhaeghe, Guy, 1951–
A good man / Guy Vanderhaeghe.

ISBN 978-0-7710-8608-3

I. Title.

PS8593.A5386G66 2011   C813'.54   C2011-902101-3

We acknowledge the financial support of the Government of Canada through the Book Publishing Industry Development Program and that of the Government of Ontario through the Ontario Media Development Corporation's Ontario Book Initiative. We further acknowledge the support of the Canada Council for the Arts and the Ontario Arts Council for our publishing program.

Although a number of historical figures appear in this novel many of their actions have been invented and their motivations for others purely imagined. The rest of the characters are entirely fictional and any resemblance to persons living or dead is purely coincidental. This is a work of fiction, not history.

Printed and bound in the United States of America

McClelland & Stewart Ltd.
75 Sherbourne Street
Toronto, Ontario
M5A 2P9
www.mcclelland.com

I   2   3   4   5   16   15   14   13   12

To Margaret,
For everything.

A
Good Man

ONE

July 25, 1876

THOUGHTS OF MOTHER early this evening. She came back to me complete, the memory like a fist slammed to the heart. Father always called her "the dragon without scales" to diminish her, but he was like the wolf blowing on the brick house of the third little pig. She did not tumble or collapse under his scorn, not once. Even when he chose the little maid from Quebec, Solange, over her and decided to live as man and wife with his skivvy in the house in Ottawa, Mother maintained what Father mockingly described as her irrepressible dignity. That phrase was never a joke to me; her dignity was real, hard as diamonds. When she decamped to Toronto, it was not because she was fleeing scandal and sympathetic glances as everyone in Ottawa assumed, but because Toronto was where she was born, where she grew up, where she was wooed and won by the man whom the papers always identify as "the lumber baron, Mr. Edwin Case," a man who, prosperous as he was even in those days, would never be rich enough for her parents to overlook his rough and ready ways, to forgive him for snatching her up and carrying her off. Philomena Case, née Edwards, simply marched back home, head held high, and sunk her roots back down in the flinty soil of her family.

Grandmother Edwards was long dead by then. Grandfather lasted two more years after Mother's marriage fell apart. Grandfather Edwards did not trust the man who had disgraced his daughter to continue making payments to her once his father-in-law's watchful eye closed on the scene. Which means he did not know Edwin Case, who, tenuous as his sense of honour is, is still capable of twinges of bad conscience. Grandfather left Mother the old house in Toronto and a tidy sum to ensure she would be provided for until the end of her days.

The memory of the end of her days is what reared up its head and laid its basilisk eyes on me tonight. In the weeks before she confessed to me her foreboding of death, I noticed nothing except that she seemed a little pale, a little tired, but whenever I dared an observation on her health she said it was nothing but the oppressive summer heat. When the leaves changed, so would she. Or so she claimed.

Then came the afternoon I found her in her bedroom on the second floor, sitting by the open window, flicking bread crumbs to the birds on the lawn below. Nothing unusual in that, it was a daily ritual, but she happened to be wearing an old evening gown, and that was more than strange. Poor Mother. I once overhead a friend of hers say, "Philomena is the only woman who can wear a silk dress and leave the impression it is a hair shirt." Perhaps putting on that dress was a signal to me of who she was, a lady long on character, short on style. Mother knew herself.

She held up a cheek to me and I brushed it with my lips. A woman chary of displays of physical affection, but this much was permitted. I stood at her side, watching the mob of sparrows quarrelling over the dry crumbs, hopping about, flapping their wings, pecking at one another.

"Greedy beggars," I said.

"The pot calling the kettle black. You, constantly dunning your father for money," she said, but fondly. She pointed to the dressing table. "I have something for you there. Please bring it over."

I crossed the room. The item lay beside Father's wedding gift to Mother, the silver comb and brush that he had had proprietarily engraved with *P.C.*, the initials of the new name he had bestowed upon her. Mother's present to me also had initials stamped on its red morocco cover: *W.C.* For the first time, I held the little book whose blank pages would chastise me for a decade. I christen them tonight with Mr. Turncliffe's ink.

"For your birthday," Mother explained.

"It doesn't speak very well of me when my own mother can't recall the date of her only child's arrival in the world. My birthday's three months off."

There was no smile. "Sit down, Wesley," she said.

"You are being very mysterious. Why are you in that dress? Are you going out tonight?"

"No, I am not." She paused. "I give you this today because in three months it may not be possible."

It was second nature for her to veil her feelings. She had raised me to do the same, but my hands began to tremble. I recalled Dr. Cowan had paid her a visit the day before. My voice faltered. "What is it? What has that old quack said to you?"

Her answer was no more emotional than it would have been if she were reporting gardener O'Reilly's opinion on the condition of this year's tea roses. "It was not what Dr. Cowan said, but rather the manner in which he said it. He prescribed rest. That is the cure-all for what ails you when what ails you cannot be cured." She looked down at the sparrows. "If your father were here, Dr. Cowan would have given him the diagnosis. With me, he thinks, Frailty, thy name is woman, and says nothing. I expect that you will soon be called to his consulting rooms and given the news. I thought you deserved a warning." She hesitated. "Whatever he tells you, don't keep it from me."

My wits and tongue betrayed me. All I could offer was stumbling, anodyne drivel.

She turned from the window and threw me a look of warning. No cheerfully silly words. Keep them to yourself. I neither

3

want nor require them. The late-afternoon sun was full in the window behind her, shaping her dark and solid in my eyes. But at the edges of Mother's silhouette, the streaming sunlight flared in her hair, glinted off her shoulders. She was sculpted by shafts of light, chiselled by radiance.

Mother would frown at that description. Tall for a woman, long-legged and long-armed, she towered over Father. It embarrassed him, her height. And then she was saddled with what she wryly referred to as "the fleshly embodiment of the Edwards' family motto – 'first before all,'" a nose so salient it entered rooms well in advance of the rest of her. She thought of herself as homely, but in that moment, in my eyes, she trumped beautiful.

A mirror shows traces of Mother to me. My height, my gangly arms and legs, my own prominent beak, my own "first before all." What I wish most to see is some evidence of her strength wink back at me, but that is one quality a pier glass can't reflect. When I returned from the consultation with Dr. Cowan I tried to feign strength. With counterfeit stoicism I repeated his words: Tumour in the lower bowel. Unquestionably malignant. Unquestionably inoperable.

Mother only nodded and said, "Thank you." For the first time in my life I heard her sounding frail and lost. It set me off, my shoulders heaved.

"My dear boy, so much like his father," she whispered, half to herself, half to me. An observation that continues to bewilder me. I have inherited nothing from the Baron but his temper. But perhaps seeing me weep reminded her of some scene that occurred behind closed doors back in the days when matters came to a head over the maid Solange. Had Father stood before her, tears spilling down his face, as I did then? Had he too realized what he was losing? Unlikely. If Father cried, it was because he could not have his cake and eat it too.

I see I have walked out before the horse. I must backtrack to the moment Mother gave me this book, a moment when I could still dismiss her premonition of death, a moment when she glowed in her old-fashioned evening gown, and she said, eyes flitting between the squabbling sparrows and me, "I have a confession to make. You may think it insignificant, but I assure you it is not." She pointed to the journal resting on my knees. "When I turned fourteen, your grandmother gave me a diary such as that, and it has had a great effect on me. I have kept it faithfully." She pondered a moment, lips tucked in thought. "No, I must be exact. When I say I have kept it faithfully, I do not mean to imply I write an entry each and every day. That has always struck me as far too self-regarding. But each year, on my birthday, I draw up a summation of my character. Where I have failed, where I have succeeded. I recommend the practice to you. It need be no more than a few lines, but they must be unsparingly honest, which means you must bear witness to all your qualities – both good and bad. The mind has a way of making a detour around uncomfortable truths unless it is forced to focus on them. And putting something down in ink – well, I think it concentrates the mind wonderfully – like the prospect of hanging," she said. "And ink has another advantage. It is permanent. It does not permit you to escape it or yourself, as long as every now and then you make a point to review what you have written. Any time I choose to I can compare the girl of fourteen with the woman I have become."

I felt I knew what she was alluding to, felt Mother was making reference to the sooty cloud of trouble that had hung over my head for nearly a year. Just a month before, Alice had broken our engagement. The statement Alice's father had forced me to sign, which declared his daughter blameless in our suddenly interrupted march to the altar, laying all fault with me – this was common knowledge in Mother's circle. My erstwhile fiancée had ensured that by circulating her father's idiotic document among all her friends, beginning with the bridesmaids. And that document, onto which I had contemptuously scratched an angry signature, had bolstered suppositions about my bad conduct at the Battle of Ridgeway. Mother was certainly aware of such gossip. That I had failed to do my duty was dinner-party talk among all the "better people" of Toronto. Nevertheless, it was only talk; my name had never appeared in the newspapers; I was not subject to the sort of public finger-pointing that pursued Lieutenants Colonel Booker and Dennison and led them to demand military courts of inquiry to examine the accusations of incompetence and cowardice made against them in the press. As could have been predicted, they had been exonerated because key witnesses were not called. But if the big fish had escaped, there were still minnows such as me darting about in the muddy waters of the disgraceful affair, ready to be scooped up in the persistent journalists' sieves.

Fearing she might touch upon the rumours surrounding me, which she had so far always studiously avoided, I hurried to deflect her. "And have you changed? Are you a different person now than you were when you were fourteen?"

Her brow furrowed. "Changed? On the whole I should think not, but I have always wished to recognize things."

"Recognize what things?"

"When I was fourteen, I drew up two columns, entitled Greatest Weaknesses, Greatest Strengths. Under Greatest Weaknesses, I wrote, 'I want too much.' Under Greatest Strengths, I wrote, 'I want too much.'"

That was unexpected and intriguing. "And what was it you wanted?"

"I didn't know. I still don't know. But you, Wesley, don't even realize that wanting is a possibility."

Mother gave me this journal when I was nearly twenty-four and all at sea, my ship going down under me. I have carried it with me for ten years and, until tonight, never set down a single word in it. Now I cannot seem to stop scribbling. Why? Is it because I will soon risk the money Mother left me, try to amend my stumbling life, and I dread the prospect of failure? Does some part of me wonder that the urge to defy Father makes me rash? Or am I uneasy that the past is yet to present its bill and demand payment? At any rate, unlike Mother, I seem unable to sum myself up in a few lines, look at myself directly as that fourteen-year-old girl was capable of doing.

Hours after the memory of Mother visited me, I put this journal, Father's most recent letter, a stub of candle, and a box of lucifers in my pockets and trudged up the knoll to the Métis grave-yard. By the derelict wooden crosses that stand askew as if shoul-dered aside by Death in a hurry, I sank down on a boulder to think. The heat of the day was still stored in the stone. I fondled its pelt of rough lichen while the acrid odour of timber burning far away to the south in Montana Territory stung my nostrils.

I gazed down solemnly at what I will soon say goodbye to, the fort, whitewashed palisades glaring in the twilight. A sprinkling of lights several hundred yards north of it marks the tiny settle-ment, which sprang up overnight, watered by a generous shower of Mounted Police dollars. The Billiard Emporium, the mercan-tiles of T.C. Power and I.G. Baker, the laundry shack of the black washerwomen, Molly, Annie, and Jess, who scrub my shirts and unmentionables, Claggett's bedbug-infested lodging house, the cabins and soddies of Indian traders, Métis carters, wolfers, and hide hunters.

Night sounds all about me, the quavering, desolate howling of coyotes punctuated by a high-pitched yipping and yapping, the persistent ratcheting of a cricket, the furtive scurrying and rustling of mice in the parched grass. Overhead, the moon, a fingernail paring hemmed by stars that smouldered weakly through the haze spread by forest fires hundreds of miles to the south, but which, here and there, by an optical trick of the same smoke-thickened air, pulsed like banked coals, red, glowing.

I took Father's letter out, lit my candle, and scanned the words that bobbed about on the page in the trembling light, the most spiteful passages which I now take the trouble to reproduce here.

So what have you done, but sit on the cheeks of your bloody arse, your hands pinned beneath them? I tell you that you have squandered yet another opportunity – first the law, come to nothing – playing at journalist, a penny-a-word scribbler! but did I stand in your way, God forbid? and that thrown up too – then, apprenticing yourself to an architect, you, who couldn't draw a shithouse with a ruler. Finally, for once, you took my advice and agreed to enter the North-West Mounted Police. I thought, an active life, fresh air, etc. might clear you of the doldrums. And what do you do? You refuse to accept a commission. You, who had experience of command; who had been a captain of the militia. But no, you preferred to scrape by as an underling, as a mere sub-constable. To wrap yourself in martyrdom like your mother. Do you know what that signals to the world? That you are either an idiot, or so frivolous and irresponsible that you couldn't escort an old woman across a street without leading her under the wheels of a wagon. You have no idea of the high regard in which the public and press holds the Police here in the East, none whatsoever. And if you had deigned, I say deigned to accept a commission, and kept your snotty nose clean, you would have returned home covered in glory. Nothing clears scandal out of people's minds like success. And scandal is what you created by virtue of your shameful last act of military service.

And then the Baron struggles for a more conciliatory tone, and becomes simply offensive.

All right, what's past is past. I have spoken to a few people, and smoothed your way back into civilian life. I have succeeded in buying out the last year of your term of enlistment in the Police. As of July 31st your obligations to the force are legally fulfilled – at considerable cost to me. The question remains as to what is to be done with you. I have spoken to Sir John A. Macdonald about the possibility of finding a safe riding for you. He did not commit – unlike you, he looks before he leaps – but he left the impression your candidacy is not out of the question, which is his way of saying he wants to hear the ring of gold in the bottom of the party bucket. I will oblige him by producing that sound. All signs point to an election within the year so you must get back here to Ottawa, reacquaint yourself with and make yourself pleasant to the men who count. You are university educated, you can turn a phrase, you are more intelligent than your actions testify to, and I shall provide all necessary funds for a campaign. A seat in the House is yours for the asking. If you apply yourself, in a few years you might find your lazy bum on the Front Bench. Let me emphasize, my friends will be your friends if you offer them your hand. Return home and we will begin to sort all this out. I anticipate you at the earliest possible date. There is no time to lose.

Since I could not take him by the shoulders, shake him, shout, "Let me be!" I blew out the candle, consigning Father and his blather to the shadows. It is the place for him; he is a shady man. So why do I take the trouble to copy choice selections of his tirade into this journal? Because at some future date I shall surely wish to relive my triumph over the Baron. He may puff himself up for unlocking my cell door, assume that I will meekly do his bidding, fulfill his defeated ambitions by becoming his parliamentary proxy, but if he thinks that will happen, he has another think coming. In the two months since this letter arrived I have had plenty of time to make my own plans, to prepare to roll the dice and become a rancher. A chancy business, but I have enlisted Joe McMullen to help me bring it to fruition. So to hell with Father. The struggle between his higher organ, which prompted him towards the world of politics, and his lower organ, which urged him towards Solange, was settled long ago. His lower organ won. Let him live with the consequences of it.

Certainly he could not have foreseen the present situation when he decided my future and delivered it to me in this damnable letter. But by now he surely has realized that by springing me from the Police before my term of service has run out, he has inadvertently rubbed more dirt on the family name. Everyone will assume that this was done to save my topknot from the Sioux. As long as three weeks ago, when a civilian dispatch rider for the U.S. Army brought us the report of Custer's defeat, I understood that this would be how my early exit from the Police would appear, a coward scampering out of danger.

The courier had few details of exactly what had occurred at the Little Bighorn and what the consequences of it would be, except to say that deliveries of mail and supplies from Fort Benton to Fort Walsh were suspended until the Sioux threat passed. Deliveries have not yet resumed. Which means that no message from Father can reach me. I am certain that out there somewhere, a letter penned by him is held captive in a mailbag, a letter that pleads with me to immediately re-enlist, that reminds me how useful that act would be in future political campaigns. Wesley Case out on the stump, parading himself as the man who rallied around the flag in his country's hour of need.

When Major Walsh galloped back to the fort on a lathered horse a few days ago, completing the last stage of a mad dash across the continent that carried him from Hot Springs, Arkansas, to Ottawa, then on to Fort Benton, he immediately assembled the men to address them. Unfortunately, he did little more than confirm that Custer and the troop he had personally led into battle at Little Bighorn had, in fact, been utterly annihilated. Walsh related this calmly, as if to leave the impression that he gave us the whole truth and nothing but the truth. His quiet authority did a good deal to steady the men. But I found his silence about where the Sioux were, or what steps the Americans had taken to pursue them, a significant omission.

As Father is fond of saying, connections are the harness that pulls your wagon. I did not hesitate to use them to my advantage with Major Walsh. I may be a lowly sub-constable now, but he has not forgotten the time we spent together training at the School of Cavalry in Kingston. The Major believes he owes me some consideration as a former colleague; my request for a few words with him was not refused. When we met, I tried to leave the impression that I had come simply to inquire after his health and to remind him that my term of service expires at the end of the month. But the Major, clearly preoccupied with weightier matters than my departure from the Police, only acknowledged my imminent return to civilian life with a brusque hitch of the shoulders.

Then I went to work to find out what he had avoided saying at the assembly. After all, what happens in Montana has a bearing on my future. If one prods Walsh gently, circumspectly, he opens up. Soon he was giving me the substance of a brief meeting he had had with Major Ilges, commandant of the Fort Benton Army detachment. Ilges confided to him that rumours of what the troops sent to recover the corpses at the Little Bighorn had seen are circulating throughout every Army post in the West. Bodies stripped of every stitch of clothing and left to bloat in the sun. Faces pounded to mush with stone hammers. Corpses quilled with arrows. Private parts lopped off and stuffed in mouths. One of the officers of the 7th Cavalry, who sported a magnificent set of sidewhiskers, had his cheeks cut off to decorate a scalp shirt. Now, Ilges says, every man in the Army with a pair of Burnsides is in a panic to shave them off. He intimated to Walsh that these reports of atrocities have demoralized the rank and file to an extraordinary degree. Nightmare has walked out into the daylight. The shock given to the generals' systems by the Sioux victory appears to have induced paralysis in the high command. It is all dithering and hand-wringing at the top. Few steps are being taken to see that the Sioux are swiftly dealt with.

If there is paralysis in the Army, the rest of the country is having a fit of hysterics. That much is evident from the stack of newspapers that Walsh collected hurtling his way to Fort Benton and which he passed on to me before I left his office.

What a farrago of lunacy they contain. Glowing approval for schoolboys in Custer's hometown, who laid their hands on their McGuffey's Readers and swore a solemn oath to make short work of Sitting Bull if he ever crosses their paths. Praise for the showman Buffalo Bill, who portentously announced that he was abandoning his Wild West Show tour because his country requires his services in the wilds of Montana. Ludicrous claims that Sitting Bull is no Indian at all, but a dark-skinned former West Point cadet expelled from the academy, who, nursing an implacable hatred for the Army, has made common cause with the Sioux and is ready to vengefully employ his knowledge of military science against his former colleagues. There can be no other explanation for Custer's whipping than that he received it at the hands of a white man. The buck-naked, dirt-worshipping polygamist savages that the newspaper scribes denounce could not have dealt him such a blow.

And if this renegade is not to blame, others are plainly culpable. The Army is crammed with bummers, drunks, the dregs of the slums, foreigners. The Indian Department is a nest of pacifist, mollycoddling Quakers who teach the Indian one thing and one thing only: contempt for the weakness of the white man. Cleanse the Augean stables, the journalists cry, sweep them clean, clear this stink from the public's nostrils.

Adding to the hysteria is the timing of the defeat. News of the disaster at the Little Bighorn reached the Eastern Seaboard shortly after July 4, and not just any ordinary July 4 but the grand celebration of the hundredth anniversary of the founding of the Republic. A country feeling its oats, flexing its muscles, vigorous and rich, cocksure and confident, has seen the impossible happen, the unthinkable become fact. Sitting Bull has spoiled their glorious Centennial, pissed on Custer's golden head, the head of a genuine Civil War hero, the head of someone who has recently been touted as a future President of the United States. Somehow a wedding and a funeral got booked for the same hour in the same church. The joy of the Centennial, the joy of the great Exposition in Philadelphia, is drowned in a wave of gloom.

But after a little reflection I realized that I had witnessed this madness before. Papers are papers, I suppose. I remember the days when the tone of our own respectable Canadian journals was every bit as frantic. The savage stalking the land then was the dipsomaniacal, ring-kissing, bony-shanked bogtrotter. Beware, the Irish Republican Army is massing on our border, a tribe of drunken pillagers and arsonists. Take heed, the secret society of Fenians in our midst is readying a massacre of Protestants that will make the gutters of Toronto and Montreal run with blood. The Irish in our customs service are passing on shipments of contraband arms and ammunition to their co-conspirators. Priests are turning their churches into weapons depots; the sacristies are heaped with revolvers, rifles, and pikes. Come St. Patrick's Day, Catholic graves will be opened and weapons retrieved from coffins for a dreadful day of murder and destruction; the countryside will be lit with burning barns and granaries.

A particle of truth feeds any panic. When I learned of D'Arcy McGee's death at the hands of a Fenian gunman on Sparks Street, a byway so familiar to me that I could feel the cobblestones through the soles of my shoes as I read the column announcing his demise, the word *peril* became real for me. And the invaders did come. I fought them. The bright brass IRA button of that young dead soldier still burns in my eyes. But for the rest, the nefarious priests, the plotting Irish hod-carriers? Ghosts of our invention, steam rising from overheated imaginations. Run a bayonet through steam, it passes blindly through a fog. Any flesh it strikes is likely to be innocent, any damage done, done to a bystander.

And while sitting in the graveyard on the hill, surrounded by revenants and wraiths, moodily gouging the sandy soil with the toe of my boot, another ghostly presence intruded. I sensed a stirring, a flickering against the trees on the hillside to my right.

It froze me on my boulder; I strained to make it out. A trembling cloud of midges, a vague form drifting out of the forest shadows, swimming into the meagre moonlight, bit by bit knitting itself into a horse and rider.

A Sioux wolf, a scout? A horseshoe clinked against a stone, and I knew then whoever the man was, he was white. Another five-hundred-dollar-a-day dispatch rider bringing a warning from Fort Benton? Feeling my presence, the horse halted. Its startled whinny roused the man dozing in the saddle. Peering blindly up into the darkness, he called out, "Who's there?"

There was a querulous confidence in his voice. The cemetery hill shielded Fort Walsh from his view so he had no reason to assume he was addressing a white man. I shouted down to him, "No need for alarm! I am with the Police!" and got to my feet to show myself.

There was no reply; he simply sat gazing up at me, immobile as an equestrian statue planted in a town square. I relit my candle and held it aloft to reveal myself. The night so calm the flame stood up like an exclamation mark.

Horse and rider crossed to the foot of the hill and began to leisurely negotiate the clumps of cactus and scrubby juniper that scatter the slope. Guided by my tiny beacon, the rider took his own sweet time, keeping me foolishly standing there. At last he jerked his horse to a stop before me, offered no word of greeting or acknowledgement, and again sat looking at me. The candle carved a closet of illumination, a space of uncomfortable intimacy out of the night. He remained absolutely still, lips frozen in a queer, dismissive smile. His dress was as odd as his manner. Nothing suitable for rough travel, a black derby squared on his head, a black frock coat, black trousers, a soiled white shirt, an equally filthy celluloid collar. A bank clerk cruising the wilds. But the body stuffed into those clothes was not the body of a pen driver; it was a block of solid flesh hammered into the notch of the saddle. Face cut square, jaw nearly as wide as the broad forehead, small, neat ears laid flat to the temples as if pinned there by tacks. The eyes, almost colourless, pale as rainwater in a pan, flat, depthless.

"My name is Case. Constable Wesley Case," I said. His eyes slid away, a furtive movement, as if the name had pushed them off me and turned them to the whitewashed walls of the fort. Stupidly, I said, "You are at Fort Walsh."

His head swivelled back to me. The mute found his voice and it was unequivocally rude. "Is Major Walsh back?"

"He returned several days ago. Do you bring a message to him?"

"Why would I have a message for Walsh?"

"Because most men with a scrap of common sense know better than to go traipsing about in the wilds putting their hair on offer to any Sioux warrior who happens along," I said, irritably. "I presumed only important business would bring you here. And that would be business with Walsh."

"Looking for a man name of Gobbler Johnson is my business. You know a fellow called Gobbler Johnson?"

"The name means nothing to me."

"Well, maybe he found it convenient to trade that name for another. But he can't lose a turnip-size goitre." A huge fist went up, pressed itself to his throat. "That ring a bell?"

"No."

He shifted his weight in the saddle, causing the leather to gasp a complaint. "I guess I'll have a look-see round here. Turn a few rocks over, see what's under them."

"If you're looking to make trouble with this Gobbler Johnson – think twice. Major Walsh knows how to deal with mischief-makers. Fair warning," I said.

"Fair warning," he repeated. "Don't concern yourself on account of me. I'm mild as milk."

"Maybe, but give me your name. For Walsh."

"That's very policeman-like of you." He ran his pale eyes up and down me. Then he said, "Michael Anthony Sebastian Dunne." He pointed to the journal that hung forgotten in my hand. "Last name ends in an *e*. Maybe you'd like to write it down for the Major."

"I'll remember." I blew out the candle and went to step around his horse. Dunne pulled his foot from the stirrup and thrust out his leg, barring my way.

"Put your damn leg down," I said.

He eased his boot back into the stirrup. "I do hope Major Walsh found relief for the St. Anthony's fire in those hot springs down in Arkansas. I hear it's a most plaguing condition. What he's facing, he'll need to be fit as a fiddle."

"The state of his erysipelas is no concern of yours."

"Sundays we pray for the health of the Queen. And Walsh is as good as a prince in these parts. Ain't it natural to ask?"

I tapped the insignia of rank on my sleeve. "Walsh does not confide personal information to a mere sub-constable."

"Oh, I don't think you're no mere constable, Wesley Case. Far from it."

His impudence was irksome. "Do you pretend to know me, sir?" I said.

Dunne looked past me down to the settlement's wan lights. He remarked, "Somebody in Fort Benton give me the name of a fellow who rents beds hereabouts. It just went and lost itself. Maybe you know it."

"Claggett," I said.

He nodded. "That's it."

"I put you a question, Dunne. I want an answer. Do you pretend to know me?"

Gravely, he shook his head from side to side. It was like watching a boulder teeter. "No, I don't know you from Adam," he replied, giving a twitch to the reins. His horse gave a crow hop of surprise, brushed my shoulder with its flank, and broke into a shambling trot. I watched Dunne roll down the hill, broad shoulders tossing about like the gunwales of a barge in a heavy sea. Then horse and rider dissolved back into the liquid blackness from which they had emerged.

Midnight has come and gone hours ago. I have missed lights out and there will be hell to pay for it. Sergeant Major Francis will have me back on punishment detail. A small price to pay for a night of privacy. I write at a table in the back of the Billiard Emporium, which Mr. Halston Turncliffe has frugally outfitted with Fort Benton castoffs, two pool tables with cracked slate beds, and cues crooked as a dog's hind leg. At my back are three shelves of tattered books and newspapers. For a one-penny fee, two-month-old copies of the *Illustrated London News*, and slightly newer editions of the *Minnesota Pioneer*, can be rented. For books, Mr. Turncliffe charges a nickel a day: blood-and-thunders that offer a corpse every chapter, higher literature for the higher minded, a spine-cracked, dog-eared miscellany that includes Carlyle's *History of the French Revolution*, the collected works of Sir Walter Scott (minus *Rob Roy*, *Ivanhoe*, and *Old Mortality*), and seven or eight Dickens novels.

Tonight, I play scholar in the Bodleian of the Cypress Hills. About eleven, when the last of the billiard players left, Mr. Turncliffe threatened to evict me, but relented and provided me with a coal-oil lamp and pen and ink when I waved two bits under his nose, enough to send him happy to his bed in the backroom.

"You might think of keeping notes," I remember Father saying to me at the Ottawa train station when he sent me off to the Police. We were wrapped in a cloud of locomotive smoke and cinders. "Adventures in the West and so on. More than one man has done well from a thing like that. It could get your name about, even if it's only a pamphlet for distribution on the hustings. Something patriotic, with mustard in it. That would set you apart from the average pol."

Both parents demanding I produce an account of my life. One, so I might find myself. The other, so I might find fame, the brightest currency in politics. Mother suggested a few lines; Father a pamphlet. Now that I have begun to spill, I wonder where it will stop.

TWO

WALSH'S RECENT RETURN has put B Troop on its mettle. By night, the men diligently thumb the *Regulations for the Instruction, Formations and Movements of the Cavalry* and the *Instructions for the Sword, Carbine, Pistol, and Lance Exercise*; by day, they execute the prescribed drills under the watchful eye of officers. The Major wants them ready to fight. Today, as midday approaches, two seven-pound mountain cannons and their gun teams wait for the artillery instructor Standish's command to go into action. The horses stamp, toss their heads, lash their tails, their trace chains jingling. Standish bellows, the drivers whistle, slap reins down hard on rumps, the guns surge forward, wheel spokes blurring, dust boiling, caissons bouncing, cannon barrels wagging as Standish roars above the din, "Look lively, you damned unwashed limbs of Satan! Turn them bloody horses! Bring them guns about, hard!" The gun carriages cut a savage arc, the barrels swinging round on target, a distant hill beyond the thin silver thread of Battle Creek. The drivers haul back on reins, the caissons skid to a stop, gunners scramble down from the boxes to unhook and sight the artillery. But they do not fire. Ammunition is in short supply. Every precious round is being held in reserve because it may be needed if the Sioux come.

The drumming of hooves, the clatter of gun carriages ended, a long-drawn-out cry of "Timber!" is heard from a nearby hill, followed by a resounding crash, a fusillade of cracking and popping branches. Chaff and dust puff from the trees like breath on a winter morning. A black murder of crows hoarsely caws, scolding the wood gang threatening their nests.

Case is hard at work just outside the palisades, digging a latrine trench. The Sergeant Major was not satisfied he was suffering enough under his first punishment detail, infirmary duty. At present there are only five bedridden, haphazardly diagnosed by Surgeon Kittson as if he were dealing cards from a deck: one malaria case, three beaver fever, one bloody flux. The infirmary may be hot as an oven and pullulating with bluebottles the size of hummingbirds, but for two days Case had scoured shit-spattered bedpans, changed sweat-soaked sheets, cooled brows, dispensed barley water, beef tea, and the surgeon's favourite specific, Perry Davis Vegetable Pain Killer, with such cheerful alacrity that the Sergeant Major took it as a sign of calculated insubordination. Sergeant Major Francis is British Regular Army, retired from the 13th Light Dragoons, and even Walsh is a little in awe of a veteran of the Charge of the Light Brigade, one of the foolhardy immortalized in verse by Lord Tennyson, a poem so famous that a handful of sub-constables have actually read it. As the men say, even the Sergeant Major's old pecker springs to attention when he salutes.

Francis has harboured a grievance against Case since the day he learned he had refused a commission, an insult to the Queen and the service. So it came as no surprise to the Sergeant Major to learn that Case had managed to get himself bought out of the force, and he means to carve his pound of flesh out of the whingeing coward while he still has time to do it. This morning he pulled Case off orderly duty and put him on hard labour "excavating a sanitary convenience," a latrine trench a dozen yards long and eight feet deep. Case has been warned that if he dawdles or shirks, he will get a week in the lock-up and if that sentence extends beyond the remainder of his term of service, tough titty for him.

Stripped to the waist, Case streams sweat under the yellow glaring eye of the sun. Each swing of the pick bites away a tiny chip of earth; he may as well be digging up a cobbled street. Every half-hour he scrapes up these shards with a spade, flings them up on a mound beside the trench. An iron hoop of pain tightens around his kidneys. He pauses, wipes stinging eyes with a forearm, flexes blistered hands as he watches two officers listlessly knocking a tennis ball back and forth over a drooping net. They play with all the enthusiasm of convicts breaking stones. But Major Walsh, in his youth a celebrated rugby player, cricketer, canoeist, and boxer, is a great man for the games; like Wellington, he believes they prepare men for the battlefield. The Major limed the tennis court himself, and his junior officers know he takes favourable note of those who use it.

Case returns to work. The rhythmic thud of the pick, the whistle of his breath fills his ears. A shadow falls on him, and he looks up to see the Sergeant Major scowling down at him from the lip of the trench, legs planted wide, arms akimbo. "You call that a proper hole?" he barks. "I've known whores with bigger ones than that."

"I daresay you have, Sergeant Major."

"Cheeky bastard and bloody useless besides," says Francis. "An idiot with a teaspoon could have done a neater job of work."

"I'm not in the right frame of mind," says Case. "It distresses me to think that I, the master builder, will soon be long gone from here and never able to witness the joy I've brought to others."

"Not gone yet. You're mine until the thirty-first." Francis crooks a finger. "Get yourself out of there and follow me. Major Walsh wants a word."

Major James Morrow Walsh sits, spurred boot spiked on his gouged office desktop. Trouser leg rolled to his knee, he studies the scrim of rash on his calf. In Hot Springs, the Frenchman, Dr. Dupont, had taken one look at the distinctive eruptions on his limbs and passed judgment. "The *peau d'orange*." That's precisely what this morning's new outbreak looks like, orange rind, shiny and reddish-orange, riddled with tiny pores. Dupont had warned him, "You must remain *tranquille, Monsieur. Toujours tranquille*. Mental disturbances excite the erysipelas." Yesterday, Michael Dunne had gained an audience and disturbed the uneasy balance of his mind, and now he is suffering the consequences, chills, a loss of appetite, fatigue, aching joints.

Lately, it has been impossible to remain *tranquille*: his stay in Hot Springs spoiled by rows with his wife, followed by a dressing-down from the minister of the interior, then Dunne had come wriggling into his brain like a greasy worm.

News of Custer's defeat had reached Hot Springs on July 6. The telegram from Minister Scott ordering him to Ottawa arrived the next day. He had read that as a very good sign, recognition of his accomplishments. After all, he had graduated from Kingston's School of Cavalry with a first-class certificate. He had seen what the Commandant had entered into his official record. "Walsh is the smartest and most efficient officer that has yet passed through the school. He is a good rider and particularly quick and confident at drill. I thoroughly recommend him to the attention of the Adjutant General." Surely this file must have been brought to the attention of Secretary Scott; surely the minister had recognized the cut of his jib and realized that a man with his military skills was best suited to deal with the possibility of a Sioux attack. So without a moment's hesitation, Walsh had fired off his reply in a telegram to the Department of the Interior. "Will depart within 24 hours."

Knowing the storm this decision would cause, he had not consulted Mary in making it. From the moment they and their young daughter had taken up residence in Hot Springs' most stylish and fashionable spa hotel, his wife had launched her campaign to get him out of the North-West Mounted Police.

Mary wanted an ordinary husband, cozily camped in her parlour behind a newspaper, and she immediately went to work to drag him home to Prescott, tamed and in chains. It didn't matter a whit to her that he had proved unsuitable for every other job he had ever had, discharged as a locomotive engineer for "running the rails recklessly," a failure as a mechanic, then his disastrous stint as an irascible hotel manager.

Their trunks were barely unpacked, he was preparing himself to go off to a bathing cabin to take the waters, when she said, "I have spoken to Jenkins and he is willing to give you another chance at running the North American Hotel. Of course, you would be *on trial*, Jimmy darling, but if you would buckle down all would be well. We could resume family life in Prescott and repair your fragile health."

She always called him Jimmy darling when she had a scheme up her sleeve. Turning to her, bath towel slung over his shoulder, he said, "If you think I'll return to that, then you must be mad, Mrs. Walsh. Listening to old spinster ladies complain about drafts, and flies in their water pitchers, grinning docilely at two-bit peddlers of dry goods while they bitch about lumpy mattresses, I'd sooner put a goddamn pistol to my head and scatter my brains over the walls. Never. And do not return to this topic again." That had set off the hysterics, the crying fits, the accusations that all he wanted was to get back to his "copper-skinned sluts." Walsh was susceptible to women and women to Walsh. Mary knew that from her own experience; she had gone to the wedding altar big as a house.

Walsh often muses that if ever there was a skirt he shouldn't have lifted, it was Mary's. And the timing of his marriage couldn't have been more unfortunate because five months after the knot had been tied with his pregnant bride, the militia was called out to put down Louis Riel's insurrection on the Red River. And he had had to stay behind, sand a cradle, and curse his luck. His wife had robbed him of his crack at glory. By God, she wasn't going to do it again.

When he told her he was off for Ottawa, that he was leaving the next day, Mary flung herself down on the bed and sobbed herself into a migraine. A little later, Cora sombrely crept into the room where her father sat with a railway timetable open on his knees, planning his escape route, and tucked her head into his side. As he studied departure and arrival times, he toyed with her curls.

No other child had a fonder papa than Walsh; Cora was his dearest girl, his angel, the light of his life. Each year, a thousand miles from Prescott where his beloved daughter was blowing out her cake candles, Cora's birthday was celebrated in the Cypress Hills. On the wall over her father's chair in the mess hall her name was spelled out in horseshoes. The room was decorated with bunting, paper chains, NWMP pennants, and Union Jacks. B Troop reverently toasted her, and Walsh answered the toast with a rambling, emotional speech that exhaustively catalogued his daughter's peerless virtues. He always ended it with eyes humid and glistening.

Shortly before he left for the train station, little Cora had climbed up on his lap and asked, "Will Mother be better soon?"

"When I am gone, Mother will be right as rain."

Very gravely, Cora said, "I won't be. Stay, Papa."

"That is impossible. You must understand, Cora, it is Papa's work that buys you your bread and butter, your cocoa that you love so much, and your pretty dresses. That is why he must go, to see you happy and content."

From the bed, Mary broke in; she had been feigning sleep. "Liar, liar, liar," she moaned, her voice choked in the pillow. "You care for nobody but yourself."

He rained kisses on his daughter's face, set her on the floor, and closed the door on the whole sorry business. Within the hour he was flying north, racing away from the future his wife had plotted and back to what he was sure he had been born to do. He sat and watched a fiery confetti of locomotive sparks whirl by his window in the darkness. When dawn broke, he counted the telegraph poles flashing by, each one bringing him closer to Ottawa, to his destiny. The burgeoning cornfields, the apple orchards, the fat cattle seemed fertile promises. Washington clattered by, Baltimore, Philadelphia, New York, Montreal, and finally his train chugged into the national capital's train station.

Travelling light as he was, there was no need to pause to find lodging. He strode directly up to Parliament Hill, brown Gladstone bag swinging in his hand. Walsh had never met Secretary Scott, but what he had heard about him didn't impress. By all reports, he was a very queer duck, a vegetarian, a teetotalling, *saintly* Catholic. A nun with a beard. He expected to have his way with him.

But almost immediately things began to go amiss. A snotty clerk was not convinced of the urgency of Walsh's mission; he was curtly told to wait his turn in a queue of shabby-looking office-seekers and petitioners. Two hours later, at last ushered into Secretary Scott's office and introduced, he couldn't restrain himself from acidly remarking to the minister, "That officious little majordomo left me kicking my heels in a corridor half the afternoon."

Scott, a parched, bony-looking fellow with a long white beard hanging down his shirtfront like a bib, slowly raised his eyebrows and said, "I have a great deal of business to get through in the course of a day. People need to be sifted." That said, he opened a file, scanned it. Without preamble he announced, "It is the view of the deputy minister of justice, Mr. Richards, that if the Sioux cross the border it will be somewhere in the vicinity of Wood Mountain. I concur with his evaluation." Walsh could not disagree, but it irked him that this was presented as if it were some astounding revelation. It was not news to him. He had ridden over every inch of that ground, and felt that his opinion should have been solicited. That would only have been polite. He frowned and put a sour pucker to his mouth, but Scott did not notice. "Since you are in charge of the police detachment nearest Wood Mountain, the expectation is that you will be the first representative of the Crown these tribesmen will encounter. That is why I have called you here – to clarify the position adopted by the governments of the Dominion and the United Kingdom in regard to the Sioux." With emphasis he added, "And to give you instructions on implementing the same."

"I am at your service," said Walsh, unable to stifle a half smile. The old stick's pompous self-regard was amusing.

"Indeed you are, sir. Indeed you are." Scott eased himself back in his chair, began to comb his beard with his fingers. For some time, the secretary scrutinized him with an intense gaze that made him feel he was a bug under a magnifying glass. Finally, Scott said, "You will patrol the border – assiduously patrol it, ceaselessly patrol it. If any party of Sioux, no matter how small, crosses into our territory, it is necessary that I be immediately informed by wire. Be exact and detailed in your transmissions. This is of the utmost importance since I am charged with relaying all information to the head of the British legation in Washington. Do you understand?"

"Yes."

"Exactitude is of the utmost importance because the governments of Great Britain, the United States, and the Dominion of Canada have agreed to cooperate fully in managing the Sioux threat." His look was stern. "I regret to say our government has got off to a very bad start with the Americans. They have informed me they suspect us of withholding vital intelligence from them. You, it appears, bear some responsibility for their disgruntlement."

That was a bewildering accusation. Affronted, he said, "Me? What the hell is it I am supposed to have done?"

"It is not what you have done, sir, but what you did not do. Isn't it true that a great gathering of Indians took place in early June in the Cypress Hills, *your* territory – Peigans, Blackfoot, Bloods, Gros Ventres, Crow, and, most notably, the *Sioux*? How is it that the newspapers report it and I was left in the dark? The *Daily Globe* claims that as many as fifteen thousand natives convened there. Why was I not informed of that? Why weren't the Americans apprised of the situation? Why did you not relay a dispatch to the garrison at Fort Benton?"

He was determined to give as good as he got. "May I remind you, sir, that at that moment I was on the point of taking sick leave in Arkansas? I had already surrendered my command at Fort Walsh to Assistant Commissioner Irvine."

"That is a dodgy answer. You were still *in situ*. The Cypress Hills is your bailiwick, not Irvine's. You had local knowledge. You might have shown some initiative and alerted the department of this convention of savages."

"I have never been faulted for lack of initiative. No one has ever said I do not take things in hand."

Scott waved away his objection. "You did not take *this* matter in hand, and because you didn't, the Americans are unhappy. They say it was the Sioux who called this powwow, and that its purpose was to weld all the tribes into an alliance to drive the white men from the plains. Quite rightly, the Americans are angry that they received no news of this extraordinary congregation of red men. In their eyes, our oversight was tantamount to wishing them harm. They assert that if they had received notice that the tribes had assembled in such numbers they might have anticipated such a large encampment of Sioux and North Cheyenne on the Little Bighorn. With such intelligence in hand, Custer might have averted disaster."

"That's a big might. If pigs had wings they might fly."

"I ask you again to explain yourself. Why, before leaving your post for Arkansas, did you not dispatch a rider to Fort Benton to give the U.S. Army this news?"

"I have already explained. Assistant Commissioner Irvine was in charge. He is my ranking superior and I did not see it was my place to read him his duty. Your questions about why a messenger wasn't sent might better be put to him." The instant the words left his mouth he felt regret for criticizing a fellow officer to a trumped-up duffer like Scott. Quickly, he added, "But why

26

would Irvine take such a step? How could he know what the Indians' purpose was? Do you expect that one of them would pull him aside and say, 'By the way, just in the interests of fair play, I want to let you know we have all decided to exterminate the white man. I would get ready if I were you, old sport.'"

The secretary drew himself up in his chair; his hand fumbled about on the desktop and found a pencil. It broke in his fingers with a savage crack. When he spoke again, his voice was soft and menacing. "Assistant Commissioner Irvine has been made aware of my displeasure. But that does not mitigate the fact that the Cypress Hills is your beat, Sub-Inspector Walsh. I am gravely disappointed."

"If I may speak frankly, I am not a mind reader, Mr. Secretary, nor a crystal ball gazer. I could not foresee a future when we would bundle into bed with the Yanks. If I had sent a message to Fort Benton, and Custer hadn't gotten himself so soundly spanked, perhaps our neighbours would have accused me of spreading rumours intended to disrupt their commerce and terrify their population."

"You do not have a crystal ball? Then let me be your crystal ball. I will predict your future. From this day forward you will not keep the Americans in the dark about anything whatsoever that might affect them. You will provide the commander of the garrison at Fort Benton with any and all intelligence that could conceivably assist the Americans in conducting a successful campaign against the Sioux. And, sir, you will do it expeditiously and with good grace."

"So you are ordering me, who has sworn an oath to our majesty the Queen, to put myself in the service of a foreign power – to ferry information to Major Ilges, that ass in Fort Benton, like a servant carrying plates to the master's table?"

"Let me remind you that I too have sworn an oath to Her Majesty," the secretary said frigidly. "It is her interests that I am entrusted to safeguard. Both the Dominion of Canada and the government of Great Britain wish no friction to arise with the United States. We wish no outburst of that anti-British feeling which so frequently is excited in the American public and in the Congress. That would be highly regrettable."

"These are very vague principles for my poor soldier's head to con. I'm a straightforward man and I'd like a straightforward answer. If the Sioux take refuge on the Canadian side, how am I to respond to their presence?"

"Do everything possible to persuade them to return to their country."

"If your aim is to please the Americans, I do not think that would do it."

"You should recall who you are speaking to, sir. Do you permit your subordinates to address you so impertinently?"

"I apologize," said Walsh, "but I am struggling to make a point. If I were Sitting Bull, I'd sure as Christ want a safe harbour from the American Army. I think persuading them to give up such a refuge would fall on deaf ears. If they refuse to go, what am I to do? Do you expect me to expel thousands of Sioux warriors with the ninety men I have at my disposal at Fort Walsh? Or is it the government's plan to reinforce us with militia and British Regulars?"

"No military will be deployed; it would impose too great a cost on the Treasury. Besides, we have no desire to incite a war with the Indians, to repeat mistakes that have been made south of the border." Scott tangled his fingers in his beard and gave it an irritated tug. "However, if the Sioux do come, it is imperative that we do everything to prevent them using Canada as a base of operations against the United States. If we fail in this, we provide an excuse to the American Army to deal with the problem, not on their soil, but ours." Scott paused. "This cannot be allowed to happen. When Americans pay a visit, they have a habit of staying. Think of California, New Mexico, Arizona, all lost to Mexico. There are still plenty of annexationists in Congress looking for a justification to relieve us of territory."

"Britain is not Mexico. She would not sit idly by and allow such a thing to happen. It would mean war."

"Perhaps. It is true Britain is not Mexico. She possesses a vast empire. Which is to say there are many pots on Britain's stove that require tending. One may boil over before it is noticed. I," said Scott primly, "do not want to be that pot."

"A mere three hundred police scattered over the entire North-West, how are we to do what you demand? Custer lost nearly that many at the Little Bighorn. You expect us to do the impossible – me in particular."

Scott hunched forward, enunciating very slowly, very clearly, "If you are not up to the task then I must find a man who is."

For the first time, Walsh felt how unbearably hot and humid the room was. He realized he was sweating profusely. Yet the old man across the desk from him looked cool as a cucumber. Maybe it was the thinness of his vegetable-nourished blood. He caught a whiff of Scott's musty suit, the distinctive odour of mothballs. That stink summed up the old codger, a man who gave more thought to protecting a threadbare suit than he did to ensuring the safety of the North-West Mounted Police he had sprinkled all over the West. "Such a man does not exist," he finally replied, after a stubborn silence.

"Major Walsh, do you wish to tender your resignation?"

Walsh shifted on his chair, cleared his throat. Mary's hopes were two ticks away from being fulfilled. Who was James Morrow Walsh if he wasn't *Major Walsh*? "No," he said quietly, "I do not wish to tender my resignation."

"Are you prepared to follow the directions of this department, faithfully, without hesitation or mental reservations? Think carefully before you reply."

"I am."

Scott leaned back in his chair; the stench of camphor retreated. "You have many admirable qualities, Sub-Inspector Walsh. Commissioner Macleod thinks very highly of you. You are an efficient officer, you are brave, you have inspired a remarkable loyalty and admiration in the men of B Troop. In a word, you are a leader. But I have heard other reports on your character and seen proof of them today. You go your own way; you act as if you were a law unto yourself. I am here to inform you you are not a law unto yourself. You are an instrument of government policy. That is all. You are a tool. *My* tool. You are on trial."

On trial. Exactly Mary's words when she told him there was a job waiting for him as superintendent of hotel chamber pots. "Do you wish to correct any of my observations?"

"No, let them stand."

"Very good. I am glad we see eye to eye. I think it advisable that you seize the earliest opportunity to embark for the West. If you require travel funds, apply to my clerk for a chit."

"Thank you."

Scott fished a hunter watch out of his vest pocket, glanced at it. "I believe I am running behind in my appointments."

"Of course." Walsh stood abruptly; his chair skidded back.

"Good day, Sub-Inspector."

"Good day, Mr. Secretary."

It was a little before six o'clock when Walsh walked out into the sweltering day, hand tightly gripped to the handle of his bag. The sky was grey and heavy; he felt as if he were drawing breath through a steaming-hot washcloth. Shivering with rage, he stalked along the bank of the Rideau Canal, his anger slowly bleeding away into bleak despondency. He stared numbly at the heavily laden boats wallowing their way somewhere. His mind, struggling to parse what had just happened to him, was as sluggish and difficult to steer as a coal barge. He couldn't understand what had just transpired. Scott had as good as called him untrustworthy, a harum-scarum fellow. Absolute rubbish; he is sound as British sterling. Who had answered the call to duty before you could say Jack Robinson? James Morrow Walsh. He could have begged off, pled illness; there were plenty who would have done it, and kept their soft seat in Arkansas. Not a speck of gratitude tendered to him;

instead he had been scolded, chided, threatened like a jam-fingered child.

Was he suspect because he had received his commission from Sir John A.'s Conservatives? Did the Liberal Scott read treachery in his face? It couldn't be that. Plenty of other officers had received their appointments from the Tories. Surely it was known he didn't give a fig for politics.

It had to be that Scott objected to him on moral grounds. Heard that on occasion he avails himself of the services of sporting women in Fort Benton, does a little of what the men like to call "tipi creeping" when he visits Indian camps. One look at Scott was enough to tell you that the twig between his legs hadn't had its bark peeled back in a coon's age. Mr. Secretary ought to read Surgeon Kittson's annual medical report with more attention. That would give him an education in human nature: the number of cases of clap Kittson treated every year at Fort Walsh.

Perhaps somebody had told the old teetotaller he keeps a bottle in his desk. The Territories may be officially dry, but circumstances require the law to be winked at now and then. Sometimes difficulties arise between officers, and a drink is called for to settle them. Whiskey eases disagreements. It's a question of sustaining morale. As the actress said to the bishop, "One spot is always wet and welcoming, milord." In the Cypress Hills, that wet and welcoming spot is his office.

Enough, thinks Walsh. With a violent jerk, he rakes his boot off the desk and snatches down his pant leg. Enough returning to past humiliations like a dog to its vomit. He thrusts himself off the chair and hobbles to the window. Gazing out the dusty, spy-speckled pane, he sees men going from bakery to mess, their arms stacked high with loaves of bread. Walsh feels the erysipelas throb in his own knees as he watches the veterinary surgeon run his hands up and down the cannon of a horse, examining it for swelling. The square of the fort is a bright box of noonday sun; the Union Jack hangs limply from the flagpole like a dish-cloth on a peg. Louis Léveillé, his favourite scout, sits on the stoop of the guides' quarters, contentedly sucking on his pipe. There's a man who could teach Scott a thing or two about loy-alty, how it's earned. If you're foursquare, straightforward, Léveillé is yours until kingdom come. If he asked Léveillé to douse himself in kerosene and set himself afire, the guide would ask for a match. But underhanded, sneaky sorts like Scott can't grasp the power of frankness to bind men together. They dance you down a tightrope and are only too pleased to see you fall.

And that thought turns Walsh to Michael Dunne. A sneaky, conniving, underhanded bastard if he's ever seen one. Two days ago, Dunne had slid into his office, stuffed into that tight black suit of his like a sausage in its casing, the staring, glassy-eyed son of a bitch. Started bombarding him with insinuations, hinting at political and diplomatic tangles that Scott had never breathed a word about. Baffling him with what ifs, hints that the wicket was stickier than he could have dreamed, and suggesting that if Dunne's palms were greased he could see to it that the roof didn't fall down on the good Major's head. It was all so exasper-ating he had ordered the fellow out of his office, and Dunne had risen to his feet, a smile pasted on his mug that said: More fool you, Walsh. The next day he departed Fort Walsh, gone like fog in the sun. But not without leaving behind something that had ripened into doubt.

What he wants is advice, and he thinks Case may be the man to give it. Politics is the storybook his father read him on his knee; he's sucked its tricks up with his mother's milk. If there's anyone familiar with the backstairs of power and sensitive to its cold drafts, Wesley Case is that man.

And then, the man he has summoned appears. Francis is steaming across the square, looking fit to explode a vein, and Case, wearing a bemused smile, is trundling along behind him. Walsh returns to his desk and makes a show of being occupied with paperwork. In moments, he hears the Sergeant Major's gravelly voice muttering something to Case, followed by a tap on the door.

"Come in!"

Francis and Case enter; the Sergeant Major quivers like a tuning fork when he gives his salute. Case's obeisance is more perfunctory and lackadaisical.

"Constable Case, sir!" Francis's voice booms in the small room.

"Thank you, Sergeant Major," Walsh says. "You may leave us now."

"Very good, sir." Whipping off another salute, Francis wheels round and marches smartly out of the office, so forcefully that the floorboards shake.

Walsh catches a glimpse of Case's blistered palms. He shakes his head. "You must see if Surgeon Kittson has some salve for you. A fine fellow, Sergeant Francis, but given to extremes." The Major gestures towards a chair. "Come, no standing on ceremony. Take a seat."

Case does, gingerly places his hands on his knees. Taking a bottle of whiskey and two glasses from his desk drawer, Walsh says, "Let us pull a cork. There's something on my mind that needs airing. It requires the wisdom of Solomon, which means you." He sends Case one of his famously winning smiles. "And maybe you'll be good enough to do this old campaigner a service when you've heard me out."

For a half an hour Case listens closely as Walsh expatiates on what happened in Ottawa between himself and Secretary Scott. As the Major talks, he grows more and more agitated, comes out from behind his desk and begins to stalk furiously round the room. He fulminates against the dismissive way he has been treated, how he has been asked to make bricks without straw, and how, worst of all, he has been ordered to play handmaiden to Fort Benton's commander, Major Ilges. Then the storm spends itself; he drops down on the chair behind his desk, refills their glasses, and, without preamble, raises another topic. To Case's surprise, he begins to question him about his plan to set himself up as a rancher near Fort Benton with Joe McMullen.

"I expect that's on hold for the time being," says Walsh with circumspection, "that you'll hang about here until things quiet down in Montana."

"No. I want to start looking for properties as soon as possible. McMullen will accompany me. He won't hear of me making the trip alone," Case confesses ruefully. "Joe thinks that without him, I'd blindly ride into the whole Sioux nation. He'll have to come back here to wrap up his affairs as quickly as he can, before returning to join me in Fort Benton."

Walsh is unable to suppress his distaste. "Yes, B Troop's horse breaker has announced he has quit on me. Good luck with him. I warn you, the man's so lazy he won't trouble to scratch his ass – just in case it might stop itching on its own – he'd hate to waste any effort. Why you hired that layabout is beyond me."

"I didn't hire him. He's my partner. I need a man who can show me the ropes, and he has experience as a cowhand. And no man knows horses better than McMullen. I provide the capital, he works alongside me and teaches me the hundred and one things I don't know about ranching. I consider myself damn lucky he agreed to come in with me for twenty-five per cent of the profits."

Walsh greets the notion that McMullen is a bargain with a dismissive shrug. Case is sure he would like to say more, but is checking himself, and the Major restraining his impulses is highly unusual. Walsh sits moodily flicking his thumb against his chin. As if speaking aloud the thoughts darting in his head, he abruptly says, "What Scott charged me to do – mend fences with the Yanks – it didn't come off so well. I mean my meeting with Ilges in Fort Benton."

Case suspects this is an understatement. "How so?" he asks.

"I've never liked that Ilges. Pompous German bastard. Couldn't bring myself to lick the beanpole's boots. He took offence. There was a bit of a dust-up." The Major sounds a tad remorseful about whatever occurred. He shifts uncomfortably on his chair, as if waiting to receive absolution from Case. But it is withheld. Finally the Major says, "I was thinking that since you are going to be in Fort Benton – perhaps you could pay him a visit. Smooth things over between us."

"If you would like me to pay him a courtesy call on your behalf, I will try to do what I can." Case watches the Major. It is clear that he has more on his mind.

"I've been thinking how useful it would be to have a gentle-man on the spot who is a little more discreet than myself. You know how I am, Case. I'm apt to flare. It nettles me to be at that bastard's beck and call. It's not in my nature to spend my days fixed to a chair, cracking my brain trying to figure out how to write a *tactful* report that won't make him bristle. That's *politics* and I have no talent for it, but politics is what Scott is asking me to do. There I'm like a blind man groping in the dark. I can't close my fingers on the proper thing to say or how to say it. But you might say it for me. You have a nose for that sort of thing. It's in your bloodline."

"I can hardly take that as a compliment, not coming from you."

"Well, that's not all you are. You were a soldier once. I remember how high you stood in the examinations on tactics and strategy. A very good classroom soldier," he qualifies, un-generously. "That could be of great benefit. I mean to say you could give me a second reading of Ilges's view on the military situation." Walsh adds coaxingly, "Why, you could even winkle things out of him he might be reluctant to divulge. It's my sus-picion that all the traffic in intelligence is going to go in one direction – to the Americans. And we get nothing in return."

Case turns this over in his mind. "What precisely are you asking me to be? A buffer? An intermediary? Or a spy?"

The glint in Walsh's eyes rivals the glint of his tunic's well-polished buttons. "Let's say a bit of all three," he says delightedly.

"That would describe it. I could pass information – how would you put it – that needs a *light* touch to you. You could sand the rough edges off it. I have a habit of putting things in a way that catches in a lot of people's throats."

"That means stepping outside of official channels. Highly irregular, to say the least."

Suddenly Walsh averts his eyes, directs his gaze to the blazing square outside his window. When he speaks again his voice has a beseeching tentative quality to it. "I need to keep Major Ilges happy. If he is not happy, the secretary of state will not be happy. I believe Scott is itching to show me the door. I do not want to go out that door. I am asking you to help me keep that from happening."

The naked honesty of Walsh's appeal takes Case entirely by surprise. The Major is the last man he would have expected to stoop to supplication. More surprising still is how quickly Walsh's plea tips the scales of his sympathy. "Let us talk about this later when I have had time to think about it."

On hearing that, the Major swivels around eagerly. "I owe you that much at least," says Case. "You have extended courtesies to me that a sub-constable had no right to expect. I am grateful for that."

"Glad to have done it," says Walsh, his confidence recovering. "Once we were brothers in arms. Comrades."

"There are obvious difficulties," warns Case. "Somehow, Ilges would need to be persuaded to deal with me."

"You'll twist him around your little finger. No doubts on that score."

"He will need to see there's benefit for him in this arrangement. You would have to be willing to accept the terms I am able to negotiate."

"Certainly, certainly," says Walsh.

"I would need a letter of introduction. A letter that informs him I speak for you. I would want to compose it myself, so as to define my position. I would want you to copy this letter out in your own hand and put your signature to it."

"No argument from me. Bob's your uncle."

It strikes Case that Walsh's manner is too offhand, too airily casual, he's assuming too quickly that he has already tucked him in his pocket. "All this is merely musing aloud on my part," he states. "I have not agreed to any of this. Far from it. I will need to mull this over, as I've said, before I give you my answer."

Disappointment clouds Walsh's face. Grudgingly he says, "If you must. I am in no position to dictate terms."

"Well then," says Case, beginning to rise, "the Sergeant Major has pressing business for me."

"Set that aside." Walsh peremptorily motions him to sit, forcing Case to subside back down on the chair. "There's another matter I need to speak to you about. That fellow Dunne you cautioned me about came to see me. The scoundrel wanted money to keep watch on the Irish in Fort Benton, can you believe his gall! I chucked the insufferable rascal out of my office. The next day he slipped this under my door." Walsh removes several sheets of paper from a drawer and thrusts them at Case. "I don't know what to make of it."

The handwriting lurches across the pages.

Dear Major Walsh,

    I think you should rethink. Here is my warning and argument concerning trouble brewing for you in Montana. Fort Benton is a Democratic town, entire. The party is run by Irish and Southerners. Neither has any love for President Grant nor Republicans and will not think twice to give them any pain they can. Nor to us. It is a well-known fact the Irish hate us loyal subjects of Britain and grab every chance to stab us in the back. Now with the Sioux in uprisal and talk running wild here that the red men will flee to Canada, these Irishmen say if we take these Indians in we are the foes of honest Americans everywhere and it's Perfidious Albion all over again, up to her devilish tricky ways. These Irishmen mean to stir up trouble in Montana and all over the United States on account of this, and make it as hot for us as possible. I know this because I live above the Stubhorn Saloon that is run by an Irishman by name of Dink Dooley where all the Irish hang about blackening our good name. I hear things continual about how they want to stick a pointy stick in our eye and how the Sioux will give them a chance to do it. The Southerners will back them in any ruckus with the Republicans because they hate Grant for licking them in the war. They all grouse it's up to the President to keep the Indians in hand and he's botching the job. All the citizens are hot under the collar because of this. So here is a double-edged sword to cut us Canadians backwards and forwards and it is swung at us by Irish traitors. In case you mistake me, I am Orange through and through and loyal to Our Sovereign Majesty the Queen. Depend on it.

Now I will name you the worst of the rascals who need watching and why.

1. John J. Donnelly, Fort Benton lawyer and politician. Holds rank of Colonel in Irish Republican Army. Known to have taken part in two attempts to invade Canada from U.S. of A. If memory serves you, recall he helped block extradition of wolfers who killed them poor Indians in your neck of the woods, up there in Cypress Hills in 1873. Led demonstrations and ralleys against England and Canada all over Montana, claiming we was interfering with rights and liberties of Americans. Everybody in Benton still admires hot-winded speech he gave here in front of banner showing American eagle twisting tail of British lion. Lawyer Donnelly struts frequent on how he got Commissioner Macleod of NWMP arrested on visit to Helena on charge of provoking false arrests of so-called innocent wolfers. I have heard Donnelly brag on this with my own ears. I bring this all back to your mind to show that these scoundrels stop at nothing.

2. Johnny Healy, Chairman of Choteau County Democrats and Sheriff of Fort Benton. You Mounted Police pushed him out of the whiskey trade and shut down Fort Whoop-Up, costing Mr. Healy plenty of hard cash in lost profits selling porch climber to British Indians. So he is no friend of yours. Fenian sympathizer and well situated to make political trouble.

3. Lastly, biggest troublemaker of them all is rumoured to be in vicinity, General John O'Neill. Three times led Irish Republican Army into Canada, namely Ridgeway, Pigeon Hill, and not too long ago went to the Red River to prod the half-breeds into rebellion against the lawful government, throw us Canadians out and petition Congress to take Manitoba into U.S. of A. Had backing of Governor of Minnesota and members of Congress. On his way to Red River attacked Hudson Bay post he thought was on Canadian territory, but same was on American territory. So Army arrested him, but he was let out of jail in a blink of the eye because authorities here in this country fear power of Irish vote and mollycoddle them something scandalous.

Now as is plain to see, I know what I'm talking about and as a good patriot I will watch these mischief-makers for you and report all plots they are hatching that comes to my attention. But as I said before you brushed me off so rude, sir, keeping an eye on these scum is dangerous business and costly in out-of-pocket expenses. But I will do it cheap, at the price of $50 a month, and if you don't think that a bargain you must be a Jew. I would think hard about my offer if I was you because I will look to your interests and those of our country. I can't speak fairer than that. If you come to see the light, I can be reached at the Stubhorn, Fort Benton.

Yours sincerely,
Michael Dunne

All the while he has been reading, Case has been aware of Walsh's boots impatiently scuffling under his desk. He only loses that sound when he comes across the name of General O'Neill, a disconcerting encounter. When he lifts his eyes from the document, Walsh eagerly demands, "So what do you make of that?"

"Dunne has a point – a small point – about the trouble the Irish in Montana may create."

Walsh's countenance darkens, believing that a criticism of him has been levelled. "You mean to say I was wrong to turn him out?"

"No, you were right to do that. This Dunne creature could be himself working for the Fenians. Or playing both sides of the fence – trying to collect a monthly stipend from you while at the same time peddling to the Irish whatever he picks up from his association with the Police. That sort of man is better kept at arm's length. It's never advisable to take snakes to your bosom."

"I thought as much," says Walsh, although it is clear to Case he hadn't.

"Nevertheless, it might be wise if you warned Secretary Scott of the possibility of Irish political agitation. I wouldn't exaggerate the peril. Simply intimate something disagreeable might be expected, give a sober alert to the government that they can take under advisement. If trouble does arise, you will look perspicacious."

Walsh leans forward over the desk. "Is it possible that Dunne is Secretary Scott's man? I wouldn't put it past the old bugger, putting me to the test to see if I show what he calls initiative."

The suspicion is so preposterous that only Walsh's anxious look prevents Case from smiling. "Hardly. The secretary has more important things to do than to lay traps for a mere sub-inspector. The minute you walked out of his office, you walked out of his mind. Only if you make a misstep will he take notice of you again." He sees that the phrase "mere sub-inspector" is not sitting well with the Major. But if he is to be of any use to Walsh, he will need to say similar things to him in the future.

Case gets to his feet. "Duty calls. Back to the pick and shovel," he announces.

"Damn it, man," says Walsh. "I'll speak to the Sergeant Major and see you relieved of that chore."

"But I don't want to be relieved of it. I haven't finished many things in my life. I need the practice." And with that he leaves Walsh's office.

For the rest of the afternoon Case chops ground, hands weeping blood, thinking of what Walsh has proposed. There is no denying that there is something flattering about being petitioned by a man who, back in the days at the Kingston Cavalry School, was so universally admired. Walsh had sparkled with promise, was a constant reminder to the rest of the officer trainees that he was the one real warrior among them. Like Blake's Tyger, he had been formed by a different hand and eye, his sinews twisted to one purpose – a life of action. All he had talked about was his yearning to be gazetted a subaltern in the British Regulars. A little hard cash could have bought him a commission, but the son of a ship's carpenter didn't have that sort of tin – or the requisite gentleman's upbringing. So Walsh had swallowed disappointment and settled for second best, a career in the Police, and now Scott was threatening to snatch second best out of his grasp. Only fear could have made Walsh beg for assistance, and that fear was what had surprised and touched Case the most. He had never guessed it was an element of the Major's character.

It is easy to want to protect him. The man is as susceptible to disaster as a toddler careering around the house with a fork stuck in his mouth. And there Case thinks he might be useful. Protect and serve not only Walsh but perhaps his country too. If Scott doesn't think he needs the Major, then he's a fool. Only Walsh can give B Troop the backbone it will need to face the Sioux.

It surprises him a little that some of his youthful patriotism remains, though he will practise what is left of it in secret, as the

Bible enjoins you to pray in secret, rather than do what his father would surely prefer and make the grand gesture of re-enlisting, parade his love of country. He has no interest in winning anyone's applause. Least of all his father's. Playing this game for its own sake is enticing. His father has always been the grand master of this variety of backroom chess. He cannot deny that also has something to do with the decision he arrives at.

That evening he frames his letter of introduction to Major Ilges. Next morning he gives it to Walsh to copy and sign. He also seizes the opportunity to ask the Major to permit young Constable Hathaway to accompany McMullen and him to Fort Benton. Walsh is reluctant. Only when Case points out that Joe McMullen will soon be returning to Fort Walsh and can shepherd Hathaway safely back to the fold does the Major give way, reassured the lamb will not be left bleating in the wilderness.

But when Case returns to his attack on the unyielding earth of the latrine trench he is not sure he has done the boy any favour. From the day he first met Peregrine Hathaway, he has been looking out for him. Hathaway's naïveté, idealism, and brimming enthusiasm have made him unpopular with the more hard-bitten and cynical of his barrack mates. Case had gathered Hathaway under his wing to spare him what misery he could, but having that particular chick tucked away at his side has not always been a comfortable fit. Hathaway is very young, and acts even younger than he is, which is often a trial. He claims to be twenty, but Case is sure that that was a fabrication for the recruiting officer, and that the lad is no more than eighteen. Peregrine has decided he, Case, is an older brother and an infallible one to boot, and carries all his problems to him, nagging for solutions.

Hathaway's latest problem is a girl he met at the New Year's dance in Fort Benton, an affair annually hosted by Major Ilges and to which a contingent of Police are always invited. To display B Troop at its best, Walsh always hand-picks the men who will attend the dance, and Hathaway's good looks and impeccable English manners made him a highly suitable selection.

There he met a young lady named Celeste Tarr, and a romantic correspondence between the two ensued. Now with mail delivery suspended, Hathaway is in a fever because several times in the past months he has sniffed in Miss Tarr's letters allusions to a rival for her affections. The boy believes only a face-to-face meeting can re-establish his supremacy in her heart. Ever since he learned that Case's departure to Fort Benton was imminent he has been importuning him to get Walsh to agree to let him make the trip too. And now he has given the boy what he wants. Two favours in two days, both granted because he was incapable of withstanding a plea for help. It will remain to be seen if no good deed goes unpunished.

Case gives himself a shake. He has digging to do, a "sanitary convenience" to finish. For the next two days he labours mightily with scarcely a pause. Evenings, he has appointments with the Major to discuss how things will be handled with Ilges in Fort Benton. When Walsh cavils or balks, Case reminds him that if he does not cooperate, his "intermediary" has it in his power to quit at any time.

The afternoon before Case's term in the North-West Mounted Police ends, he throws the last shovelful of dirt out of the trench and clambers up the ladder. Face streaked with muddy sweat, he looks down with satisfaction on what he has accomplished. It seems to him a small step in putting the right foot forward into the future.

Watching Joe McMullen tighten cinches, examine hooves for cracks and loose shoes, sling saddlebags into place, leaving nothing to chance before hitting the trail to Fort Benton, confirms for Case how wrong Walsh is to brand Joe lazy. If need be, he can act with energy and purpose. It's just that his ambitions are different from the Major's. Joe simply wants to enjoy life. He is content to be paid a dollar a head to break a string of horses for the NWMP every two or three months; the rest of the time he sits outside his cabin in the sun, regales passersby with jokes and stories, whittles sticks into toothpicks, makes friends with stray dogs, and, when the spirit moves him, goes hunting game. Right now, seeing him slip in and out among the horses, light footed, quick, and purposeful, it's difficult to credit his reputation for sloth, which he had been branded with the moment of his arrival in the Cypress Hills. Case had been there to witness that first appearance.

On a soft spring evening almost two years ago, a group of Police had been playing rounders on the parade square, when they spotted a horseman coming down the freight road from Fort Benton. The way he rode, slumped over in the saddle like a man wounded or deathly sick, caused them to break off the game and run to meet him. As they approached, the buckskin bearing the man came to a stop, ears up, watchful. The troopers edged in carefully, so as not to spook the nervous horse.

The man's chin hung down on his chest, face hidden by the wide brim of his hat. When he started to list precariously to the right they all took him for dead. Case was the first to dart forward, grab an arm to keep the toppling body from falling to the ground. As soon as he touched it, the corpse gave a galvanic twitch, Case flinched in surprise, and all the constables took a startled step backwards. Slowly the rider's head lifted, and they all got their first look at Joe McMullen, a weather-ravaged face, crow's feet flaring at the corners of deep-set black eyes, a crooked mouth, an iron-grey moustache drooping two long wispy tails below his jaws, a tall, lanky composition of sinew, bone, and stringy muscle.

McMullen broke a lopsided grin at the red tunics surrounding him. "Lord," he said, "I fell asleep and I've woke up in heaven, sitting in a bowl of strawberries. Where's the cream?" Then with no further ado, he stretched out his hand to the nearest policeman, who happened to be Case. "Name's Joe McMullen," he said. "Glad to know you."

With time, Joe McMullen's appearance in their midst was embellished into legend, an often repeated story about the idler who dozed his way from Fort Benton to Fort Walsh, dreamed his way through over a hundred miles of howling, perilous wilderness, simply drifting like cottonwood wool on a breeze, happy to settle wherever the wind carried him. Joe does nothing to deny this interpretation, simply says, "It ain't a bad trip with your eyes closed. The scenery ain't got much to recommend it."

McMullen is sheathing Peregrine Hathaway's Police-issue Snider-Enfield carbine in the boy's bucket scabbard. Hathaway is the only one in uniform, scarlet jacket and buff breeches, pillbox hat cocked on his head at a rakish angle. If McMullen is used goods, nicked and scarred, Hathaway looks fresh as a daisy even though the summer sun has burned his face livid. His habitually amazed and innocent blue eyes watch every move Joe McMullen makes.

The last buckle buckled, the last bit of gear stowed away, Joe turns to Case and Hathaway and declares, "All right, girls, tuck your skirts between your legs and get your sit-upons in the saddle. Time to go."

They trot through the gates of Fort Walsh. There is no one to see them off but the guard. The rest of B Troop is taking supper, and Walsh is abed with a bad case of chills and fever. McMullen followed by Hathaway, Hathaway by Case, they file down the Benton–Walsh trail. The day before, the Métis scouts, Louis Léveillé and Cajou Morin, had done reconnaissance as far as the Milk River and found no evidence of Sioux in the area. Beyond the border, the disposition of the hostiles is unknown. Joe aims to cover the ground between Fort Walsh and the Milk by daylight and proceed into Montana Territory under cover of darkness. When dawn comes, the party will take cover, sleep, then make the last stage of the journey to Fort Benton by night.

The descent down the southern slopes follows a snaking path; the tops of the lodgepole pine and spruce sway in a wind that brooms the sky clear of every scrap of cloud. Bit by bit, the forest thins, the last of the trees fall away at their backs, and they enter a vast stretch of browning grass that shines like a dented brass platter in the slanting sun. Hour after hour, they continue on at the pace McMullen sets to conserve the strength of their horses for the long ride ahead. Just short of twilight, Case lifts his eyes from the shadows that have held him mesmerized for so long, tall spindly-legged horses, towering riders looming on their backs, and sees the Milk River smelted by the setting sun into a trickle of molten gold.

"We'll rest here until the sun drops," McMullen declares, "let the horses drink their fill, make us some supper."

Joe gets a small fire going, one that scarcely raises a wisp of smoke, boils up corn mush, fries a pan of bacon. He dresses the porridge with salty bacon grease. The men crouch around the pot and spoon it up, eat bacon with their fingers. Nose to nose with Peregrine, Case can see he is pondering deeply on something.

"Mr. McMullen," Hathaway says uneasily, "ought we not discuss our tactics if we encounter Indians?" There is a contest playing out in Hathaway's face. He is eager for a thrilling adventure of the sort Mr. G.A. Henty's novels provided him back in his bedroom in Bristol. On the other hand, he realizes Mr. Henty is not in control of Peregrine Hathaway's story, and the plucky young hero may end up lying butchered in the grass.

"Tactics?" says McMullen. "If we bump into Sioux – I run and you come hard on my heels. If we can't outrun them, then we stand and fight." He jabs a thumb to Hathaway's Snider-Enfield slung on his saddle in its bucket scabbard. "How many rounds you got for that carbine?"

"Twenty-five."

"You fight them until you got one round left. Save the last for yourself." McMullen slides his finger into his mouth, clicks his thumb to the side of his hand mimicking the action of a rifle hammer striking a round. Withdrawing the finger, he wipes it with an exaggerated flourish on his trousers. "Son," he says, "you don't want them cats playing with you if you're a live mouse."

The three men sit in silence, contemplating American soil across the Milk. The sun is a vestige of burnt-orange dome glowing on the horizon. Bank swallows are skimming above the stream, snatching insects, curvetting, rocketing up against the dying light. McMullen carries the pans and mess tins to the river, gives them a rinse, comes back, and douses the fire. "All right," he says, "let's make a mile."

They mount, splash into the shallows of the Milk, scramble their horses up the opposite bank, fall into their former line of march. Individual stars spark into life against the dove-grey sky, the glitter steadily multiplying as the heavens turn blue-black. Soon the Milky Way hangs its trembling canopy over them. McMullen, the notorious saddle-dozer, remains alertly awake, guiding them down every twist and turn in the wagon road. Shoulders square, back straight as a plumb line, Joe is their compass needle.

Still, with every passing hour, Case feels anxiety building. It isn't McMullen's advocating self-destruction in the event of defeat at the hands of the enemy that disturbs him. It is the texture of the night itself, the way the minutes crawl by, the feeling Joe is dragging them towards peril just as years ago the train locomotive dragged him through the darkness to Ridgeway. It's the light he dreads, what it might reveal.

Even darkness is capable of revealing that he had no business bringing Hathaway along. The boy can't keep awake. Every half-hour, like clockwork, he begins to sway in the saddle, and Case has to ride up and give him a sharp poke. Peregrine mutters a shamefaced apology, promises to be more vigilant, but thirty minutes later he succumbs again. Hathaway needs looking after and, if nothing else, the Battle of Ridgeway taught Case he can't be trusted with anyone's life.

False dawn shimmers slate-green, snaps back into a final, intense blackness. Then there is a slow flush of light; a pile of cloud becomes visible in the east, heaped like rumpled bedclothes, small birds begin to chitter and whistle in the sagebrush and juniper. As day breaks, Case twists in the saddle, sweeping all points north, south, east, and west. The sun climbs; the bunch-grass and twitch grass sweat dew. He thinks he spots mounted men in the distance, clustered at the foot of a butte, but then they resolve into harmless antelope. He feels something out there waiting for him. He would prefer it to make itself known.

Hathaway turns his horse, comes up to him, looking worried. "Shouldn't you have a word with Mr. McMullen? Isn't it time to secrete ourselves?"

"When Joe finds cover he'll take it," Case says tersely. His eyes move to McMullen as he says this and sees that he has halted on a small rise and is beckoning to them. They trot to his side. Joe is staring down at a coulee, its rim scribbled with brush.

Case asks, "You thinking that's a likely place to camp?"

"Maybe," Joe answers. "But that's got me pondering." He points to a dark mass humped in the grass near the ravine.

"Buffalo carcass?" says Case.

"Looks like it. Might be Indians was using that coulee for a buffalo jump. Might be they dropped that one before it reached the gulch. Might be there's a party of Sioux down there, horses tucked away, sleeping off a feast. Wouldn't want to stumble on them."

"So we move on?"

Joe scans the horizon, looking for shelter. "Sun's up. No likely place in view. I better take a look-see."

"No. I'll go. If there's trouble Hathaway's better off in your hands." Case dismounts, draws his shiny new Winchester out of its scabbard. He passes his reins to Hathaway. "Hold my horse."

"You go afoot and are discovered, you ain't going to make it back," says Joe.

"If I ride down and Sioux horses catch scent of mine, they'll whinny. I like my chances on foot better."

Case starts down the gentle slope towards the patch of tall grass that circles the dead buffalo. He moves to the beat of his heart, a quick, light stuttering step, listening intently for any suspicious sound, sniffing the wind for the telltale smell of woodsmoke. Drawing closer, his hand tightens on the stock of the rifle and he suddenly realizes he has neglected to chamber a round before setting out. Does he dare lever one into place now, or would the click be audible in the coulee and give him away? He is heading directly into the sun, the buffalo hump swimming black in his squinting eyes.

He freezes dead in his tracks; the grass is shaking; something is stirring there. Case raises his rifle. The seed tassels of the grass convulse. A coyote suddenly appears, a long rope of purple bowel clamped in its jaws. Catching sight of him it goes absolutely still, regarding him with a yellow, fathomless stare. Case stands locked in the animal's gaze. A whiff of the ripe contents of the glistening intestines reaches his nostrils.

Then, unhurriedly, the coyote turns, and with the buffalo guts slithering wetly between its spindly legs, it carries off its prize.

The buffalo proved to have died of bad teeth and old age, half-starved, its ribs standing gaunt under a mangy hide. There were no Sioux in the coulee. The travellers had found a haven to spend the day.

Hathaway and McMullen lie sprawled on the ground, dead to the world. The horses nod on their feet. Only Case is awake, sitting cross-legged, staring up the long corridor of the declivity. It is noon; the sun, directly overhead, pours heat into the breathless, narrow confine. Its sides are a jaundiced clay, deeply eroded by prairie downpours. Out of the friable earth poke arthritic, grasping fingers, the roots of the brush and trees that skirt the coulee.

Case counts off the hours he hasn't slept, reckons them at thirty. A short time ago, he felt his body rocking, overcome by heat and fatigue. He had to put both hands to the ground to stop the alarming teetering. He is not a superstitious man but he cannot shake the feeling that what was awaiting him as he traversed the long night was the coyote's agate-eyed stare, the grinning mouth dangling entrails. When his eyelids fall, this is what he sees. And when his eyes snap back open they are blinded by the sun, bright as that brass button he had once placed on the breast of a corpse.

THREE

IN THE OXBOW RESTAURANT the blinds are drawn and the door is barred. Behind the counter of Fort Benton's finest eatery, D.B. Dagg is watching the last patron of the night demolish his meal. It's the same every evening: Mr. Dunne arrives a half an hour before the posted closing time, when the place is deserted, and orders supper. Proprietor Dagg finds this a great annoyance, but he senses it better not to express his aggravation to this particular customer. So Dagg stands, hands folded over his aproned paunch, waiting for Dunne to work his way through a flank steak, creamed onions, fried potatoes, gherkins, and two side plates heaped with biscuits. Dunne consumes his food as if it were a grim duty rather than a pleasure. Some evenings, this lack of appreciation for his restaurant's cookery prompts the owner of the Oxbow to close his eyes, sending him into a light doze, which he does now until a loud, insistent rapping on the door jerks him back into consciousness.

"We're closed!" he shouts. "Bugger off!"

A thin, piercing voice cries out, "Mr. Dunne! Mr. Dunne!"

Dunne plants his fists on each side of the plate, a fork upright in one, a knife in the other. Dagg throws him a questioning look. Dunne nods, and Dagg reluctantly goes to the door, unbarring it to reveal an urchin holding an envelope in a grimy paw. Brimming with self-importance, the boy announces, "Message from Lawyer Tarr for Mr. Dunne."

Dunne beckons and the youngster crosses to him, bare feet whispering on the floorboards. He is one of Fort Benton's whore whelps, a boy of ten in stained canvas trousers and a shirt he laid claim to when its owner got bounced naked as a jay bird out of the knocking-shop where his mother plies her trade. The shirt hangs to his knees like a filthy dress.

Dunne slits open the envelope with a gravy-smeared knife, reads the brief note. *Mr. Dunne, I will come to your lodgings at ten o'clock. Be there, I beg you. It is a matter of the utmost importance.* The signature, Randolph Tarr, is an urgent, assertive scrawl. Dunne slips the paper into a coat pocket, places both hands flat to the table, and hoists himself out of his chair, the joinery of the table wailing under the strain of his weight. Slipping a penny into the street arab's hand, he asks, "You ate?" The kid replies with a violent shake of the head. Dunne points to his plate. "Go to it."

"No sirree," says Dagg, "I got to shut down. It's half past closing time already."

Dunne turns to Dagg. "I paid hard cash for that and I got the right to do with it as I please." He draws back the chair. The boy scrambles into it to attack the leftovers. Dunne goes to the counter and counts coins into Dagg's hand. "And if the mite wants more biscuits, see he gets them," he says. "Biscuits ain't extra according to the bill of fare."

The proprietor coughs apologetically. "No they ain't, Mr. Dunne. As you say."

"And don't rush him. Rushing is bad for the digestion." Dunne adjusts his celluloid collar. "I'll see you per usual tomorrow night, Mr. Dagg."

"Look forward to it. Always a pleasure to serve you."

Dunne steps out into the night. For a moment, he hovers on the boardwalk outside the Oxbow, trying to remember the face of that other whore's catch colt. The bits and pieces of memory, a pendulous lower lip, the shine of an eye, tufts of hair that lie strewn about in his mind nearly succeed in binding themselves into something recognizably human just as it is said the bones of the dead will reassemble themselves come Resurrection Day. Then it all goes slinking off into the darkness. Dunne does the same, crossing over Front Street to where the glow from the saloon windows doesn't penetrate.

Twenty yards to his right, the Missouri coils heavy and black as if it were a river of pitch; intermittently, a pallid moon appears between tattered clouds, its reflection shivering on the water. On the riverbank, where the refugees who have come in from the countryside are encamped, cook fires are flickering, someone can be heard singing, a baby cries. It is chiefly women and children who populate the village of wagons and tents; many of the men are still out on their ranches and farmsteads, guarding their property against the threat of Sioux marauders. Others, who have had all the fight knocked out of them by years of drought, hailstorms, frosts, grasshoppers, and horse-killing outbreaks of the equine epizootic, have preferred to remain safe in Benton and let the damn Indians help themselves to whatever they want. According to their temperaments they take to the bottle, to gloomy silence, or to backhanding the missus. There has already been one suicide, a fellow who loaded himself down with a length of chain, a post maul, a branding iron, his wife's Dutch oven, and then threw himself into the river. It is said his widow professes to regret the loss of the Dutch oven, which she claims was a damn sight more use to her than her husband ever was.

Across the way from Dunne, on the illuminated side of Front Street, stands Fort Benton's commercial district. Every third false-fronted establishment is a saloon blaring a fearsome hubbub – the wheeze of concertinas, the jangle of pianos, the squeals of hurdy-gurdy girls, the whoops and curses of roustabouts, mule skinners, and bullwhackers. Drunks piss in the streets, whores toss chamber pot slops from second-storey windows and shout down to potential customers graphically detailed descriptions of pleasures on offer. Nightly, violence erupts over gambling losses, insults real and imagined, and sporting women. These disputes are most commonly settled by brawls of the eye-gouging, ear-biting variety, but occasionally knives are drawn, shots are fired, and a corpse results.

However, in the last few years Front Street has been easing its way towards respectability. Ideas of law and order might be notional and shaky, but Benton is tipping into the future, into what town boosters call progress. The men who lived the old wild life are withering on the vine. Up north, the North-West Mounted Police have lowered the whiskey trade into the ground and shovelled dirt on the coffin. The trappers who established the town as a fur-trading centre are long gone. Most of the beaver were trapped out years ago, and there is no market for the few who are still left slapping the water. The trade in buffalo hides rattles along, but each year the take of robes is a little less. It's clear to everyone that the days of the buffalo, like the beaver before them, are numbered.

There isn't much money to be had by striking off into the wilderness. Enterprise has polished its shoes, put on a frock coat, and set up shop in town. Real wealth comes to those who have cornered the market in supplying the NWMP posts in Canada, or distributing goods shipped by steamer to Fort Benton from the great world beyond. The town is the commercial hub of Montana, and expectations run high that when settlers start arriving in the Canadian North-West, Benton will play the same role there. Everybody confidently predicts it will be the next Chicago. Michael Dunne hopes that's true. Chicago was good to him, and he wasn't even in on the ground floor of the boom. It was good to Randolph Tarr too, until he got carried away with speculating.

Wedged in among saloons with names like the Jungle, the Extradition, and the Occident are new businesses catering to a more solid class of citizen. A black barber has opened Foster's Tonsorial Palace, which provides hot and cold baths, shampooing, the latest in hairstyles, and beard-dyeing, black or brown. Patrons of the Overland Hotel are assured that accommodation suitable for ladies and families is available. Mrs. E. Smith has set up shop in the same hotel, offering accomplished and fashionable dressmaking for gentlewomen. Cabinetmaker A.M. Stork promises plans and specifications drawn to customer approval. W.S. Wetzel's store lists everything necessary to provision a cozy home: shoes, clothing, staple and fancy groceries, dry goods, cigars, shelf hardware, toys, glassware, notions, toilet articles, drugs, patent medicines, paints, oils, tin ware, crockery, tools, as well as fine wines and champagne. The members of the Benton bourgeoisie are beginning to turn their noses up at the old standbys of merriment: gin, beer, Hostetter's and Plantation Bitters, Shawhan, O.K., and Eldorado whiskey, or that most potent frolic-promoter and sorrow-killer of all, pure grain alcohol.

Buds of civilization are showing everywhere, but the side of the road that Dunne travels tells a different story. The Benton levee is stacked high with barrels, crates, and bales of goods intended for every town in Montana, but freighters now judge it too risky to attempt to deliver them. The *Red Cloud* discharged its cargo yesterday and lies ready to embark passengers tomorrow morning for Bismarck – if there are any takers. River passage is not an inviting proposition. The woodhawks that supply boats with fuel have abandoned their posts. There are worries that the Sioux will attack the *Red Cloud* from the banks of the Missouri as it makes its way to the Dakota Territory. If the mountain steamer runs aground on a sandbar or explodes a boiler, who's to say Indians won't take advantage of its helpless state, board it and wreak bloody mayhem? Dunne can see the *Red Cloud*'s captain in the lantern-glow of his wheelhouse staring forlornly downriver, contemplating dangers shortly to be faced.

Dunne is closing in on his destination. He pauses to let a horseman trot by, then strides swiftly across the street, dodges into the alley between the Stubhorn Saloon and a harness maker's shop that brings him to a rickety staircase running up the back of the saloon. He goes up it two steps at a time, strikes a match on the landing, and inspects the hair he plucked from a horse's tail and pasted over the gap between the door and doorframe of the room he is renting. It is still in place.

Carefully, he peels off the hair, stores it away in a pillbox for future use, unlocks the door, and ducks into the black room. Dunne has memorized how many steps it is to the table from the threshold, precisely five. He counts them off, puts out his hand, and there is the coal-oil lamp. When he lights the wick, a small, bare, meticulously arranged room is revealed. A narrow cot pushed tight to the west wall, a position he calculated exactly. The door opens inward, so the cot is hidden from sight until the door has turned back completely on its hinges. His table is placed squarely in front of the entry. In bed, or seated at the table, he cannot be surprised. The single window is set far enough away from the landing to make it impossible for anyone to peer in on him. Even so, he keeps the blind drawn at all times.

A wood chisel rests on the lintel of the door, easily reached, something he knows from experience can do terrific damage, cut to the bone, disable a man with a single blow. There's a parlour gun nestled out of sight in the kindling in the wood box. One of the stockings laid out on the floor beside his cot holds a straight razor. His long-barrelled Schofield Russian revolver is secreted under his pillow. The short-barrelled Schofield rides in a silk sleeve sewed into the lining of his jacket. The jacket never comes off until he goes to bed.

Michael Dunne takes pride in being a cautious, careful man. He likens himself to water. It finds a way around every obstacle because it is patient. He is patient too. On John Harding's orders, Tarr had sent him off to the Cypress Hills on a wild goose chase; he had told him it was pointless, but Tarr insisted he pursue Gobbler Johnson, so he had seized the opportunity to aim this senseless errand in a direction of his own choosing, see if he couldn't persuade Walsh to employ him. That proving fruitless, he has switched his attention to Tarr. A man, like water, has to take his openings where he finds them.

Dunne catches the sound of steps on the stairs. He plunks himself down at the table, chair facing the door. There is a soft knock. "You want in, name yourself," he calls.

"Didn't you get my message?"

"A dog scratching at my door don't tell me who he is. I need to hear his bark to identify him."

"God, Dunne, you know perfectly well who I am. It's Tarr. Randolph Tarr."

"If you're Tarr, step in then."

When he enters, Dunne notes Lawyer Tarr looks to be a little under the weather, face puffy and pale, the skin under his eyes baggy and dark. Dunne points to a chair on the other side of the table. Tarr sits, holds his hands tightly clenched in his lap.

Dunne's visitor clears his throat. "I heard you were back. But since I got no news from you I assumed you didn't locate him."

"I told you he wouldn't be found there. If you and Harding would turn me loose, I'd find Gobbler Johnson sure enough. It might take time, a little money. But you got to meddle, tell me where to go." Dunne shrugs. "But I reckon whoever pays the piper gets to call the tune."

"That was Harding's call. He said Johnson always believed there was gold in the Cypress Hills. He figured he would be up there prospecting."

"You ought to have done what I said from the start. A man takes a shot at you through your office window, people see him doing a skedaddle down the street – that's attempted murder. You see to it a reward gets posted."

"Bullet lodged three feet in the wall above my head. The sheriff called it a calculated miss, said the county doesn't squander funds to capture a man who lets off a little steam firing a warning shot."

"County don't care where the money comes from as long as it don't come out of their pockets. Harding could have put up a thousand with a little extra for the sheriff, the judge. A reward brings bounty law into play. Gives me a legal right to go after

Johnson. Bring him in dead if need be. But no, you and Harding got to try to handle it on the cheap."

"Johnson came after me, not Harding, and Harding's not the sort of man who reaches into his pocket for anybody's sake but his own. And you know I can't raise a lump sum of that size."

"So why you here, then? I ain't interested in listening to you cry over spilt milk."

Tarr licks his lips. "I found this under my office door when I opened up this morning." He takes out a piece of paper from his pocket and slides it across the table. Dunne picks it up. It's stiff as a shingle, covered with words snipped from printed material and pasted to the paper. Dunne reads it aloud. "'See to it I get back what is mine or your women will burn in their beds I will chop them to bits I will drown them like kittens depend on it I will not touch you so as you have to bury them and know what it is to have something dear taken from you.'"

Tarr says, "I checked my copy of *Webster's Dictionary*. Most of the font matches. Other bits seem to have been cut from the *Fort Benton Record*. All the personal pronouns, the I's, the you's, must have come from a novel."

"Ain't you the detective," says Dunne.

Tarr says, "If I showed this letter to the sheriff, perhaps the authorities might reconsider offering a reward." There is no certainty in his voice.

"Good luck but it ain't going to happen," says Dunne, and waits.

"I suppose you're right." Tarr gives him a hopeful, pleading glance. "I'm out of my depth here. Even if I were a man with the hardness, the will – I have a legal practice to run, I can't be everywhere at once . . ." He trails off, struggling to contain his emotion. "I have no one else to call on to protect my womenfolk, Mr. Dunne, but you. I need help. The man is a lunatic."

"Well," says Dunne placidly, "a man is apt to go that way when he loses something rightfully his. You got to look at it from Johnson's side of the fence. Here's a man didn't trust the lawyers up in Helena to defend his gold claim because he believes they're all in the pocket of your friend Mr. Harding. So old Gobbler comes to Fort Benton to hire himself a lawyer. Puts his trust in Mr. Randolph Tarr to represent him. But Mr. Harding – what's the word for it – *suborns* Lawyer Tarr, and Lawyer Tarr goes all left-footed in court, doesn't present the case proper, neglects to lay out evidence, and Johnson loses his gold claim. There's something puts a itch on a man needs scratching, ain't it?" He lifts his eyebrows inquisitively. There is no response to the question. "Now," resumes Dunne, "that brings us to me, who's also been deprived of what's rightfully his. The seven hundred dollars that was due me for services rendered in Chicago walked away in your pocket when you done your flit from there. But to my surprise when I rolled into Benton I seen your name up on a signboard, Randolph Tarr, Esq., Attorney at Law. I figured you'd pay that debt, settle up like a honest man. But till this day I ain't collected nothing but promises from you, and none of them fulfilled."

"The thing is," interjects Tarr, "I walked away from Chicago absolutely busted. I had *nothing* in my pockets. You know very well that everything I owned was ashes. Seven houses gone up in the Great Fire, my own house burned to the foundations. My creditors ready to pick the flesh from my bones."

"Boo hoo, life is hard. So who owes me? You, or Mother O'Leary's cow?"

"I have always admitted my obligation. You'll get your money. It's just a question of time. Moving here incurred considerable expense. My daughter needed to be provided a suitable home. Life as a widower was not to my taste, I married again . . . these things eat up money. You have no idea. But I assure you, I'm good for it."

"If you want me to play broody hen to your chicks, keep them safe from Mr. Gobbler Johnson, you better be good for it," says Dunne. "Two dollar a day, cash on the barrelhead. And the day that money ain't handed over is the day I walk away. You understand?"

"Yes. Certainly. Each and every day. Depend on it."

"And here's another thing, Mr. Tarr. I know your opinion of me, even now when you're licking my bum hole. You think I'm dirt."

"That's not true –"

"I ain't a fool. You ain't never so much as invited me into your home. So I know what I am to you, a guard dog. I'll sleep on your porch as long as the fine weather lasts, so's not to bring fleas into your house. But don't think you can starve this dog. He'll sink his teeth in you." He pushes the letter back to Tarr with his forefinger. "If that's agreed, I'll see you crack of dawn tomorrow."

"Why certainly that's agreed. Thank you, Mr. Dunne. I am forever in your debt."

"All right then," says Dunne. "You best be gone. I take it your womenfolk is alone."

"Oh no, Lieutenant Blanchard is paying my daughter Celeste a call. I thought them in good hands with a military man in the house." Tarr rises to his feet. "But I should return without delay. And let me say again how happy I am to put this in your hands, the hands of a sterling professional."

Dunne shepherds Tarr to the door, closes it on his visitor's last ingratiating goodbye, and locks it. For good measure, he jams a chair under the knob. Then he undresses, kills the lamp, crawls into his cot, and draws the blankets up to his chin.

Dunne's breathing is quick and shallow. Sometimes, when he falls silent after talking so much, as he has tonight with Tarr, he will feel a voice slowly pulling free of his body, little by little, and go wafting about the room. The voice is flat and uninflected. He hears it now. It warns him that *someone is following*.

Each time, a picture hesitantly takes form in the ether to keep company with the words. He sees it hovering above him, a daguerreotype lifted too early from the developing bath. He can't make out what the figure in the picture is, whether it's a man or woman. He perceives movement around the knees, a skirt billowing, or perhaps snow churning as a man plunges through drifts. Around the head and shoulders of the hazy figure a multitude of bright white flecks are swarming, chemical spotting, or perhaps snowflakes whirling out of a grey and heavy sky.

FOUR

.

IT IS HARD FOR Ada Tarr to say what is producing the fine sweat she has to dab from her upper lip every few minutes – the searing sun pummelling the shingles, or thoughts of her husband's former client, Gobbler Johnson. Randolph has landed his family in a predicament; proof of how dire that predicament is has been visible on her porch for a number of days in the person of Mr. Dunne, a shotgun laid across his massive thighs. She can see him now from her parlour window.

She had married three years ago, at the age of twenty-seven. By then she had reconciled herself to a life of spinsterhood. It wasn't her looks that had kept suitors at bay. Like any young woman, she had taken stock of herself in a looking glass, and concluded that if she was not a conventionally pretty woman, the right pair of eyes might grant she was a striking one. Ada knows she possesses a good figure. Her father had liked to say she had a smile that could light up a coal bin. She is aware that lamplight lends an auburn tint to her dark and abundant hair. Her lips are full, although the upper one is a bit short. She no longer despairs of the freckles that she had tried to bleach away with buttermilk compresses when she was thirteen, buttermilking herself so frequently the housecats began to eye her like a dish of cream. Finally, her mother had put her foot down. "Ada," she had said, "do not presume to undo God's work. Never think the Lord makes mistakes." Ada is not convinced her beloved mother was right to give God so much credit. Living with freckles is one thing, but whatever was the Lord thinking when he gave her Randolph Tarr for a husband?

Of course, her mother's firm answer would be, "God did not impose Mr. Tarr on you, my dear. You accepted him."

If she had not been so miserable as a governess in the Harding household, would she have leapt so quickly to accept Mr. Tarr's proposal of marriage? That, Ada admits, isn't the only explanation for her rashness. Randolph in his mid-fifties is still a striking man, with a thick mane of pewter-coloured hair, a high-bridged aquiline nose, and an erect and commanding carriage that any United States senator would envy. His self-assurance, his refined manners, his gifts of perfume, handkerchiefs, and chocolates, the little kindnesses offered her during their courting days had cast him in a very favourable and flattering light when compared to the wind-burned and ham-fisted young farm boys who had come to woo her in the front parlour back in Ohio. More to the point, Randolph never fled the scene the way they had done after hearing her opinion on some topic such as Russian objectives in the Dardanelles, or the Dred-Scott decision. Her bluestocking ways had put them to flight.

Randolph Tarr had listened to her opinions, or appeared to listen to them, with the utmost attention. Back then Ada had judged that the difference in their ages – more than twenty years – might be a requirement for her happiness. She reasoned that a woman encouraged by her parents to have strong views, to be independent, was better off with an older man, someone confident and accomplished enough not to be frightened by a woman with ideas of her own. Randolph had seemed a man of substance, but on that score she couldn't have been further from the mark.

Shortly after their wedding, she had begun to learn what sort of man her husband was. Their brief honeymoon was spent in Helena; Randolph claimed his thriving law practice in Fort Benton could not spare him more than a few days. When the surrey rolled to a stop before her new home, Randolph had said in a most casual, offhand fashion, "Inside, my dear, I have a surprise for you. The nicest little package imaginable. My daughter, Celeste, whom you will adore and who will adore you. Let us go inside and the two of you can become acquainted."

Ada was struck dumb. She could not believe she had heard him correctly. Or perhaps this was his strange idea of a joke; he had a rather heavy-handed sense of humour. He had made no mention of being father to a child. But there inside the house, any hopes she had had that he might be giving her a leg-pull smashed up against the hard fact of Celeste, a little blond, vacuously blue-eyed porcelain doll of sixteen, to whom he announced the news of his marriage right then and there, in the same breezy fashion he had informed Ada of her step into motherhood. It was callous beyond belief; it defied the imagination. One glance at Celeste confirmed that she, like her new stepmother, had been kept in the dark about the other's existence.

Given the volatility of girls Celeste's age, Ada had expected a blaze of fireworks, but no eruption came. In an instant, the girl swept surprise from her face, simply put out her hand, and said, "I am very pleased to know you, Mrs. Tarr." Ada's bewilderment was so complete, she was so at a loss for words, that she found herself responding in the same numb fashion, greeting her new daughter with a formal handshake and a frozen smile.

But that night, when Randolph and she had retired to their bedroom, Ada had lit into him, ferociously saying, "What were you thinking, why have you resorted to this preposterous secrecy?" And Randolph had assumed an innocent, blank look and said that since they were so much in love, what difference could it really make? When she had continued to press him, he had grown frustrated and unleashed his nasty lawyer's tongue on her. He had coldly remarked, "You know, Ada, Mr. Harding did not offer me congratulations on my marriage. But he did thank me for taking a very difficult woman off his hands. I'm beginning to see what he meant."

It has taken Ada a good deal of time to understand her husband. What she has concluded is that he will do almost anything to dodge or delay unpleasantness. He likes people to think well of him, and when they don't, he finds it inexplicable. He hopes problems will miraculously evaporate. Failing to mention Celeste was prompted by Randolph's fear that his fiancée would balk, have second thoughts about his suitability as a husband. Only at the last possible moment, when there was no escaping the corner he had put himself in, had he blithely broken the news, behaving as if it were nothing but a tiny oversight and that any reasonable person would accept it as such. When she hadn't, he had struck back cruelly because it was necessary for him to make himself believe in his own innocence. Ada suspects these habits of mind are at the root of his troubles with Gobbler Johnson.

As to Celeste's unusual reaction when they met, at first Ada had assumed the girl was so under her father's thumb she dared not evidence surprise at anything he had chosen to do. Now she knows this was not the case at all. It is Randolph who is under Celeste's thumb, although she seldom feels the need to squash him. Her stepdaughter is so lethargic, so unengaged with life that she is generally content to listlessly reflect back to people what they regard as proper and fitting. However, once in a blue moon, if Celeste feels her interests endangered, then those who threaten them better duck.

Perhaps Celeste, who has few preoccupations besides her hair, her clothes, and entertaining young gentlemen who admire her almost as much as she admires herself, was quickly pleased to have another woman in the house, assumed the two of them would naturally become best of friends, imagined jolly times giggling about her beaux, dressing each other's hair, and sharing clothes and jewellery. It is difficult to say exactly what her stepdaughter may have been thinking; she is such a dim and frivolous girl.

True to form, Randolph had given her no hint of Mr. Dunne's arrival. Five mornings ago, Ada had looked out the window and seen a man seated on her porch, a brooding figure dressed all in black. Startled, she had rushed into the kitchen and excitedly reported the trespasser to her husband. With his mouth full of toast Randolph had replied, "Yes, my dear, that is Mr. Dunne. That damn Gobbler Johnson has resurfaced – sent me a threatening letter. Until I get the matter sorted out, I thought it prudent to keep a man watching over the place." Offering a placating smile, he continued to assure her that this was just a precaution, there was absolutely no need for alarm.

But Ada is alarmed, most dreadfully alarmed. After Gobbler Johnson had fired into her husband's office, she had done her best to drag out of Randolph what was behind this mad act. With customary vagueness, Randolph had drawn a caricature of an ignorant prospector who, having lost an unwinnable case, had gotten it into his head that his legal counsel was at fault. In an act of bravado, the lout had fired a bullet into the wall above his lawyer's head. Randolph had sworn there had been no genuine intention to harm him – Johnson had meant only to frighten him. And then he had conceded with a sorry-looking smile, "In that he was successful. His mission accomplished, he won't be heard from again." But Johnson has been heard from again and as a consequence, that very peculiar man, Mr. Dunne, is guarding her doorstep, armed to the teeth.

What she finds even more disturbing is Randolph's attempt to arm her, to press a five-shot derringer pepperbox on her. When he informed her that Mr. Dunne was going to teach her how to use the weapon, she had retorted that she was not going to submit to any such nonsense, he could get that idea out of his head. Her husband had turned the pocket gun over to Mr. Dunne and put the onus on his hireling to get her to accept instruction.

Yesterday, Mr. Dunne had come to the door and solemnly declared it was time for her lesson. She had done her best to hold firm against him, but he was more stubborn than she had bargained for. He had simply persevered, saying the same thing over and over again with the single-mindedness of a child who wants something and will not relent until he has it. At last, it came to her that she could drive him off only by losing her temper or insulting him. But she could not bring herself to show him such rudeness.

With ill grace she followed him out of the house to buy some peace at the price of a lesson and be rid of him. Pedantically, Dunne had explained the working of the gun to her, shown her how to cock it. Standing beside her, solicitously supporting her arm, he directed her aim towards the lone cottonwood tree in the backyard. His touch was very light and delicate, as if he thought the slightest pressure would snap a fragile bone. Then, his breath gusting against her cheek, he whispered, "Now, Mrs. Tarr, fire away." She did, two rounds, the second of which found its mark and bit off a small plaque of bark from the tree.

"Keep firing," he said. "Once he's struck you must not hesitate. You must finish the job."

But the feel of the pistol jumping and struggling in her hand like a tiny animal squeezed in her fist had been so upsetting that she had dropped the gun at her feet and walked back into the house feeling vaguely ashamed and disgusted with herself. A few moments later she heard a timid knock and went to the door.

If Mr. Dunne had been the wilful child before, now he was contrite. He blurted out, "Oh, Mrs. Tarr, I don't know what I done to offend you, but I am most grievous sorry. I only done what I was told, what needed to be done to keep you safe and somehow I . . ."

She looked down and saw the pocket pistol resting in the middle of his enormous palm.

Impulsively, she took him by the sleeve, drew him into the house, and walked him to the parlour, saying, "Mr. Dunne, I most sincerely apologize for leaving you without an explanation. You are most chivalrous and kind. I promise you I will keep that gun close. For your sake, to ease your mind." She took the gun from his hand and stowed it away in her bag. "There. It is settled."

And Mr. Dunne had beamed.

Ada Tarr turns her eyes back out the window where faithful Mr. Dunne keeps watch over her. This morning she made sugar doughnuts before the heat of the day took hold. There is a pitcher of fresh lemonade. Mr. Dunne is a robust man, the kind of man with a great hunger to feed. She gets up and goes to the kitchen to prepare him a tray.

Stepping out onto the porch she murmurs, "Mr. Dunne, would you care for some refreshment?"

And Mr. Dunne, anticipating his treat, is the very illustration of heart-felt gratitude.

FIVE

August 4, 1876

REACHED FORT BENTON two days ago. The place is strained to the bursting point with sanctuary seekers. With a bit of luck I was able to secure lodgings for Hathaway, Joe, and myself in the Overland Hotel. A Methodist circuit rider had just been evicted because he was in arrears with his bill. The offer of two weeks' payment – in advance – secured the room McMullen and I now share; greasing the palm of the bloodsucking proprietor with a little more cash got Hathaway a spot on the floor of the pantry.

Climbing the stairs to our room with Joe, I felt as if I was held together with nothing but flour paste. When McMullen stripped off his clothes and tossed himself down on his bed to sleep, I thought the glue had crumbled. I couldn't trust my eyes. Stretched out on the counterpane, Joe resembled the corpse of one of those slaughtered bandits American lawmen lash to a board and prop up against a wall so they can have their photograph taken with the trophy. I saw that he is riddled with old bullet holes. Seven. I counted them to prove I wasn't hallucinating. Maybe that sight gave me the jolt needed to shake loose that other picture from my head, the coyote's accusing eyes, the slick guts hanging from its jaws. At any rate, given a respite from that, I slept the sleep of the dead, did not wake until three o'clock in the afternoon.

McMullen was up and about by then, spry and chipper, ready to embark on a tour of the saloons. He is determined to have a high old time in town before he returns to Fort Walsh to sell his cabin and its contents and collect his backpay from Walsh for breaking a string of mustangs for B Troop. No love lost between those two men, largely because Joe has never been able to hide his amusement at Walsh's vanity, his taste for "dressing up." The first time Joe saw the Major swanning about in a fringed buckskin shirt, a dress sword, and a slouch hat – which like a fussy milliner he had decorated with an eagle feather and a long silk scarf – he feigned wonder and amazement, saying within earshot of the Major that "Buffalo Bill himself could learn a thing or two from our very own eye-dazzler on how to primp and preen and prance." It didn't help Joe's standing with the Major either when it got back to him that B Troop's horse breaker was calling the hero-worshipping constables who sported imperials in admiration of their commander's own dashing beard "Walsh's Chinny Chin Chin Hairs." The Major is not a man to be mocked; he holds a grudge.

Joe did his best to coax me to join him in a night on the town, but I begged off, pleading fatigue. I felt a contemptible sneak when he finally left, but I need to be discreet regarding my business with Major Guido Ilges. Joe is such a garrulous fellow that he is apt to drop a careless word on some occasion. This is a matter that requires circumspection.

Setting out to pay my call on Ilges, I had no idea of the character of the man I was about to encounter. Once or twice, when I'd been on leave in Benton, I had noticed him going about the street in uniform, but that hardly qualifies as acquaintance. And Walsh had been of little help in providing insight into his American counterpart. If the Major gets off on the wrong foot with a man, as he did with Joe, it blinds him to any virtues that individual might possess. "Six-foot-six of stogie-smoking, sauerkraut-farting Prussian" was the best he could do to sum Ilges up. The only useful thing for me in that description was the reference to Ilges's weakness for cigars, so on my way to the post I stopped off at Wetzel's General Merchandise to buy a peace offering to deliver along with the letter of introduction I carried in my pocket.

The tinkle of Wetzel's bell, the aroma of oiled floorboards, sugar-cured bacon, coffee, soap, leather, pickling brine, boiled sweets, cheese, lanolin, and kerosene took me back to those happy Saturday mornings before what Mother euphemistically called the Great Disruption – a phrase that always capitalized itself in my boy's mind as the title of a mysteriously arcane book whose meaning I could not grasp. But when I was five or six years old, long before the Great Disruption, long before Father flung himself at the feet of the scullery maid, every Saturday morning he and I would stroll down Ottawa's streets to, as he put it, "take a look at the accounts" at Case's Merchandise, son and heir, hand in hand. By then, Father's business concerns had expanded beyond logging. The Merchandise was only one of his many enterprises and a very minor cog in his money-making apparatus, but to me it seemed his crowning achievement. Other boys may have dreamed of being Captain Cook, Francis Drake, or General Wolfe, but I can remember only one overweening ambition – to succeed lucky Mr. Tunbridge and to someday manage the Merchandise and take charge of that treasure house of mints, harnesses, oranges, enamelled pans, nuts, shovels, dates, shotguns, bolts of cloth, and gingersnaps. I wandered up and down the aisles touching and smelling all the wares, stood gazing up at the stamped-tin ceiling, mesmerized by the play of sunlight on its shiny surface while Mr. Tunbridge and Father examined the ledgers in a backroom. On those Saturdays I felt a happiness that seemed inextinguishable.

When I told Wetzel's cordial clerk that I was looking for a box of cigars for the commander of the garrison, he was delighted to inform me the Major was a regular customer and to point me to Ilges's favourite brand, manufactured by Kennedy Bros. of Canaan, Indiana. With the box tucked under my arm, I proceeded through the town. Fort Benton has suddenly become a gloomy place now, displays little of the rollicking high spirits I remember from my last visit here. Out-of-work river rats and freighters hang about on corners, hands stuffed in empty pockets, mourning the whores and whiskey a shortage of funds puts out of their reach. Poke-bonneted countrywomen eye the prices in shop windows, hands folded up in their aprons, calculating how to feed their families on a thin dime. All were so wrapped up in doleful thoughts that I did not merit so much as a glance as I made my way down Front Street – except one from a billy goat perched on a hogshead, chewing on an old flour sack.

Near the post I passed an encampment of soldiers, reinforcements in transit to face the Sioux. They are bivouacked hard by an alkali flat, and when a wind comes up, it raises a blizzard of dust. That afternoon it was blowing, and a spectral picket line of horses powdered in bitter white alkali was standing there, heads hung low in the heat. The soldiers sat drooped on campstools, or wandered about with a haunted, aimless air, their blue uniforms turned ashen. They looked to be at the end of a long campaign rather than at the beginning of one.

I gave the officer of the day Walsh's letter of introduction, requested him to give it to the commander, and asked him to inquire whether Major Ilges would be so good as to grant me an interview. After a short wait, I was ushered into his office, a large, airy room spartanly furnished with a few cane chairs and an oak filing cabinet. Ilges was seated behind a baize-covered desk, a big map of Montana Territory on the wall behind him. He was wearing a green eyeshade and was toying with the letter he had just been given. When he stood to shake my hand the room suddenly seemed to shrink, the ceiling to lower. The man dwarfed everything in sight.

Although his manner was professionally amiable it was also distinctly wary. His English is fluent with only a slight trace of the Deutsch. We passed a few pleasantries and managed to achieve an absolute unanimity of opinion on the weather: hot and with little prospect of rain. I gave him the cigars, accompanied with the white lie that they came with the compliments of Major Walsh. Ilges's eyebrows gave a skeptical bob when he heard that, but he politely replied, "That is very kind of him." At his insistence I helped myself to a cigar. We sat down and passed a few moments of awkward silence camouflaged in smoke.

Then, suddenly, Ilges embarked on an anecdote about a bizarre decree passed by the Prussian government which had forbidden the smoking of cigars in public unless they were fitted with a wire mesh to prevent their ends coming into contact with women's crinolines. The Kaiser feared for the ladies' lives, feared mass incinerations in the ballrooms of his kingdom. As he related this, Ilges's accent noticeably thickened. It was as if he were performing in a music-hall skit, lampooning an officious German puffing away on his own terrible incendiary device. Finishing his story, he looked me steadily in the eye and said, "Ah, the Germans. So obsessed with rules, with order. Ridiculous, nein?"

I suspected this self-parody was a response to the tantrum Walsh had confessed to throwing, some slur he had probably cast on the Teutonic race in the heat of the moment. I took my time replying. "Don't mistake me for Walsh," I said. "I am a cautious man. Unlike him, I have a taste for order."

Ilges gave a pat to the letter of introduction lying on the desktop. "That is what Walsh says in this. He claims you are a rational man. That you calculate like an abacus." I could see him studying me closely, and was pleased to think that in choosing to describe myself as an abacus I had intrigued him. "He mentions you bring me a proposal – one that he hopes I find agreeable. I am not convinced agreement between the Major and me is possible. The last time we met was not a pleasant occasion. When I spoke of my intention to keep a copy of any report I sent him, and suggested that he do the same with any he submitted to me, Walsh was outraged. He said I had insulted him by suggesting he was likely to distort any information I provided him. I hurried to assure him my motives were simply this: if any of my superiors in this time of crisis charged me with being negligent in the performance of my duty, I wanted proof to the contrary. But Major Walsh stormed out of my office." A brief smile flitted over Ilges's lips. "I do not want my crinoline set aflame by President Grant's cigar."

I was realizing that the man did not conform at all to Walsh's disparaging description of him. Then my eyes fell on a framed daguerreotype on his desk, which depicted Union officers gathered around cannons, and what I took to be a captured Confederate flag. Ilges was easily recognizable among them because of his great height. Walsh, who has yearned for battle and never seen it, must have felt the thorn in his paw when he saw his counterpart in Fort Benton pictured this way. I said, "Major Walsh was wrong to view your actions in such a light. Yours was an eminently sensible precaution. He sees that now." I paused before adding a qualification. "What you say about establishing a record is all very well, but I think you would acknowledge official correspondence has its limitations."

Ilges took off his green eyeshade and carefully stowed it away in a small mahogany box. I sensed that was a stratagem to mask that his curiosity had been piqued. "In what sense?" he asked, careful to display no particular interest.

"I'm sure that it is your experience that anything to be read by a higher-up encourages circumspection, a certain guardedness in the writer."

Ilges conceded that with a slight dip of the head.

"Here we are talking about an even touchier situation, one in which the governments of our respective countries are demanding you and Walsh to keep each other fully apprised of developments on your side of the border. But we know that *perfect* frankness is not possible."

"Do we? It is very kind of you to speak for me."

It was a mild reproof, accompanied by a faint smile, but I felt the force of it. "I beg pardon, Major. Perhaps I am too much in love with abstractions, but permit me to pose a hypothetical. Let us say that you provided an estimation on the morale or fighting quality of the troops in the field, or passed an opinion whether your generals were likely to succeed or fail in suppressing the Sioux uprising in the next few weeks or even months. How would that sit with the higher authorities? It would not be appreciated." I shrugged. "But surely that is exactly the kind of information that would be very useful because it bears on the possibility of the Sioux arriving in Walsh's vicinity. It would influence how, when, and where he readies himself to meet the threat." I paused. "I could think of other instances of a similar kind. But no matter how pertinent such information could be, no one would commit it to writing for fear of being seen to criticize those in command."

"So this is what Walsh is proposing?" demanded Ilges with some asperity. "That I pull his fat from the fire and leave mine to burn?"

"Far from it," I assured him. "On the face of it, it may appear you have more to give in such an exchange than Major Walsh. The telegraph office here surely provides you with updates on the latest military developments, troop movements, and so forth. Steamboats from downriver bring news and rumours concerning the Sioux from every place they pick up cargo and passengers. In that sense, you have a great advantage over Walsh, who is isolated from the wider world. But he has resources you do not. His half-breed scouts are welcomed in all the Indian camps. He and his troopers go wherever they please, unmolested by any of the northern tribes. I put this question to you with the greatest respect – does the American army have that freedom of movement, those kinds of friendly relations with the Indians?"

"I admit that we do not," he said grudgingly.

"Presently, no one knows where the Sioux are. They must be located before they can be beaten. Other Indians are likely to know their whereabouts. Walsh has access to those Indians, he can go straight to the horse's mouth."

I could see Ilges was weighing what he had just heard. Coaxingly, I said, "I am well aware of the size of the garrison here, Major. It is small. Hardly adequate to protect Fort Benton and its outlying areas if the Sioux arrive here. Am I correct in assuming that you do not have sufficient soldiers at your disposal to reconnoitre the border area?"

"The answer is obvious. I do not."

"Walsh is as eager to know where the Sioux might be as you are. Let me put you another hypothetical. If his Métis scouts and police patrols extended below the line, might that not be useful to both of you if something were learned about the hostiles' location? Of course, the question is rhetorical because no government will countenance extraterritorial incursions. They are a violation of national sovereignty, no matter how practical they might be." There I left it hanging.

Ilges wore a doubtful look. "You are suggesting Walsh and I go behind our superiors' backs."

"I am suggesting that you strike a gentleman's agreement so that you can do exactly what you have been charged to do. You have been ordered to share information fully, but your hands are tied. As the crow flies, Fort Benton and Fort Walsh are separated by less than a hundred miles. Everyone expects that if the Sioux make for Canada, they will pass this way. This is your ground. You will be held responsible if a mishap occurs here."

Ilges sat thinking. When he spoke, I detected indecision in his voice. "I cannot refute what you say, but I am not prepared to act recklessly."

"One could say that under the circumstances the advantages outweigh the risks. Yes? The authorities will settle for nothing less than success. I suggest that what I and Walsh propose offers the best chance of achieving it." I hesitated before adding, "I tell you this in confidence. Major Walsh fears that if he does not produce results, no explanation for failure will serve to satisfy his masters. They will have him out on his ear."

"He left no such impression with me," said Ilges.

"Walsh does not admit fear. He is constitutionally incapable of that. But I heard it in his voice when we talked about these matters."

With great caution, Ilges said, "And how would this utter frankness, this perfect honesty, be achieved?"

"I plan to establish myself here in Fort Benton. If you were amenable, I could act as an honest broker. Anything sensitive could pass through me. As a civilian, my communications with Walsh would naturally be assumed to be personal and private. They would not be subject to scrutiny. Whatever you told me that could be viewed askance by your superiors I would convey to him by letter. Whatever Major Walsh wrote me I would pass on to you verbally. Whatever you learn from each other unofficially," I said, laying stress on the word, "can appear in your reports without mentioning from whom it came – present it as hearsay, your own deductions, the fruit of your own intelligence gathering, however you wish. Or do not pass it on at all. That is for each of you to decide."

He shook his head. "I am an orderly man. It goes against the grain."

"I understand your reservations, but in a crisis like this it seems to me the gravest danger to you and Walsh is to be regarded as having failed those above you. In times of panic blame is seldom allotted fairly." Ilges was listening closely. "All one has to do is read the papers. Do you see any willingness on the part of Congress or President Grant's administration to shoulder any blame for Custer's defeat? No. It is shifted to those lower in the chain of command, men like you and Walsh. I have read a good deal about the damage foreigners have done to your army – the Irish and others," I said. "Some would even like to lay the defeat at Little Bighorn on the shoulders of the Italian trumpeter who carried Custer's order for reinforcements to be sent up – it is claimed his English could not be understood. A battle lost because of an accent." I paused. "Some people make better scapegoats than others."

"My English is more than serviceable," said Ilges stiffly.

"I regret to have put it so brutally, but you know what I'm saying. It is not a question of an accent but of origins."

"I need some time to think about this," he said.

"I can ask for no more," I conceded, getting to my feet. "But before I go I have one last thing to say. I know Walsh's character. I can interpret him, read him. He is a volatile man who, in the heat of the moment, does not always mean what he says. It can be useful to you to have the services of a translator."

"Why would I consent to any of this, put myself in your hands?" he said as if musing aloud. "You are Walsh's man."

"Believe me," I told him, "I am no one's man – at least in the sense you mean."

"Then why are you doing this? What do you hope to gain?" Ilges looked genuinely perplexed.

"I only wish to make myself useful. To be of assistance to my country. And if I succeed in doing that, I will be of assistance to you too, Major Ilges. Like it or not, the powers that be have yoked you and Walsh together. The question now is whether or not you will pull together." That said, I left him.

If the Major and Ilges are a strange pair, Walsh and I may be a stranger one. He sees everything in black and white. There are no greys in his world. I suppose it falls to me to point them out to him.

Walsh once told me that he envied me. When I asked how that was possible, he said I had had the great good fortune to see action at the Battle of Ridgeway and he had not. The Major has a strange idea of good fortune. When I saw General O'Neill's name in that document Dunne left with Walsh, I was brought back to the moment that the Irish hero had looked down at me from the back of his horse, the contempt with which he treated me after our defeat, the haughty glitter in his eye. In such circumstances, I doubt Walsh could have swallowed O'Neill's condescension the way I did.

But to speak the truth, the scorn of the enemy did not cut me very deeply. It was the disdain of Pudge Wilson, brother officer, erstwhile friend, that slashed me to the bone.

SIX

CASE AND MCMULLEN HAVE given up hope that Peregrine Hathaway will show. The three had agreed to meet at six o'clock for supper at the Oxbow, but when the hands of the wall clock pointed to six-fifteen, McMullen said, "Enough is enough. Time, tide, and Joe McMullen wait for no man. I'm ordering."

It's now nearly seven-fifteen and McMullen is looking forward to a night of frolic. This afternoon he paid a visit to the Tonsorial Palace and still smells powerfully of bay rum; his freshly shorn temples gleam white, and the moustache he had had the barber wax into a set of bristling whiskers twitches and vibrates as he chews his pork chop. "Most likely the pup's piddling on that girl's door post, marking his territory," Joe observes to Case.

"Perhaps. He feels that territory under threat. The visit he paid her he found a rival in the parlour, and beat a hasty retreat. Yesterday, the young lady's mother told him the object of his affections could not receive visitors because she was resting her voice. Peregrine took that as a flimsy excuse, a sign Miss Tarr didn't want to see him. He believes that his adversary has won the day."

"Then he better give it up. Two fellows contending for the warm regards of a young lady – that's dangerous business. I learned that lesson years ago. Almost got myself killed over a sweet young thing by name of Lurleen." McMullen gives a sly grin. "Don't tell me I never acquainted you with that episode?"

"No, but you will. I see it coming at me like a runaway carriage."

"Lurleen," says McMullen, "was the one who come between me and my boss, Fancy Charles. Fancy had a woodhawker's station about a hundred mile downriver from here. Made his living selling fuel to the steamboats. Old as Methuselah, but lord almighty that man could chop and buck wood. Damn near killed me trying to keep up with the old bastard. Now of course woodhawking ain't exactly my line, I don't care for work that comes with blisters, but a empty belly leads to compromise. Ain't that so?"

Case nods. It is the only thing a man can do once McMullen starts one of his anecdotes bouncing downhill.

"Anyways, after that first day on the end of a bucksaw with Fancy, I was so tuckered out I didn't have the strength to force a fart, and just as I was dropping off to sleep I heard something peculiar." Joe's eyes widen in mock awe. "It was the voice of a young gal. Coming from t'other side of the cabin. Now you best believe, a voice coming out of nowheres was a shock to the system, but what it was saying, why it made the hairs on the back of my neck stand straight up." Joe pauses, and with a thoughtful air adds more white gravy to his plate. "She was saying, 'Lurleen been thinking about this all day. Lurleen been having nasty thoughts all day about what she's going to do with Fancy's peeder.' Well, I sat up in bed and ran my eyes every which way looking for that girl. But she wasn't to be found. It was old Fancy himself talking in that high, sugary, girly voice, addressing his very own carrot. And it was the same thing next night, and the night after that, and the night after that. Now he might been old as dirt, but Fancy worked his peeder just as hard as he did his bucksaw. No sooner we crawled into our pallets of a night and Lurleen would start whispering to Fancy's doowinkle, telling how she'd been wanting it all day, studying on exactly what she was going to do to it, and what it was going to do to her."

"Joe, you lie whether it's called for or not. Just to keep in practice."

McMullen solemnly crosses his heart. "No, sir, hope to die if this ain't the unvarnished truth. Three weeks I had to listen to that dusty old coot and Lurleen carrying on in a bed not eight feet from my own. And every morning Fancy would get up and go about his business as if he was in his right mind, felling cottonwoods and whistling away, happy as a lark. But it was coming near to destroying me. Hearing him and Lurleen carry on in that fashion each and every night was making me desperate jumpy and nervy. So one afternoon I hoists up my courage and I says to Fancy, 'I ain't deaf, you know,' and he looks puzzled and says, 'Who said you was?' like he didn't have any notion to what circumstances I might be raising. So next time we settles down in our cots, I thinks to myself, 'Well, see how it suits him, a taste of his own medicine,' and before Lurleen can start romancing him, I says, 'Hello, Mr. Joe, Lurleen come to pay you a visit this evening. Slide over and let me get in alongside you, you handsome man.' And then Lurleen cries, 'Oh my good Lord, but ain't it *big*!' And I went on to say a good deal more to commend my privates, but I won't burn your tender ears by repeating it all."

"And that did the trick? You got him to mend his ways?"

"Mend his ways? No, sir, it did not. It made him *jealous*. Why every time I turned around, there he was staring at me, hate writ all over his face. And you never seen a more terrible sight than old Fancy Charles with a double-bit axe in his hands, calculating when and where to split me like a chunk of cottonwood. I could see my days was numbered. But lucky for me a steamer hove to a couple of days later, so I seized the chance, resigned from woodhawking without giving notice, piled aboard that boat just as she threw off her mooring lines and started downriver. I took leave of the sweethearts from the deck rail. 'Goodbye, Lurleen! Goodbye, Fancy!' I hollered. 'Never meant to come between you two! If you have a boy child, Lurleen, name him after me!'"

"Joe, you stretch the truth like taffy," says Case, smiling despite himself.

McMullen makes a show of hurt feelings. "Well, I take offence to that. And if you got to call me a liar, you might put the word interesting before it." Then he raises his eyebrows and says, "Hello. Judas bouncing up and down on a railway jigger, here comes trouble."

Case cranes his neck to see Peregrine Hathaway wending his way through the tables, face shining like a bull's-eye lantern, waving a piece of rolled-up paper. He drops down on a chair beside Case and announces, "Miss Celeste *did* have to rest her voice. She wasn't trying to avoid me."

"Your elders was speaking," says Joe, "don't interrupt." He aims a finger at the boy's breastbone. "And another thing. I don't hold with tardiness. You and me leave for Fort Walsh four o'clock tomorrow afternoon, on the dot. If you ain't ready to go – you get left. I ain't going to dawdle about playing pocket pool with myself on account of you ain't learned to tell time. Punctual is polite."

Hathaway is oblivious to McMullen. "I feel so bad having doubted her sincerity, Mr. Case. But look, it's all explained," he says, unfurling a poster on the table. Case and Joe lean over and read.

CITIZENS OF FORT BENTON TAKE NOTE!
You are cordially invited to an
EVENING OF MUSICAL ENTERTAINMENT!
COME ONE, COME ALL!

A free-will offering will be collected, all proceeds intended for the relief of friends and neighbors driven from their homes and occupations by the continuing menace from Sioux hostiles.

Fort Benton's own, the charming and talented
MISS CELESTE TARR, shall offer a selection
of songs both sacred and secular, accompanied by
MRS. RANDOLPH TARR on the pianoforte.

MOSES SOLOMON, ESQ., has generously donated the
use of the *MAJESTIC STAR SALOON* for this charitable
endeavor. Mr. Solomon graciously extends an invitation to
the entire populace of Fort Benton, of every age and sex.

The sale of alcoholic beverages of any variety or
description whatsoever shall not take place during
the duration of the concert, nor any disorderly conduct
deleterious to a full appreciation and enjoyment of the
musical program be countenanced.

Program to take place
AUGUST 6TH, EIGHT O'CLOCK SHARP!

**ALL WELCOME WHO KNOW HOW TO
CONDUCT THEMSELVES!**

"Miss Celeste is to sing, gentlemen. That was why she had
to spare her voice," says Hathaway. "I knew her to be charming
and beautiful, but I had no idea, none at all, that she is also musi-
cally accomplished. It will be a splendid evening. The two of you
must both come to see her."

"Well," says McMullen, "I ain't coming because never mind I
did go, I'd have to hear about it all over again from you, Peregrine,
mile after mile all the way back to Fort Walsh. So I'll save time and
rely on your report. Besides, I already made plans. A fellow in the
Extradition Saloon was praising up four whores who got stuck
here in Benton when the stage stopped running to Helena. Two
sets of twins, identical, can't tell them apart. One pair of Irish and
one pair of Swedes. The Irish ladies is said to be skinny as

greyhounds and plastered with freckles. He said if it weren't for the weight of them freckles those shed hens would lift off and fly skyward in the least breeze. But the Swedes is so plump, pink, and substantial, a cyclone couldn't tip them over. I think I'll have a go at one of each set." Joe stands, gives his pants a hitch. "You best come along, Wesley. It'll be a experience."

Case shakes his head. "No, Joe, I shall pass a chaste evening at the recital with Peregrine. One of us must set him a good example."

"Well, boys, I wish you joy listening to the sweet songstress warble." And with that, McMullen begins to saunter through the Oxbow, nodding pleasantly to total strangers, passing remarks on the dishes. "My, don't them short ribs look a mouthful! Don't Mr. Dagg's cook have a hand with the parsnips!" Then, from the doorway, he gives Case and Hathaway a cheery wave, settles his hat on his newly cropped head, and is gone.

A saloon bartender guards the door of the Majestic Star equipped with a bucket he shakes menacingly in the face of anyone trying to enter. Donations do not appear to be *voluntary* as advertised. When he rattles the bucket at Case, its bottom reveals a pond of silver floating several paper bills. Case contributes two dollars to the pail; the bartender moves aside and he and Hathaway cross the threshold of the Majestic into a jammed room.

Instantly, Peregrine begins to squirm his way through the mob, heading for the front of the room where the saloon's piano stands, displaying a vase of brown-eyed Susans to lend a refined, feminine air to the evening's proceedings. But Case has no intention of pursuing Hathaway through this crush of humanity, choosing first to take his bearings.

The saloon is hot as a boiler room, steaming with the animal heat of closely packed bodies. All the faces around him are beaded with perspiration. The odour is as extreme as the heat, the vinegary, pickling brine smell of sweat laced with the barn-yard aromas of manure, horse, and mule given off by teamsters, bullwhackers, and hoop-legged waddies. An undercurrent of river mud and fried catfish wafts off the boatmen; the hide hunters and wolfers stink of old blood, the sharp tang of rusty iron. Add a dollop of spilled beer, sweet and yeasty, the reek of cheap tobacco, and Case feels his eyes are about to water with every pungent breath he draws.

The din is terrific. Despite the owner's assurances that tonight decorum and propriety will rule, the inexorable inching of the hands of the clock towards the hour of the concert and the suspension of the sale of alcohol has led to a panic among the Majestic's customers. They are swarming the bar, banging glasses on the zinc top, jostling for position, shouting and gesticulating to catch the attention of harried bartenders who scurry back and forth slopping whiskey into out-thrust shot glasses.

Case's gaze falls on the Majestic's proprietor, Moses Solomon. The one serene, still point in bedlam, he stands with his back propped against a beer barrel, squinting at the room through a haze of blue tobacco smoke. His beard is biblical, long and forked. He wears a crimson satin waistcoat buttoned over a white linen shirt; the red satin rosettes on his sleeve garters perfectly match the colour of his vest. His hairstyle is Disraelian, ruffled sissy-boy waves that sweep over his ears and seem scarcely in keeping with his fearsome sobriquet, Moses Mayhem. Case had learned that when Solomon had established Fort Benton's toniest saloon, the citizenry had not appreciated his success, and had subjected him to a barrage of insult and calumny. But one day Solomon had turned on two of the most persistent Jew-baiters and shot them down on a corner of Front Street. Since then, people stepped very lightly in his presence.

The skull-cracking uproar, the stench, the sweltering temperature, the tight press of bodies is almost too much to bear. Hathaway has disappeared, swallowed up in the crowd, and Case is at the point of beating a strategic retreat when he sees

Major Ilges looming above the throng, beckoning him. It's a struggle for Case to reach the Major but when he does, he discovers a relatively calm island in the stormy saloon, a row of chairs reserved for the town's notables in front of the piano, most of them already occupied.

"So glad to see you, Mr. Case," says Ilges. "Will you be my guest? I'm sure Lieutenant Blanchard would surrender his seat so you might sit beside me." The officer asked to relinquish his place shows no evidence of a willingness to surrender anything but withdraws with a sullen, put-upon look as Case demurs accepting. But finally he has no alternative but to settle down on the gracelessly vacated chair.

The Major immediately launches into introductions to the Fort Benton quality. In turn, Case is presented to a young dentist who has just opened a practice in town, the pressman of the *Fort Benton Record*, a goggle-eyed druggist, and Dr. Cornelius Hooper, Fort Benton's most accomplished surgeon. The town's biggest fishes follow: the merchant princes T.C. Power, Mr. Hamilton and Mr. Baker, the Conrad brothers, and the tycoons' wives. The gentlemen are solemn and sober in black broadcloth. The ladies are bedecked, bedizened, and loaded down with jewellery, lavishly swathed in yards of taffeta and silk, and severely corseted.

Ilges insists on describing Case as a young man come to Benton seeking business opportunities. Hearing that, most of the leading businessmen's faces take on a bored, patronizing look, a look that says, How often have I heard that and how often have I seen the results – bankruptcy. Apologetically, Case qualifies the Major's description. "Not so much business as ranching. In a small way."

One of the Conrad brothers remarks, "If it's land you're after, now's the time to plunge. Some of the cattlemen are looking to sell up. The recent troubles have them spooked. If you want to drop by the office sometime, I can give you the name of one or two who are looking for a buyer. I don't touch land myself. It's not liquid."

"Very generous of you," says Case, becoming aware that the racket is subsiding to a low murmuring and expectant shuffling of feet.

In this instant of almost quiet, Major Ilges leans over, puts his mouth to Case's ear, and whispers, "What we spoke about the other day – I have weighed things carefully. I am agreeable. Come to see me tomorrow."

"Very well. I will indeed."

Behind them, Moses Solomon bellows at those still lingering hopefully at the bar, "Stand back! Clear off! Immediate! Music about to begin!" Fort Benton's princes of commerce brace themselves on their seats as if a tooth-puller were approaching, while their wives coyly survey the scene over fluttering fans, straining for a glimpse of the musical entertainment. Case hears one of the women say, "Now young Miss Tarr is a dear, sweet thing, but the way Mrs. Tarr acts is another matter. So very *superior*." As his eyes search the room for a glimpse of this superior woman, he spots Hathaway loitering hard by the improvised stage, a smile on his face, his Adam's apple dancing as he swallows his excitement.

There is a voluntary parting, a shifting and stirring of the multitude to make way for the Tarr family. With a stately and measured tread, Randolph Tarr escorts wife and daughter, one on each arm, their white gloves perched on the sleeves of his best frock coat like obedient doves. The saloon falls into a respectful hush as blond, pink Celeste and dark-haired, pale Ada advance on the piano.

Case is surprised to see Michael Dunne stalking along behind the Tarr family, his colourless eyes restlessly sweeping over the assembly. Briefly they hold on Case, and Dunne bares his teeth – whether in a smile of recognition or a challenge Case can't decide. When the procession halts before the piano Dunne looks a bit befuddled, at a loss as to what to do or where to go. But then he collects himself and plods to a location near Hathaway where he folds his arms over his chest and assumes a look of self-important, alert readiness. Tarr ushers his womenfolk to their respective places, gives a courtly bow to each, and takes a chair that has been held open for him beside Mr. T.C. Power.

Case nudges Ilges and asks, "That fellow Dunne skulking about there. What connection does he have with this?"

"It's said an unhappy client of Tarr's has threatened the peace of his household. Apparently Dunne has been hired as some sort of bodyguard." Ilges juts his jaw disapprovingly. "But I think his presence is hardly necessary here."

Ada Tarr is fussing with her music, and Miss Celeste is offering the room her profile, one slender, gloved hand resting on the piano top. The thrust of her chin, the way her stance displays her figure to full advantage, suggests she has spent hours posing before a mirror, indulged in many finicky adjustments and sidelong glances at herself in the glass. The cuirasse bodice of her lilac gown displays a slender waist and gives an upward thrust to plump, girlish breasts. An intricately beaded polonaise bustle, elaborately pleated and ruffled, cascades behind her to the floor. A thick plait of white-blond hair dangles over her left shoulder like the tail of a docile cat; her tiny mouth is vivid with lip rouge. She stands as perfectly still as a Wedgwood figurine.

Her stepmother is another picture altogether. Ada Tarr is dressed in a modest high-necked grey gown, hair primly parted down the middle and drawn into a tight bun. But she wears a wry, enigmatic smile at odds with her severe and spinsterly appearance. She makes Case think of the older, unmarried sister at the wedding, the one who knows unflattering comparisons are being made between her and the bride, but remains determined to rely on her own estimation of her worth.

Moses Solomon is making his way towards the front, a piece of paper clutched in his hand, a sure sign that a ponderous introduction is about to be delivered. Seeing him coming, Ada Tarr tilts her head at her stepdaughter and slams out a thunderous chord, transfixing the publican in his tracks. The melody established, Celeste's high, tremulous voice scrambles after it, and Solomon scrambles back to the refuge of the bar.

"Shall we gather at the river, / Where bright angel feet have trod, / With its crystal tide forever? / Flowing by the throne of God?" sings Celeste, so invitingly that the roughnecks stare at her pretty shoes, as if this vision's feet are those described in the hymn – bright and angelic.

The chorus impending, Ada Tarr's right hand leaves the keyboard in a commanding gesture that urges the audience to join in the refrain. And they do, at first in a tentative mumble that slowly swells into fervent disharmony. "Yes, we'll gather at the river, / The beautiful, beautiful river; / Gather with the saints at the river / That floats by the throne of God." As the last words of the chorus are bellowed, her hand flies up again, then gives a downward chop that axes them into silence as Celeste commences the next verse. Three more times Ada's hand flashes a trainman's signal and the chorus rumbles into action like a locomotive, three more times she slashes it down, slamming on the brakes.

Case, like everyone else, sings on cue, but unlike the rest of the audience, he feels irritable, growing increasingly annoyed at Mrs. Tarr's imperious manipulation of them, at the mildly sardonic twist to the conductor's lips. Still, despite a vague feeling of hostility, he can't keep his eyes off her, off that shockingly white, luminous face.

Just like that, "Shall We Gather at the River" ends. A ripple of uncertainty runs through the audience. Is it sacrilegious to applaud a hymn? A few waddies and teamsters begin to clap and whistle, but before the acclaim can secure a toehold, Mrs. Tarr arches her eyebrows at Celeste and they launch into "Come Home, Father." The lugubrious air proceeds, Little Mary pleading piteously with Father to leave the bar because Brother Benny, lying cradled in Mother's arms, is deathly ill. But Father, crazed by demon drink, refuses. Back home, Benny expires, the last words on his lips a wish to kiss Papa good night.

When the last line comes, Case can hear a good many demon drinkers in the audience snuffling and clearing their throats. He catches the sound of a stifled sob, disguised as a cough as Ada Tarr bustles her stepdaughter headlong into the next selection. And that is how the evening's program unrolls, song following song without a pause, "Grandfather's Clock," "I Dreamt I Dwelt in Marble Halls," "Oh, Come, Angel Band," "Brother's Fainting at the Door." Celeste delivers them with her eyes fixed on a corner where wall meets ceiling; each is sung with the passionless, mechanical tunefulness of a music box, her body stiff as a pikestaff.

An uncanny, clenched tension builds in the room. Case can sense the men's struggle to master the sentiment these songs and hymns have stirred up in them. Since they boomed out "Shall We Gather at the River," they haven't been able to give vent to their feelings; even the release that a stirring ovation could provide them has been denied. Everything they've heard is a catalogue of woe, regret, and loss. Case is certain that the old hymns, the old songs have awakened homesickness: memories of a kitchen in Massachusetts, a stretch of black, muddy field in Ohio, a moor purpled with heather in Scotland, a green pasture spotted with red horses in Kentucky.

And more. Death hovers in all these tunes. Like a man who takes a drink of water and tastes silt when he comes to the bottom of the glass, they feel mortality on their tongues. A dying child, a clock in a parlour stopped by an old man's last heartbeat, a soldier expiring on the doorstep – not even a lavish sugarcoating of sentimentality can sweeten the bitter taste in their mouths.

Only when the rousing finale comes does the crowd shake off its gloom. It is "Garryowen," the song that the newspapers have reported the 7th Cavalry marched off to, bound for the Little Bighorn. "Our hearts so stout have got us fame, / For soon 'tis known from whence we came; / Where'er we go they dread the name / Of Garryowen in glory."

An eruption comes with the first words. An outburst so violent that Miss Celeste flinches; her eyes fall from that distant spot she's been contemplating and swing to the bellowing mouths. Now is their chance to march against death, to put it on the run with a stirring tune. Trample it under their boots. There is a ruckus of concussive hand clapping, foot stomping. Shot glasses jump on the counter; ceiling lamps rock on their chains, dust puffs up between the floorboards as if the sallow revenants of Custer's slaughtered men are resurrecting. Miss Celeste's voice is lost in the roar. Her lips keep silently forming the words as Mrs. Tarr gallops the tempo, beating the keyboard harder and harder, trying to end this wild demonstration by whipping on the song to its finish. Smashing out the last chord, she leaps up from the piano bench, flaps her hands at the audience to drive home the point "Garryowen" is over and done.

But there's no quelling the riot. A black fireworks of shapeless, battered hats pitches into the air, a deep-throated holler comes as the mob surges forward, heaves up against the backs of the chairs holding Fort Benton's most eminent citizens. Everyone is shoved and rocked; there is a scramble to get to their feet to avoid being upset on the floor. The Benton ladies are scowling, jerking shawls into place; their husbands tug down coattails and try to look imposing, but can't quite manage the trick. A moment of confused indecision and then Fort Benton's finest begin to make a hurried exit from the scene, the men hustling their womenfolk towards the door with stealthy, shamefaced haste. In moments, the front row empties, all except for Mr. Randolph Tarr, who looks like the one forlorn courtier left to hold the palace while royalty flees.

A walleyed prospector shouts, "Give us another song!" a demand bolstered by wild cheers. Remembering Custer's death has got the mob's blood up; their mood is jovially belligerent, but they might turn ugly-sour if they don't get what they want. Near the piano, Celeste is clinging to her stepmother's hand like a little girl, blue eyes popped wide with fright. Mrs. Tarr turns the cold stare of a judge threatened with losing control of the courtroom onto the boisterous horde.

They're all chanting "Song! Song!" at the top of their lungs, and Celeste appears to be contemplating burying her face in Mother's skirts. Ada shouts, "Gentlemen! Gentlemen! Please! Please, gentlemen!" Gradually, the clamour dies down. "We thank you for your very generous approbation, which is much appreciated," declares Ada sternly, "but Miss Celeste's voice is not strong, and must not be overtaxed. She must decline an encore."

Case glances to Peregrine Hathaway, whose face is worriedly knotted at the sight of Celeste's distress, and hopes to God the boy doesn't attempt to intervene. Mr. Tarr certainly shows no signs of coming to the ladies' succour, aside from offering the room a timid, appeasing smile over his shoulder.

"You then, Missus," shouts someone. "You ain't used your voice up. You give us a song. It's for a good cause, them that's been turned out of house and home. We'll pay. What say, boys?" A coin sails through the air, strikes the piano, clatters to the floor. And then pennies come flying from every direction, a shower of copper hail, bouncing all around the Tarr women, Celeste ducking and cringing, one arm thrown protectively over her head while Ada cries out, "Stop! Stop! Stop *now*!"

The storm of change peters out and the men switch to clapping and stamping, a bullying drum roll. Mrs. Tarr steers Celeste over to her father and leaves her in his care. He gives a few ineffectual pats to his daughter's back that only result in Celeste's head drooping even lower. Ada Tarr strides back to the piano, stares at the rabble until they fall silent. "All right," she says quietly, "I'll give you a song."

Bowing her head, she pensively shoves a coin about on the floor with the toe of her shoe. She begins to hum, searching for the melody. The audience strains to catch the tune but in the beginning it's unidentifiable, nothing but a low, tentative drone. Gradually, the hum begins to strengthen, and as it does Ada Tarr's head begins to lift, eyes clenched so tightly shut that a pearl of moisture gleams in their corners, her hands spasmodically opening and closing, clutching for whatever the music is that she is hearing in her head.

Everyone recognizes the song when she begins to sing, but Ada Tarr has slowed the tempo, turned it into a dirge, a long-drawn-out lament. Her voice is grating, harsh, wiping all the verve and bounce out of what was once a rollicking challenge to the secessionists by the North. She has taught a familiar song to speak a new language.

"We live in hard and stirring times, / Too sad for mirth, too rough for rhymes; / For songs of peace have lost their chimes, / And that's what's the matter."

Case can feel the room breathless behind him as she stands there like a blind woman, hands opening and closing as if trying to grasp and pull some form out of the darkness she has surrounded herself with. "That's what's the matter, / The rebels have to scatter; / We'll make them flee, / By land and sea, / And that's what's the matter." Somehow she succeeds in making boisterous defiance sound hopeless, painful and poignant. Against their will, Mrs. Tarr drags the audience along with her through every single verse of the song, darkening and wringing sorrow out of words that no one guessed held sorrow in them. And when she finishes, no one moves, no one makes a sound. Then, whatever has taken possession of Ada Tarr drains out of her. Her face relaxes; her hands drop to her side; her eyes open, washed clear and shining.

There is no applause, only an angry mumbling, the scrape of boots shifting irritably on the floor. The spell of her performance broken, all they are left with is the bare and literal meaning of the words, an insult to every Southerner in the room.

Someone says, "Bitch."

In the front row, Randolph Tarr's head gives a twitch.

"I'll say good evening now." Ada's voice is even and pleasant. Head held high, carriage impeccable, she walks into the audience, files down the narrow corridor that opens for her, serenely passes through a gauntlet of hostile looks. Dunne rushes after her and overtakes his ward just as she is going out the door of the saloon.

The men drift back to the bar, many muttering and shaking their heads in disgruntled amazement. Solomon's doorman is already busy harvesting coins from the floor. Case feels a tap on the shoulder and turns to face Ilges. "Look at poor Lawyer Tarr," the Major says, "calculating how many clients he's likely lost tonight. Given all the Southerners in this town, a man would think he had been dropped down in Georgia. Having your wife rub your customers' noses in their defeat – it's not good for business."

Tarr and his daughter have only one well-wisher: Peregrine Hathaway, who is showering a visibly dismayed Miss Celeste with frantic compliments, compliments she seems incapable of appreciating in her distraught condition. Despite this, Peregrine slogs on, a trooper of good cheer.

Case turns away from the distressing scene. "I'm going to leave now," he says to Ilges in an undertone. "Would it suit if I came by at four o'clock tomorrow afternoon?"

"Yes," says Ilges, "that would suit."

Case departs without bothering to attempt to collect Hathaway. Outside the Majestic, he pauses to draw in a draft of cool, fresh air and give a glance to a sky speckled with ice-chip stars. Then he starts for the Overland Hotel, boot heels thudding hollowly on the planks of the boardwalk as Ada Tarr, that strange woman, insinuates herself into his thoughts.

Up the street, he sees two figures that bring him to a halt. Mrs. Tarr and Mr. Dunne stand in the shadows of Wetzel's mercantile. The great slab of Dunne's body is tipped so close to her that she is forced back against the storefront. He appears to be pressing some argument or declaration, emphasizing whatever he is saying with vehement bobs of the head.

Dunne's aggressive posture, his way of boring in on the woman, connects to what has just transpired in the saloon – the song, the hostile reception to it. Something arises in Case's brain, a picture comes to him of a small man, his trouser bottoms soggy with melted snow, shrinking back against a wall in the Queen's Hotel in Toronto, trembling, as he's berated. The words *Dunne, bloody Dunne* suddenly come to Case and he wonders if he might have the answer to why Dunne acted as if he presumed to know him that night in the Cypress Hills.

Now Dunne is gallantly holding out his arm to Mrs. Tarr. She hesitates before taking it. A decorous advance down Front Street begins; they look like a long-married couple out enjoying a pleasant evening stroll.

SEVEN

THE AFTERNOON FOLLOWING THE disastrous concert, Ada Tarr sits on her sofa, a book on her lap and her husband's straight razor in her hand, taking a wicked satisfaction from the sharp *snick* that accompanies each angry snap of her wrist as she slits the leaves of *Daniel Deronda*. Randolph is very particular about shaving with a keen razor. He would be scandalized to see her using his to cut the pages of a novel.

It had been her intention to keep George Eliot's latest, delivered by post from Chicago six weeks before, in reserve for when the snow flies, something to light dreary winter nights. But now she is desperate for something to take her mind away from last night and her anger at her husband. The quarrel after the concert was a vicious affair. Randolph had been apoplectic about her singing an anti-Confederate song, but coldly so, which is his fashion when he is truly furious. Ada knows he suspected she had chosen that song purposely to give offence, but he wouldn't come right out and say what was on his mind. If he had, she could have explained. Told her husband that thinking about the deaths of Custer's poor boys had led her to think about her own brother Tom's demise on a battlefield more than ten years ago. She could have mentioned how, as she had pushed that coin about the floor with her toe, trying to summon up what she should sing, she had come to recall the

96

night Tom had told the family that he had enlisted. She had *seen* them, her parents, herself, Tom, all singing her brother's favourite song, a young man's foolhardy war anthem. Instead of clinging to him and weeping, they had striven to give him the brightest, cheeriest send-off they could.

She had sung that song in memory of the darkness and sadness they had not expressed that evening. Nothing more. True, she had leapt before looking, but if you didn't do that now and then, you were apt to pass your days unable to feel life at all.

Randolph had been determined to make her pay for what she had done, but he had been just as determined not to reveal the real reason he was so upset with her. So there had been no mention of the potential damage he believed had been done to his business, no mention of the clientele he feared she might have offended. She knew her husband never stooped to talk of money. That was beneath a gentleman. But believing himself a gentleman did not stop Randolph Tarr from continually *thinking* of money, of loss and gain. So he criticized not the substance of the song itself but rather the way she had performed it, sneering, "It is beyond me how a respectable married woman could caterwaul in public like that in such a vulgar, unladylike fashion, like the lowest of music-hall sluts."

Of course, she had given as good as she got, saying that if he thought she had behaved in an unladylike way, how much more ungentlemanly it had been of him to browbeat the women of his household into exhibiting themselves before a crew of rowdies in a saloon. Why? Because he wanted to parade himself before the town as a *philanthropist*. If he had given it a moment's thought couldn't he have predicted what result that would have on Celeste? Didn't he see the toll the evening had taken on her? The state she was in?

There is nothing that can set Randolph off quicker than the suggestion he is not an exemplary father. He had begun to shout, and she had too, and that had brought Celeste to the top of the stairs in her nightgown where she stood in hysterics, screaming for them to stop, which sent Randolph bounding up the stairs two at a time, to wrap his sobbing daughter in his arms, happy to prove he was as considerate and sensitive a father as any young girl could wish for.

That scene, if any more were needed, demonstrated her stepdaughter's unsoundness. The acorn does not fall far from the oak, and as with her father, there is something hidden, unfathomable, unknowable about that girl. Ada cannot, for the life of her, decide whether Celeste is playing off Lieutenant Blanchard and Peregrine Hathaway against one another, or whether her behaviour simply testifies to a complete and utter absence of feeling for anyone but herself. Right now, she is off picnicking with the sincere, doting English boy who has been mailing her a blizzard of letters ever since they met at last New Year's Ball at the military post. Celeste had insisted on reading these letters aloud to her and her replies to him. Was Celeste taking her into her confidence to prove she was loved, or was she seeking approval for the romance? Likely her motives are as unclear to the girl as they are to her.

It's Ada's guess that Celeste's new admirer, Lieutenant Blanchard, son of a prominent Philadelphia family recently posted to Fort Benton, is destined to win her hand, not the sweetly innocent and steadfastly devoted Peregrine Hathaway. As far as she can tell, it isn't Blanchard's wealth and social position that has turned the girl's head. Nor can it be his looks that have captivated her. Lieutenant Blanchard is pear shaped and waddles like a duck. Ada believes Celeste is so smitten with him because he does not defer to her wishes. All her previous suitors fell all over themselves trying to please her, but Blanchard is an astoundingly self-important and self-satisfied young fellow who expects Celeste to second all his opinions and cater to his every whim, which includes preparing him custard to soothe his chronic dyspepsia.

Is it possible that these two really love one another? It makes Ada feel mean spirited to ask the question. And it naturally leads to another. Has *she* ever really loved Randolph Tarr? At the time of her engagement she was sure she did, but perhaps she had deluded herself and made what her mother had always disparagingly referred to as a *marriage of convenience*.

Four years ago she had found herself alone and penniless. The typhoid had carried her father off; two days after he succumbed, her mother lay dead of the same malady. Her brother had been in the grave for over a decade. The little family property that existed had to be disposed of for a pittance: a set of china, a family silver service. The Jessups did not own a house, but lived in a teacherage supplied by the school in which her father taught. She had had to vacate it to make way for the new schoolmaster, crate up her mother's books, take the train to Chicago, and begin a search for a suitable position. When she had read Mr. John Harding's advertisement for a governess in a newspaper, she had immediately applied. Helena, Montana, was a distant, unknown place, but Ada was what her father called a plunger, and she dove heedlessly into these waters. Her ideas of a governess's duties were hazy and ill defined, derived from her reading of English novels. She was soon to learn that if her own notions of what should be expected of her were vague, her employers' were even foggier. The Hardings did not read English novels. They disdained novels of any description whatsoever.

Mr. Harding had made a bundle in the Helena goldfields as a prospector, but unlike many others of his kind, he had held on to his wealth and steadily added to it. He bought up claims that others believed were played out, introducing innovations such as giant sluices and steam-driven ore crushers capable of squeezing out the last ounce of remaining gold from the stubborn stone. In time, these profits had given him the means to erect a mansion high above Last Chance Gulch and the hardscrabble, smoky town that had given him his start. Ada soon learned that she was expected to make Mr. Harding's daughters fit to inhabit the stately quarters he had built for them. It was clearly his view that if gold could be extracted from rock, surely the same could be done with his Martha and Jenny. That was what she was meant to do, to refine them, to teach them a bit of music, a smidgen of geography, a dab of French. Mr. Harding also stated that his girls must be taught to recite a little verse; he didn't care what it was, as long as it was improving, edifying, and suitable for young women's lips because it was his plan, sometime in the future, to send his daughters and their mother to Europe for a look-see, and he didn't want Jenny and Martha sticking out like sore thumbs over there. Although it was left unsaid, he apparently judged his wife's manners and education were irremediable – Europe would have to make do with Dolly Harding just as she was.

Mr. Harding seemed to think that sprucing up his girls for the Grand Tour was the equivalent of making them presentable for church; all that was necessary was to give them a quick scrub behind the ears and remind them to clean their fingernails. However, Ada soon learned that beating the names of European capitals into an anvil would have been easier work than insinuating them into the heads of the young Harding ladies. As far as they were concerned, their father's money lent them all the allure they would ever need.

But the greatest obstacle to educating Martha and Jenny proved to be their mother. Mrs. Harding had married her tycoon when he was still merely a prospector, and she was sure everyone remembered her former occupation – Army laundress – and that all of Helena was maliciously gossiping about her and looking down their noses. She was especially suspicious of the hoity-toity governess. In Mrs. Harding's mind, Ada, like the charwoman and the scullery maid, was a servant and she had better not forget it. She needed taking down a peg, and Dolly Harding was the woman to do it. From the beginning, Mrs. Harding took to calling Ada "Little Miss Grace and Diginity" to her face. Ada bore this for a month until one day her exasperation spilled over and she corrected the mistress of the house's pronunciation in front of her daughters. "I think you mean to say," she said, "that I am Little Miss Grace and *Dignity*."

Her parents had always encouraged her to stand up to injustice, to resist bullying, to exhibit independence of mind, and to defend her rights, but upon reflection she could see that humiliating a persecutor was not necessarily the same thing as demanding respect. She had only to think of how her own gentle father would have conducted himself in a similar situation to see the error of her ways.

Her father had always spoken his mind. But he had done so out of principle, smiling away personal insults. It was his Quixotic idealism that had backed him down the teaching ladder. In the beginning, he had been a professor of Latin and Greek at a distinguished preparatory school in New England. There he had intervened on behalf of a boy who he felt was being persecuted by a small-minded, vindictive headmaster. When the headmaster persisted in making the boy's life a living hell, her father had written to the boy's parents criticizing the conduct of the headmaster and suggesting that they remove their son from the school. When it came to light what he had done, he was immediately sacked. After that, her father had passed through a series of increasingly less eminent schools where his gentle but stubborn resistance to arbitrary authority had led to a series of further dismissals, a steady descent arrested only when there was no place lower to fall, and he landed in a one-room school in an Ohio backwater, where the dreamy scholar spent his last years drumming the three Rs into farmers' sons and daughters.

Of course, Ada had always believed her mother's causes, enthusiasms, and wilfulness had contributed to her father's professional decline. His colleagues, the parents of his students had all found her mother a little more eccentric and idiosyncratic than was proper for a schoolteacher's wife. Her abolitionism would have been perfectly acceptable in New England society if her espousal of it had been a little less fervent and wild-eyed. Some called her John Brown in a skirt. An ardent disciple of Mrs. Amelia Bloom, she had been a passionate advocate for rational and hygienic dress for females, marriage law reform, and votes for women. But people found her tiresome and annoying because she insisted on promoting her views at the most inappropriate times, at dinners and tea parties where it was understood that the conversation should be both amusing and decorous. Some tongue-waggers said that the only question upon which Mrs. Jessup's views departed from Mrs. Bloom's was the temperance issue. Mrs. Jessup liked her sherry; many were of the opinion she liked it far too much.

Ada admits that the sherry sometimes got the better of her mother, who found their reduced circumstances difficult and wearying. But then she would brighten, pull herself together, and say to her children, "Poverty cannot affect the treasure we store up in our minds. That is incorruptible. We Jessups may be forced to live low, but let us always strive to think high."

This was training ill suited for life with the Hardings, who thought the worth of anyone was best measured by the balance in their bank book. Day by day, friction between Ada and the Harding females grew, and she found herself subject to obloquy, contempt, and petty harassment. For a year she had lived a dreadful life in that dreary, cold house, and her pride – fierce since childhood – had taken a pummelling. It had taken all her will to maintain her dignity, to carry herself as if she could withstand every slight, but in the privacy of her room, her courage ebbed away and left her sobbing in a pillow.

When Dolly Harding demanded his husband discharge the governess, he flatly refused, but it wasn't because he admired her teaching and her spirit. Whenever she crossed a room, Ada could feel his eyes flicking at her haunches. One afternoon, after his wife had made a particularly noisy complaint about Little Miss Grace and Diginity, he had summoned her to "sort things out." While he admitted his wife could be difficult, he urged Ada to be a little more "accommodating to Mrs. Harding's ways." During the entire speech his eyes never strayed from her breasts.

Three days later she made up her mind to go to Mr. Harding and negotiate her freedom from this insufferable bondage. The terms of her contract stated Miss Ada Jessup was to receive her salary yearly, on the anniversary of her first day of employment. She said to Mr. Harding that clearly the present situation was unsatisfactory to all concerned. She proposed that if he were good enough to release her, she would accept a trifling sum, much less than the wages she had already earned. She would settle for travel expenses to get her back to Chicago.

"A bargain is a bargain, my girl. If you have it in mind to leave, you will go with nothing" was Mr. Harding's stark reply.

Shortly after this, handsome, courtly, attentive Randolph Tarr had come to provide Mr. Harding with legal advice. And one thing had led to another.

No more crying over spilled milk, Ada warns herself. Randolph's razor lies in her lap. The house is quiet as a tomb, except for the feeble buzzing of an exhausted fly on the window-pane behind her.

But Ada's restless mind will not settle and wanders to Mr. Dunne. Why did he not object to Celeste's leaving the house with Peregrine Hathaway today? After all, he was most insistent last night about not letting her out of his sight. Is she herself more delicate, more in need of guarding than flighty Celeste? Of course, the circumstances are different; Celeste is in the company of a young police constable. Or maybe Mr. Dunne was hesitant to provoke her because she flaunts her detestation of him to his face. Celeste cannot be prevailed upon to lift a finger for him; she will not even consent to carry a glass of water out to the porch for the poor fellow.

It all falls on Ada's shoulders to make him comfortable. Any small kindness she shows him is greeted with excessive gratefulness. If the guard dog had a tail, it would thump at the sight of her. If she happens to make a comment on the weather, he nods his head with excessive enthusiasm. A drink of water on a sweltering afternoon, a piece of bread and butter sprinkled with sugar and cinnamon, a ham sandwich, a bowl of stew prompts him to rhapsodize about her goodness and thoughtfulness.

When she invited him to take supper with them in the house the other evening rather than eat out on the porch, which he insists on doing, he refused the offer, but she is sure she saw his eyes moisten with appreciation. Ada finds these displays of emotion more than odd; she finds them embarrassingly disconcerting.

And although Celeste's aversion to Mr. Dunne cannot be justified, Ada has to admit it is difficult to *like* the man. It isn't that his compliments and effusions are insincere – they're too sincere, too *extreme*. His deference verges on the pathetic.

Yet last night he had shoved his usual deference aside just as he had when he had forced that shooting lesson on her. Of course, by trying to set off from the saloon on her own she had broken one of Randolph's cardinal rules. *Go nowhere alone.* Mr. Dunne was not going to permit that. And from his point of view, he was correct. After all, he had sworn to Randolph to protect her. With little mincing, shuffling steps he had backed her into the wall of Mr. Wetzel's store. She had felt cornered in every conceivable way, pinned by those pale, unblinking eyes, half suffocated by the heat of the heavy body that stood mere inches away from her own. And the way his insistent murmuring had surrounded her, rustling like musty curtains in a draft, "Missus, I got to watch over you. Missus, you got to let me do my job. Missus, you got to listen to me. Missus, please." In the end, what choice did she have but to succumb to his pleading? All those sibilants hissing in her ears, the stove-like warmth of his body had dizzyingly overcome her. And when Mr. Dunne had offered his arm, how could she refuse his awkward gallantry? Yet she had been reluctant to touch him, to touch even the cloth of his sleeve.

Slowly, Ada turns her head to look out the window. There is Mr. Dunne. How can he bear to sit out there, hour after hour, staring at empty prairie and the ugly backside of an ugly town? Is it monumental patience or is his mind as empty as the howling wilderness that confronts him?

Ada picks up her husband's razor and resumes slitting the

pages of her book, releasing George Eliot's characters to keep her company, relieve this sense of smothering loneliness.

Peregrine Hathaway has gone missing. When the boy didn't show up for either breakfast or dinner, Case said to McMullen that maybe they should try to find him; perhaps it had slipped his mind that he and McMullen were to leave for Fort Walsh today.

"I already told him four o'clock sharp. Let him mind to his own business. You worry about that boy too much" was all that Joe had to say.

But Case does feel responsible for Hathaway. He got Walsh to agree to let the boy accompany him to Fort Benton, and he feels obliged to see that what he's borrowed gets returned. He makes a quick tour of the town just on the off chance his young friend has decided to make a few purchases before he heads back to Fort Walsh. Finding no trace of him, Case returns to the Overland to get directions to the Tarr residence. The desk clerk tells him it can be found a half mile behind the town and adds, "A big white house. And not whitewashed, mind you, but *oil-painted*."

Case can see that oil-painted wonder now, a few hundred yards off at the end of the dusty buggy track down which he is tramping, a two-storey frame house with a long gallery porch running along its entire front. It is a little past one o'clock; the sun is directly overhead, doing its best to shrivel him and the stringy, yellowing weeds that line the trail. Everything is still except for a brace of hawks wheeling about in the pale sky, riding the scorching updrafts rising from the skillet-flat prairie.

He feels irked by Hathaway's irresponsibility, resentful that it will no doubt bring him into proximity with Dunne. He is resolved to make no mention of the time years ago when he first saw the scoundrel backing a man into the corner of a hotel lobby, hissing his contempt in his face. The memory of this, and hearing Walsh's report of his meeting with the man, has told him all he needs to know about what he is. Surely a paid informer then, the lowest of parasites, and most likely a petty criminal to boot, as such types often are. A man beneath notice, and that's how he intends to behave towards him, as if he were no more significant than a flyspeck.

And then there is the awkwardness of seeing Mrs. Tarr. Meeting that eccentric woman is not a cheering prospect. He best not make any mention of being present at the concert. What could one say about that? Compliment her or commiserate with her?

As Case trudges on, drawing nearer to the house, he spots Dunne, a black heap on the porch. Trying to assume a confident air, he even attempts a nonchalant whistle, but the walk has parched his mouth so badly he gives it up as futile. When he comes within hailing distance, he tenses himself, expecting some dismissive salute, but Dunne doesn't blink an eye or utter a sound. He simply fills a chair, legs spread wide, a shotgun resting across his bulging thighs. Only when Case's boot strikes the bottom step does Dunne grind out three words.

"He ain't here."

Case refuses to respond, strides up the stairs, crosses the porch, and gives a crisp knock to the door.

Dunne says, "You deaf? I just told you that young fellow you're looking for ain't here."

"Don't presume to know my business, Mr. Dunne."

Ada is in the kitchen preparing a jug of iced tea, rinsing sawdust off one of the last shards of ice that have survived the summer in the icehouse, when she hears a rap on the front door. Thinking that Mr. Dunne must have finally found the courage to ask for something, she goes to the door, wiping her hands on a dishcloth. But what greets her is a stranger on her doorstep, a tall, lanky fellow in an oatmeal tweed suit, sombre eyes shadowed by a broad-brimmed straw hat.

"Beg pardon for this intrusion," the man says, looking non-plussed because she has caught him trying to rub the dust off one of his shoes on the back of a trouser leg. "If I may introduce myself – the name is Wesley Case, and I've come looking for Peregrine Hathaway. By any chance is he here?"

Ada recognizes the visitor's name because it frequently appears in Hathaway's chatty letters to her stepdaughter. The young Englishman is always singing Case's praises to Celeste, lauding him as the epitome of a scholar and gentleman, a mentor and dear friend. "Mr. Hathaway was here, but he and my stepdaughter have gone on a picnic," she says.

"That's what I tried to tell him, ma'am," Dunne calls out tri-umphantly. "But he didn't listen to me. Preferred to disturb you."

"Thank you, Mr. Dunne. It is quite all right. I am not incon-venienced at all."

"It's a matter of some urgency, I'm afraid," Case says. "Do you know where I might find them?"

"I should think some spot along the river, but where exactly it is impossible for me to say. They could be anywhere."

"Did they set an hour for their return? I apologize for press-ing you, but I need to speak to Hathaway."

Ada gives a small smile. "I would not expect them to be too very long. Celeste does not care for hot weather very much. Not even in the company of an admirer. She sunburns dreadfully. But if you would care to come in and wait for Mr. Hathaway to return, you are very welcome to do so."

Case tucks her a little bow. "If it would not be too great an imposition, Mrs. Tarr, that might be the answer to my predicament."

Ada ushers him down a short hallway and into the parlour. It is a cozy, cluttered room that drives a spike of homesickness into him – not for the cavernous place in which he and his par-ents had rattled around like three dried peas in a barrel, but for the rather ordinary houses in Ottawa's Sandy Hill where he had gone to play with his schoolmates, to eat bread and jam, to take shelter from the cold winds that blew down the long corridors of his own home.

The wallpaper is patterned with blowsy pink roses; there is a horsehair sofa, a loveseat, several leather armchairs, a spinet, an oak sideboard, a scattering of mismatched occasional tables, and, wonder of wonders, a tall, glass-fronted bookcase, its shelves crammed with reading matter.

"I was making myself a pitcher of iced tea. Perhaps you would care for a glass?" asks Ada.

His tongue is threatening to stick to the roof of his mouth. "That would be very kind. Thank you."

"Make yourself comfortable," Ada says, motioning him towards the sofa before she heads for the kitchen. But Case doesn't sit. He roams about the room, picks up a book lying on the sofa, glances at the spine. *Daniel Deronda*. He doesn't recognize the title; it must be Eliot's most recent. He replaces the novel and shifts to the bookcase, which holds a surprising amount of philosophy: Bentham, Mills, Burke, Locke, Hobbes. There are numerous abolitionist pamphlets and bound numbers of a journal called *The Lily*. Several shelves contain the usual English poets, the plays of Shakespeare, novels by Hawthorne, Washington Irving, Thackeray, Trollope, and Defoe. There is much more George Eliot, including the essays.

He startles at the bookcase, embarrassed, when Mrs. Tarr enters the room. Clearing his throat, he says, "Your husband has a fine library."

She carries a lacquer tray holding two glasses of iced tea. Her black eyebrows lift and a mocking smile tucks the corners of her mouth. "My husband's library? It is mine, Mr. Case. Or rather it was my mother's – which I have augmented over the years. Mr. Tarr never puts his nose in a book – except a law book." She puts the tray down on an occasional table, hands Case a glass of tea, and motions him to take a seat on the sofa. He is preparing to sit when she rushes over, snatches up something and drops it in a drawer. Before the drawer closes, he catches a glimpse of a straight razor. What use could she have been making of such an article?

He seats himself on the sofa; she takes a chair directly in front of him, presses the cool glass to her forehead. It crosses his mind that Mrs. Tarr is not wearing a corset; he sees an inviting curve of belly and feels a disconcerting charge of desire. Immediately, he deflects his attention to the wallpaper above his hostess's head. He hears her say, "My mother used to claim that one can learn more about a person by scanning their books than could be learned by years of acquaintance. Do you think that true, Mr. Case?"

He doesn't know how to take that. Is he being chastised for snooping? He can't be sure because of her smile, which may or may not be ironical. Perhaps she is trying to needle some reaction out of him just as she did with the crowd last night. Maybe it is her hobby to play *agent provocateur*.

"I have no opinion. I have never considered it." Instantly, he regrets how brittle and stuffy that sounds. How foolish. If he is not careful he will soon be blushing. He takes some tea to hide his unease.

But Mrs. Tarr only laughs, leans forward eagerly, breasts swelling against the cloth of her dress. "It is only small talk, Mr. Case. Not a matter of life and death. Give it a go."

He senses she is trying to conduct him, direct him the way she did the audience the previous night. He is to spring into action at her command. Well, if that's what she wants, he will. Trying to adopt her insouciant manner he says, "If I were a medical man and those books were symptoms, I would diagnose a case of mortal seriousness." Even worse, he thinks. Ponderous, silly.

Case detects a mercurial flash of intelligence in those dark eyes, a slight colouring of her extremely pale skin. But she looks more intrigued than angry. Whatever the woman thinks seems to register itself on her face. "Mortal seriousness? Particularly deadly for a woman, I take it. And what is the cure, Doctor?"

"A dose of Dickens is what I would prescribe, ma'am." He crosses his legs; his foot begins to flick impatiently up and down. He wills it to be still.

"Oh, I don't think Dickens will do," says Mrs. Tarr. "My mother could not abide Dickens. She said his characters resembled no human being she had ever met. She called Dickens false to life. It was the gravest charge she could level." Her eyes fall on Case's shoe, which has resumed a frantic jigging.

He uncrosses his legs and shoves both feet firmly to the floor, grips both knees hard to keep them from bouncing. "I would say that it is all to Mr. Dickens's credit that he gives us the sort of characters he does. I find them entertaining. Who would read a novel just to meet the same bores they encounter on their daily rounds?"

"Click, click, click," says Ada, and sticks her tongue impudently in her cheek.

"Beg pardon?" says Case.

"The sound of swords crossing. I do enjoy a fencing match, a lively discussion about the respective merits of artists. It has been ages."

"I hate to disappoint you, Mrs. Tarr. I am a shallow man. So shallow that if I were a puddle and you stood in me you would scarcely wet the soles of your shoes." His eyes dart to the George Eliot novel lying beside him on the sofa. "So shallow that I don't have a taste for sermons masquerading as stories."

This only amuses her, which he finds even more aggravating. Mrs. Tarr remarks, "I think your opinion of yourself does not do you justice. Peregrine Hathaway speaks very highly of you, Mr. Case. With him it is Mr. Case this and Mr. Case that. He finds you fascinating."

The mention of Hathaway reminds him of the boy's feckless behaviour. "What or whoever fascinates him is not much of a recommendation. I've seen him held mesmerized for an hour by a cricket in the corner of the barracks." The way Mrs. Tarr is looking at him makes him feel even more prickly. He adds, "The boy doesn't bear listening to."

"I like the boy. I especially like how many things delight him. We would all be better off if we had his talent for happiness."

"And he would be better off with a swift kick in the pants. Today he has inconvenienced everyone dreadfully."

"You are not very forgiving towards your friends," says Ada, and for the first time Case sees that face, which hides nothing, showing disapproval.

Case's hand bumps *Daniel Deronda* and, before he realizes it, he's up on his feet and shoving the book at her. "Your novel, Mrs. Tarr," he says. "I'm sure it will be better company than I have been. I thank you for the tea, and for observing my faults of character. If Hathaway appears within the next hour would you be kind enough to tell him he had better get down to the Overland? That said, I think it is time I relieved you of my presence."

Mrs. Tarr takes the book, opens it, lowers her eyes to the page, and says, "Very well. If that is what you prefer."

Her eyes do not lift from the book. Case sees she is actually reading. His petulant outburst fizzles. He crosses the parlour, mortified. Just then the back door rattles open; he hears the sound of hurrying footsteps, excited voices, a peal of laughter. The picnickers have returned.

Ada Tarr closes her book. "What a timely intervention, Mr. Case," she says mildly. "So fortuitous for you. And just in the nick of time."

EIGHT

August 9, 1876

THE AFTERNOON OF McMullen and Hathaway's departure for Fort Walsh, I had a long and satisfactory talk with Ilges concerning the present military situation. Next day, I dropped in on Mr. Conrad to see if he would help put me in contact with gentlemen interested in selling their land, as he had offered. Through his good offices I was directed to Mr. Worthington. Most momentous of all, yesterday I wrote to Father to inform him of my decision to remain in Fort Benton, take up ranching, and commence a useful life. Bluntly put, to turn to any other occupation than politics. Nothing to do now but batten down the hatches and brace myself for the hurricane that I suspect will soon come roaring westward from Ottawa. Having set my heart on Mr. Worthington's property I intend to make him an offer – pending Joe's approval when he returns from Fort Walsh. I am satisfied Mr. Worthington's asking price is dirt cheap and the ranch a most attractive package. A thousand acres situated a mile from Fort Benton, a four-room house constructed of lumber, a small barn, several granaries, three hogs, six draught horses, a bull, fifty bred-heifers and cows, twenty steers, plus miscellaneous and sundry agricultural implements and machinery. Best of all, part of the property sits on a bend of the Missouri,

providing ample water for livestock. I believe it a sound invest-
ment of the capital Mother left me.

Nothing to do now but await McMullen's return, but waiting
isn't easy. Feeling skittish last night, I sat drinking in my room
until just short of midnight when I crawled into bed half-drunk.
I dreamed a terrible nightmare. I was lying on a slab of marble,
absolutely naked. It came to me where I was; the surgical theatre
of a medical school. Nearby was a small trolley holding a tray
littered with bone saws, scalpels, and forceps. Over it was bent a
surgeon in a white apron, inspecting the tools of his trade. A powerful odour of formaldehyde wafted about the room. Suddenly
I realized that I had been mistaken for a corpse and that I was
about to be subjected to an autopsy, dismembered piece by piece.
I tried to shout, to scramble down from the slab, but my vocal
cords and limbs were paralyzed. Hundreds of medical students
seated in a semicircle of steeply raked benches gazed down at my
naked body with detached and clinical curiosity.

In the very last row of the theatre I spotted Pudge Wilson
in the midst of his little band of acolytes, the Lilies of the Field.
He was leaning forward, his elbows on his knees, watching the
proceedings with avid interest. The look on his face told me that
he was the only person in the room that knew I was alive and
that he was looking forward to the moment when I would be
opened up in agony, when those cruel forceps would clamp and
pluck the organs from my body.

And then I lost sight of him, my view blocked by the surgeon bending over me. I saw the glittering scalpel poised in
his long, delicate fingers, poised to make the first incision, and
made a hopeless attempt to scream.

I woke whimpering, drenched in sweat.

It is no surprise that in my dream I cast Pudge as the all-
knowing one. He always prided himself on being the master of
every situation. William Tewkes Wilson even selected the nickname for himself. Good-humoured self-mockery had no part in
that; he simply wanted to forestall anyone else from saddling

him with a less amiable-sounding sobriquet, one more in keeping with his true nature. By naming himself he claimed ownership of himself, just as in naming us the Lilies of the Field he laid claim to owning us. It falls to the master to name his dogs.

What a little clique of young wastrels we were. Tommy Richards, Packard Trelawney, Caleb Morrow, and Wesley Case, boys whose fathers' prosperity gave Pudge the notion of christening us the Lilies of the Field. As a Church of England bishop's son, William Tewkes Wilson had had enough scripture drummed into his head that the appropriate Bible passage was always on the tip of his tongue. "'Consider the lilies of the field how they grow; they toil not, neither do they spin: And yet I say unto you, That even Solomon in all his glory was not arrayed as one of these,'" he intoned one day with sonorous sanctity, making a gesture that resembled a priest gesticulating in the pulpit, illustrating how the lost sheep are drawn back into the fold.

No, we had no need to toil or spin. Our fathers arrayed us in bespoke tailoring; we wore handmade boots on our feet; our faces were shaved and patted with scent, our hair cut and dressed with lime cream by Toronto's most exclusive barber, fresh off the boat from England.

Not to say that membership in the Lilies was simply carefree and easy; it had its obligations. Pudge decreed that our shoes must always be polished bright as a new penny, but our cravats sloppily knotted. Servants buffed shoes, but gentlemen tied their own cravats – let the contrast be stark. No more than three fobs to a watch chain, tie pins forbidden. As Pudge liked to say, "I will not be mistaken for a vulgar Jew like Disraeli." Drunkenness required, a minimum of four times a week. Attempts on the virtue of servant girls an absolute necessity, although I believe only Pudge lived up to the high standard he set for the rest of us – he had the necessary streak of ruthlessness to get what he wanted.

At his insistence the Lilies joined the militia. Anyone could call himself a gentleman – haberdashers were unscrupulous enough to refer to themselves in that way – but officer and gentleman was a distinction beyond the grasp of shopkeepers. Besides, regimental balls, cotillions, parades, and military picnics added a little spice and variety to what passed for society in a dim, parochial backwater.

Pudge was midwife to the Lilies; he guided our first steps, and soon was leading us everywhere by the nose. We provided him with a mission in life, a mission he pursued with the same single-mindedness that evangelicals pursue the baptizing of black babies in Darkest Africa. He wanted to introduce a bit of flair into dreary, sabbatarian Toronto, to thumb his nose at our elders and their dreadful solidity. "It is our duty," Pudge was fond of declaring, "to shock Presbyterians into gaiety."

He wished to turn us into walking advertisements for the Gracious Life. But in the end we scarcely differed from those shabby, defeated men who shuffle up and down Yonge and Front Streets strapped into sandwich boards that urge on the public miraculous patent medicines, shoddy hardware, bad tobacco. No one sees the shufflers. They become the signs they carry. And like them, I too became invisible, wore a sandwich board too, one hand-painted by Pudge, with no mark of my own on it.

He surprised us all by marching us off to the saloon bar of the Queen's Hotel to finish our education, not the most picturesque or salubrious academy, and a surprising choice for the usually fastidious Pudge. Hard by the lake, the Queen's was a victim of the harbour's weather and nasty smells. In winter when gales came ripping off Lake Ontario, slapping sleet and wet snow to the windows, the fireplace moaned and coughed smoke, and all its patrons with their feet up on the bar rail smelled like wet dogs. Summer did nothing to improve it. When the ships and tugs stoked their boilers, a greasy black fog of coal smoke swirled along the docks, and everybody hurried through a free-for-all of smuts and cinders. The hot, oppressive air stank of rotting vegetables, ripening fish, tar, horse manure, and tallow. As for scenic views of the lake, they were limited to glimpses of grey-blue snatched between the barriers of hulls, casks, drays, towers of stacked crates, the sky a tangle of spars and masts, smears of dirty canvas sail. A din of stevedore curses, screaming steam whistles, squealing winches, clanking and clattering chains rattled the hotel's windows.

What attracted Pudge to the Queen's was the group of men who clustered around a trestle table there every evening, hard-eyed, malarial-looking fellows who wore their hair longer than was customary in Toronto. Drawls dripped from their tongues like thick molasses; their antique courtliness hearkened back to an earlier time. That was my first impression of the secession men, the Southerners who had escaped from Union prisoner-of-war camps and made their way to Canada, the sympathizers of the Cause from Ohio and Indiana who belonged to grandilo-quently named societies such as the Knights of the Golden Circle and the Sons of Liberty, the agents doing Jefferson Davis's business in our midst. Fifteen thousand of them was the number estimated by the newspapers. It was an open secret that the Queen's was their unofficial headquarters, the place where they hatched their plots against the North. The authorities turned a blind eye to them and their conspiracies. If our powerful neigh-bouring nation, which had coveted and menaced our lands since the War of 1812, chose to tear itself to pieces, our govern-ment had no objection.

To Pudge the secession men were romantic figures and his admiration for them was boundless. Like them, he was proud as Satan. Maybe his father the bishop had kept him on his knees too much as a boy; for Pudge a bowed head did not come easily. He liked to say, "Each rereading of *Paradise Lost* only confirms for me how much more interesting a world it would be if the Devil's rebellion against God had succeeded." He was all for rebellion and rebels.

The first night Pudge led us on a pilgrimage to the saloon bar of the Queen's he had the good luck to find an empty table next to the secessionists'. As soon as he heard their accents he set to attract their attention by behaving in a manner even more outrageously flamboyant than usual. When their eyes turned on him, he solemnly, reverently, lifted his glass in a toast to them. The Southerners didn't seem to know what to make of this. Fiercely, Pudge whispered to the rest of us, "Damn you, raise your glasses." We did. Still, they did not respond, but Pudge stubbornly kept his tumbler aloft, and so did the rest of us, looking like boys preparing to catch rain in our glasses. And finally, Pudge caught his raindrop. The Confederates slowly lifted their glasses to return the compliment. Pudge had paid obeisance; King Cotton was pleased.

Under Pudge's orchestration, ever so gradually we insinuated ourselves into the Southern gentlemen's favour. The toast had given Pudge his toehold, and whenever we trooped into the saloon, he would give them a friendly nod or wave of the hand, pass some amiable remark on the weather. At last one night all his efforts were rewarded: they invited us to join their table for a drink. Pudge replied that that was most hospitable of them but we could agree only if they would accept a bumper of champagne from us. And they deigned to do so. And I paid for it because that was the duty of the son of the Lumber Baron, to scatter his father's coin.

The Lilies were the only patrons of the Queen's ever invited to sit with the Dixie boys and we were all flattered by the great privilege extended to us. We hung on their table talk. The war or politics were seldom mentioned; most of the time the secession men debated the finer points of dogs, horses, and women. Once, an entire evening was devoted to the Southerners' anecdotes about famous duels and the gallant men who had fought them: Andrew Jackson versus Charles Dickinson, Secretary of State Henry Clay versus Senator John Randolph, Congressman William Graves versus Congressman Jonathan Cilley. Hard on the heels of that, Pudge obtained a copy of the Irish Code Duello, the catechism of duelling, which he read obsessively. Pudge liked to imagine himself spilling blood and garnering applause for the stylish, punctilious way he did it. He frequently interrogated the

Southerners on the finer points of the code of conduct in an affair of honour. But in dull, unchivalrous Toronto, duelling was illegal, and blowing another man's brains out or running him through with a sabre would earn you a trip to the scaffold. Which was why Pudge could indulge in bloody fantasies with no fear of being called upon to act them out. Luckily for him. His ample girth would have made him a target hard to miss.

Most evenings we spent with the Southerners the conversation ran light and free. I still find it hard to reconcile my memory of these charming, cultivated fellows with what I learned they had done. The long-jawed, hooded-eyed Virginian, John Yates Beall, was the epitome of the refined and cultivated gentleman. He tried to take the Union warship *Michigan* on Lake Erie, free Confederate prisoners held on Johnson's Island, and burn Detroit to the ground. Later, he turned to derailing trains around Buffalo and got hanged for his sabotage.

The avuncular Dr. Luke Pryor Blackburn carried himself with the quiet distinction of a man who had received a commendation from the Queen for his selfless, charitable work during the yellow fever epidemic in Bermuda. What would the Widow of Windsor have thought of the good doctor if she had known he had brought the bedding and clothing of the Bermudan fever victims to Canada and was dispatching it all over New England, hoping to spread an outbreak of yellow jack among the Yankees? Or that he had sent a fine suit contaminated with the bodily secretions of a fever victim to President Lincoln as a gift?

And then there was the happy-go-lucky Robert Martin and the inveterate punster John William Headley, who went down to New York and set fifteen hotels and Barnum's American Museum ablaze with Greek fire.

Their hatred gave them all a serene conscience, a conscience that I saw troubled only once, and that was out of regard for a lady's feelings, the beautiful widow of one of their former comrades. Madame Francine Boisclair Stewart had made her way from New Orleans to Toronto to nurse her husband, an escapee from a Union prison camp who had contracted a mysterious wasting illness there. Despite all her efforts, she was unable to save his life. Even after his death she remained in residence at the Queen's, where we often saw her seated in the lobby drinking tea, watching people come and go, earnestly searching the newspapers for the latest reports from the front. One afternoon, Giles Postlethwaite, who was clearly the most influential and respected of the secession men and their informal leader, introduced the Lilies to this flower of Southern womanhood. From that day forward, all the Lilies paused to offer her our compliments whenever we crossed the lobby. On one of these occasions Pudge brashly asked her why she did not return to her home in New Orleans – what was keeping her in dreary Toronto? Although her English was impeccable, she chose to answer in French. With a faint, sad smile, she whispered, *"Parce que je suis tombée amoureuse de Monsieur Stewart."* Her reply was not really an answer but it was so mysteriously romantic that from that instant on we all fell a little in love with her. No one tumbled harder than I. Could any naive young man of twenty-one have resisted her? A woman so devoted to her husband's memory, so loyal to her love, that she could not bear to leave the seedy hotel where he had drawn his last breath?

But as I was to learn, Madame Boisclair Stewart's devotion to Mr. Stewart and her ardent support of the Cause came to be a source of consternation and embarrassment to her husband's friends. In those newspapers she so earnestly searched for war news, she came across troubling accounts of the atrocities committed by Southern forces at Fort Pillow. Naturally she turned to Mr. Giles Postlethwaite to ask whether these reports could possibly be true or were they simply foul Yankee lies? He was only too happy to assure her they were most certainly fabrications, but the more she read about what had transpired at Fort Pillow, the more Madame Boisclair Stewart brooded. Repeatedly, she badgered Mr. Postlethwaite with the same questions. Could General Nathan Bedford Forrest's troops have possibly executed both white and coloured troops under a flag of surrender? Could it be true what the Northern papers said, that the nigras had been nailed to logs, the logs soaked in kerosene and put to the match, the poor devils roasted alive?

In the presence of the Lilies, Mr. Postlethwaite seldom spoke of the war, but Madame Boisclair Stewart's constant pestering threw him into so great a state of agitation that he could not hold his tongue. "I told her a lady should not contemplate such things. In her present delicate, grieving state she will undermine her health if she doesn't let it go. But she won't let it go. Is it true? Is it true? When I maintain it is nothing but damn Yankee mendacity, she wants to know how I can be certain it is a falsehood. Can I prove it?" He looked around the table at us as if he half expected someone to pull a proof out of his hat that he could take to the sorrowing widow. When no one said a word, he tilted his chair back and stared up at the ceiling. "She said that if these things happened, her husband's suffering and death for the South has no meaning. I'd like to be able to set that little lady straight on that point but it can't be done given her rocky state of mind. I'd like to say to her that whatever happened at Fort Pillow, Tom Stewart would have approved of it and taken a hand in it if he were there. He would have had no doubts that if Nathan Bedford Forrest gave those orders, they were right and fitting. The General has been selling slaves and running nigger yards all his life, and there isn't a man living who knows more about nigger nature and how to deal with it than he does. Maybe the General reckoned a lesson needed to be taught to runaway slaves that throw in with the North. That a lesson needed to be learned. And the way to do it was to burn some black bastards and shoot down a few nigger-loving Yankees waving a white flag." He shrugged. "But you can't explain that to a widow suffering from the hypo, a woman so cast down and melancholy she can't produce a sensible thought in her head."

Postlethwaite fell moodily silent, and Pudge, sensing an evening of gloom threatening, suddenly pointed out a man at a table near one of the windows. "Madame Boisclair Stewart does not know the meaning of the word melancholy," he said. "I give you the very picture of despondency, gentlemen. There he sits, broken and bereft. It's a sight to melt your heart."

All heads turned towards a fellow who had been haunting the bar for weeks. A beard began at his Adam's apple and crawled up his cheeks to his eyes, which were an oddly pale shade of blue; he wore a pea jacket, and a seaman's cap tugged so low its visor shadowed most of his face. He was staring blankly into a tankard of ale that he turned slowly round and round in his fingers. If the rest of us had hardly taken note of him, Pudge certainly had. He believed sailors and dockworkers had no business frequenting the saloon bar distinguished by the presence of cavaliers such as Postlethwaite and company, and that the man needed to be taught his place.

"My friends," said Pudge, turning his voice sombre and resonant, speaking loudly enough to make sure the sailor by the window could hear, "look upon misery incarnate, known to seafarers everywhere by the sad appellation the Lugubrious Helmsman." The Helmsman's eyes slowly lifted to Pudge, then just as slowly fell back down to his drink. "I have heard," said Pudge, "that years ago, after long and anxious expectation, the Lugubrious Helmsman finally achieved his heart's desire, the captainship of a coal boat fresh from the shipyards, the noble *Clinker*. This long-awaited promotion finally provided him with the means to marry his robust, strapping sweetheart and even to buy her her first pair of shoes, which she so proudly sported the day of their wedding, as enamoured of her footwear as she was of her groom. Now," Pudge continued, "although you wouldn't think it to look at him in his present state, in those happy days the Helmsman was a man of a poetical, metaphorical turn of mind. He thought it only fit to board *The Clinker* and his virgin wife at one and the same time. He was determined to have her maidenhead on the maiden voyage of his vessel. It was his plan for the fond couple to pass their first night of connubial bliss upon the Helmsman's beloved coal packet.

"So they set sail, but before the Lugubrious Helmsman could clamber into his hammock to slap bellies with Mrs. Helmsman, a great storm, a most terrifying blow, put *The Clinker* in peril. The Lugubrious Helmsman was a scientific seaman, well versed in the navigational arts, familiar with trigonometry, algebra, and even arithmetic. As his craft floundered about in heavy seas, he took a stub of pencil, made rapid calculations on the back of an envelope, and discovered *The Clinker* was carrying a cargo exactly two hundred and fifty-five pounds beyond her capacity. If that precise weight were not immediately jettisoned, the noble *Clinker* would go to the bottom.

"He turned his eyes on his wife. By a tragic coincidence this was exactly the weight of his new bride. The Lugubrious Helmsman was a man of warm human sentiments, but he knew his duty to his owner – to deliver the cargo and protect his ship at all costs. Three sacks of coal overboard, or the love of his life? He was torn, gentlemen, you cannot imagine how he was torn. But in the end he did the right thing, tenderly placed his wife in a lifeboat, set her adrift, and called out a teary, heartfelt promise to return and collect her when the tempest abated.

"But despite his wife's putting her mighty back into it, pulling at the oars for all she was worth, sometime in the night her lifeboat went down. When dawn arrived all the Lugubrious Helmsman found of her was one very large wedding shoe bobbing on the waves – which from a distance he had mistaken for her lifeboat.

"And there," cried Pudge, with an exaggerated quaver in his voice, "he sits! Tortured by remorse, a shadow of his former nautical self, gazing into the fathomless depths of his nut-brown ale where his bride's face can be seen as in a glass darkly, crying out her plaintive recriminations, overwhelming him with waves of regret mightier than those mighty breakers against which she strove that night and which consigned her to Davy Jones's locker!"

Pudge could be so very tiresome.

I got up and walked out. They were all laughing; I do not believe anyone noted my departure except for Pudge, who always studied his audience to gauge its appreciation of his extempore performances. That was the moment I should have expressed my disgust by making a show of going to the Helmsman and apologizing for my friend, but I did not. Madame Boisclair Stewart occupied my mind. It was her I sought. I found her in the lobby, turning newspaper pages with her slender white fingers. I went up to her, intending to tell her the truth, to say that those bodies spiked to charred logs that smoked in her mind were real. But at the last moment, I saw that uncertainty would be less cruel than the truth, that she needed some scrap of belief in her husband and what he had given his life for. I only said, "Mrs. Stewart, may I offer you tea and cakes?"

"Why, Mr. Case, how lovely," she said. "Do sit down."

That was, I suppose, the moment I resigned from the Lilies. There was no formal break between Pudge and the others and me. With Pudge in particular that would have been impossible. With both of us serving in the same militia company we could not help but cross paths. But from that day on, our relations were marked by a guarded politeness. Although I stopped frequenting the bar of the Queen's, I did not quit visiting the hotel. Almost daily Madame Boisclair Stewart and I met in the lobby for small talk, tea, sugar buns and petits fours. I would have liked to have done the unspeakable, to fervently declare to her, "Mrs. Stewart, how very completely I agree with you that murder committed under a white flag, by Greek fire, or diseased bedclothing dishonours your gallant husband's memory. That is not war, Mrs. Stewart." And how wrong I would have been because that is exactly what war is, Greek fire, infected clothing; desperate, mindless ferocity. The facts, as Father would say, are bars to beat your wings against.

It was about the time Madame Boisclair Stewart informed me that she was going to leave Toronto to live with a female cousin in Missouri that I last laid eyes on the Lugubrious Helmsman. Forlorn and heartsick at the prospect of her departure, I was pacing the lobby waiting for her to appear when I glimpsed the

Helmsman buttonholing a little man with a Macassared kiss-curl pasted to his brow, a long scarf draped over his shoulder, and a violin case tucked under his arm. A picture of Bohemian poverty, shabby overcoat sprinkled with melting snow, trouser cuffs soggy with slush, shoes soaked, and miserably shivering.

But then I realized he wasn't shivering; he was trembling with fear. The Helmsman was menacingly pressed up against him, had driven the little violinist backwards until his shoulder blades bumped hard against the wall, and was berating him in an urgent, scolding whisper. Suddenly he took him by the collar, turned him towards the saloon, and gave him a fierce shove. The musician stumbled, hesitated, glanced back over his shoulder at the Helmsman, and scooted into the bar. For a moment, the man in cap and pea jacket stood watching the door; then he swung round on his heels, strode past me, and shot out of the hotel.

Inquisitiveness led me to follow the man with the fiddle into the saloon. He had already posed himself near the counter, violin tucked under his chin, an embarrassed, self-conscious smile stuck to his face as he lightly ran his bow over the strings while he tuned his instrument. People seated close to him cast amused and puzzled looks. I lifted my eyes to the secessionists' table at the very back of the room where a handful of regulars were in deep conversation. None of the Lilies was about.

The violinist struck up a tune that brought the Southerners' heads up with a sudden jerk. The room went still. The fiddler mistook these reactions as signs of musical appreciation. The tip of his pink tongue licked his lips; his head began to weave from side to side; his kiss-curl gleamed and radiated oily confidence. He began to sing in a high, nasal voice as piercing as the noise his violin was making, and my eyes slunk off him, fastening on those wet trouser cuffs that draped his thin ankles. "John Brown's body lies a-mouldering in the grave, / John Brown's body lies a-mouldering in the grave, / But his soul goes marching on."

I could not look at him. Then there came a sharp bang and clatter that swung me round to search its source. Postlethwaite was on his feet behind the trestle table, one hand clenching the lapel of his jacket in an orator's pose, head flung back, eyes startled and staring. Overturned on the floor behind him lay his chair. His colleagues were slowly rising, dressing a line against the plaster wall. A ripple of uneasiness ran the length of the room; people shifted in their chairs, craned their necks, darted glances from the Confederates to the fiddler, who sensed something was wrong but could not divine what it was. Feeling himself losing his audience, he sang louder, sawed his fiddle harder, and grinned a wobbly, ingratiating smile. Postlethwaite was leading his men out in protest. With their canes held slanted across their chests, with the utmost gravitas they were moving through the other patrons, murmuring apologies whenever someone had to shift a chair to clear a path for them, dignifying their displeasure with the utmost courtesy. As they approached the door near which I was standing, I stepped aside to let them pass. At that very instant, I heard the violinist singing, "The stars above in Heaven now are looking kindly down."

Perhaps Postlethwaite remembered what he could not bring himself to say to Madame Boisclair Stewart – his speech about the necessity of teaching the enemy a lesson. He veered away from the door. The other three shifted their shoulders and followed him, making for the fiddler, whose voice went even shriller with every step they made towards him. I suppose sheer terror kept him doing what he was doing, just as the mouse will keep nibbling on a seed as the snake glides towards it.

Only when the Confederates halted face to face with him did he finally stop, lift his bow from the strings, and timidly say, "Gentlemen?"

"You damned dirty dog," said Postlethwaite quietly, and slashed his cane down on the little fellow's collarbone. Then the others went at the man; walking sticks rose and fell, chopping him to his knees with meaty thuds and sharp cracks. Between the legs of his attackers, I glimpsed the musician's lips, moving in a soundless, plaintive protest. A ring of bowed backs hid him from my sight and the beating went on. A walking stick snapped; the gold knob flew off, skittered across the floor, sizzling in the gas lamplight. I shouted something to them. Something about they must stop or they would kill him. As I did there came a shrieking of whistles, and nightstick-brandishing constables swept into the room.

From beginning to end, the attack could not have lasted more than a minute. The Southerners offered no resistance to arrest, meekly held out their wrists to be manacled. The constabulary showed no interest in the victim, who was creeping about the floor, bloodied and dazed. When I went to him, he seemed incapable of understanding that someone was trying to help him. His hands kept pawing, his knees jerking, as he scrambled about the floor. I had to take hold of his collar to stop him from going under a table. Feeling my knuckles touch the back of his neck, he gave a small incoherent cry, rolled over on his side, pulled his thighs up against his chest, and began to whimper something through his broken teeth. I had to put my ear to his mouth to hear what he was saying. "Done. Done. Bloody done," he muttered, over and over. At the time I took him to mean he was done for, or done in.

It seems strange to me now that I gave so little thought to the exemplary speed with which the Toronto Police had arrived on the scene. But knowing what I know now, I see that they must have been standing at the ready, or perhaps been summoned by the Helmsman, who had left the hotel in such a hurry. After all, he had bought himself a fiddler, told him what to play, and knew what the consequences would be.

Two musical provocations in two saloons, both of which offended the sentiments of the South. Seeing Dunne hunched over Ada Tarr like a black bird of prey summoned the image of the cringing fiddler. Bloody Dunne. Keeping close watch on the Confederate table for weeks had made him familiar with all the Lilies. Perhaps our friendliness with the secession men had made us subjects of suspicion for whomever Dunne was working for – the Police, maybe Union agents. He may even have been charged to make inquiries about us. I certainly had no interest in him. Until the night Pudge held the Lugubrious Helmsman up to public ridicule I had paid him no more notice than I did the chairs and tables that I walked by in the saloon bar of the Queen's.

Pudge Wilson and Michael Dunne, two figures from the past, linked in my mind by the former's humiliation of the latter. Michael Dunne, no stranger to the auction block, paid to provoke the secession men, eager to sell himself to Walsh, owned at present by Randolph Tarr. So contemptible a creature he doesn't merit a second thought.

Pudge Wilson is a different matter. If I refuse to think of him by day, he visits me in my sleep. All these years he has burrowed himself deeper and deeper inside me. There seems to be no ridding myself of my malignancy until some surgeon inhabiting my nightmares miraculously cuts it out of me, or I do it myself.

August 11, 1876
Fort Benton

My dear Walsh:

Your initiative in sending Cpl. Rampton and Sub-Const. Charles to deliver mail to Fort Benton has caused astonishment in the town, seeing as overland postal delivery here on the American side is still suspended, it being considered too risky a venture with the Sioux still at large. Rampton and Charles's arrival is a fortunate circumstance for me since I have recently met with Ilges, and am pleased to report he appears ready to cooperate in every way with the proposal I put to him on your behalf. You will see evidence of that in what follows.

The latest news has come to him via two half-breed scouts, Baptiste Pourier and Frank Grouard, who until lately were attached to Gen. Crook's force on the south fork of Goose Creek. They rode into Fort Benton a few days ago. Grouard was granted leave to receive treatment for a venereal complaint that had rendered him unfit for duties. Pourier accompanied him because Grouard was judged incapable of making the journey alone.

These men told Ilges that Crook has avoided pursuing the Sioux ever since he engaged the Indians at Rosebud Creek six weeks ago. The only step he took to prosecute a campaign was to send out a large reconnaissance party of what he described as "hand-picked men," led by a green young officer, Lt. Sibley. Grouard and Pourier were Sibley's civilian scouts. Pourier said that not long into the mission he spotted Sioux on their trail and informed the Lieutenant they were being followed. Sibley dismissed his warning and halted his troop so he could brew himself a pot of coffee. The coffee had scarcely begun to boil when the Sioux attacked and drove the soldiers to take refuge in thick timber. Pourier was certain the Indians would set fire to the tinder-dry woods and burn them out. He managed to convince the Lieutenant that their only chance of escape was to leave their horses and make their way on foot through the forest. It was a catastrophic retreat. Carbines were lost fording streams; men discarded their ammunition to lighten their flight. The half-breeds report that one exhausted soldier who couldn't keep pace was abandoned and that Grouard, incapacitated by his disease, would have met the same fate if Pourier had not carried him on his back. The scouts related to Ilges a litany of hardships they had suffered: days of heavy rain succeeded by freezing nights, a starvation diet of wild turnip augmented by a few fledgling ground birds the troopers captured by hand. If one of Crook's civilian packers had not stumbled on them, they maintain the entire party would have perished from hunger.

A correspondent from the Chicago Times, John Finerty, was a member of this sorry expedition. You can be sure his account of it will be cast as a tale of heroic survival rather than the debacle it was. I advise you to present the full details of this fiasco to Secretary Scott to drive home to him that the American troops in the field show few signs of adapting themselves to war as it is fought by the Indian. No doubt Scott is receiving optimistic assurances from American sources as to the progress of the campaign. Military leaders will always assure their political masters of a sunny outcome – it is what their bosses desire to hear. But it is better that Scott hears the truth. (I suggest you say that this information came to you from your Métis scouts who in turn received it from their kinsmen Grouard and Pourier.) There is a bad smell about this business and it is wiser to accustom Scott's nose to it by degrees than have the stench break full force in his nostrils at some later date.

It is Ilges's opinion that the only chance the Americans have of crushing the Sioux before winter comes rests with Gen. Crook and Terry who, after many weeks of delay, are finally preparing to launch a campaign in the Rosebud–Powder River country. They have four thousand men at their disposal. However, Ilges confided to me that he is not optimistic about their chances of success. He judges such a large force too difficult to supply in the wilderness, too slow and cumbersome to pursue a well-mounted foe. What's more, Terry and Crook share joint command and Ilges says that may prove a recipe for disaster. Every officer in the West is aware of the personal antipathy that exists between the two generals and their long-standing professional jealousy.

The bad relations that exist between Terry and Crook is, I suggest, not a point you should raise with the Minister, but I think you might offer Ilges's opinion of the military situation as your own – that such a large force is not suited to the hit-and-run style of fighting favoured by Indians. On the other hand, the Army's likely inability to come to grips with the Sioux does have a silver lining – for the time being the Sioux will feel no need to seek sanctuary in Canada.

I would advise that you also send a copy of whatever report that you render to the Secretary of State to Commissioner Macleod. Make it a <u>ditto</u>. Two identical copies of a report in two different sets of files provide you with a record of diligence that cannot be disputed.

Sincerely yours,
Wesley Case

P.S. I was disappointed that Rampton and Charles brought me no communication from you. You may have nothing yet of consequence to pass on, but I still believe it is important that you remain in touch with me so that I can provide Ilges with assurances that you are living up to your end of the bargain.

NINE

TIME HANGS HEAVY on Ada Tarr's hands; she feels her home has become a penitentiary. Her daily chores completed, she has nothing to do but fill the interminable hours with her thoughts and *Daniel Deronda*. Yesterday she came across a passage in the novel that she underlined with a sense of savage vindication. Miss Eliot had written, "Some of them were a very common sort of men. And the only point of resemblance among them all was a strong determination to have what was pleasant, with a total fearlessness in making themselves disagreeable or dangerous when they did not get it." Randolph described perfectly.

But then she fell on what Miss Eliot had to say about Gwendolen Harleth, a most exasperating, arrogant, preening female character. "Whatever she could do so as to strike others with admiration and get in that reflected way a more ardent sense of living, seemed pleasant to her fancy."

Ada has to ask herself if that wasn't exactly what she had done during Mr. Case's visit. Hadn't she attempted to impress him with her intelligence, her love of literature, her enthusiasm for things intellectual? Hadn't she wanted to receive the admiration of a cultivated man, so as to stoke her own *more ardent sense of living*? What else was that but a coy opening gambit, to ask him if one could not know a person best by studying their library? Hadn't she hoped to be extolled for reading Bentham and Mill by someone Hathaway had described as a "university man"? Her face goes hot to think of it.

Peregrine Hathaway's praise of his friend had led her to believe Mr. Case and she would have much in common; she had made the assumption he would be just as eager as she to discuss *something*, that an educated gentleman would be pleased to have a little enlightened conversation. So she had proceeded with headlong self-confidence. She had *darted* at him, which is a habit of hers, giving way to her impulses because they too encourage *a more ardent sense of living*.

She admits she created an awkward situation, but Mr. Case hadn't eased it by greeting friendly overtures in such a chilly and superior fashion. Pleading that he was stupid hadn't fooled her. That was pure condescension, his way of saying: Permit me to be gallant. Permit me to pretend to be just as empty-headed as you undoubtedly are. It's only good form.

But when she had continued – maybe pushed him is nearer the truth – in a direction he did not wish to go, he had reacted as Miss Eliot said most men did when displeased; he had turned disagreeable. Distinctly disagreeable. True, it was hardly her place to accuse him of not being very forgiving towards his friend Hathaway. That was impertinent. Another reminder not to *dart* at people, people she hardly knew, with her opinions.

Laying down her novel, Ada glances out the window and sees Dunne staring out across the prairie. He looks utterly absorbed. What, she thinks, can he find in a blanket of brown grass, a cloudless sky, to hold his interest?

The answer to Ada Tarr's question is nothing. Nothing in the landscape interests Dunne. What interests him is the contemplation of a sensation new and utterly foreign to him, a vast, oceanic contentedness. Hour after hour, day after day, his mind fondles those small favours dear Mrs. Tarr so generously bestows on him, those little gestures of esteem and affection that speak more loudly and truly than words ever could. He dwells on angel food received from the hands of an angel, on the way she hovers about him, fluttering like a butterfly around a flower. Are you thirsty, Mr. Dunne? Is there anything I could bring you to eat? He has heard her try to persuade her husband to let him take his suppers inside with the family. It doesn't matter to him that the argument was lost. It's enough that Mrs. Tarr wants him close to her.

Her regard for him is the sweetest victory he can imagine over all those – like Randolph Tarr – who believe he can be used for their purposes then dropped down the privy hole like the corn husks they wipe their arses with. Lately, he had sensed that Tarr was about to do just that, that he had convinced himself that the threat from Gobbler Johnson had passed and he had no more need of a guard. But Tarr had been very wrong on that score because one morning he discovered Gobbler had killed a dog and dropped it on the threshold of his office. After that scare, cowardly Randolph had come home in a panic and ordered him to redouble his vigilance. As if a man like him needed to be told how to protect the ladies of the household. Did Tarr think Michael Dunne would ever let any harm come to that dear lady? Did he take him for a feckless idiot?

He has compiled a long list of such people who had treated him as though he didn't own a thought of his own, beginning with his father, who had thought him no better than a dumb beast of burden. "Strong back, weak mind. It's a waste of money trying to teach him anything" was his father's explanation when he dragged him out of school at the age of eleven. The elderly, doddering schoolmaster, Mr. MacIntyre, had attempted to convince his father he was making a mistake. As young Michael looked on from a corner by the stove, MacIntyre and his father had debated his future as if he were no more capable of understanding what hung in the balance than the three-legged stool on which he was perched.

MacIntyre had said, "You must understand, sir, your boy has a most remarkable mind. Let me give you a proof. One afternoon I showed him a chronology of the kings and queens of England. He looked at it for only the briefest of moments, turned it over on its face, and repeated them letter perfect, names and spans of reigns exact! I tested him again with an ornithological album of South American fowl – birds he could not possibly be familiar with. I gave him an instant to study each page, closed the book, and asked him to give the name of each bird. He did so without hesitation, omitting none!"

"Parlour tricks," Dunne senior grumbled, glaring at his son, who was making himself as small in his corner as he possibly could. "On all other counts, the boy's a simpleton."

"Yes, yes," agreed MacIntyre, "young Michael is a little tone deaf to other subjects, no feel for higher literature, or poetry, perhaps –"

Dunne's father leaned over, spat into the tobacco can between his feet. "That ain't what I mean. Left him to rig a pulley the other day. He couldn't figure it out. Came back and it was a cat's cradle. The lad is a dolt."

"But Mr. Dunne, the narrow mind is frequently a concentrated mind. One might say it specializes. Now your son's attention to detail, his remarkable memory, these are qualities that go to make a prodigious clerk. Give him a little more schooling, then you might put him in a bank."

"Where I'll put him is betwixt plough handles. One thing I'll give him, for his age he's strong as a ox, but no more suited to thinking than one. What he's fit for is swinging a axe, a mattock, a scythe. I know what that boy's good for, and I won't waste him on what he ain't."

And that was that. For the next twelve years Dunne wasn't wasted. The yoke settled on the ox's shoulders. He pulled stumps, picked rocks, shucked corn, ploughed, reaped, and sweated. What no one realized was that the ox was growing horns. No one suspected its fury. One day, glancing up from hoeing the corn patch, his father saw smoke writhing up between the shingles of the barn. Flames were shaking a red rooster comb along the roof by the time he reached the farmyard, bellowing for every Dunne on the property to form a bucket brigade. When Michael did not turn out to sling water on the flames his father assumed the worst, ran circles around the barn, howling and beating his temples, calling, "My boy! Michael! Michael!"

But Dunne was not inside the barn; after leaving the candle burning in the manger straw, he went into the house and calmly chopped his father's strongbox to pieces with a hatchet. From its splinters he scooped up two dollars in paper banknotes, thirty-seven cents in American coin, and a single English shilling. By the time his father gave up shouting his name into the conflagration, Dunne was nothing but a silhouette stamped at the end of a country lane.

Heading southwest, the ox plodded down the Ottawa Valley. For the first week, fearing an arrest warrant might have been issued for him, he travelled only by night, under cover of darkness. When day broke, he wormed his way into thorny thickets, haystacks, whatever hidey-hole he could find. He made no attempt to buy supplies at country stores, but provisioned himself by foraging in gardens and orchards and raiding chicken coops for eggs. Once he got well down the road from the scene of his crime, he breathed a little easier and ate a little better. It was harvest time and farmers were willing to exchange a bed in a barn and three square meals for a day's labour. This made for a long, slow journey but it left the money from the strongbox untouched.

It was early October before Dunne reached his destination. Following the long, sloping artery of Yonge, he walked down into the heart of Toronto, a country boy dazed by the city. Everywhere pedestrians were sprinting recklessly in and out of traffic, risking life and limb in daring street crossings. Vans, wagons, carriages, cabs racketed by, iron-rimmed wheels shrieking on cobblestones, their chassis rattling like a load of bouncing planks. Even though the sky was serene, clear of clouds, Dunne heard a low, ominous rumble of thunder gather behind him. Perplexed, he turned, and scarcely had time to spring out of the way of two men rolling empty beer casks down the edge of the street.

Newsboys on every corner brandished papers in his face, gleefully announcing famine and epidemics in places he had never heard of, battles lost and won in the War Between the States, stupendous loss of life in train wrecks and ship sinkings. A man, his beard clotted with egg yolk, stood on the sidewalk proclaiming the end of time in a spray of spittle. A drunk was yelling at him, "Shut it! Shut it! Or it'll be the end of *your* time! I'll see to it!" Passersby scurried by without giving them a second glance. Farther up the street, two goods wagons blocked an intersection. The drivers were up on their feet in their vehicles, shaking their fists at one another, hollering, "Give way, damn you! Give way!"

The roadway was a relief map of cobbles, yellow lagoons of horse piss, slippery hillocks of manure flapping canopies of iridescent bluebottles. The whirling flies made Dunne's brain swim as he stared down at them. He had come to the city imagining he would find streets paved with gold that would lead him *somewhere*. Instead, beset by noise, havoc, confusion, he had no idea where to turn. In a panic he stumbled down Yonge until he found his way blocked by the lake. He gave it the briefest of glances, turned and tramped back uphill, desperately sucking air. His feet hurt and a headache was pummelling his temples. In front of a tailor's shop, he squatted down on his hams to take stock of things, but the pawky-faced owner came out and ordered him off. The man had a tape measure hung around his neck. Dunne was tempted to strangle him with it.

All afternoon, he trudged the streets trying to find some peaceful spot where it would be possible to connect two thoughts together. Only when a coal-smoke Toronto dusk began to darken the thoroughfares did he find it, the shadowy grounds of a massive red-brick Methodist church. Leaning an elbow on a tombstone in its graveyard, Dunne counted his money into his palm, a pitiful amount when weighed against the extravagant rates for accommodation he had seen posted outside fleabag hotels and dusty-windowed rooming houses. Life in a city was dearer than he had ever dreamed. As he closed his fist on his few coins and crumpled paper money, he saw that the evening service had concluded, and the congregation was filing sedately down the steps of the church.

Catching sight of a vagabond in the churchyard, one of the congregants, Mr. Hind, indignantly marched over to demand a word with him. He was a parchment-skinned, desiccated, elderly gentleman who had all the stern self-confidence of those who have pulled themselves up by their own bootstraps. At the last deacons' meeting he had raised the issue of vagrants who hung about begging from parishioners and used the graveyard as a doss-house and lavatory. There had been some soft tut-tutting and weary head-shaking on the part of the other deacons, but no one had seemed ready to take steps, to take action. Hind was about to.

"You," he said to the young fellow in a harsh, ringing voice, "don't bother coming cap in hand here, bothering honest people. And there'll be no sleeping rough in the cemetery either. Clear off."

"I ain't asking no money from nobody. And I ain't intending to sleep here neither. I was just looking for a quiet spot to think is all."

The phrase "to think is all" struck home with Mr. Hind. Was it a discreet allusion to a crisis of faith, to the spiritual confusion that so often beset the young? At just such an age he himself had been prey to religious melancholia, but had managed to flail his way up from the dark depths to bathe in God's beneficent light. Suddenly, this young man seemed a worthy object of fatherly concern. Hind saw himself sculling a lifeboat to the rescue of a sinking soul.

The old man dramatically swept his arm to the tombstones that surrounded them. "It is not here you will find rest for your soul, my young man." Then he pointed emphatically to the church. "What you seek lies there. In the midst of the living body of Christ eternal."

Michael Dunne followed the finger taking shaky aim on the double doors creaking shut on the backs of the last of the departing parishioners. "I ain't looking for rest," he said. "I'm looking for work."

This was a deflating response; it was disappointing to have to ship oars in the midst of soul-saving. But Hind had a practical side to him also, and a mere three days before, he had found it necessary to dismiss his man of all work when it had come to light that he was engaging in highly irregular relations with the neighbour's parlour maid. Hind's eyes narrowed in appraisal. This sturdy lad was obviously healthy and strong. And, of course, the firm guidance of a Christian master and the atmosphere of a godly household would be of great profit to the young fellow. Here was a situation of benefit to both parties.

"Can you drive a team of horses?" Hind demanded.

"I was raised up on a farm. I can drive anything that's got four legs."

"Not afraid of work?"

"I said I come off a farm. There it's nothing but hard work."

"What's your name?"

"Michael Dunne."

Hind's eyes bored into him. There was a time he had hired Catholics, colleens fresh off the boat who came cheap. Frustratingly, however, they had all clung to their rosaries, resisted being Methodized. Their intransigence had led Hind to swear off engaging them. He was not a man who liked to be reminded that not everything could be moulded to his will. "Irish, that name, isn't it? You're not a Papist? I don't employ those who bend a knee to Rome."

Without a moment's hesitation Dunne said, "Me? My colour's Orange. King Billy's my man."

A shadow of skepticism passed over Hind's face. The answer had come a little too swiftly. But the width of this prospect's chest and shoulders was promising. "Very well," Hind said. "I pay a hundred dollars a year. You will have a room in my house and meals at my expense. I provide male servants with three shirts, two pairs of trousers, socks, and undergarments every twelfth month. A new suit of clothes every four years. I keep a teetotal house. My name is Rupert Hind. Mr. Hind to you."

Dunne immediately accepted the terms offered and followed his benefactor into a new life.

Hind had made his fortune provisioning railway construction gangs and lakeboat crews with the very cheapest of weevily food-stuffs. Driving hard bargains and slicing the loaf thin had won him an imposing home, a square, ugly blockhouse built of russet brick that cowed an elm-lined street. Its architecture resembled that of the church he attended. The interior was solemnly church-like too, furnished with hard chairs constructed to wring repentance from buttocks, walls painted a Protestant eggshell white, the air an eye-watering compound of varnish and vinegar. Dunne's attic room was as bare and cold as a cell in debtors' prison.

Compared to the heavy labour he had been sentenced to on the farm, his work was relatively light, but he was constantly at the beck and call of his new master and mistress. The ox was transformed into a patient dogsbody. He mucked out the stables, curried the horses, polished carriage fittings, mended harness, chopped wood, stoked the furnace, shovelled snow, cut grass, trimmed hedges; planted, manured, watered, weeded, and harvested the vegetable garden; made repairs to the house, walked the master's two Irish setters daily, ran errands to the shops, and drove Mr. and Mrs. Hind about in their carriage wherever they wished to go, any hour of the day or night.

Dunne performed all these tasks with consummate diligence and attention. Even when he learned his counterpart down the street got paid twenty dollars a year more for doing the same work, he never complained or betrayed resentment. The schoolmaster's belief that he had the makings of a prodigious clerk had taken root in his brain. He was alight with ambition. He had a plan. If he beavered away, proved himself loyal and efficient, perhaps Mr. Hind would consider him for a post in his company offices. In the meantime, he was making himself fit and suitable for such employment. No one was aware Dunne was studying a primer on double-entry bookkeeping, which he pored over whenever he could steal a spare minute from his busy days. Late at night, as he did accounting exercises in his attic room, the figures he entered with such lip-licking precision in the columns took on an eerie significance for him. The black numerals he inked were the bricks with which he was building his dreams. They were the hard, solid support for his future. They were *actual*. They were *real*. It was in such things he sought salvation.

But Dunne did not rely simply on competence with numbers to win him a place in Mr. Hind's firm. He memorized acres of the Holy Book, which he dropped into every conversation with his employer, giving proof of both his piety and power of memory. Sometimes he got carried away spouting scripture, which brought a flicker of irritation into Mr. Hind's eye and made him scuffle his feet impatiently on the floor. Still, Dunne doggedly persisted in making a good impression. At morning and evening prayer, obligatory for all servants, he sang hymns and entreated God with a fervour that incited giggling fits in the maids.

From the other servants Dunne held himself imperially aloof, not because they laughed at him and pulled faces behind his back, but because in his heart of hearts, he knew he was not one of them. Michael Dunne was destined for better things. He was training himself to think like a master, to note the delinquencies and shortcomings of household staff because the time would come when he would be a master himself. Several times, he took it upon himself to inform Mr. Hind of misdeeds and trespasses committed below stairs. He reported that the butcher had given the cook an emolument to ensure she kept placing orders in his shop. With a sad, reluctant air, he informed Mr. Hind it was Alice who had been responsible for breaking one of Mrs. Hind's prized vases. His employer appeared to be very happy to be enlightened on these matters. Of course, tattling made Dunne no friends among his fellow servants, but that signified no more to him than a cabbage fart in a windstorm.

Finally, after eighteen months of sterling service, Dunne respectfully buttonholed Mr. Hind and asked whether he would consider him for a clerkship. Something humble, of course, but a post that would offer opportunity for advancement if he proved capable. Mr. Hind stared at his handyman as if he had gone barking mad. "Why, Dunne, you are deficient in experience. I need practised men," he said sharply.

Dunne interrupted, mentioning the bookkeeping primer, the midnight oil he had burned improving himself. Mr. Hind turned slippery, muttered something evasive. When Dunne persisted in arguing his case, his master grew angry. "Not now! Can't you see I am busy? I have visitors arriving from New York tonight. A thousand things to see to! Understand?"

The set of Mr. Hind's shoulders, the way the tip of his cane angrily stabbed the floor, drove home to Dunne that all his hopes had been illusory. Hind would never give him fair play, never give him a chance. The old man had imagined his faithful dogsbody's big paw wrapped around a pen and realized what a ridiculous sight that would make, had considered what impression his man of all work's Ottawa Valley accent and country manners would make in a commercial establishment, what a preposterous figure he would cut before customers. Hind briskly dismissed his servant and marched off to see to the preparations being made to welcome his visitors from the United States.

Americans had been frequent callers ever since Dunne began to work in the Hind household, a great itinerant pack of anti-slavery men, so many of them that Dunne had wondered if there wasn't a factory in New England dedicated to their manu-facture. A flock of wing-collared, frock-coated, starchy-shirted old ducks, quacking the same thing through their bills. *Free the slaves! Lift the poor black man up!*

Dunne wondered why, if Hind was so much in favour of giving the Negro a boost, did he want to keep his boot planted on his white neck? He had driven his employer to enough meetings and lectures, stood at the backs of enough halls to have seen how these famous pamphleteers and orators could bring crocodile tears to Hind's eyes with the mere mention of shackles, whips, and slave auctions. Every abolitionist who came to Toronto to raise money to extirpate the Great Abomination was an honoured guest in Hind's home, and managed to stick a hand in his pocket.

But then in the summer of 1863, two months after he had dashed Dunne's hopes for advancement, Mr. Hind descended into a period of profound despair. For days he sat in his study, face buried in his hands, and everyone tiptoed about the house as if there had been a death in the family. Mr. Hind subscribed to a bundle of newspapers from near and far, some of which arrived by post from distant points, including New York and Boston. Being a frugal man, when Mr. Hind was finished with them they were turned over to his handyman to light the stoves and draw the drafts in the fireplaces. But before he put them to the match, Dunne, not having given up trying to improve him-self, read them assiduously. From what he read, he soon became convinced Mr. Hind's black mood had something to do with the riots that had recently broken out in New York in opposition to President Lincoln's new Army draft. For three days mobs had run wild, attacking and burning government buildings, until soldiers and artillery arrived to clear them from the streets. According to the newspapers, poor whites held the Negroes responsible for the draft, resented that their blood was to be sacrificed to buy the black man's freedom. The Negroes soon paid a price for that, were assaulted and murdered by the rampaging gangs; even a Negro orphanage was laid siege to and set ablaze with the children trapped inside.

From experience, Dunne had learned that his employer's moods were accurate barometers of what was in the newspapers. Union successes gladdened him and Union defeats darkened his countenance. But nothing before had thrown him into despondency the way the news of the slaughter of New York's Negroes did. The carnage there shook the old man to the core. When he finally emerged from the study, he was much changed. Hind had always been a hard man, but the newspaper accounts he had brooded over had cold-chiselled his face into the terrible, righteous mask of an Old Testament prophet.

A few months later, Dunne's employer began to entertain Americans of a very different stripe from the soapy old codgers who had formerly cluttered the premises, flashy young fellows who sported yellow waistcoats and loud windowpane-checked trousers. These men never orated or peddled pamphlets; they simply lolled about in an upstairs bedroom for a night or two, playing cards, smoking foul cigars, and passing round a bottle, which, to Dunne's astonishment, his teetotalling employer turned a blind eye to.

One of Dunne's duties was to ferry these rakish fellows back and forth from the Union Train Station. He picked them up when they arrived and drove them back to the depot when they departed. During these trips, his passengers didn't deign to exchange a word with him, but Dunne listened intently to the slangy, jokey code they talked and which they assumed he was too witless to decipher.

"Well, I hope the fish are biting down Windsor way. With the border so close, I like to get them into the frying pan while they're still wet and fresh!" And another would say, "Last time I didn't even have to call those wild tom turkeys around Mount

Forest out of the bush. They trampled each other trying to climb into my game bag."

It wasn't long before Dunne saw that these shady strangers threw their own shadows. He began to notice strange people and peculiar occurrences in the street outside the house. One morning while raking leaves, he observed a furniture van that sat in the roadway for two hours, then drove away without making a delivery. Another day a workman spent most of the morning up on a ladder checking a gas lamp – and peering into the upper windows of the Hind house. There were others, a suspicious birdwatcher with binoculars, and a man who walked a fat old dog for an eternity, toing and froing up and down the same few blocks near the Hind property until the animal sat down and refused to move, and his owner had to carry the exhausted animal off in his arms.

Then one October afternoon, as Dunne was greasing the hubs of Hind's carriage, he glanced up and saw a figure framed in the double doorway of the carriage house. The fellow had carefully posed himself there to create a picture of devil-may-care self-assurance. His thumbs were hooked in the armpits of his waistcoat; his bowler was cocked down over one eye; he was flicking a toothpick up and down in his jaw. "Now that's a landau to beat all landaus – a regular beauty," he said, and sauntered over.

Without offering a reply, Dunne dipped into the grease and resumed lubricating the wheel. This did not discourage the stranger; on the contrary, it drew him in even closer, so close that he filled Dunne's nostrils with the cloying smell of his pomade.

"Getting ready to take Mr. Hind's American friends on a sightseeing tour? Toronto displays itself to advantage this time of year, the colour of the leaves and what not. Don't you agree?"

"I ain't stupid. I know why you're here," said Dunne.

The man produced a gold sovereign, waggled it at him enticingly. "It's yours, mate, you give me the Yankees' destination."

"I never know where they're going," said Dunne. "Hind gives me their hour of departure. But if you take a gander at a railway schedule, it ain't hard to figure where they're likely headed."

"So what's their hour of departure?"

"Hind ain't give me my marching orders yet. But there's time yet. He always gives a day's notice."

"Well then, you and I are the best of friends already," said the man. "Aren't we?" He pressed the sovereign into Dunne's palm. Dunne stood staring down at the engraving of St. George's horse trampling the dragon. When he looked up, he saw the man's face was stretched in a wide, elastic grin that revealed a notable gap in his front teeth. He looked ready to swallow him whole.

"The name's McCorkle. And yours is –?"

"Dunne."

McCorkle tipped his head in the direction of the door and smoothly suggested, "I think we should step outside. Just in case someone happens to come to find you to run an errand. In that case, I'll be looking for a certain house and you'll be giving me directions."

Dunne followed him out into slanting sunshine. From a neighbour's yard, the smoky incense of burning leaves wafted over them. A blue jay cocked its head at McCorkle, its attention captured by the piece of chalk he was casually tossing from hand to hand. "So when you get the departure time from Hind, this is what you do. Note the hour here," he said, writing down *10:45 a.m.* on a plank of the carriage house. "Make the figures small. We aren't a commercial concern – no need to advertise," he said. "I'll be checking it regular. When I get the hour" – he swiped the wall with his sleeve – "gone." He handed Dunne the chalk.

Dunne thought for a moment. "I wonder why a fellow happens to carry chalk with him everywheres," he said.

"In my line of business," said McCorkle, "there are plenty of things to mark. Maybe a carriage of interest, or maybe a door that needs looking into or opening. By my associates, I mean. But those are details you don't have to bother your head about."

"Well, if it's your line of business maybe you ought to think longer and harder about the marks you leave lying about. No numbers," Dunne said. "Do it so." He drew four lines, ran a diagonal through them. "Five." Marked another four and slashed them with another diagonal. "Ten. Say it's ten forty-five, I take it to the lowest hour. Ten o'clock. It don't hurt any of you fellows to kick your heels in the train station waiting a few minutes. I put a little dot on top of the lines if it's a.m., a dot under them if it's p.m." Dunne illustrated, then wiped his marks clean. "If Hind was to catch sight of a number like 10:45 writ down on his property, it's likely to remind him of a time he just give me. It's likely to make him wonder. But this looks like somebody counting off something. What? Maybe the number of days until it's time to grease the wheels on the carriage again. I might say that if I was asked."

McCorkle shrugged. "If you're so damned skittish – do as you like."

"I like best what's in my interest. And I ain't said I'm about to do it neither." Dunne paused. "I'm just saying how's the right way to do it if a fellow *was* to do it. The way I'm thinking now is that a damn sovereign ain't worth losing gainful employment for."

McCorkle jabbed the dust of the lane with the toe of his boot. "If we had a permanent arrangement, more sovereigns would follow in due course. Seeing how well-placed you are, that could be advantageous to both of us."

"I think you better explain how that arrangement would work."

"I take it you post the family letters?" asked McCorkle. Dunne nodded. "Then it shouldn't be difficult for you to drop me a note when you learn Mr. Hind is receiving guests. Send it to Dan McCorkle, care of the Brandywine Tavern, Front Street. Once I am alerted, we'll proceed just as we have discussed today. I, or someone else, will check the carriage house wall until we receive news about when Mr. Hind's guests are leaving" – he flashed a smile – "on business."

"And how do I get paid?" said Dunne. "You didn't happen to mention that."

"If you have a bank account it could be deposited there."

"I don't trust banks. I want cash laid in my palm," said Dunne.

Irritation showed on McCorkle's face. "The other servants may begin to speculate if we're seen too much in one another's company – as you have already proved, the help knows more than one would expect."

"Whenever I tip you about visitors, the next Thursday afternoon I'll come to the Brandywine. That's my half-day off. You can give me my money then."

"I have my duties. I can't be dancing attendance on you. My time is valuable."

"I'll be saving you time aplenty. There'll be no need to keep men hanging around watching the house like you do now. You got a departure time, all you have to do is be at the station, board the same train, and follow them. As far as your precious time goes, you got a bargain."

McCorkle sucked his cheeks. "All right," he said at last. Then he added, "You're a dark horse, Dunne."

"Yes, I am," said Dunne. "And nobody rides me for nothing. Remember that."

Dunne finds it sweet to recall how good it had been to strike Hind in his soft spot, hit him in the breadbasket of his nigger love. Sweeter still to know that he had no inkling his plans were being confounded. There's the difference between a man such as Michael Dunne and those cocks of the walk that have to crow and flap their wings, let everyone know they've had a triumph. Knowing he's won is satisfaction enough for him. After all, secrets are power. Let them loose in the world and the power escapes with them.

Just as the newspapers had helped him to deduce the reason for his employer's gloom that past summer, now they helped him deduce who the whiskey-drinking Yankees were. He put two and two together and decided the old man was aiding and abetting crimpers and substitute brokers. As people said, the conflict raging to the south was a rich man's war and a poor man's fight. The wealthy had a way to escape the draft that had sent poverty-stricken New Yorkers on a wrecking spree. For three hundred dollars, an exemption from conscription could be purchased from the government. Men of lesser means, for whom raising such a sum was a stretch, could buy themselves a substitute, negotiate a cheaper price with some hungry wretch.

But the article writers pointed out that the flesh dealers couldn't get enough recruits in the United States to supply the demand. The crimpers had now come to Canada and were tricking gullible farm boys into selling themselves into military servitude for a few Yankee dollars. Worse still, there were claims that young men were being shanghaied, filled with beer and strong cider, then spirited across the border in the dead of night, or simply tapped on the head with a cosh, loaded into a wagon, and bundled off against their will. Editorials demanded that an end be brought to the chicanery and kidnapping, reminded the government that the recruitment of British subjects by a foreign power was a crime, and that it was their duty to protect honest citizens from these thugs. But from everything Dunne read, the trade in cannon fodder seemed impossible to suppress. If a broker was promised two hundred and fifty dollars from some boy's family to find a replacement for him, and the broker could nab a Canadian hayseed for fifty, it made perfect sense to Michael Dunne why men would run the risk of arrest and continue in such a profitable business.

Not that Dunne thought Hind was helping crimpers and substitute brokers for hard cash; he was sure his employer believed he was furthering God's holy work by assisting the Union to harvest soldiers for its army. But as far as Dunne was concerned, Hind had as good as opened his house to slavers. If trading in black flesh was an offence in the sight of God, wasn't it a hundred times worse, a thousand times worse, to buy and sell a white man? Hind would sooner wash the feet of a darky with his tears than give a man who had been his *slave* for two years, who had practically got down on his knees and begged for a chance to better himself, the slightest consideration. The old hypocrite had put his thumb to Michael Dunne's head and pushed him down just as his own father had. People who did that paid a price. Hind's would be to pay wages to a man working against him. It delighted Dunne to serve two masters, Hind and McCorkle, betray the first in the interests of the other, and pocket the money of both.

And so it went on for months, chalk marks rewarded with sovereigns, although as far as Dunne could see without much effect on the tide of brokers and crimpers. They still continued to arrive from the States. When he questioned McCorkle about what results were being obtained, all that McCorkle could do was make lame excuses. He said that the crimpers were slippery fellows and careful not to incriminate themselves. They needed to be caught red-handed to provide the evidence a court required to convict them, and that was a difficult thing to do. But, McCorkle added smugly, the mere fact that they knew they were being watched was making them so cautious that their catch was growing ever smaller and smaller. That was almost as useful a result as putting them behind bars. Dunne knew what to think of that explanation. McCorkle was a bungler and so were the people who worked with him.

Then something occurred that changed Dunne's comfortable situation. He found it necessary to report some bad news to McCorkle. Several articles of Mrs. Hind's jewellery had gone missing, and everything pointed to the substitute brokers having stolen it. Mr. Hind felt this as a crushing blow, twice over. The men he was aiding had abused his hospitality, and reporting the theft was out of the question. The police would oblige him to answer questions about the people he had entertained and that meant compromising himself. So when Mrs. Hind unleashed her ire on him for the loss of her geegaws, her husband contritely offered a solemn pledge never to entertain people of that sort again.

Never would Dunne have believed that Hind would so easily draw back the hand he had extended to pull the Negro out of the mire. The goose that laid the golden eggs had been well and truly cooked. The crimpers and substitute brokers would never again darken his master's doorway. It was all over.

But two days later Dunne received a message from McCorkle asking him to drop by the Brandywine Tavern at three o'clock on his next half-day off. Something needed to be discussed. When Dunne presented himself McCorkle was not alone. Sitting beside him was a tiny man with a shovel-shaped beard, deep-set eyes, and an aggressively crooked nose whom McCorkle introduced as Stipendiary Magistrate Gilbert McMicken. The title signified nothing to Dunne, but the moment McMicken opened his mouth he knew this little bantam ruled the roost. Turning to McCorkle, he said in a harsh, scraping voice, "Off with you."

Surprise glimmered on McCorkle's face, surprise quickly succeeded by disappointment. "Shall I wait outside or –"

"No reason to wait. I don't know how long this will take."

When McCorkle had left, the magistrate said matter-of-factly to Dunne, "I'm a frank man. McCorkle urged me not to meet with you. He thinks you may have lost your nerve and tattled to Hind. He sees no other explanation for his sudden break with the crimpers."

"Here's the explanation," said Dunne. "They lifted his wife's jewellery. She laid down the law to him. Said she wouldn't have them in her house again. I told McCorkle all about it."

"Indeed you did, indeed you did," said McMicken. "Yet how very strange those substitute brokers should put their cozy, safe nest in jeopardy."

"Well, they're a tribe of money-hungry rascals. Maybe the itch in their fingers overruled their good sense. The arrangement I had with McCorkle – I was doing all right by it. Why would I wreck it? And if I'd gone squealing to Hind about McCorkle like some fat hog stuck under a gate, would I still be in Hind's employ?"

McMicken eased back in his chair, stroked the tabletop with his fingertips. "McCorkle says you're an extremely cautious, an extremely wary man. He reads that as timidity, a lack of fortitude. I thought it might point to something else. A quality I'm looking for." He smiled grimly. "I've come to see. Put a few questions to you."

"What questions?"

"Have you formed an opinion about who McCorkle is? Who he represents?"

"I took him for a peeler. Otherwise, I wouldn't have got mixed up with him."

"Yes," said McMicken, "I'm sure an upstanding citizen such as yourself would wish to render every assistance to the police. But I ask myself if you ever wondered why the police were willing to pay so exorbitantly for your civic-mindedness?"

"No."

"I think you did, Mr. Dunne. I think you concluded you were not dealing with ordinary, run-of-the-mill peelers."

"Well, maybe not ordinary peelers," said Dunne guardedly. "Detectives. I figured McCorkle for a detective."

"Yes, a detective. Of a kind," McMicken said. He stared hard at Dunne for a moment. "Have you liked your work? Did it suit you?"

"Good enough."

"The thing is," said McMicken, "at present I have a pressing need for men. You may be the kind of man I require, or you may not. I would need to examine you on your suitability. But there is no point in beginning that examination until I know whether or not you are interested in being employed as a detective."

"Same sort of wages – I'm interested," said Dunne.

McMicken gave him a wintry smile. "There is another thing you must be aware of before we proceed. What we are going to speak of is confidential. If I were to hear that you blabbed about anything I have to say I would be obliged to do you a great deal of damage. Let me assure you that I have that power, and I would not scruple to use it." He paused. "So what do you say? Are you ready to continue?"

McMicken reminded Dunne of nails, hard and sharp. He sensed the little bugger would not hesitate to do him harm. "I don't blab," he replied. "Ask McCorkle."

"I assure you I did ask McCorkle. You would not be here if he did not testify to your discretion." Dunne saw he was growing impatient. "But I want to hear from your own lips that if you decide you wish to hear me out, you will keep your mouth shut about any matter I touch upon."

"I will," said Dunne. "Go on."

McMicken resumed talking in his frosty, level way. "Some months ago I was put in charge of the Western Frontier Constabulary created by Attorney General John A. Macdonald. We are a force of detectives who do not concern ourselves with ordinary villains, burglars, robbers, pickpockets – common criminal riffraff. We have one task and one task only – minimizing awkward, unpleasant situations that arise in our midst from the conflict going on to the south of us. One might say our work is *political*. Do you understand the implications of that?"

"No."

"What I mean is that it is political in the sense that the constabulary is more closely monitored and directed by the government than is customary. Attorney General Macdonald has a hand in the day-to-day running of our affairs. He and I have had a long personal relationship. I have done him many favours in the past and he has returned them," McMicken said significantly. "He has my sworn loyalty. The efficient working of the Frontier Constabulary depends on loyalty, loyalty that binds the highest link in the chain of command to the lowest. Which is to say I look after my people. I take care of them." He paused. "We have made a beginning in our work, but I am discovering that not everyone we have employed has the proper outlook. We need men who don't let their private opinions interfere with their work. Could you be such a man?"

"I don't have no private opinions," said Dunne.

"Everyone," said McMicken emphatically, "has private opinions. The question is, can a man shelve them as required? At the behest of his superior?"

Dunne looked at him blankly.

"Very well," said McMicken, "let me illustrate from my own experience. A short time ago, I obtained a commission from President Davis's government to assist Confederate escapees from Union camps to make their way back to the South. There was no pecuniary award attached to this work. I accepted it because I sympathize with the Confederacy's struggle against the tyranny of the North. It was also my firm belief that an independent South would be in the interests of British North America because it would diminish the power of the United States on this continent. If they were weakened we could breathe easier." McMicken pondered for a moment. "Nevertheless, I resigned this appointment. Do you know why?"

"No," said Dunne. "I ain't got no idea."

"Because Attorney General Macdonald requested me to. It is his view that it is now clear that the South has no chance of winning this war. The writing is on the wall. And in the light of the script he reads there, we must modify ourselves to a new reality. This means placating the North. Whatever feelings of distaste this causes me, I have set them aside. Whatever wind Attorney General Macdonald fills my sails with is the wind I steer by. This is the sort of loyalty I speak of."

"Which means you ain't interested in arresting crimpers any longer. Because the winds has changed."

"In a nutshell." McMicken made a wry face, as if his own observation had injected a bitter taste in his mouth. "President Lincoln's government has made a vigorous demand that we take action against Confederate conspirators resident here. In Mr. Macdonald's opinion, it is only wise that we give full attention to this request. At present, we have a Southern plotter in our custody, a man called Bennett Burley, implicated in the Confederates' attempt to launch an attack on Detroit from our soil. Unfortunately, we were not successful in capturing the ringleader, John Beall. President Lincoln's administration is not happy Beall avoided our nets. It is necessary they be mollified."

"And how you going to do that?"

"In the past, our courts have frequently proven unwilling to extradite Southerners to face justice in a Northern court. Mr. Burley's extradition hearing is pending. There is no doubt that in this instance he will be given over for trial in the North. *That* is already decided. However, the secessionist men here in Toronto will do everything they can to prevent him being surrendered to their enemies. They may attempt to spring him from the Toronto jail, or, more likely, try to free him when he is escorted to the border." McMicken tapped the table with his index finger, a soft insistent noise. "It is my responsibility to see the Southerners do not succeed. If Burley makes an escape, the Lincoln administration will accuse us of colluding in it. That would be most unfortunate." McMicken's eyes suddenly seemed to be regarding some far distant place. "But as you can imagine, this reversal of policy in regard to the North has produced difficulties. Men have had to be shifted to new purposes. Chop and change produces gaps. They need to be filled. At present I am short a pair of eyes and ears."

"Meaning you want to buy mine."

McMicken laid his hands one beside the other on the table and studied his nails. Dunne understood that this was a calculated effect, the depiction of a thoughtful man easing into an important decision. "That remains to be seen. Ordinarily I would wish you had a little more seasoning, but we are stretched very thin. The best of my people are taken up with the riskiest work. The role I am considering you for is not dangerous – it simply requires that you observe the comings and goings of certain individuals."

"And what is the wages for that? Watching comings and goings."

"In the past you have received a sovereign for each piece of information divulged – that is the piecework rate. Now you would go on the regular payroll. It would certainly be considerably more than you earn from Mr. Hind. And if you did stellar work, there would be bonuses."

"All right," said Dunne, "I'll take it."

"You have misunderstood," said McMicken. "I need to satisfy myself that you are right for the job. McCorkle disparaged what he called your 'morbid suspicions,' said you were 'dull as ditchwater.' But ditchwater has its uses. It's very difficult to see to the bottom of ditchwater, isn't it, Mr. Dunne? It's difficult to ascertain what lies beneath it. On the other hand, sometimes murk is simply murk. Nothing but stupidity. I need to know which it is with you."

"I ain't stupid," said Dunne. "I'm a damn sight smarter than McCorkle."

McMicken ignored that. "I am looking for a man with a grasp of detail, a mind for particulars, a sticky memory, powers of concentration and focus. I have found this a useful tool for testing those qualities in my men." McMicken reached inside his jacket and removed a sheet of paper, which he slid across the table to Dunne. "Have a look at that," he said.

Dunne stared down at the strange configuration on the page.

	5	2	3	I	4
2	A	B	C	D	E
I	F	G	H	I/J	K
5	L	M	N	O	P
3	Q	R	S	T	U
4	V	W	X	Y	Z

"That," said McMicken, "is a cipher known as the Polybius square. You take the number at the top of the grid, follow it with the number down the side, and you arrive at a numerical co-ordinate for a letter of the alphabet. For instance, A would be 52. Do you understand the principle?"

"Yes," said Dunne.

"It is a system for secret codes. But I have also found it a useful tool for testing the mental acuity of recruits. I give them half an hour to memorize it and then see how well they do translating letters into numbers. I would like you to take thirty minutes to attempt to master it."

"Put it to me now."

"You haven't understood. First, you must commit it to memory."

Dunne tapped his temple. "She's all up here."

McMicken smiled dismissively. "A," he said.

"52," said Dunne.

"V."

"54."

McMicken arched his eyebrows. "Apple," he said sharply.

Dunne momentarily contemplated the frame in his mind. "52, 45, 45, 55, 42."

"Banana," said McMicken quickly, dissembling his astonishment.

Dunne looked perplexed.

"So?" said McMicken.

"I don't know how many *n*'s is in it."

"B-a-n-a-n-a," spelled McMicken rapidly.

Without hesitation, Dunne rattled off the numbers.

"Well, well, well," said McMicken. "I am in the presence of a prodigy."

"I take it prodigy means I pass your test."

"Yes, yes, indeed you do," said McMicken with a distracted air. He returned the Polybius square to his pocket, gathered himself and said, "I think you would do nicely."

"I ain't reporting to McCorkle," said Dunne. "He's too loose in his methods."

"Of course not. To me. Consider yourself now under my special care."

"Your special care doing what?"

"In observing the Southerners who congregate in the Queen's Hotel. I will provide you with descriptions and the names of the principals so you can identify them. Since Beall has fled the scene, a man called Postlethwaite appears to have assumed leadership." McMicken's crooked nose twitched. "We have time to sound the situation because they are anticipating a favourable outcome in Burley's extradition hearing. They do not know there has been a change in attitude to their activities. They think things will play out as they have in the past. When the judgment doesn't go as they expect, they will look to other means to free their friend. That will be the crucial time. You must note their comings and goings. The more details the better, dates, times, anything of importance. I will want to know which of them vanish from the Queen's Hotel and which remain. Whether they mass their forces there or disperse them. Such movements will give some indication of their plans to free Burley – whether they intend to attempt to spring him in Toronto or when he is under transport to the American authorities. All this will require the utmost patience and alertness on your part. Do you understand?"

Dunne nodded.

"All these particulars will help us determine whether it is possible to cut the head from the snake in one blow, or whether we have to send people chasing it through the grass. If the Confederate plotters can be taken out of action just before Burley is to be handed over, that would be the happiest, most satisfactory outcome. There are several possibilities to bring that about." McMicken got to his feet. "But these are matters for future discussion. For the present, tender Mr. Hind your resignation – or simply disappear. As you choose. But leave his house immediately." McMicken took out his wallet and handed Dunne a small bundle of dollars. "Here is the necessary to rent a room and re-establish yourself. Once that is done, provide me with the address." He passed Dunne a card. "You may reach me here by letter. When you write, use the Polybius square cipher. It will be the means of all our future communications." McMicken placed a hand on Dunne's shoulder. "Grow a beard. A man has two faces to choose from. One with a beard, another without it. Sometime in the future you may want to reclaim your old face."

Dunne watched him leave, a tiny, brisk, purposeful man, hardly bigger than a boy.

The very next day, Dunne gave Mr. Hind notice he was quitting his employ and left the old man raging against the ingratitude of servants. He carried off all his belongings in a single carpet bag, his clothes, McCorkle's sovereigns, the scanty wages earned from Hind. Mrs. Hind's missing jewellery also went with him. He saw now that stealing it had not been wise. But his desire to injure Hind had got the better of him. He would be careful not to make such a rash mistake again. Still, it had all come right in the end. McMicken's promise of his "special care" left him feeling like a pig in clover.

But that situation cannot hold a candle to the one he finds himself in now. His days are exceedingly pleasant. There is the pleasure that comes from extracting his pay from Randolph Tarr each and every day and watching him squirm whenever the lawyer is reminded of what he is still owed for services provided in Chicago. It doesn't matter that Tarr, in return, treats him with contempt, and doesn't want him in the house. After all, this only excites greater kindness, greater gentleness on the part of Mrs. Tarr. He would sooner have her sympathy than sleep in a feather-bed or eat a meal off china.

When he stares out at the empty countryside, when the hot wind burns his cheeks, he is entirely occupied reviewing his past and planning his future. His most private thoughts are formulated courtesy of the Polybius square, as if he were afraid some outside presence might be trying to read his mind. He thinks, over and over again, 333142 3252234233.

She cares. She cares.

Sometimes, when all the Tarrs are asleep, he eases open the front door and slowly edges his bulk into the house. He stands staring up the dark stairway that leads to the bedrooms on the second floor, heart wildly beating in anticipation of the ascent. Then he begins his slow, careful, stealthy climb, moving on all fours, supporting himself on his palms and his toes, distributing his weight as evenly as possible to minimize creaking and squeaking from the steps.

Reaching the top, he continues to creep, testing each plank as he makes his way to Ada Tarr's bedroom door. It is always left ajar to encourage the circulation of air. Of all the happy surprises he has received during his stay with the Tarrs, the most gratifying of them all was the discovery that Mr. and Mrs. Tarr do not share a bed.

Dunne never enters her room. He remains crouched in the doorway, listening to the sound, to the rhythm of her breathing. Whenever his mother produced another infant, Dunne remembers her warning everyone to see to it that the cat was kept out of the house. "They suck a baby's breath," she said.

That is what Dunne would like to do with Ada Tarr, to draw the warm breath from her lungs and take it into his.

TEN

JOE RETURNED TO Fort Benton from the Cypress Hills by
the middle of August, far more quickly than Case had expected.
One afternoon he stomped into the Overland Hotel and
announced to his partner, "I sold my cabin and contents to a
no-nothing Englishman. McMullen's flush." When Case gave
him his own news, that he had scouted a promising property
and would like Joe's opinion on the livestock before clinching
the deal, McMullen said, "No better day than today." That afternoon they toured the Worthington ranch; Joe made an inspection of the cattle and horses, and allowed as he thought the
asking price for land and livestock to be fair. Then he added,
"But the price ain't everything. Be sure this is what you want.
Don't be going into this thing blind."

But Case was sure, burning to begin the purposeful, independent life he imagined for himself. There was a substantial
letter of credit deposited in the Fort Benton bank that he could
draw on. At last he had somewhere to put that money to a
worthy use. The next day, Worthington and he signed the document of purchase in Randolph Tarr's office. When he came out
of the lawyer's, Case found Joe and a pretty sorrel mare with
dainty hooves and trim legs waiting for him out in the street.

Joe tossed him the halter shank. "She's yours," he said.
"I reckon a cattleman needs a cow pony."

Case was surprised at how much this gesture touched him, but still felt obliged to protest McMullen's generosity.

Joe's only response was, "I got to throw *some* money into the pot in this poker game. Otherwise, I ain't a player."

That very day, Case sold his former mount to the proprietor of the livery stable. Then he and Joe bought supplies, and soon were riding past the Tarr house under Dunne's watchful scrutiny, headed for their new residence, a four-room, wind-buffeted shack, lonely in a sea of drab grass. Mr. Worthington had decided on a clean break with the past, as if in doing so he could shed the bad luck and misfortune that had dogged him for years. Aside from a few personal items to which his wife had a sentimental attachment, he had lumped the rest of their goods into the purchase price: rickety furniture, chipped dishware, dodgy pots, threadbare linens, and tarnished cutlery. Worthington meant to travel light, get clear of the accursed place as fast as he could.

Case had bought a bottle of Monongahela whiskey to celebrate his acquisition. Lifting a glass to the shabby surroundings, he said, "To our new venture, Joe."

McMullen lifted his glass to his lips, took a parsimonious, sombre swallow, and made no return to the toast.

Joe's silence, his serious mien, bewildered Case. "This is a happy occasion. Why the dark face?"

"I know why I'm here, but I ain't got no idea why you are," said McMullen so softly that Case had to strain to catch his words. "I'm fifty-three year old and it only come to me recently that the way I've lived – spending free and gadding about – hasn't left me so much as a pot to piss in. I'm about finished making my living bucking out rough stock. It come to me I'm facing a hungry old age and there ain't much time for me to correct that prospect. So I naturally got to thinking, is Case going to stick this? Because if you ain't in it for the long haul, my twenty-five per cent of nothing is nothing."

"Listen, Joe," said Case, "I'm not going to run from this. I want to build something here. Something that I can point to with a little pride. Up until now, my life's been short on anything of that description." Case realized that this confession had been more self-revealing than he would have liked, so he tried to temper the earnestness by adding a wry note. "Maybe it's time I earned my bread from the sweat of my brows."

Joe nodded solemnly. "If it's sweat you want there'll be aplenty of that in store for you. Starting tomorrow we got to get the bung out of our asses. Worthington put up but one cut of hay. We're going to have to make another to get them cattle through the winter. And we ain't got much time to do it."

"Whatever you say."

"All right then, this is what I say. Tomorrow, I'll start mowing buffalo wool. It makes good feed but it's short, scanty grass. Down near the river, the pasture grows higher and ranker, but there's too much driftwood and suchlike laying about to use a horse-drawn mower. It'll need to be hand-cut and hand-raked. That's your job." Joe hands Case an apologetic smile. "And don't think I'm trying to shirk my share of the sweat riding a mower. It ain't that. Horses has jumpy, nervous dispositions. A mower is a fearsome contraption to them, chattering and clicking away behind them. They're like to bolt. If there was a runaway and you got jolted off the seat, that mower blade would chew you to pieces. I'd be scooping you up with a teaspoon to get enough bits in a coffee can to bury."

"Well," said Case, "I appreciate your concern for my well-being."

Joe looked relieved. "Now that I been assured you mean to sweat, it wouldn't do no harm to take another tot to celebrate. But only one," he said. "After that the cork goes in the bottle. We got to make an early start tomorrow."

Case has been reaping hay for three weeks. As soon as the dew burns off the grass, he starts for the river on his little mare, a scythe propped on his shoulder. At the beginning of the day the morning sun is nothing but a soft, warm hand on his back. But in an hour or two, it turns hot as a stove lid, leaves him dripping sweat. By quitting time, the collar of his work shirt is starched with a rime of salt; crusty white stains loop the armpits.

The first week of mowing was agony. At dawn, he woke and creaked to the kitchen in a harvester's stoop, back knotted, fingers curled into bird claws, frozen in the grip he had held locked to the handle until sunset the day before. A dull ache scoured his shoulders and the cords of his neck. But now he has found a rhythm to the work, an efficient action that swings the long blade back and forth, its weight sweeping it to and fro like a grandfather clock's pendulum.

His body is toughening up; hard buds of callus are forming at the finger joints, and the skin of his palms is turning to rawhide. McMullen counselled him to piss on his hands to harden them, a suggestion he flinched from. But he did listen to Joe's admonition that a sharp scythe is half the job, and whenever he pauses to take a breather, he gives the blade a few passes with the whetstone in his pocket, keeps it wickedly keen and glinting, sharp enough to shave a mouse, as McMullen says.

Now that his body has stopped torturing him, Case takes real pleasure in the way the tall grass tumbles with every pass of the scythe. It's like being a boy playing war, toppling lead soldiers over. He likes the way grasshoppers spurt out of the seeded heads, their wings blurring in a papery-sounding whir. Sometimes they land on his shirt, cling there, antennae twitching, bulbous eyes trained on him. He never bothers to brush them away, holding to the tempo of the work, to the dance of the job. At intervals, the grass ahead of him explodes, a prairie chicken heaving up from a tussock with a rush of beating wings, or a rabbit bursts from its hiding place, scut twitching frantically. More than once he has struck a garter snake, which took a twisting, writhing ride on the scythe blade. Now he keeps an ear cocked for the dry-pea rattle of a diamondback. He doesn't want to sweep a rattler out of the grass and have it come sliding down the scythe handle to strike him.

There are cottonwoods, willow thickets, cactus patches, and piles of bone-white driftwood heaved up when the Missouri was in spring flood that he must work around. At the tail end of summer, the river is at its lowest ebb. Geese and ducks promenade sandbars that hunch their backs out of the slack, greasy river. Stray feathers and down waft about, speckling the biscuit-coloured water. The riverbank is scribbled with green-and-white goose shit.

The waterfowl are flocking early, a sign, Joe says, of a hard winter coming. Great wavering flights of sandhill cranes streak the pale blue skies. At dawn, the geese lift off the river to feed, booming their sad, nasal honking, pinions whistling. Returning later in the day, they glide down like a lazy autumn blizzard. Wings spread cruciform, webbed feet braced for the shock, they plough furrows in the river, bob about for a few self-satisfied seconds before clambering up on a sandbar with a matronly waddle.

Occasionally, the rhythmic, repeated movement of the scythe induces in Case a dream-like state where scraps from his past blow about in his mind. Strange, disconnected bits. The unholy terror he felt at the age of three when the barber went to work on him with his big, shiny scissors, how he had screamed, fought, and struggled in the chair. Until that day his mother had been the one to cut his hair. It was her gentle hands he wanted on his head, wanted to hear her say, "All done, my handsome little man," to feel her giving his earlobe that little tweak, his signal to scramble down from the chair.

Christmas Eve, carried out of doors in his father's arms. The old man laughing, the smell of port on his breath, a new toboggan waiting in the back garden with an apple crate set on it. There was straw in the crate. His father nestled him down in it. A night so cold his nostrils stung, but the straw warm as a feather tick. Staring up at a blue-black sky, the stars bobbing with every tug to the towline. A carol the old man had sung, the creak of the frozen snow under his boots. He had wished that ride could go on forever, just as he had wanted his mother's hands to never lift from his head. He had been content. They had all been content. The world itself had been content in those days. That's how he remembers it.

But Case does his best not to let memories of the past intrude, nails his mind to the present, the gurgling song of red-winged blackbirds – *conka-ree conka-ree* – the agitated whistles of warning and alarmed chorus of *cack cack* as they ride the tips of willows, swaying in the wind. He fixes on a snag in the river where an eagle perches on a single branch poking above the waterline, staring at him with a hanging-judge's cold eye. He glances over to his red mare mincing in her hobbles to a fresh patch of grass, watches her dip her nose in it.

He sets himself goals – to reap the grass between this boulder and that wild rose bush before he eats. An empty belly, the promise of satisfying it, hurries the ripping whoosh of the blade, fills the air with the sweet, sappy smell of fresh-cut hay. When he reaches that wild rose bush, he collects the packet of sandwiches stowed in his saddlebags, settles down in the shade of a thicket of willows, their leaves hanging like tattered ribbons, fills his mouth with bread and cold bacon, dried apples and raisins.

At the end of the day, Case trots up to the ranch house in an amber mist of dust. Joe is preparing supper. McMullen's domestic streak, his housewifely pride in his own cooking, came as a surprise to Case. There's a fire going in the yard, a cast-iron pot banked with embers and a skillet baking sourdough bread.

Case stables Sally, shakes out a ration of oats in her manger, and goes to the house for a good scrub-down and a change of clothes. When he comes outside McMullen hauls a bucket filled with bottles of beer from the well where they have been left to chill since morning.

Without a word, they tip the bottles and take the first long swallow. Joe swipes away a dab of foam from his chin with the back of his hand and says, "I allow I'll finish mowing tomorrow. Then commence with the raking. How you coming along?"

"Making progress. Slowly but surely."

Joe squints to the west where the setting sun is a blood blister. "If it stays fair a bit longer, we catch no rain, we should be all right."

"What's Delmonico's got on the menu tonight?" Case inquires.

Joe raises the lid off the pot with a stick. Chunks of fatty beef, parsnips, carrots, potatoes, onions bubble in thick brown gravy. It smells of wild sage. "Sourdough's done," he says, jerking the skillet from the fire. He takes out his jackknife and cuts the bread like pie, spears a slice and holds it out to Case. It's piping hot; Case washes each yeasty mouthful of it down with a swig of yeasty beer.

"It ain't a bad life if you don't weaken," says Joe, belching softly, "but if I had your money, I'd sit on it. Live high on the interest. Live easy."

"No, you wouldn't."

"Wouldn't I? What'd I do, then?"

"Spend it on horses. Then you'd sit on your ass and admire them all day."

"You might have that about right. It's a weakness." He scuffs the ground with his boot heel. "You know," McMullen says, "that damn Walsh told me to my face you was crazy for taking me on. But I ain't completely dead lazy. Nor all tomfoolery and lightheartedness, am I?"

"No, you aren't, Joe. I don't know where I'd be without you."

"Don't put everything on me," says Joe sternly. "I'm in your corner, but it's your fight. You got to do whatsoever you need to do to come out on top. I popped a man's eyeball out of his head with my thumb one time. It was that kind of man, that kind of fight. You got to make up your mind to do the necessary."

Case almost lets that pass unchallenged, then, abruptly, he says, "You make it sound easy – knowing what's necessary."

"I reckon it is."

"No, it isn't," says Case with a heat that surprises him. "I thought I saw what was necessary once. It wasn't. A man's dead because of my bad decision."

"It's none of my business to ask questions," says Joe carefully. "But what you just said sounds accidental, not purposeful. There's a difference."

"The longer I've thought about it, the less sure I am which it was."

"Well, if you can't answer that maybe you're thinking too hard. Turning round and round in circles like a dog chasing its own tail. Maybe it's time you stopped. Picked yourself a direction to go." Joe moves to the pot. "Enough said. Let's eat."

The fatty meat is succulent, tender; peppercorns erupt heat in the mouth; the aroma of sage fills Case's nostrils every time he lifts a spoonful. The second beer tastes even better than the first. Evening gathers round them; a pale moon hangs itself in the sky; the prairie turns blue. McMullen gets to his feet and announces he is turning in. Despite his bone-tiredness, Case can't bring himself to retire. An owl keeps him company on the ridge of the small barn. The yellow lamps of its eyes shift about like the beams of a tiny, compact lighthouse.

He nods off, wakes with a jolt so violent it almost tumbles him off the step where he sits. He sees the last embers of McMullen's cook fire throbbing in the darkness, gets up and draws a bucket of water from the well. He stands staring down at the hot coals, and wonders if everything he has seen, tasted, felt today mightn't have been pointing him in the direction of happiness.

Then he tips the bucket and puts the fire out.

By the last week of September haying is almost completed. Case and McMullen have finished five tall haystacks and are building the last. It is a fine, mild autumn day, shirtsleeve weather. Case is pitching hay to McMullen from the load on the rack. Every forkful he hoists to the top of the stack sprinkles a prickly shower of dust, chaff, seeds, and stems down on him. They lodge in his hair, spill down his collar, and glue themselves to his sweaty skin. He is covered in a fiery rash; his eyes are red and swollen and he streams snot. He blows his nose with his fingers, wipes them on his pants. When he glances back up to Joe, he sees him looking off intently into the distance, eyes shielded with a hand.

"What is it, Joe?"

"Somebody's coming."

"Who? You recognize him?"

"Ain't a he. It's a visitor in a skirt."

Ada Tarr had risen early to bake cakes while it was still cool. She thinks best when her hands are busy. Randolph's behaviour has been of increasing concern to her. Ever since he saw the nonchalance with which Mr. Case had bought himself a ranch, her husband has been quizzing her about anything Peregrine Hathaway may have divulged about his friend's financial circumstances. She tells him she knows nothing about Mr. Case's pecuniary position, his prosperity or lack of it.

Lately, her husband's usual energy seldom shows itself. When it does, there's something desperate and feverish about it. He's like a gambler on a losing streak, seeking salvation in the turn of a card. Perhaps this explains his interest in Mr. Case; he speaks vaguely of enticing him to invest in some commercial enterprise that would make them both a fortune. Randolph says he is tired of the law.

Ada believes he is just plain tired. Last night he fell asleep over his supper like an old man, his mouth hanging open. She wonders if it isn't the worry and strain brought on by this Gobbler Johnson business that has aged him so. Even his habits have changed; once a prim, picky eater, now he devours everything in sight. When once he was abstemious, now every evening he drinks beer as if it were water. Randolph claims his kidneys need flushing, but she is sure it is his anxieties that he is trying to rinse from his mind.

Looking out the kitchen window at the beautiful autumn day, Ada wonders if this might not be as good a time as any to muster her courage, approach Mr. Case, and ask him to do her that favour she has been pondering for some time. Besides, she feels she will go mad if she doesn't slip the bonds of this tiresome seclusion that Randolph's troubles have imposed on her. She wants to feel the sun and breeze on her face, to stretch her legs, to fill her lungs with fresh air.

Her mind made up, feeling light and happy, she hurries up the stairs. Celeste is in the sewing room working on yet another dress meant to bewitch the pompous Lieutenant Blanchard, so absorbed in her stitches she doesn't notice her stepmother pass by.

She dresses quickly in her prettiest blouse waist – the one with the long, scalloped, flowing sleeves – a straw bonnet with a spray of yellow cloth roses, and a pair of fine grey kid gloves that perfectly match the colour of her walking skirt. She glides past Celeste's door unnoticed and swiftly descends the stairs to the kitchen, where she wraps a freshly baked pound cake in cheesecloth and stows it in a wicker basket.

The only one left to evade is her warder, Mr. Dunne. She must steal out the back as quietly as possible. With her hand on the doorknob, she suddenly remembers the pepperbox derringer. It has become second nature always to have it near to hand. Mr. Dunne insists on it. He even asks to see it before they walk into town to do the shopping. She puts no trust in it as a weapon. Ada is certain she could never use it against another human being. But she has come to feel it is a charm against danger, against evil. Just as her grandmother was convinced an iron knife buried under the doorsill kept witches from entering the house, Ada has begun to believe the little pistol is what has kept Gobbler Johnson at bay. It may be superstitious nonsense, she feels a little abashed by it, but what's the harm? She darts into the parlour, takes the derringer from her reticule, and puts it in the wicker basket with the cake. One quick glance at Dunne through the window to make sure that he is where he should be and she is out the back door and gone.

Ada Tarr covers the half mile to the ranch at top speed, constantly looking over her shoulder, half expecting to see Dunne. Only when the squat and homely Worthington house comes into view does she stop to catch her breath. The day is far warmer than she had thought; her face is hot and flushed, her hands are perspiring in the kid gloves, which she impatiently tugs off. Giving a triumphant slap to the side of her leg with them, she resumes walking. Her successful escape, eluding Mr. Dunne, has left her giddily exhilarated.

Case and another man walk into the ranch yard and stand watching her approach. She hails them with a wave. "Mr. Case! Beautiful day, is it not?"

He returns her salute, arm lifting slowly like a drowning man going down for the last time, but offers no other greeting, no word of welcome.

Seeing Mrs. Tarr draw nearer, Case suddenly realizes what a sorry picture he must make. He starts to rake his fingers through his hair, searching for errant straws, thinks of the swollen, bloodhound eyes that stared back at him out of the mirror this morning, of his ridiculously red nose. With Ada Tarr ten steps away, he glances down and is mortified to discover a slug track of snot streaking the sleeve he's been using all morning to wipe his nose. Case hides that arm behind his back. There she is, face to face with him, smiling and squinting into the sun. "Forgive the intrusion, Mr. Case. But my family has delayed too long in welcoming you to the neighbourhood. I thought it high time that oversight was corrected." She holds up the wicker basket and says, "I have brought you a little something – a pound cake I baked this morning. Hardly a proper housewarming gift, but –"

McMullen jumps in enthusiastically. "Pound cake! Why, ma'am, if you'd have handed us a pound of gold we couldn't have been happier! Would we now, Wesley!"

"Certainly not," says Case. "Much appreciated, Mrs. Tarr. Very kind." He sees Ada inquisitively studying Joe, face tilted under the brim of her straw bonnet. "Excuse me, I have lost my manners. Mr. Joseph McMullen, allow me to present to you Mrs. Randolph Tarr. Mrs. Tarr, Mr. McMullen."

Joe doffs his hat and says, "Mrs. Tarr, I'm very glad to know you." Then he astounds Case by winking at her. "I guess a genteel lady like you expects to get her hand kissed on occasions like this. But I ain't going to try. My performance would just disappoint you."

Even more astounding than Joe's wink, his barefaced flirting, is Ada Tarr's response, a full-throated laugh of delight. "Why, Mr. McMullen," she says, "a plain, democratic American handshake will be every bit as good – if not better."

Joe takes hold of the proffered hand with two fingers and a thumb and gives it a delicate waggle. "Miz Tarr, if you would give me the pleasure of escorting you and your pound cake to the house, we'll have us a slice." He lowers his voice to a stage whisper. "But I got to warn you of the lamentable state of our quarters on account of Mr. Case going uncivilized out here in the wilds. The man has turned our little home into a bear's den. No matter how I harp at him, he just won't tidy up after himself."

Joe chicken-wings his arm to Ada; she takes it and the two sail off laughing, leaving Case to follow along behind. Inside the house, Joe insists on dusting Mrs. Tarr's chair before she sits, gives it a conspicuous flogging with his handkerchief before he's satisfied it's fit to receive their guest. "Now you make yourself comfortable, Mrs. Tarr," he says, "and I'll brew us some strong coffee."

"Mr. McMullen, do not bother –"

But Joe is off to the stove. Watching Joe's performance, seeing how much Mrs. Tarr enjoys this monkey business, Case experiences a twinge of annoyance. Disgruntled, he plops down on a chair at the table.

"I trust I have not interrupted your work," Mrs. Tarr says to him.

But Joe is back at the table with plates, forks, and knives, and he answers before Case can get a word out of his mouth. "And thank God you have, Miz Tarr. Because Mr. Case here is a blamed slave driver. Chases me out of my bed every morning before the crack of dawn, waving a stick."

Case is growing more irked by the second. "Pay no mind to him. Joe has liberal views on what constitutes the truth. In fact, he treats it with prodigious latitude."

McMullen puts his hand to his breast and draws himself up ramrod straight. "As God is my witness, Miz Tarr, what I say is the unvarnished truth. But now I have went and contradicted him and he'll take me to the woodshed for it when you're gone. Don't ever contradict or cross this man. It stirs him up something terrible."

Ada's lips curve in a half smile. "Yes, I have had experience of it." Case flushes bright red and McMullen throws him a puzzled glance as Ada reaches down for the basket at her feet. She produces the cake, sets it down on the table, and unwraps the cheesecloth.

"Why, look at that, ain't that a cake!" Joe exclaims.

"Very fine," mutters Case.

"Gentlemen, it is a simple pound cake, not the Elgin Marbles."

"A lady as humble as she is kind and good," Joe says. "I hope you don't mind me saying what a fine thing you and your daughter done, throwing that benefit concert for the misfortunates."

"That concert," responds Ada dryly, "is an event best left unremarked and forgotten."

"I can't agree nohow. Why, all that music and singing, trust me, I ain't going to forget it in a month of Sundays."

"For God's sake, Joe, there are bounds," Case snaps at him. "You weren't even there."

"I didn't say I was there. I said I wouldn't never forget it. Why? Because young Peregrine couldn't talk of nothing else all the way to Fort Walsh. Now if you'd have told the lady how you enjoyed it I wouldn't have felt it necessary to risk a compliment."

"You were there?" Ada asks Case.

"Yes, yes, certainly," he says quickly. "A very memorable evening."

Ada's mouth twists ironically. "Mr. Case, it seems every time you are present I show myself at my best." Then she points to the stove. "Is that the coffee I hear on the boil?"

"Yessir. Let me take it off the fire. Let the grounds settle." Joe hands her a knife. "I'd be obliged if you'd be mother and cut the cake, Miz Tarr."

Ada touches Case's hand as Joe tends to the coffee pot. "I require a word alone with you. Please volunteer to walk me home." It is less a request than a command. She eases back in her chair as Joe returns.

The cake eaten, the coffee drunk, Ada gathers up her basket and gloves, rises from the table. "And now, gentlemen, I must take leave of you. I have passed a very pleasant hour in your company. Thank you for your hospitality."

"Miz Tarr, you're very welcome. As welcome as the flowers in May."

Ada turns to Case and waits. He lurches to his feet. "Mrs. Tarr, might I have the pleasure of escorting you home?"

"Most kind of you. I would be pleased."

"It's a poor day you don't learn a lesson in something," says Joe. "Now why didn't I think of that?"

"Always another day, Mr. McMullen," says Ada, smiling. "Always another day."

Joe roguishly tucks his tongue in his cheek. "Tomorrow?"

"Goodbye."

"Day after tomorrow?"

"Good*bye*, Mr. McMullen."

Once outside, they are both at a loss for words. Ada studies the ground, biting her lip, as they walk along in silence.

Eventually, Case finds himself saying, "There was something you wished to speak to me about?"

"You must find this all very curious," she says, sounding hesitant. "I debated at length the propriety of this, but in the end – well, it is a matter of conscience."

"Conscience?"

"Yes. It concerns Peregrine Hathaway. Something needs to be done. He must be told the truth."

"Told what truth?"

"How else to put it but directly? My stepdaughter, Celeste, is involved with a young officer at the post. I think it is serious. I have told Celeste she has a duty to inform Mr. Hathaway where her affections lie. I said to her she must write and make the situation clear to him. She refuses. She says that Peregrine never harboured any illusions she welcomed his attentions. Which seems to me patently untrue."

"I should say so. At least from his perspective."

Ada gives a curt nod of agreement. "The next time he comes to Fort Benton he will be on our doorstep to pay her a call. I should hate to see her turn him away and humiliate him. He is owed an explanation, but Celeste will not give him one. She says to do that would put *her* in a humiliating position. I know the girl. She will not change her mind." Ada pauses. "So you see, I have come to a dead end."

"Indeed."

"It struck me that if a friend, an older man whom he trusts and admires, could show him how things stand, gently lower him down from the clouds and set his feet firmly back on earth, that would be the kindest solution. Would you consider writing him such a letter? For the boy's own good? As a favour to him? A favour to me?"

Case takes a moment to answer. "Yes. If you think it necessary."

"You sound as if you have reservations."

"Mrs. Tarr, I am a cautious man. It is my nature. I do not like meddling in other people's personal affairs. This is not an errand I welcome, but I will do it. Writing such a letter will require a good deal of thought."

"But not too much thought. Or too much time."

"As little of each as possible."

"You have my gratitude, Mr. Case. I mean that most sincerely. I knew you would put the boy's interests first."

"You have put the boy's interests first. I am merely your agent."

Ada halts. "You see, I have done it again."

"Done what?"

"Been insistent. Just as I did the day you came looking for Peregrine. I have *pushed* you. I think you are not a man who likes to be pushed, Mr. Case."

"No. Perhaps not." He makes it sound as if this thought has never struck him before.

"And since I am a woman who does not care to be pushed myself, I should have known better. It was rude of me when you paid your first visit . . . to try to make you speak of things that I find amusing and you do not."

Case shakes his head. "I would like to correct your impression of that afternoon. It was I who was rude to you. I was very short-tempered that day. Hathaway's irresponsibility put me in a foul mood. I have no excuses for my behaviour. I was a guest in your home. An uninvited one, I might add. I imposed my company on you –"

"And I was glad you did," Ada interjects. "I was happy to know you. The way Peregrine spoke of you – I thought we might have a good deal in common." She smiles faintly. "I was eager to make a friend of you and my eagerness made me act foolishly." She stops and subjects him to a searching look. "You are taken aback."

"I am taken aback. I have no talent for friendship."

"From what I have seen, I think Mr. McMullen would disagree. Young Hathaway certainly would. He believes you kind and decent." She pauses. "Shall I put that description to the test? Will you be so decent as to shake my hand? Be so kind as to let bygones be bygones? Come now, let us be friends."

Case looks down uncertainly at the white hand held out to him. His fingers close on her palm; the softness and heat of it are disturbingly intimate. He holds it for just a moment too long and then lets it go.

"There," she says, "my conscience cleared on two counts. A good day's work." Briskly, she straightens her shoulders. "You know, when winter rolls round, if time hangs heavy on your hands – you are welcome to borrow any of my books."

"That is a very kind offer."

There is a mischievous glint in her eye. "Of course, I will not press George Eliot on you."

"Perhaps you should. Perhaps it would be good for me."

"But your opinion of her was so very disapproving and decided –"

"All second-hand, paraded as my own. I knew a man who often passed disparaging judgments on her work. I merely parroted him."

"And who is this critic?" demands Ada, laughing. "So if our paths ever cross I can box his ears."

"His name?" Case says, more to himself than her. "It hardly matters."

But it does matter, he thinks. Pudge Wilson.

They recommence their walk. In a short time, Mrs. Tarr's house comes into view. Suddenly she stops and says, "I think it best we part here. I did not announce to Mr. Dunne that I was paying you a visit. I slipped off. Now I must steal back into the house through the back. How very wicked of me," she says, giving him a pert look.

"Your secret is safe with me, Mrs. Tarr."

"Well then, I'm off."

"Goodbye, Mrs. Tarr."

Case watches her go briskly down the trail, skirts switching.

ELEVEN

AT THE BEGINNING OF September, Case had found Walsh's first brief communiqué awaiting him at the Fort Benton post office. It informed him that the Major had sent his two most dependable Métis scouts, Cajou Morin and Louis Léveillé, below the border to visit the Assiniboine to see if they could learn anything from that tribe about the whereabouts of the Sioux. The Assiniboine professed to know nothing about the Sioux's movements, asserting that they had had no contact with them since the days before the Battle of Little Bighorn, when Sitting Bull had sent an emissary to the war chief White Dog, promising him a hundred horses if he would join forces with Bull against the Long Knives. Case immediately brought this news to Ilges's attention. The Sioux chief's attempt to strike an alliance with the Assiniboine gave credence to the rumours that Bull was making overtures to other tribes to draw them into war with the Americans. It hadn't been much to give Ilges, but it was something.

Case hadn't heard anything more from the Major, which he found exasperating. If Walsh wanted him to keep Ilges happy, the Major needed to make an effort. Walsh's aversion to paperwork might be one reason for his silence, but it was Case's guess that the Major was piqued because Ilges had provided no recent updates on the progress of the Crook-Terry campaign. Perhaps he suspected Ilges was holding back on him. If he did, more fool

Walsh. Since the end of August, no one knew where Crook and Terry were. It was as if the wilderness had swallowed them up. Then, in the last week of the month, Ilges had a visitor, and he brought with him a great deal of insight into the situation.

September 30, 1876
Fort Benton

My dear Walsh,

If in your last report to Secretary Scott you did as I urged you – suggest that the joint campaign of Gens. Terry and Crook would come to naught – you will have been well served, may even have earned a reputation for perspicacity in Ottawa. An officer who, until recently, had been attached to Gen. Sherman's headquarters passed through Benton en route to join his regiment for active service against the Sioux. He is an old friend of Ilges from Civil War days and they spent an evening discussing the most recent developments of which this gentleman was fully cognizant given his position on Sherman's staff. He was as full of gossip as an egg is full of meat. According to him, the whole campaign turned into an unmitigated debacle because of the animosity and petty jealousy that rules relations between the two men. On August 25th Crook separated his force from Terry's control on the pretext of providing protection for the settlements in the Black Hills of Dakota Territory. The real reason appears to be he could not abide Gen. Terry's company any longer. Crook led his men into unfamiliar territory with meagre rations and inadequate supplies. The difficult terrain coupled with many days of cold rain soon took its toll on soldiers and animals. By September 7th, many of the troops were exhausted, stricken with acute dysentery, and suffering from exposure because they had no tents and each man had been issued only a single blanket. Within ten days of separating from Terry, the force was facing starvation and had no alternative but to slaughter and eat the majority of their horses.

Given the seriousness of the situation, Crook dispatched Capt. Mills of the 3rd Cavalry with 150 troops and 50 pack mules to hasten to Deadwood in the Black Hills to secure provisions. Shortly after setting out, Capt. Mills came upon signs of a large body of Sioux. Scouts found their encampment near a place called Slim Buttes. Mills thought the Indians vulnerable to attack because the bad weather and heavy rain was keeping them hunkered down in their lodges. He attacked at first light and took the Indians by surprise, but he did not press forward, giving the Sioux time to place warriors in a defensive position to cover the escape of the women, children, and elderly. Mills ordered a second assault, but that was met with stiff resistance. By then, warriors had arrived from Crazy Horse's band, which Mills hadn't realized was camped nearby. By the time Crook appeared with reinforcements, the initial advantage had been squandered, and the engagement petered out into an inconclusive standoff.

Ilges's friend said that the Army is determined to put the rosiest complexion on what they glorify with the title "The Battle of Slim Buttes." It will be painted as a great victory. To describe it so is the height of absurdity. True, Sioux horses were seized, food stores and tipis taken; nevertheless, casualties among Sioux fighting men were very light. Most of the Indian fatalities were women and children, and sustained during the first attack on the village. The officer who divulged all this to Ilges believes American losses were equal to those inflicted on the enemy. He was disgusted by what appears to have been near mutiny among the American troops after this fight. Contempt for the incompetence of the leadership was given vent to by the rank and file, and Crook's vain attempt to take his men to the Black Hills was openly and disparagingly referred to as "The Starvation March." After the battle, soldiers refused to obey orders to assist the ill and wounded. The rule of the day was "Every man for himself." Even junior officers are said to have shown signs of disaffection.

What should be of most concern to Canadians is the present reluctance of any American commander to come to grips with the enemy. Ilges's friend said that Terry was so unnerved by Crook's abandonment of him that he immediately withdrew to Fort Abraham Lincoln. It is reported that Gen. Gibbon has retired to the safety of Fort Shaw. Crook's bedraggled, sick, and footsore command is licking its wounds at Custer City. Once his men have recovered, he intends to make his way to Camp Robinson, Nebraska, where his troops will remain in garrison for the foreseeable future.

It is clear that until some active, resolute American officer is willing to prosecute a campaign against the winter camps of the Sioux where they are most assailable, to harry them continually so that they cannot hunt and provide food for their families, this situation is not going to be speedily resolved. Come spring, the Sioux are expected to resume hostilities, inciting terror among the population. At present, most civilians have returned to their farms and ranches – circumstances leave them no other choice – and things have returned to what might be called a normal footing here in Montana. Nevertheless, this lull cannot be regarded as permanent. I would advise you to make it clear to Secretary Scott that this matter is going to drag on and any hopes he may harbour that the Americans will force the Sioux to capitulate in the next few months are ill founded. The government of Canada cannot take an overly optimistic view, but must keep a cautious watch on developments, and consider every contingency. Scott must not think that the Americans will pull a happy result out of the hat. It is evident that Sitting Bull's ears are not going to be taken hold of easily. He is no obliging and compliant rabbit.

This brings me, finally, to a delicate matter. Maj. Ilges has been questioning me as to why you have failed to supply any intelligence recently. I cannot emphasize the importance that you keep in touch. I know you are a busy man with many things on your mind, but please write me as soon as possible. It is important that we be seen as acting in good faith.

I await your speedy response.

Yours truly,

Wesley Case

October 14, 1876
Fort Walsh

My dear Case,

Thanks for yours of the 30th. Let it be known to the Sauerkraut Farter that I am, as per usual, ever vigilant in his service. My men are constantly in the saddle, combing the border between Fort Walsh and Wood Mountain for Sitting Bull and his cronies. Tell Herr Ilges that on several occasions I have sent my people over the line to the American side to scout in places the Yankees studiously avoid going for fear they might find the enemy there and be obliged to face them. Which is very prudent tactics given the whippings they have been handed every time they bump up against the foe. Further inform Ilges that as of yet I have not a goddamn thing of any real consequence to report.

Of course, tell him all this as sweetly as possible so as not to offend his tender, girlish sensibilities.

Yours truly,

Maj. James Walsh

October 27, 1876
Fort Benton

My dear Walsh,

Your last letter does you no credit, sir. I will say
no more.

Here is the latest generously provided, I might add, by
the man to whom I did not pass on your insults. He received
it from a dispatch rider from Fort Buford. Things may be
looking up. There is an American officer who appears to
have some fight in him, Col. Miles of the 5th Infantry. On or
around the 15th of October Sitting Bull attacked a United
States Army supply train. When the Indians disengaged, a
written demand was found on the trail purportedly signed
by Sitting Bull (it is unclear who may have written it,
perhaps a half-breed in Bull's camp) warning that unless
Miles pulled out of the Tongue River country the consequences for him would be dire. This resulted in a two-day
parley between Col. Miles and Sitting Bull in which both
parties adamantly insisted that the other must yield. Miles
demanded the unconditional surrender of the Indians.
Sitting Bull demanded that all soldiers depart the Yellowstone
district and that the Tongue River Post and Fort Buford also
be abandoned. Negotiations broke off amid acrimony and
recriminations. Miles chose to immediately advance on the
Indians. The so-called Battle of Cedar Creek did not result
in success for either side, but when the Indians quit the fight
Miles did not do as his predecessors have done and choose
to call it a day. Instead, he set off in dogged pursuit of the
Sioux. Due to this initiative he overtook a large group of
Indians (regrettably Sitting Bull was not among them) and
forced the surrender of some 400 lodges that pledged to
return to the Cheyenne River Agency.

Yours truly,
Wesley Case

November 11, 1876
Fort Walsh

My dear Case,

    I admit it; I am a mule. Ilges is a packsaddle cinched to my back and when it galls my withers, I kick and buck. I know that much about myself. That's why I asked you to act as my spokesman. You can muffle my braying. You think before you speak.

    Yours truly,

    Maj. James Walsh

With the haying completed, the pace of ranch work eased a little. McMullen was worried that they still did not have enough feed to carry the cattle through the winter and persuaded Case to buy a supply of oats from the mill in Benton. Joe took on the task of freighting the grain from town while Case occupied himself with small jobs: patching the roof of the house, repairing the corrals, and setting out twice a day to round up strays and return them to the herd. The weather remained fine and Case revelled in the sunny days. The six tall stacks they had built gave him a feeling of accomplishment whenever he rode by them; the sight of his cattle contentedly grazing filled him with the pleasure and pride of ownership. Already he was making plans for the future. Even before he had left Fort Walsh, negotiations were under way to persuade the natives to sign treaties with the government. It was only a matter of time before the tribes were removed to reservations, the country opened up to settlers. Homesteads and grazing leases would be granted, and Case had it in mind that when that happened he might sell his land, pocket the money, and he and Joe drive their herd north to less expensive pastures. He sometimes wondered ruefully if he hadn't more of his father's head for business than he had ever imagined.

As to his father, Case had had no answer to his letter that announced to the old man that he would not be returning to Ottawa. He could only conclude that his father had decided that stony silence was his only recourse, seeing that his fury could not be expressed in words. It seemed to Case that all his correspondents were dilatory in replying to his missives. After spending a great deal of time dithering about how to compose a tactful letter to Peregrine Hathaway that would gently bring home to him how he really stood with Celeste Tarr, he had opted for bluntness. He had always found any discussion of the personal and private to be embarrassing, even painful. This he put down to his mother's influence. "Hearts are not meant to be worn on the sleeve," she liked to say. "They are hidden from sight for a reason. They require protection." As yet, there had been no reply from Hathaway.

He had considered that he might pay Ada Tarr a visit to tell her that he had written to Peregrine as she had asked. The temptation was very great, and it was a struggle to remind himself that great temptations often lead to great disasters. Perhaps the Case men had a fatal weakness, an attraction to women that they had no business pursuing – his father a scullery maid, he a married woman. There was no point in tormenting himself with what he couldn't have.

The first winter storm arrives in mid-November, a cold surprise. Case and Joe awake in the dead of night to a shrill, keening wind that shakes the ranch house. The windowpanes chime with blasts of hard, granular sleet and then the gusts begin to trowel a mortar of wet snow over the glass. The two men stand shivering, peering out as the storm draws a white curtain down on the world. All Joe says is, "First light, we better get those cows in."

It is still blowing hard when morning spreads a milky, peaked light, the snow wiping chalky smears over the landscape.

It robs them of breath when they ride out into it, drives cold needles into their eyeballs. The wet snow blankets their clothing and the coats of the horses. The force of the blizzard has ripped the herd to rags; here and there five or six dazed cows huddle together, rumps backed into the gale. Joe and Case prod the reluctant cattle on towards the haystacks where they can find a little shelter. Then back they go into the flying snow to chase down a few more strays and shepherd them home. For eight hours they roam the storm, gloved hands welded to reins, rocked in the saddle by buffets of wind. By five o'clock, the sun is so obscured by a gauze of snow that scarcely any light breaks through. Four cows are still unaccounted for, but Joe says they have to give up the hunt for fear darkness overtakes them, making it impossible to find their way home, which would be the end of them.

At last, they stagger into the house, light the stove, and, like beetles shedding their carapaces, they peel off their snow-caked garments to roast themselves by a roaring fire as they massage their fingers and stamp their feet on the floorboards. Soon a lightning-like stinging starts up in Case's numb toes, sets him hopping with pain. It's all he can do to choke back a whimper. Joe holds a frozen ear cupped in one hand, and sucks the frostbitten fingers of the other. His face has gone a queer zinc grey; he begins to shake uncontrollably. "Christ," he says, "I'm taking myself to bed. I advise you do the same. A slow melt serves best."

Case follows his advice, crawls into his cot. He can hear the chatter of Joe's teeth clear across the room. Between clicks, McMullen jerks out, "In a few minutes, when I thaw, I'll make us some hot food." That never happens because Joe drops off. Soon Case slides into a deep, dreamless sleep. Six hours later, he wakes with a nagging feeling that something has gone missing, and soon realizes that what is gone is the querulous whine of the wind, which had been present in his ears for twenty-four hours. A dead calm reigns. Case twists his head on the pillow and listens intently, hears nothing but the boards of the house contracting, the cold snapping its bones. Bundled in his quilt, he gets up and feeds the stove as much wood as the firebox will hold, scrambles back into bed. Bit by bit, the elbow joint of the stovepipe reddens in the darkness. Case drifts off again.

Next morning it takes two of them to shoulder open the door. A snowbank lies curled up like a large dog on the threshold. The snow gleams with a faint tint of indigo as if it had been rinsed in laundry bluing. The sun is a blurred, hazy whirlpool sucking all the colour out of the sky.

"Christ," says McMullen, "she's cold as a pauper's coffin."

Case shivers in the doorway. The only signs of life are the smoking noses of the cattle, the steam rising from freshly dropped dung, the famished bawling as they mill around the fences that ring the haystacks. The two men plod through the crusted snow, grapple their way up the icy sides of the stacks, and begin to fork feed down to the cows.

The first snowfall marks a revolution in the Tarr household. Given the severe turn in the weather, even Randolph can't argue that Dunne should remain sleeping on the porch bundled up in a buffalo robe. But he tries to keep him quarantined as much as possible. Dunne never eats with the family, but takes his meals separately in the kitchen. He sleeps there too, on a pallet by the stove. Randolph and Celeste treat him with open contempt, leaving Ada to bear the weight of his doleful presence. For the best part of the day, Randolph is at his office and Celeste spends most of her time in the sewing room, working on her finery. When Lieutenant Blanchard pays her a call, Celeste banishes both Dunne and Ada from the parlour, exiling them to the kitchen. On the first few occasions when this happened, they simply sat at the table drinking tea and making stilted conversation, or rather Ada did the talking, Dunne only seconding whatever she said with a fervent, disconcerting enthusiasm.

Now to avoid such awkward moments, Ada busies herself with baking, but can sense him following her every move. Sometimes it makes her hum with frustration. It's like having a begging dog underfoot, or a greedy child, eyes pleading for a taste of sweetness. So she feeds him raw cookie dough and spoonfuls of cake batter to appease his hunger, never guessing that Dunne is famished for something else.

Looking at him, licking a blob of cookie dough off his finger, slowly sucking a gooey spoon, Ada can only think, *Poor, poor booby*. Yet this poor booby is souring her life. Randolph is right; it's impossible to share a house with the man. Now that he keeps watch in the parlour, her favourite place to read and think is spoiled. It's not that Dunne chatters at her when her nose is buried in a book, as Randolph or Celeste frequently do, it's that his efforts to remain silent, to not disturb her, are so very distracting. He ostentatiously tiptoes across the floor. When he shifts his legs, or crosses them, he does so with such excruciating care that she'd like to shout at him, *You're not building a house of cards. Just cross your legs and have done with it!*

And there is something else. Ada is beginning to wonder if the steady gaze he directs out the window doesn't sometimes detect, mirrored on the surface of the glass, the look of distaste on her face when she glances over his way, distaste for a man whose only crime is doing his best to make himself agreeable. When this guilty thought crosses her mind, Ada will set down her novel, one of those books in which the most charming man is invariably the most wicked, and ask, "Mr. Dunne, could I interest you in a cup of tea?"

And Dunne always says, "Don't put yourself to any trouble, Missus, not on my account."

Despite his aggravating humility, she pulls her face into the brightest smile she can muster and assures him, "It is not a trouble at all, Mr. Dunne. It is my pleasure."

A week after Mr. Dunne took up quarters in the house, Ada descends the stairs one morning and hears Randolph and the bodyguard talking in the kitchen. Whatever is being discussed is a serious matter, Randolph's tone alerts her to that; she has heard that scolding urgency before, directed at her when she has displeased him. Dunne's responses are flat, monosyllabic.

Both men fall silent when she enters the room. She sees a bag at Mr. Dunne's feet, the one he used to bring clothing and personal effects from the Stubhorn. His shotgun lies across it.

"Good morning," says Ada, glancing first to her husband, then to Dunne. Randolph makes no reply. He is blinking furiously.

"Good morning, Missus Tarr. I trust you slept well," says Dunne.

"Moderately well. And you, Mr. Dunne?"

Impatiently, Randolph taps his foot on the floor. "Ada, please go back upstairs. Mr. Dunne and I have business to conclude."

Randolph does not look well; his eyes are haggard, his lips a sickly mauve. Dunne looks insufferably pleased. "What has happened?" she demands.

"Mr. Dunne is leaving us this morning," Randolph answers.

"When was this decided? As usual, it seems you have kept me in the dark about your plans."

"Mr. Dunne is unhappy here."

"No I ain't."

"It's settled," says Randolph, raising his voice. "Your services are no longer required."

"I don't understand," says Ada.

"No, you don't. And that is why it is not your place to interfere."

This is not the tone to take with Ada, not the thing to say. She turns to Dunne. "This comes as a great surprise to me,

Mr. Dunne. But if you must go, allow me to offer my gratitude for the service you have rendered us. A service that has eased my mind very much." She extends her hand. "Thank you, sir."

Dunne hesitates, takes hold of her fingers, and simply holds them, unable to lift his eyes from the amazing sight of their linked hands. "Missus Tarr," he says, "you are a peach. To have made your acquaintance . . ." His voice falters; he looks up and colour rushes into his face. "Words do not do you justice, Missus Tarr." He stoops in a sudden bow, snatches up his bag and shotgun, and flees out the back door.

Randolph drops down on a chair. "Well, I'll be damned. What facility you have, my dear. I can't eject the hooligan, but you butter him up and out the door he squirts."

Ada may feel relief at seeing Dunne go – but that only makes her more acutely aware of the disgraceful treatment her husband and stepdaughter subjected the man to. They were the reason she felt it necessary to pet him up, and now she is being mocked for it.

"Why have you sent him away?"

"Leave it alone, woman," snaps Randolph.

"Here we have lived for months in fear of Gobbler Johnson – bullet holes in the wall of your office, dead dogs on your doorstep – and now all danger from him has evaporated. Is that what you're saying?"

"Gobbler Johnson, Gobbler Johnson," he mutters, "I'm sick of the sound of the name. If you need an admission from me, I will make it. I lost my head. I panicked. I fell prey to an old man's senile, impotent threats. All Johnson meant to do was give me sleepless nights. He succeeded. Now are you satisfied?"

"That is not all. Something else has changed. Tell me."

"If you insist on harping at me like a fishwife I'll give you my answer. I am stony broke. One step short of bankruptcy. I lack the money to pay Dunne." He sags in the chair, shoulders hunched in defeat.

"Where has the money gone? What are you saying?"

"It is not so much a case of it going as it is of it not coming in." Randolph fretfully rubs at his eyes. "A good deal of my income came from the business I did with Harding. He is a man who requires a good deal of legal advice. But now he has dispensed with my services."

"He must have provided you with reasons."

"Harding doesn't give reasons, neither does he explain himself. I was his faithful dog. I rolled over, sat up, fetched the stick at his bidding. And what good did it do me?" he says bitterly.

"Harding is not a man who concerns himself with doing good to others. He certainly did me none. You might have learned a lesson from the way he treated me."

Randolph gives Ada a look filled with such vindictiveness that it takes her breath away. "You and your damned insufferable sense of superiority. How many times did I have to listen to Harding complain about how you squabbled with his wife, sneered at his daughters. A man like that doesn't forget such things. Lord," he groans, "maybe it's you I have to thank for this. What was I thinking when I married you?"

It comes as a shock to Ada that her husband could entertain the same question that has so long perplexed her.

TWELVE

DUNNE CLUMPS UP THE stairs to his room above the Stubhorn, pauses on the landing to gaze back over the snowy roofs of Fort Benton in the direction of the Tarr residence. A slim finger of smoke beckoning to him above the horizon, a reminder that right now Mrs. Tarr will be preparing baking soda biscuits for breakfast. The thought leaves a flaky, hot, buttery taste on his tongue. She knows they are his favourite.

Dunne enters his quarters. It is no warmer inside than it was outside. Nailheads are capped with a fur of frost; the only window is glazed with ice. He reaches up and puts his hand to the chisel resting on the ledge above the door; making a circuit of the room, he ritualistically touches all his totems, those items that quiet his mind: the parlour gun stowed in the wood box, the straight razor secreted in one of the socks on the floor by his cot. He takes the Schofield Russian revolver from the waistband of his trousers and slips it under his pillow. He runs his fingers over the short-barrel detective-model Schofield nestled in the silk sleeve sewn into the lining of his jacket. Everything is where it should be; everything is in order. It feels safe enough to light a fire.

He spreads his hands above the stovetop. As he waits for the room to thaw, his breath steams from his nostrils; the heat of his happiness makes itself visible in the freezing air.

Dunne knows the truth of it. Whatever Tarr might say, he hadn't packed him off because he couldn't pay his wages. It wasn't because that snotty bitch Celeste objected to having him around. It was because he had *alienated* the affections of the lady of the house. Jealousy was why Tarr had shoved him out the door. *Affections alienated, affections captured.* All of the smug legal phrases Tarr had mouthed in those Chicago courts, how does he feel now that he knows they apply to him? And those last caressing looks Mrs. Tarr had given him when they parted, the fond way she had let her hand linger in his fingers, how had Tarr felt when he saw that?

Mrs. Tarr is his for the taking, if not tomorrow, then some-day soon. He knew it as soon as he spotted those crusty white speckles on the toes of Tarr's glossy lawyer shoes. Grand Da's workboots had been spotted with them too, dribbles from the old man's cock. That had set him on watch for other evidence. It was all there. Tarr's thirst, his hunger, his fatigue; Grand Da had shown all those symptoms too. No one can say that Michael Dunne isn't clever, hasn't a nose for details; he overlooks noth-ing, no matter how small. Not him. He had stolen up to Tarr's room, tasted a few drops of piss from his chamber pot. It was liquid sugar. He has the sugar diabetes. He will waste away just like Grand Da did, will slip into the dark sleep of a coma. Randolph Tarr is dying and doesn't know it.

This is the best of all possible secrets. Soon he will sit on Tarr's chairs, eat off his plates. Tarr's debt will finally be paid in full, with interest. Soon he will lay his head on Mrs. Tarr's breast in a bed that Tarr bought. But that last thought is so arousing, so stimulating, it is necessary to place his thoughts elsewhere.

Dunne's brain is a furnace. He goes to the window and presses his forehead to the melting ice, slowly rolls it from side to side, scrapes frost from the pane with his nails, stumbles to the bed and crashes down on it like a felled tree. He lies there, fingers stuffed in his mouth, sucking on the ice trapped under his fingernails. All his life people have handed him dangerous, dirty jobs, wanted him to clean up their messes, asked him to smooth the stony way, and when he did, they cast him off, turned their backs on him. They were all the same, the skinflint Hind, McMicken, who had turned him out into the street when he had had no more need of him, the debt-dodging Tarr. Shifty-eyed, lying scoundrels, every one of them.

Of them all, it was McMicken who had wounded him worst. "You will be my special care," he had promised. And at first, when he had come under the great man's wing, he had felt warm and safe, cradled against the dove's breast, but then, just like that, McMicken had pushed him out of the nest. The good work he had done, the risks he had run, in the end they earned him nothing more than a handshake and an offhand goodbye. There was gratitude for you. The crimpers he had handed the magistrate, the Confederate wheels he had jammed a stick into at the danger of breaking his wrists – that counted for nothing. And when the War Between the States had come to its bloody end, and the Irish veterans of that struggle had marshalled to make war against Canada, who had McMicken relied on? Michael Dunne. "You're the man," he had said to him. "Who could doubt your sincerity with that bogtrotter name and the potato written all over your face?" And so he had undergone another conversion, from Proddy Dog back to Cat Licker, from frequenter of the Queen's Hotel to regular of Michael Murphy's tavern on Esplanade Street. There he had become a dues-paying member of the Hibernian Benevolent Society, an organization that employed mysterious signs and passwords, was divided into companies led by captains and lieutenants, all at the beck and call of none other than President Michael Murphy of Esplanade Street. After serving his apprenticeship there, he had been initiated into the Toronto Circle of the Fenian Brotherhood established by the head centre for America, John O'Mahony, and received his card identifying him as a member in good standing.

McMicken had congratulated him on his good work, slath-
ered on the flattery, told him no one was so clever as he, that no
one could have infiltrated the nest of conspirators as quickly as he
had done. The first test of his Fenian loyalty had come when the
Orangemen of Toronto announced they would burn an effigy of
Guy Fawkes, a provocation to all freedom-loving Irishmen. The
Hibernians had been called out to parade their opposition, and
he had assembled with them, a pike on his shoulder. With military precision they had marched along College, several hundred
strong, ready to put the run on King Billy's boys wherever they
encountered them. That fifth of November night, as their boots
thundered in the midnight streets, he had made sure that Michael
Murphy, Esq., took notice of Michael Dunne. He was in the fore-
front of every charge against the jeering Proddy corner boys, and
dealt out a ferocious, bloody beating to any Orangeman whose
coat collar he could snatch, earning Michael Murphy's praise as
an Irish patriot of the first water, an example to all. His reward
was to be selected for Murphy's own personal guard, which was
charged with protecting the leader in street actions.

Michael Murphy's favour and confidence put him in the
very middle of things, like a spider crouched at the centre of a
web. Any movement, on any strand of the Fenian web, sent
tremors to the centre. His first success was tipping McMicken
that an employee of the Toronto Savings Bank by name of
Cullen would soon receive a coded telegram, a telegram that
would be assumed to be a confidential financial communication
because it would be addressed to a fine, upstanding commercial
concern. But its real recipient would be Michael Murphy, already
busy preparing to assist a Fenian invasion led by B.D. Killian.

McMicken had seen to it that the telegram was intercepted
at the telegraph office and a copy made of it before it was delivered. Dunne had seen the original itself because Michael
Murphy had triumphantly waved it under his nose. A decade
later he still had it by memory.

Trg gjraql fvatyr zra ernql sbe beqref ol ghrfqnl pubbfr
qevyyrq naq grzcrenapr zra vs lbh pna cnpx rdhvczragf naq
nzzhavgvba ernql sbe rkcerffvat jurer qverpgrq zra bg sbyybj.

X

Get twenty single men ready for orders by Tuesday choose
drilled and temperance men if you can pack equipments and
ammunition ready for expressing where directed men to follow.

K

An alphabetical code so simple it could be busted easy as a
poached egg, and Murphy so puffed up at how he was pulling
the wool over John Bull's eyes that he swelled with pride.

When the news came that Killian intended to cross over in
New Brunswick, Murphy had decided that it was only fitting that
he be there to welcome the invaders to British North American
soil. "Dunne," he had said, "I want you at my side. Hand-pick four
other good men to accompany us." Off they had raced by train for
Campobello Island. When he had informed McMicken of where
they were headed and why, he had been surprised to learn that
the Stipendiary Magistrate had no intention of stopping them.
McMicken explained he was going to let Murphy tie his own
noose, hang it around his own neck. A little more evidence of trea-
son and it would be possible to convict him of a capital crime. Of
course, McMicken was duty-bound to let the government know
what was in the wind. He did, and the politicians hoisted his shirt-
tail and buggered him good. Attorney General Cartier saw the
threatened Fenian attack as the perfect opportunity to cast himself
in a heroic light. He sped from Montreal to Cornwall, called out
the local militia, blocked the tracks, pulled Murphy and his companions off the train, and put them under arrest.

So he, Michael Dunne, true and faithful servant of the
Crown, found himself languishing in the cracker box that
Cornwall called a jail, waiting for McMicken to show up and
finagle his release. But when the old fox did arrive, he made it

clear that his agent could not simply be discharged; the dimmest Irishman would deduce that he was an informant. No, the only option was for Michael Dunne to make his escape from custody and take Murphy and his whole bloody crew with him. Prime Minister Macdonald's attorney general's rash exploit had put paid to the whole scheme. Simply put, now there wasn't sufficient evidence to convict these wretches of anything, let alone see them hanged. If they were brought to trial, the courts would have to set them free. The fat would be in the fire when Murphy and his men complained publicly of being hounded and persecuted because of their race. They were unwavering in their claim to be innocent vacationers, bound to Campobello to take the sea air. Macdonald's government would look like bunglers, the opposition would flay it in Parliament; the newspapers would raise a hue and cry from every quarter. Under the circumstances, a jailbreak was the preferred solution to the problem. Let the Fenians scamper for the States. Flight was as good as an admission of guilt. The Cornwall prison was under local control; no blame could be laid on Ottawa's doorstep. As to the guards – McMicken would have a word with them, see to it that they did not investigate any excavating. He would see to everything for the good of the country. "Start digging," he had said. "Make the dirt fly like badgers."

It had taken them a single night to mole their way under the shallow foundation of the prison using spoons, tin cups, and a metal chamber pot. The gimcrack jail was a joke, built to hold no criminal more desperate than the town drunk. They found a skiff tied up on the river. They rowed across the St. Lawrence to a hero's welcome in the United States.

Lying stretched out on his bed, arms folded across his breast, staring up at the ceiling, he feels a dull misery when he thinks of his years of exile in the States. Once there, McMicken insisted he stay. The prison escape he had engineered put him beyond suspicion. The membership card issued by the Fenian Brotherhood was a passport not to be wasted. It gave him a pass into Irish Republican Army circles. McMicken wanted his prized agent where he could be most useful, in America, where the Irish operated with impunity and without interference from the authorities. He wanted him in the thick of things.

So he had gone wherever McMicken demanded he go, insinuated himself wherever useful things could be learned, helpful information harvested. He had been bounced from Boston to Cincinnati to Detroit to Chicago and finally to New York. He had done everything asked of him. Enlisted in the Irish Republican Army, turned out faithfully for military drill, attended patriotic rallies and huzzahed the golden-tongued orators, shook collection boxes for the cause in poor Irish neighbourhoods, twisted the ears of the better class of Irishman to buy bonds issued by a still non-existent Irish government. He became a darling of the leadership. They bestowed on him the nickname "the Indefatigable Dunne."

He was every bit as indefatigable in McMicken's cause. His reports transmitted in numerical code were precise, detailed, and written with a fluency he could never achieve in English. His involvement in IRA military exercises allowed him to give estimates of quantities and kinds of weapons and the locations of arsenals. He could report backroom conversations – even hour-long speeches – nearly word for word. He carefully noted down bond sales and donations, allowing McMicken to take the political temperature of the American Irish, whether it was truly hot or cooling. Cheering a fiery speech cost nothing but, as McMicken was fond of saying, coughing up hard cash is a different thing entirely. The true measure of commitment is the number of nickels and dimes in the collection plate.

As the months passed, Dunne had begun to know what it meant to be bone-chillingly afraid. The kind of fear that tightened your nut-sack and puckered your arsehole every hour of the day. The Fenians talked openly of the terrible revenge they visited on their own. Any man discovered a traitor was meat for slaughter. They eradicated the powerful as nonchalantly as they did the humble foot soldier. D'Arcy McGee had got his bloody comeuppance, a bullet on Sparks Street in the nation's capital, for recanting his old revolutionary views. People who didn't hesitate to murder a member of the House of Commons wouldn't give a second thought to snuffing out Michael Dunne's candle. Even McMicken had grown wary after McGee's assassination. The Fenians had let it be known that they had marked him down for death too. McMicken lived like a hunted man, trusted nobody but his sons to guard him. The McMicken boys went everywhere with their father, armed to the teeth. McMicken himself carried a brace of pistols under his frock coat.

Dunne reckoned that it was time he followed the Stipendiary Magistrate's example. If McMicken relied on pistols then Michael Dunne would rely on pistols too. He began to haunt New York's shooting galleries, working hard to improve his marksmanship. Soon he loved shooting as much as he loved the Polybius square. Both demanded perfect focus, paring the world away to a column of numbers or a target. After a month of steady application he could stitch a pattern on a bull's eye the diameter of a teacup. In another two weeks he had shrunk it to the size of a silver dollar.

Those days he lived in the Bowery, a once fashionable area of New York that was now home to criminals, the poorest of the city's labourers, the lowest bums and tramps. On every street there were German beer gardens, saloons, brothels, and theatres offering lewd and vulgar entertainments. None of this had any attraction for Dunne – he despised immorality – but the district offered anonymity. The Bowery was a wasteland populated by transients; people came and went; no one remarked sudden appearances or disappearances; questions about your business were likely to awaken suspicions that the questioner was a stool pigeon.

Dunne resided in a peeling ruin that had, in better days, been an imposing townhouse but which had decomposed into a warren of noisome rented rooms. Its tenants were a cut above many citizens of the area simply because they worked. The jobs they did – scrubbing laundry, digging ditches, shining shoes, swamping out saloons, mucking out stables – sent them out of their beds every morning at dawn and kept them toiling away until darkness fell. An empty, silent building was perfect for a man in Dunne's line of work. He could compose his reports in peace. It provided a safe location to conduct IRA and Fenian business.

The only two people who didn't evacuate the building during the day were Rose and her fourteen-year-old son, Billy, who lived on the same floor as Dunne. Neither caused him any concern. It was common knowledge in the building that Rose spent her nights flat on her back in a knocking-shop owned by a toothless madam known as Polly Gums. When Rose reeled home in the morning, smelling of gin, she immediately pitched the boy out of their quarters so he wouldn't disturb her beauty sleep. From nine o'clock in the morning until dusk, when she sashayed out of her room twitching her broad behind, Dunne never laid eyes on her, and assumed she was dead to the world, well dosed with laudanum, the whores' favourite cure-all. Rose was no more capable of noticing anything going on around her than was a corpse in a funeral parlour.

As for Billy, he posed no threat either because he was a soft-head, a simpleton who mooned about the hallways, softly and tunelessly humming to himself, or crouched on the front stoop like a gargoyle, his cornsilk hair a tangle of cowlicks and rooster tails, his mouth hanging open slackly as if he were inviting houseflies to lay eggs on his tongue. Everywhere Billy went, he clutched a daguerreotype in his hand, a studio portrait of himself taken when he was about a year old. Constant handling had darkened it with a patina of grease and dirt so dense that the infant's image seemed to be taking form in shadows, or emerging from a grim thunderhead.

Nobody got by Billy without being pestered to look at his portrait. He plucked at people's sleeves, cried out to each and every passerby, "Look at Baby Billy! Look at me!" The tenants of the building ignored his pleas, bustled by him, thrust him aside, or if he latched on to them and refused to let go they handed him a slap to the head. Dunne was the only one who couldn't escape him. Once accosted, he couldn't move. The daguerreotype of the gloomy baby held him fascinated, the high-pitched, piping cries of "Look at Baby Billy! See! See!" rooted him to the spot as if his feet had been pierced with spikes. He would stare at the portrait until the boy snatched it out of his hands and ran down the corridor clutching it to his chest, shouting, "Mine! Mine! My picture!"

Each time this happened, Dunne felt a little more frightened, a little more hollow. He could not understand why a mother would memorialize one of nature's mistakes in a daguerreotype. Had she been drunk when she took the baby to the photographer? Or could it be possible that she felt something for a mush-head that nobody had ever felt for Michael Dunne?

Then one day it came to him that Billy might provide the solution to something that someone had said to him and which had recently been scurrying around in his brain like a rat in a wall. For the next few weeks, he reviewed and put in place all the necessary steps. One Saturday afternoon, Dunne sought out Billy. He found him lurking in a stairwell. When the boy thrust the daguerreotype at him to be admired, Dunne asked him if he would like to have a "big boy picture" taken.

It took some time for Billy to untangle what was being said to him. When he finally comprehended, his willing eagerness was everything Dunne had hoped for. Immediately, he began an insistent whining. "Now, take Billy's picture now. Right now. Now." He continued to chirp these words even as Dunne took him by the hand, led him out of the back of the dwelling through the privy yard and down a maze of garbage-strewn alleys that delivered them into busy Canal Street.

It was an overcast spring day; there was a smell of rain in the air, and a ceiling of dark cloud hung above the city. Dunne hailed a cab. The novelty of a ride in a hansom finally plugged Billy's gob. To keep the gawking boy from toppling out the window and into the street, Dunne had to hold on to his belt all the way to the East River dockyards.

When they dismounted from the vehicle Billy found the stupendous din of the wharves terrifying. Tucking his picture securely into one armpit, he clamped his hands to his ears to hold out the shriek of tugboat whistles, pulleys, and winches, the hiss of donkey engines, the shouts of sailors and dock men. Dunne took him by the shoulders and manoeuvred his goggle-eyed charge past all the hazards, the cranes and chugging steam engines, the files of sweating longshoremen who came staggering down the gangplanks bent double under their loads and threatened to trample the frightened boy underfoot.

When he got him into the area of warehouses, clear of the worst of the noise and the frenzied activity, Billy calmed down. Dunne steered him to a building that had once housed a sailmaking concern but was now unoccupied and in a very bad state of repair, the majority of its windows boarded up, its roof shedding shingles, its walls sprinkling paint flakes around the footings. Dunne knew it well. Eight months before, he had negotiated with the widow of the former owner for its rental. Several firms had made the widow offers of purchase, but she had refused them all because she had delusions about the value of the property. While waiting for the right price, she was willing to let it to the athletic club that Dunne represented. These supposedly ardent boxers and gymnasts were all members of an Irish Republican Army cell. The warehouse provided them a place to bayonet sacks of oats and to hack away at one another with wooden swords, safe from prying eyes.

Dunne, having selflessly volunteered to open the building on cold winter mornings and fire up the stove to warm the place before the others arrived for training, had the key to the turnip-sized lock. He let Billy and himself in.

The interior was musty, damp, and dismal. The windows had been set high on the walls, just below the roof, to catch all the sunshine possible to light the sail-stitchers' work. But stone-chucking vandals had broken many of the panes in the deserted building and they had had to be planked up to keep out snow and rain. It was a dim, shadowy place.

Billy asked, "Where is the picture taker at?"

"I'm the picture taker," said Dunne, pointing to the thickest crop of shadows. "I set up my camera there."

Billy blinked owlishly, then made a move to investigate, but Dunne caught him by the collar of his shirt, swung him around, and marched him to a chair set before a sheet of sail canvas that had been tacked to the wall. The oddments that hadn't been cleared from the building when the business had closed had supplied everything required for the picture taking: a spool of waxed cord, remnants of canvas, sailmaker's needles. All he had needed to provide were six whiskey jugs filled with water and stopped with corks, which rested on the floor a few paces from the chair where he was busying himself posing Billy. He had delivered the jugs the day before.

When he got the boy squared away, Dunne checked the light. He had selected the spot because the casements above the chair still held glass and admitted daylight. Despite the grey day, he was satisfied they provided enough illumination.

He made a few more fussy adjustments to the boy's position, lifted his chin with his finger, turned his shoulders a little more to the left. When he was satisfied with his composition he knelt down so the boy's eyes were level with his own and said, "You must keep very still. If you move, you will spoil the picture. Do you understand?"

Apparently Billy did. He didn't dare nod an answer to the question; he held himself rigid, motionless. Dunne left him there and strode towards the spot where he had told the boy the camera waited. Yesterday he had measured the distance to where the deepest darkness began – fifteen paces. He counted them off, turned to face the boy.

It seemed to Dunne that Billy's pale features and white-blond hair were attracting every gleam of light that penetrated the sooty windows, were reflecting it back to him like a smooth and radiant moon. He cocked his ear to the racket coming from the docks. It was loud enough; it would serve. Beneath the squeaks and squeals, the steady pounding of steam engines, he could detect something else, a brisk pattering on the roof, a growl of thunder, then a full-throated roar of wind. The clouds that had threatened rain earlier were unleashing a downpour.

Billy, tense with anticipation, sat frozen in place. The windows above his head were instantly convulsed with streaming water. The precious light glowing on the boy's face began to wane, he was fading from sight, darkening and receding, like the features in the little portrait he held on his knees. Billy was becoming indistinct, his countenance blurring and swimming as the rain snaked down the windows. Just as the boy hovered on the point of disappearing entirely, Dunne raised his arm, aimed, and snapped Billy's picture with a muzzle flash.

To Dunne, the walk back to the body felt a great deal longer than fifteen paces. Most of the blood and grey brain matter had struck the canvas backdrop, just as he had calculated it would. Billy was still in the chair, but his body was grotesquely contorted, the head thrown back over the chair back. Dunne pulled the sheet of canvas down from the wall, spread it on the floor, lifted Billy and placed him on it. To weight the burial shroud, he laid five whiskey jugs alongside the body. Then he began to sew up the canvas with a long, rusty sailmaker's needle. That task completed, he used the water in the one remaining jug to scrub away whatever blood had splashed to the floor. The spots couldn't be completely eradicated, but forty years of spilled tea, melted wax, and tar drippings had stained the floor so much they would hardly be noticed.

There was nothing left to do but wait for full dark. He sat down beside the body, wrapped his arms around his knees, remembering what that man had said to him in the shooting gallery. Until he had started to practise there, the fellow had been acknowledged the best shot in the borough and he hadn't liked having his reputation challenged by a newcomer. One afternoon, after having watched Dunne stitch a tight pattern on a target, the gentleman in question had said to him, "The eye in a bull's eye is only paper. It's a different matter when what you are aiming at can look back at you. I know that. I was in the war."

He had pondered that remark for some time, regarded it up and down and from every side until he thought he understood what had been said to him. He had been told that a gun was only a tool. He used it well enough on paper, but that wasn't what it was meant for. The question was: When the time comes that you need to use it to kill, will you be able to?

In Dunne's opinion, most people did not look far enough into the future. The day might come when he would be discovered as a spy, and his life would depend on proving to himself that whether it was a bull's eye or a human face before him, it made no difference to Michael Dunne, he would not hesitate to discharge his weapon into either.

He knew now he was capable.

When Dunne could no longer see his own hand held up before his face, he hoisted Billy over his shoulder and walked out into the night. There were fewer people about on the docks, mostly drunken merchant seamen returning from a spree on the town, and a few gangs of longshoremen unloading urgent cargo by lamp- and torchlight. They took no notice of a man toting a roll of sailcloth. At a spot on a deserted wharf shielded by a stack of timber, Dunne paused, looked about him, and tipped the bundle off his shoulders into the river. For a moment, it bobbed and floated, then the jugs did their work, slowly dragged it down into the depths.

Dunne turns on his side and, as he always does when he wants to be most lucid, speaks aloud in pure numbers, in the language of the Polybius square.

"22,11,55,55,14 12,11,33,52,45,45,42,52,23,42,12."

Billy disappeared.

For a time when the voice had said to him that someone was following he had thought the voice might be referring to Billy. That instead of drawing back into the shadows of the picture, Billy was emerging from them. But now Dunne sees how absolutely wrong he had been. There is no doubt. *Billy disappeared.*

Today it became obvious to him that the someone who is following can be none other than Mrs. Tarr. She is coming to him. That voice he had once thought sounded as flat as the tapping of a telegraph key had been a fault in his hearing. He is sure that the next time it speaks to him it will be in Mrs. Tarr's warm tones, will be coloured by her loving character. And that hazy form will assume a definite, happy shape, grow ever more recognizably *her* with every step it takes towards him. And that slow, cloudy billowing about the knees that might have been anything – Billy wading up out of the river, a man tramping through snowdrifts – will sharpen until it becomes that particular skirt, the one he so admires on Mrs. Tarr. And those bright, hovering flecks about her head and shoulders will grow ever stronger and light her face ever more clearly. He is certain of it. It is only a matter of time.

THIRTEEN

December 8, 1876

AFTER NEARLY THREE MONTHS, I have received Father's
response to my news that I am proprietor of a ranch and have
no intention of standing for Parliament. His style of communication is, as ever, sharp and to the point. He says my ingratitude
has given ample proof that the raising and educating of me has
been a waste of time and money, and that trying to talk sense
into me is pointless.

> Do not think that in defying me you do me an injury.
> No, you only harm yourself. I am done attempting to
> save you. If the Prodigal Son is bound and determined
> to end his days as a swineherd (or in your case a cow-
> herd) so be it. For years you have been shooting yourself
> in the foot and I should not be surprised if, sooner or
> later, you do not put the pistol squarely to your head and
> pull the trigger. You have shown a foolhardy tendency
> to do harm to yourself before. I am referring of course
> to the statement you were asked to prepare for my solic-
> itors when it looked as if you would soon be facing
> public disgrace. All that was required was a simple out-
> line of your actions, "I did this and then I did that." But

you had to beat your breast in a frenzy, indulge yourself in weepy self-recrimination. My advice to destroy that nonsense was the last time I can recall you ever listening to me. So for your own good, heed me one last time. Rid yourself of that ranch like you rid yourself of that foolish document. Do not squander the money your mother left you because I assure there will be nothing coming your way from me if you persist in your recklessness. Be assured, I will wash my hands of you.

It comes as a great relief to me to be finally disowned. Father always believed that making me his heir gave him an incontestable right to meddle in my affairs. He let himself think that the threat to disinherit me was a sword held over my head. He has let it descend now, to no effect.

If the Lumber Baron knew that "statement of fact" still existed, he would question my sanity even more than he does now. I still have not been able to cast it aside, still wrestle with the memory of the Battle of Ridgeway as Jacob wrestled with the angel. Like Jacob, who put the thigh of the angel out of joint with a touch, that day has the same power over me; the faintest recollection of it can leave my mind limping.

I always knew what Father's purpose was in having me write that account – to give his lawyers a document they could examine so as to decide which "facts" should be emphasized, which expunged. He wanted a dress rehearsal of evidence so his solicitors could coach me on how to present what had occurred, if a trial could not be avoided. My day in court never came, but I continue scouring those pages, trying and retrying myself. Yesterday, I took them out and reviewed my actions as I have done so many times before. The judgment is the same as always. So why do I pursue it, over and over again? Because it seems that sometimes even the convicted man is uncertain of the real motives of his crime.

On the morning of December 29 a chinook arch appears in the western sky, a shelf of red-and-yellow cloud that is a presage of the warm wind that soon comes spilling down the slopes of the Rockies and roaring across the plains. In a matter of hours, the temperature rises forty degrees. Snowdrifts slump; icicles rain a quick, steady drip down on the heads of pedestrians, and Fort Benton's streets turn to muddy paste. Heavy winter coats are cast aside and men stroll around in their shirtsleeves. By the second day of the "snow-eater," the ground lies brown and bare, but on the thirty-first the mercury plummets as quickly as it shot up, turning cold enough that Case dons his buffalo coat to ride into Fort Benton for Major Ilges's New Year's party. Joe had spurned the invitation, saying, "I ain't one of the quality. Their occasions ain't for the likes of me. Tonight, I'll bay at the moon with my own kind. From a saloon."

After stabling his horse at the Benton livery, Case strikes off for the post, footsteps ringing on a roadway hard as iron, frozen puddles crackling under his heels. There are carriages parked outside the garrison, their teams blanketed against the cold, noses buried in feed bags. Soldiers loiter near the gate, passing a bottle back and forth, faces lit in the ruddy glow of pipe bowls. From inside the mess there comes the prodigious tootling and thumping of a military band. Case mounts the steps, gives the door a push, and enters a room already so crammed with guests he has difficulty finding a peg on the wall on which to hang his coat. A covey of ladies has taken roost near a spindly, now desiccated Christmas tree hung with forlorn strings of popcorn and decorated with tiny candles whose flames flap and hover on the point of extinction every time the door opens or closes. The greatest social event of the year has brought out the competitive instincts in all the women, even the dowagers, who have decked themselves out in satin and taffeta and loaded themselves down with all the jewellery their necks and ears can support. Expansive tracts of bosom are on display, and a constant, coquettish fluttering of painted fans agitates the air. The blaze in the fireplace, the exertions of the dance, the densely packed crowd lend a tropical atmosphere to the mess. The band is flirting with heat prostration, mopping their faces and swigging from tankards of beer as they take a break from playing.

Case lingers by the doorway, running his eyes over the room. Ilges had told him that he had received a message from Walsh announcing that this year the Police would break with tradition and not be attending the New Year's Eve party. Despite this, Case had still entertained the hope that Walsh would see the wisdom of putting aside his pique and accepting the hospitality of Major Ilges, which might have gone some way towards mending relations between them. But there isn't a scarlet tunic in sight.

Case knows he is no dab hand at hail-fellow-well-met; there is no question of inserting himself into any of the clusters of men exhibiting a loud and easy camaraderie. Instead he takes a stroll down the long buffet table, sidling past a punch bowl, bottles of wine and liquor, platters of glazed ham, turkey, roast beef, venison, and buffalo boss ribs, scalloped potatoes, candied yams, fruit pies, custard, compote, trifle, and fruitcake. But once the collation has been surveyed, there is nothing left to do except jam his hands deep in his trouser pockets and try to look amused by the passing scene. Then he sees Guido Ilges approaching him, resplendent in his dress blues, Civil War decorations winking, looking as if he has spent as much time polishing up his smile for the occasion as his orderly has putting a shine to the Major's brass buttons.

"Ah, Mr. Case, so good to see you! But there is nothing in your hand! You are dry! Jeffries," he calls to one of the sweating privates acting as carvers and barmen, "serve this gentleman a cup of that excellent punch!"

The punch, Case discovers, is a rather tepid, watery brew reeking powerfully of cloves and cinnamon.

"It is my mother's receipt," confides Ilges. "We all looked forward to Christmas, just because of it. Papa used to say, 'If I could have got the secret of your mother's punch without having to marry her, you children would never have seen the light of day.'" So as not to leave the wrong impression, the Major adds, "It was a joke." A boisterous mazurka strikes up, sending the gentlemen rushing to the ladies to claim a partner. "A military band," observes Ilges, raising his voice and leaning into Case's ear to make himself heard, "is perhaps satisfactory for the dancing. But I long for the sound of a piano and singing. As it was at home," he confesses. For a moment, Ilges remains sunk in nostalgic reverie. Then his face darkens at the sight of two men who have just come in from the cold and are lifting their coattails to warm their rumps by the fire. One of them, a man in a fawn-coloured ditto suit and paisley waistcoat, is J.J. Donnelly, prominent Benton lawyer and Democratic politico. When Case had first arrived in Fort Benton, he had taken the trouble to have Donnelly pointed out to him, remembering the strange document Dunne had given to Walsh regarding the Irish threat in Fort Benton. By repute, Donnelly is one of the most influential of the town's Fenian rabble-rousers. The other man, a tall, bony, pigeon-chested individual, is unknown to him.

"The gall of that Collins," says Ilges, looking angry enough to spit. "I warned him he was not welcome at my post. And now he sails in with Donnelly. It's a provocation."

The Major's fury, the linking of Collins to the notorious Donnelly, prompts Case to ask, "And what has this Collins fellow done to stir you up so?"

"He's been trying to recruit my Irish enlisted men to join some colony scheme in Nebraska, painting it as a Garden of Eden, buying them drinks in the Stubhorn, filling their heads with nonsense. But what he is doing is tantamount to encouraging them to desert. He claims to be an immigration agent. It's outrageous. And now he has the cheek to walk in here as if he owned the place."

As the mazurka ends, Donnelly spots Ilges, gives him a friendly wave, corrals Collins by draping an arm over his shoulder, and begins to walk the immigration agent over to Ilges and Case just as the band launches into a waltz.

"My god," Ilges mutters. "The effrontery of those two."

Donnelly, seemingly impervious to the chill coming off the Major, positively radiates bonhomie. "There he is, our convivial host himself! Will you allow me to say, Major Ilges, that I cannot recall, in all my years, a finer commencement to a New Year! A bang-up job, sir! First rate in every respect."

"Too kind," says Ilges, bowing coldly and perfunctorily, tightening his lips.

Donnelly is squinting at Case in a fashion meant to be taken as humorous. "And all sections of society represented. It is the defrocked British policeman Mr. Case, isn't it? Known to me by reputation, seen passing in the street, but never before met face to face."

The word *policeman* has curdled Collins's face with disdain.

"Not defrocked – retired," says Case.

"Ah, yes, my mistake. Not defrocked, but perhaps *reformed*? Put the nightstick away in favour of ranching, isn't it? I commend you." Donnelly quickly steers for another shore. "Major, I have come to present to you my great good friend Mr. Patrick Collins. It seems a little bird has been twittering falsehoods in your ear about this gentleman, and I have come to correct any misrepresentations you may have heard."

Collins hasn't taken his eyes off Case. "Maybe it wasn't a bird at all. Maybe it was a lobster-back, who clamped his claws to Major Ilges's ear."

"Ah, dear me, dear me," says Donnelly, "not the best of starts, Patrick. You must forgive him, Mr. Case. Two years in prison, you know, for advocating the cause of Irish liberty. No love lost between Mr. Collins and the English police. We have touched a tender spot, a very sore and tender spot." Donnelly gives Ilges a knowing wink. "A very fervent fellow, Mr. Collins. It may be why you may have been misled about him. He has a missionary's heart, the soul of a Redemptorist priest. Wants to save the poor, give them a chance in this cruel world, see they have a little parcel of ground that is all their own, a bit of sod to scratch a living from. He burns with that noble goal – sometimes so hotly his intentions are mistaken."

Collins adds, far more loudly than is necessary to make himself heard above the music, "As General O'Neill is fond of saying, 'If the Irish cannot be free in Ireland, let them be free in America.'"

"Exactly," says Donnelly, "nail struck fairly on the head. The General seldom misses the nail. An energetic, enterprising fellow is the General. He has already planted a hundred colonists on the ground in Nebraska – a town sprung up – O'Neill City – a lovely spot. Grand, bustling place."

"I am delighted to hear it," says Ilges. "I have no objection to the General's enterprise. Only to the inducements this gentleman makes to my soldiers to desert."

"Well, there's the rub, Major, there's the misunderstanding. Mr. Collins spoke only to soldiers whose term of enlistment is drawing to a close. And those poor fellows have to make their way in the world, and there's no more honest life than that of the agriculturalist – am I correct, Mr. Case? Haven't you found that to be true?"

"Indeed," says Case, affecting a lack of interest in the conversation, shifting his gaze to the couples swirling by.

"There you have it, Major Ilges, from a man who knows whereof he speaks. But you see, when the commanding officer leaves the impression something is not on the up and up, what's the ordinary soldier to think? What headway is likely to be made with them?"

"Men with experience in the West are worth their weight in gold," volunteers Collins. "Most of our colonists arrive straight from the slums of Boston and New York. They don't know a hawk from a handsaw. They need guiding hands, need to be shown the ropes by fellows who know a thing or two."

"Yes, soldiers," says Ilges, "they know a thing or two. Well versed in raising crops, seeding, ploughing, and so forth. It's what we train them for."

"Ah," says Donnelly, "the Major is being facetious."

Collins manufactures a sneer. "Or bloody insulting."

Case turns back from watching the dancers and says to Collins, "Perhaps neither."

"Meaning?" says Collins.

"Perhaps the Major is too polite to question you about your strong preference for soldier colonists. It is curious. Guiding hands, you call them. To what purpose?"

"Don't stick your nose in what isn't your business. Unless you want a fist in it."

"Patrick," warns Donnelly, "temper."

"I will take the fist in the nose under advisement," says Case. "General O'Neill should do the same. His nose got broken several times before, putting it where it wasn't wanted."

"The peeler has forgotten the Battle of Ridgeway. The way I remember it, the Saxons shat yellow there, had to wipe their arses with the butcher's apron – that blood-soaked rag, the Union Jack."

"Indeed we did shit yellow. But you, sir, conveniently forget how your crew turned and ran when they heard British Regulars were moving up. They scuttled for the border with their tails between their legs. I would say both sides distinguished themselves equally on that occasion."

Collins steps forward, thrusts out his jaw at Case. "I invite you to take the air with me," he says.

"Enough," says Ilges. "Mr. Collins, you are not welcome here. Leave, please."

"Out I go," says Collins, "when this bastard walks out the door with me."

"I think not," says Case. "I am very comfortable where I am."

Ilges throws a look at Donnelly. "Will you talk sense to your friend?"

Donnelly shrugs. "Aspersions have been cast on Irish honour."

Ilges raises his hand to two junior officers and beckons. "Very well. Then I will have these gentlemen escort you out."

Ada Tarr, Celeste, and Lieutenant Blanchard's arrival at the New Year's party was delayed because Randolph would not give up trying to get a shoe on his foot. That morning his axe had glanced off a piece of wood he was splitting and had clipped him below the ankle. The wound had looked small and trifling at first, but by suppertime Randolph's foot had swollen to alarming proportions. He iced the bruise for hours, even cut the sides of an ankle boot to be able to get it on. Nothing had worked. When Ada had volunteered to remain at home in case he needed anything, he had quashed that idea. What impression would be left if neither of them were present when Celeste made known the news of her engagement? People might conclude her parents had some objections to the match. No, Ada must accompany the happy couple, beam joy, and explain the father's absence.

Ada has no desire to act as her husband's proxy, to smirk and simper over congratulations in his stead, to pretend to be as pleased as he is by Celeste's choice of husband. On the other hand, going to the party would present an opportunity to speak to Dr. Strathway and prevail upon him to come to the house to examine Randolph. For weeks she has been insisting he seek medical advice for his worsening condition, his listlessness, and all his other symptoms, but Randolph refuses. He has a terror of doctors, seems to believe that illness and contagion cling to them and might rub off them onto him.

Celeste and Lieutenant Blanchard's engagement is hardly a week old, but Ada is already heartily sick of the groom's smug talk about "my Cessie's sparkler," her stepdaughter's constant ogling of her ring. But relief is in sight. In a matter of days, the pair will be heading to Baltimore, where Celeste will live with a married sister of the Lieutenant's who he has decided is equal to the task of instructing his fiancée in the social graces expected in a Blanchard wife and in seeing to it that his precious diamond in the rough is buffed until she acquires the necessary dazzle. The Lieutenant's ultimate destination is Washington, where he will serve out the last months of his term of enlistment as aide-de-camp to a general who owes his father a favour. This will keep him close to his fiancée and allow him to supervise his sister's work as she puts the final touches to Celeste's training before the girl is revealed to Baltimore society at a fashionable wedding. Lieutenant Blanchard has thought of everything. A certain Mrs. Upham, a recent Benton widow who desires to return to Pittsburgh, will act as their chaperone on the trip east. Blanchard has offered to pay her expenses and travel fare so that appearances are preserved, all the proprieties observed. The Lieutenant is obviously a planner.

Randolph is ecstatic about all this. His last words to Ada were, "It falls to you to represent the Tarrs tonight." What a ridiculously grandiose way of putting it. As if she were being charged to present papers of accreditation to the Court of St. James's. The poor man, so eager to rise in the world, so avid for prestige that he is willing to ride up the social ladder clinging to his daughter's back like a monkey. How he had fussed over what his "representative" was to wear tonight, limping over to peer worriedly into her wardrobe, clucking like an old broody hen until he had made his selections, a sleeveless Prussian blue shot silk gown, a jet necklace and matching set of earrings her mother had left her. "Both set off your complexion so nicely," he had said. "It is your best feature. White as pure milk." Seeing him so let down at missing the party, looking so old and tired, had nearly brought tears to her eyes. "I'll be back as soon as possible to give you a report," she had told him.

"Not too soon, my girl," he had said. "Give them a show. Do the family proud."

As soon as they enter the mess, before Ada can dispose of her redingote, Celeste skips her way across the floor to a bundle of girls preening under the eyes of six or seven young men grimly holding up a wall with their backs. Blanchard follows his fiancée, mouth pursing in a self-satisfied smile when he hears the first squeaks and shrieks of amazement produced by Celeste waggling her ring finger under her friends' noses.

Ada scans the crowd for the doctor, hoping to catch a glimpse of the old duffer's shiny bald head. The band has taken a break and partiers are milling about on the floor. Many of the men are already boisterously drunk and those who have wives find themselves being warned away from making another foray on the drinks table with timid, pleading looks or a barrage of anxious whispers and stern head-shaking. It is, Ada thinks, just another dismal mural of the married state, and a scene so true to life that Celeste should be forced to paint a copy as a warning to her of what lies in wait.

But these scenes of dissension are eclipsed by another. People are craning their necks towards a commotion on the far side of the mess. A number of blue-jacketed officers and several civilians are violently gesticulating, voices raised in anger. Whatever the disturbance, Ada sees that Wesley Case is in the middle of it. A tall man gives him a stab to the breastbone with two fingers, hard enough to make him recoil a step or two. When the man deliberately aims his fingers at Case's chest again, Case strikes his arm aside.

The rest is a blur of movement. All at once Case reels backwards from a blow. The soldiers spring on the tall one and pinion his arms while Case wipes blood from his face, flicking it to the floor with his fingers, smiling queerly. People whisper and point as he calmly removes his coat from a peg and pulls it on. Ada hears Major Ilges call out to him, but Wesley Case gives no reply, simply walks out the door.

The Major bobs his head to the officers, indicating the door at the back of the mess, and strides after them as they hustle the guilty party to the exit. She sees the lawyer Donnelly trundling along beside the Major, making some protest inaudible to her. Ilges ignores whatever he is saying, jerks open the door. Out goes Wesley Case's attacker and after him Mr. Donnelly. Major Ilges emphatically kicks the door shut on their backs.

All at once, there is a cascade of excited talk. For an instant, Ada hesitates, then gives a hitch to her shoulders and marches after Mr. Case. Outside, the sudden darkness disorients her, leaves her blinking uncertainly on the step, which is feebly lit by the fanlight above the door. She makes out a shadow pacing by the carriages.

"Mr. Case," she calls, "are you all right?"

He stops and peers at her. "Mrs. Tarr?"

"Yes. What are you doing out here? Come back in and be attended to."

"I am waiting for the man who struck me." He pauses. "It would be better if you were not here when he appears."

"Major Ilges had your assailant put out the back door. They must have crossed to the road from there. It is pointless lingering there anticipating him. Come up here, into the light, so I can take a look at you."

"I'd prefer not to."

"Don't be foolish. I insist."

For a moment he hesitates, then enters the weak glimmer shed by the fanlight, climbs the steps, and stands looking at her. She sees two fresh, fat worms of blood crawling out of his nostrils, more red smudged on his chin and cheek.

"If you won't return inside, let us see what can be done out here. Please, sit beside me," she says, easing herself down on the top step, and gathering her skirts tightly about her legs.

Case gingerly places himself at her side. "I take it you saw it all," he says. "The ferocious peck I gave to his fist with my beak?"

"Yes, and I see the results." Ada opens her reticule, takes out a handkerchief, and holds it out to him. "You might wish to make use of this."

Case studies the handkerchief for a moment. "Mrs. Tarr, you embroider beautifully," he says. "I will not ruin it."

Ada thrusts the handkerchief under his chin. "Spit," she says quietly.

Case's eyebrows lift, but he does. Putting the heel of her hand to his brow, she tilts his head back and begins to wipe away the blood.

"There," she says, balling up the handkerchief, shoving it back into her reticule. "Now tell me, what led to that contretemps?"

"Politics. History. Man's injustice to man," he says with a sardonic smile.

"That's very cryptic."

"It seems my person represents the British Empire. My assailant felt compelled to strike a blow against tyranny on behalf of Ireland."

"And you were hanging about out here, hoping for a chance to strike him back."

Case shakes his head. "I know, I know. *Mea culpa*." He sits in silence for some moments, then suddenly says, "I wrote Hathaway as you requested."

"Yes, he mentioned that. I saw him in town several days ago, here in Fort Benton. He had come to – what was his phrase? – to 'right the ship.'"

Case looks perplexed. "My understanding was Walsh was not giving his men any leave to visit Benton. How did Hathaway manage to get granted an exception?"

"Well, it seems the boy took the matter of leave into his own hands. Hid under the tarp on a freighter's wagon returning here from Fort Walsh. I suppose you would call him a stowaway."

"The term is deserter. That's what his superior will call him. What got into the idiot's head?"

"He was determined to plead his case with Celeste. The first time he came to the house she was off shopping with Lieutenant Blanchard. I informed Peregrine that my stepdaughter and Lieutenant Blanchard were recently engaged, and he said you had written him how things stood between them. That was the reason he had come. It was rather heartbreaking, the state he was in. I had a long talk with him but it did no good. He returned the next night, quite inebriated. My husband had to warn the boy off the property. It was a distressing scene."

Case hunches forward, elbows planted on his knees, his breath a golden vapour in the faint light. Inside, the band is tooting and thumping. "Well, well," he says finally, "I have never known the boy to drink before. There must have been tears shed in heaven that day."

"It is all highly regrettable."

Case straightens his shoulders. "I'll need to talk to him – bring him to his senses," he says decisively. "If necessary I'll take him back to Fort Walsh myself. He may have earned himself a few days in the guardhouse for being absent without leave, but he'll survive that. It'll be a salutary lesson to him." He pauses. "Did he say where he's staying?"

"I'm afraid he's already left, and he was not off for Fort Walsh, but bound for Helena. Randolph said they were laughing about it at the stagecoach office. Peregrine was highly intoxicated when he bought his ticket, so much so that they put him up top beside the driver fearing he might be sick inside and inconvenience the other passengers. Everyone thought it a great joke."

Case sits considering this. At last he says, "I tried to warn him in the plainest of terms to give Celeste up. I said this was not the first time a girl showed a boy the door – that in fact it was a very common occurrence, but no one had ever died of it. With time, deathbed recoveries were total."

"Oh dear," says Ada. "That sounds rather unsympathetic."

Case gives an exasperated shrug of the shoulders. "What else should I have done? Parade my own personal experiences, regale him with lovelorn anecdotes?"

"If you had them to give, yes. It might have helped him to understand."

"You sound doubtful that I do. I suppose you think a man like me has never suffered from a broken heart, or a woman's coldness?"

"I did not say that. There's no need to bristle."

It had begun to snow; fat flakes are wafting down, swaying lazily. The clouds momentarily part and the moon's cold eye gleams down on them. Case stares moodily up at it, shifting from side to side as if he is trying to tip anger from his shoulders. He says, "I was engaged to be married once. But a month before the wedding my intended broke it off. A fine example of woman's constancy."

"Oh, that is most unfortunate," says Ada carefully. "But perhaps it was not simple fickleness – who knows what lies behind such decisions."

"I do," says Case sharply. "What lay behind it was rumour." Instantly, she can see how he regrets this admission. As if to forestall inquiry from her he adds quickly, "She demanded I deny the gossip."

"But apparently your answers did not satisfy her."

"Answers? I gave her no answers. Why should I submit to being interrogated by a woman who pretended to love me? I would not give her the satisfaction. That's the difference between young Hathaway and myself," he says brusquely. "He would have walked barefoot over hot coals if Celeste had asked it of him. And in the end none of it would have done him any good. He might bay like a dog at her door, but that door was and always will be closed to him. Unlike him, I would not make a fool of myself."

"I cannot fault Peregrine for crying out to have the door opened," says Ada softly, looking down at her feet, primly aligned on the step. "If a man rates himself so highly that he will not risk his dignity for the woman he loves, then perhaps he cares more for the good opinion of the world than he does for hers. Impulse may be foolish, but at least it speaks the truth."

When she glances up at Case to see how he has received this, she is shocked to feel his fingers closing on her wrist. Slowly he lifts her hand to his cheek and presses it there, presses it so forcefully that she can feel the bones of his face through the kidskin of her glove. Pulling up the sleeve of her redingote, exposing her arm to the falling snow, the prickle of its cold little thorns, he dips his head and buries his warm mouth in the hinge of her elbow.

It lasts only an instant. Lifting his head from the crook of her arm, he lets go his grip. Her arm drops loosely to her side. He rises and makes his way down the steps. Ada watches him disappear into the dark, into the tumbling snow. Only when he is lost to sight does she begin to slowly draw down her sleeve.

FOURTEEN

January 7, 1877
Fort Benton

My dear Walsh,

I wish to express my regret that I did not see you at
Maj. Ilges's New Year's Ball. An opportunity to improve
relations with him was missed. But this is not the season
for hectoring, so I will say nothing more, only send you
my best wishes for a happy and prosperous 1877. I trust
that you and your men have passed a merry Christmas
and welcomed in the New Year in fine style.

Something has come to my attention that I have been
looking into in the past few days. It concerns Gen. John
O'Neill of the Irish Republican Army who, if you remember,
was one of those Dunne warned you likely had plans to do
Canada injury here in the West. It appears that Dunne is
correct. A confederate of O'Neill's, Patrick Collins, has been
busy in Fort Benton recruiting Irishmen to join settlements
O'Neill is attempting to establish in Nebraska. (Collins is
fanatically anti-British. A point driven home to me by his fist
when he assaulted me at Maj. Ilges's soiree.) With assistance
from the Irish rabble-rouser J.J. Donnelly, Collins has been
circulating a document authored by Gen. O'Neill among
soldiers here of Irish descent. It is a call to arms and is of

very recent vintage, bearing the date December 8, 1876. Major Ilges confiscated a number of these that were circulating among his men, and kindly passed one on to me. I will provide you with quotes because I think it important that you supply Secretary of State Scott with statements of the General's belligerent intentions straight from the horse's mouth.

His letter is addressed to the Irish people and contains an attack on the Fenian leadership because of their reluctance to contemplate any further military action against Canada. He states, "Such men should never have embarked in a revolutionary movement or induced others to do so. They are not made of the stuff of which patriots are moulded." He further announces that these traitors no longer have any authority over him or his followers, and that it is his aim to make war on Canada as soon as it is feasible. "I hold that the Irish people, particularly the Irish Exiles whom her oppressive laws have driven from their native land, have a right to . . . make war on England . . . If we could meet England at a disadvantage at the North Pole, that in my judgment would be the best place to strike her . . . There is a long line of British frontier between Nova Scotia and Vancouver's Island, with the Atlantic and Pacific Oceans as an outlet, and there are millions of the Irish race in the United States from whom to recruit an army and man privateers to prey on British commerce."

O'Neill states without equivocation his reasons for encouraging Irish settlements in the West. "I think I can safely promise from the colonies which I have already established at least some of the young men to assist on the battle field while the older ones are raising corn, flour, potatoes to help sustain them. And I know that there are many other settlements in the western states and territories ready and willing to do their share of the work. One correspondent writes to me from the Black Hills that he has enough of men there ready to inaugurate the movement whenever ordered to do so."

I do not mean to be unduly alarmist, but O'Neill has proved to be a reckless customer in the past. If an opportunity presents itself, he will act. He ends his address with these words, "A circular of instructions for organizing immigration committees will accompany this address and the necessary information for <u>military men</u> and intending immigrants will be forwarded in due time."

It would be wise to alert the Secretary of State that something is afoot. O'Neill may be planning to launch another campaign in Red River country, hoping to spark the Métis into rebellion against the Crown. I remind you that Dunne informed you that O'Neill made such an attempt only a few years ago, and I am convinced that his failure to take Fort Garry then will not discourage him. The General has persisted in his war-like attitude towards Canada for a decade. You have evidence of his aggressive intentions in his own words. You need only to copy them down and forward same to Scott.

Yours truly,
Wesley Case

January 12, 1877
Fort Walsh

My dear Case,

Big news for you, my boy. The Sioux have come. Around Yuletide, a patrol led by Frechette went missing. I took out a search party to find him. When I located him he was low on food, and without a stick of wood to burn. He had been caught in a blizzard as he hurried back to Fort Walsh to report he had discovered Sioux at Wood Mountain. These Sioux had sworn to him that they had had nothing to do with the Little Bighorn, but Frechette saw plenty of evidence to the contrary – mules and horses with U.S. Army brands, and warriors armed with standard U.S. Cavalry issue, Sharps carbines. All spoils of war plundered from the dead.

Thought it necessary to go see the elephant for myself, so I split my rations with Frechette and his men, then set off for Wood Mountain with the eleven troopers I had under my command, leaving Frechette's party to limp back to Fort Walsh. Before introducing myself to the new arrivals, I stopped at Jean-Louis Légaré's trading post to get lie of the land. Bugger told me Sioux had paid him a visit in November. Gave him a good tongue-lashing for not sending me word immediate then subjected him to cross-examination. Légaré told me how one morning he had looked out his window and spotted twelve Indians sitting on their horses outside his store. Didn't pay them any mind. Half an hour later one of them walked in, sat down on the floor. A little later this individual coaxed the rest of his comrades in, one by one. The visitors left the door standing open despite the coldness of the day. Légaré said this proved to him they were "wild" Indians who show distaste for the white man's habit of closing himself up tight in stuffy rooms. If there's any white man in this country besides me who can read Indians, it's Légaré. For two hours his visitors sat silent as the tomb, watching him go about his business, stocking shelves, doing his accounts. Indian ways being Indian ways, Légaré said he just let them be; the watched pot never boils.

Then one of them jumped to his feet, grabbed Légaré's hand, started pumping it up and down, and announces he's the Sioux chief Little Knife. Says he and his people have crossed the Medicine Line because the Long Knives will not let them sleep soundly on the other side. Says they have heard the Old Woman is very good to her children so they have come to her country. That information imparted, they all trooped out. A few days later they came back to trade for flour, sugar, and coffee. Légaré said once again they demonstrated they hadn't had much to do with whites. Not understanding the workings of his scale, they kept yelling at it to be "solid and strong" for them, pleading with it to give them more goods for their buffalo robes.

This was clearly an advance party sent out in November to sniff out what kind of welcome they could expect in the Old Woman's country. Conclusions must have been favourable because more followed in December, a heap of them. When we reached their village, I had my troopers do a census, counted 109 lodges, 500 men, 1,000 women, 1,400 children, 3,500 horses, and 30 U.S. government mules. Give Ilges those figures with my compliments, and tell him the Yankees can breathe a little easier, a lot of their trouble has just shifted ground.

The new arrivals are camped at Wood Mountain with White Eagle's Santee Sioux who came over here fourteen years ago to escape becoming gallows' fruit at the hands of Lincoln's hangmen after the Minnesota Massacre. I calculate White Eagle is doing his best to see his kissing cousins don't cause trouble this side of the line because he doesn't want to jeopardize his haven with us. At any rate, he was more than happy to arrange a parley between the Sioux chiefs and headmen and yours truly. He introduced me to them as White Forehead, chief of all the Shagalasha, the Old Woman's pony soldiers. I wonder how Col. Macleod would take it to learn I have been promoted over his own lofty head on Sioux say-so. The leading lights in attendance at this first meeting were Little Knife, Iron Dog, Long Dog, The Man That Crawls, White Guts, The Drag, Inkapaduta, and Black Moon. The latter seems to carry the most weight in their councils.

Let Ilges know that straight off, I read them the riot act, laid down the law, told them if they wished to remain in the Old Woman's country they must obey Queen

Victoria's laws. I said she frowns on horse stealing, which in her eyes is a very serious offence. I warned them that they must not make war on any other of the Old Woman's Indians, or kill any man or woman whatsoever, because she punishes all evildoers the same, white or red, that all her children are the same to her, she plays no favourites.

Next I said that they better not entertain any idea they could rest up in the Old Woman's land during the cold, hard months and then sneak back over the Medicine Line to fight the Long Knives when the trees budded. Of all the bad things that the Old Woman disapproves of, this would make her the angriest, because she wants to be at peace with the Americans. I demanded they all swear to never do this. And they all did. So tell the Prussian that Black Moon and all the chiefs have given me their word that they will never ride out against the Americans from the Old Woman's territory, and that I am here to see they bloody well don't. And he can take that to the bank.

As to Sitting Bull and what he plans, Black Moon doesn't know or isn't saying. When I questioned him on this subject he said no man knows what Sitting Bull will do. His mind is a dreamer's mind. It is like deep water, water so deep that nobody can see all the way down to its bottom where the stones of his thoughts lie. But Black Moon is certain that Sitting Bull's hatred of the Americans is so strong that he will never surrender to them, hand over his rifle and horse to them as they demand, and go to a reservation to be kept like a cow in a corral.

These Indians are in dire straits. Plenty of hungry children who are all eyes and swollen bellies. Black Moon told me the Sioux had used up all their bullets fighting the Long Knives, and they had none left to hunt buffalo. His warriors were reduced to lassoing the beasts and closing in to stab them to death with knives. He begged me for ammunition, claiming that without it, his people could not last the winter. So I ordered trader Légaré to issue 25 rounds to every Sioux warrior on their solemn assurance it would never be used for warlike purposes. I am sure this will go a long way in making these Sioux amenable to my influence.

This brings me to O'Neill. With five hundred veterans of the Little Bighorn to keep on the straight and narrow, I have decided not to distract Secretary Scott with the spectre of some Irish bogeyman. In my opinion, the government's focus must be on assisting and strengthening my efforts to control the Sioux. I want their minds on this situation and not cluttered up with notions of Fenians skulking under the bed.

Wishing you happiness and prosperity in the coming year. Mine looks to be shaping up to be a most interesting one.

Yours truly,
Maj. James Morrow Walsh

January 18, 1877
Fort Benton

My dear Walsh,

I have passed on to Maj. Ilges all the information you furnished regarding the Sioux, which he was very pleased to receive and which he immediately forwarded to Army headquarters in the West. However, I did withhold one detail from him. I thought it best not to divulge that you had issued 25 rounds to each Sioux warrior. Your charitable impulse would not be well received in these parts. Many would interpret this action as tantamount to supplying war materiel to a bitter foe. Can I assume you will not make any mention of this distribution of ammunition in your report to Ottawa? I think Scott would share my opinion that it was a rash and impolitic step open to misinterpretation by the Americans.

As to Gen. O'Neill, I understand your point that you do not wish to deflect the government's attention from the Sioux problem. Nevertheless, I urge you to reconsider. The Fenians pose no threat at present, but the government should be alerted to their aims in this part of the world so that if O'Neill chooses to kick dust in our faces at some future date Ottawa will not be taken by surprise.

Yours truly,

Wesley Case

He had wished to write more frankly to Walsh but did not know how to do it in a fashion that would not offend him. The Major's problem was he admired Indians too much for his own good, at least those Indians who admired him in return. What Walsh had said was sensible enough – only if the Sioux felt they could trust him would they listen to him. But there was a danger there too. Knowing Walsh's nature, the closer the Major got to these Indians, the greater the likelihood he would begin to sympathize with their plight and disregard his superiors' instructions. Handing out ammunition to hunters was a generous act, but it was also unwise. When the Sioux praised Walsh for his generosity, this would only prompt him to make more gestures of a similar sort. The Major's prickliness and vanity could not be discounted either. If his own superiors did not applaud him, he would take applause where he could get it – even if that meant the handclapping came from the Sioux.

It was too early to say, but Case could not shake the feeling that the Major's foot was poised on a slippery slope. Walsh might have begged him for guidance, but when the Major was swept up in events, was in the heat of the moment, how likely would he be to tolerate a hand put to his collar to check him from sliding to the bottom of the incline?

Over Randolph's strenuous objections, Ada summoned Dr. Strathway shortly after the New Year's party to look at her husband's injured foot. After a thorough examination of the patient, the grave-faced doctor gave his diagnosis: Randolph was suffering from diabetes mellitus. The wound was trifling and would be of no consequence to an otherwise healthy man but, given her husband's ailment, it must be closely watched for signs of sepsis. If gangrene set in – the doctor tucked his jaw, pleating his chins – he could not assure her of a happy outcome.

By the third week of January, a hideous bluish-green stain was creeping up Randolph's calf. Celeste might have been able to persuade her father to submit to the amputation Dr. Strathway recommended, but she and Lieutenant Blanchard had already departed for Philadelphia. Ada certainly could not convince him of its necessity. Randolph's usual belief that if bad things were ignored they would simply go away, or right themselves of their own accord, made him resist all her arguments and entreaties. He said no quack was going to lop off any part of him. Meanwhile necrosis made its slow, remorseless advance up his leg as he lay in bed railing against the wife and doctor who were colluding to make him a cripple.

At last, Strathway issued an ultimatum to Ada. If she did not permit him to operate, she would be as good as guilty of murder. Her husband's life rested in her hands. Would she give her consent to an amputation? Ada agreed the time had come to act over Randolph's objections. The doctor asked whether she could call on any friends of her husband to assist him in the surgery. He would need strong men to help restrain him during the procedure. For Ada, the doctor's inquiry drove home a sad fact – Randolph had no friends, only clients and business acquaintances. For an instant, she considered sending for Wesley Case and Joe McMullen, but then she thought better of it given Case's behaviour on New Year's Eve.

She blurted out, "I can think of only one man I could ask. However, he's as strong as an ox. He should be sufficient to restrain my husband."

And so it was Michael Dunne who took hold of Tarr's arms and stretched him out on the mattress as if it were a rack, held him fast there, shrieking and thrashing, until the bone saw chewing its way through his femur shocked Tarr's heart into arrest and ended his life.

A woman with no family or friends to guide and assist her, Ada numbly took on the responsibilities that now beset her. The undertaker wanted to know whether the remains of the deceased were to be kept until spring arrived and the ground could be dug, or did she want to pay to have it thawed and her husband immediately interred? The thought of Randolph lying for months in the graveyard shed with ice in his hair and frost on his cheeks was too much to bear. At considerable expense, she ordered a load of coal to be burned on his grave plot to soften the earth. A telegram was dispatched to Philadelphia, relating the news of her father's demise to Celeste. Her stepdaughter's reply lamented her father's death in twenty words. She did not extend condolences to her stepmother.

Randolph's last will and testament needed to be found. She discovered it in his office desk. When she read that Randolph had bequeathed the house and all its contents to his daughter, she assumed this was an earlier will that predated their marriage. But that illusion was destroyed when she read further and came to a clause that divided equally the remainder of property between his wife and daughter. This property was a chimera. Randolph's financial affairs were exactly as he had claimed they were when he dismissed Dunne. The cashbox in his office held exactly $81.42, scarcely enough to cover the funeral expenses. A few clients appeared on the books as owing Randolph money, but the sums outstanding were insignificant. On the other hand, there were a good many unpaid bills. Her hope that Randolph's claim to be teetering on bankruptcy was a dramatic exaggeration was utterly extinguished, and replaced with a small cold anger at his irresponsibility. Her husband had neglected everything: his health, his business affairs, last of all her.

She wired Celeste news of her inheritance. An immediate response came – not from Celeste but from her fiancé. With airy benevolence, the Lieutenant informed Ada that he granted her permission to remain in the house rent-free until a decision was made about the disposal of his bride-to-be's property. He gave no hint when this might be, of when she faced eviction, but she had no intention of worrying about that now. She needed to see Randolph buried.

Fort Benton lacked a church, but she received permission to use the schoolhouse for the funeral service. She engaged a Baptist lay preacher, Mr. Clumb, to lay Randolph to rest. There was no question how Randolph would have liked to go to his grave; he would have wished to be borne there by the luminaries of the town whose esteem he had always assiduously cultivated. Her husband's ambitions needed to be honoured without passing judgment on them. There had been few enough acts of kindness and consideration they had shown one another during their married life.

So she had gone to each of Benton's merchant princes, I.G. Baker, T.C. Power, the Conrad brothers among them, to ask if they would do her the favour of serving as pallbearers for her husband. She saw how taken aback they were by her request, but refusing a grieving widow was hardly the thing to do.

The day of Randolph's burial the congregation proved to be just as indifferent to her husband's passing as the grey sky overhead. Randolph's pallbearers knew no more about him than the guard of honour at a military funeral knows about the man in the box they fire their rifles over. His funeral was nothing but ceremony and a cold one at that.

But then something extraordinary happened. Just as Mr. Clumb was paging through his Bible, readying himself to commence the obsequies, Michael Dunne came solemnly marching down the aisle, bearing an enormous wreath of silk and paper flowers. The reverence with which Mr. Dunne placed his garish floral tribute on the casket top, the way he remained standing there, head ostentatiously bowed in prayer for such a long time, swept Ada with gratitude for this tiny flame of human warmth. So when Dunne turned and began to make his way back to his seat, Ada caught his eye and offered a wan and heartfelt smile of appreciation. Despite his differences with her husband, only Dunne had shown any spirit of generosity towards the departed.

When it came time for her to follow the casket out, Ada glimpsed Joe McMullen and Wesley Case seated in the last row of chairs. McMullen's face wore a look of earnestly conventional sympathy, but Case appeared to be avoiding looking her way. His head was lowered, his eyes fixed on the fingers he held knotted on his lap. Perhaps he feared she might now harbour certain expectations. On that score, he had nothing to worry about. She was not about to latch on to any man's coattails. She had done that with Randolph and he had dragged her off to where she found herself now.

Two weeks after his former lawyer was laid in the ground – an interment that John Harding had not given a second thought to attending – the mining magnate is drowsily considering the gold, scarlet, and orange autumn leaves fluttering above him. This is baffling, since something else in the back of his mind reminds him he is warm in his bed, it is winter, and every tree has been bare for months. What's more, he can feel his wife's plump haunch nestled against his leg, and a pillow tucked under his head. When he rolls over, searching for an explanation for this puzzle, he can see the same bright colours leaping and throbbing on the windowpane. That's when his feet strike the floor and carry him to the window in a headlong rush. In the yard below, the gazebo he had erected at the insistence of his daughters and wife is enveloped in flames. Fire crawls up its pillars, greasy black smoke rolls out from beneath its cupola.

Nightgown flapping, Harding snatches open the bedroom door, runs to the stairs, and bellows to the help, "Fire! Fire, damn you!"

But the alarm is raised too late to save Mrs. Harding's charming pergola. The servants' efforts to quench the conflagration are unavailing. Master and mistress stand at their bedroom window watching the blaze until the roof collapses, cascading embers into the snow where they hiss derisively.

For the first time, Mr. Harding feels a twinge of regret at Randolph Tarr's passing. It seems that with the lawyer gone, the madman Gobbler Johnson has now put his eye on him. The next day he sends a wire to Fort Benton.

Thoughts of Ada Tarr warm Dunne during the long, cold ride to Helena. Her sweet smile when he placed the flowers on her husband's coffin has been revisited, again and again, ever since the funeral. A moment of perfect understanding.

Of course, a respectable woman is bound by proprieties, and he has sworn to himself to do nothing to endanger her reputation by paying court too early. He is perfectly content to stand aside while she observes the required period of mourning. The secret they share is enough for now. Besides, it gives him time to see to their future. He is confident that Harding summoning him to Helena will prove profitable, add to the substantial nest egg he has been accumulating over the past ten years. Ada Tarr deserves to be kept in a style worthy of her, and he will see that she is.

But as Helena comes into view, huddled in the shadowy bottom of Last Chance Gulch, Dunne reminds himself to keep his mind on the business at hand, keep his wits about him. Riding through the clamorous, soot-stained town, he scarcely gives a glance to the flash saloons and jaunty sporting houses, the imposing facades of the grander mercantiles, or the miserable log cabins and raw plank shacks of miners and prospectors that straggle helter-skelter along the creek bed. He keeps his eyes on his goal, Harding's grand house perched on a steep hill, stark against a pewter sky.

At Harding's front door he turns over his horse to a stableboy, stiffly climbs the brick steps, and gives the bell pull a tug. When he gives his name to the maid, she leads him up an impressive walnut staircase, lit by stained glass windows, to the third floor, and ushers him into a gallery-shaped room where Harding sits behind a trestle table heaped with assay reports, maps, ore samples, and lumps of brownish coal. The bitumen has shed a powdery dust over everything in the vicinity, right down to the Turkey carpet. Harding extends no welcome to Dunne, simply gets to his feet and beckons him to the window behind the worktable. Standing shoulder to shoulder, the two men contemplate the bleak ruin of the gazebo.

Harding says gloomily, "I reckon now that Tarr's dead he's turned his attention to me. Arson. To put a scare into me."

"That's the Gobbler Johnson style. He put a fire threat on Tarr. What you want done about it?"

Harding points to a humble wooden chair on the other side of the table. "Sit," he says, and walks heavily back to a leather armchair glinting with mineral grains and specks of metal. He drops down into it with a grunt, props his elbows on the low table, leans forward and says, "What I want done is a question for later. If I hire you," he qualifies. "Understand?"

Dunne shrugs.

"Tarr always bragged you up as a trained operative, but I ain't seen no evidence of it yet. Last time when you went looking for Johnson you was short on results."

"You said look for him in Missoula, which I done. Then you said the Cypress Hills. I took you at your word that you knew where he was. Well, he wasn't. I just did as I was told."

Harding picks up a chunk of rock and begins to turn it over in his hands. "Maybe it was because of them kind of lame excuses the Chicago Pinkerton Agency dropped you so quick. Tarr told me you didn't work for them more'n six months." Harding taps his temple with his forefinger. "Don't try and pull nothing over on me. I don't buy a pig in a poke."

"The Pinkertons didn't drop me. It was me waved goodbye to them."

"And what would be your reason for leaving their gainful employ, pray tell?"

"Because they put me to work as a cinder dick, riding railroad cars to see that conductors weren't slipping the odd railway fare into their pockets. You don't use a sharp tool like me for that kind of job. It was a insult."

"Sharp tool, is it? You got a pretty high opinion of yourself."

"Ain't a opinion, it's a fact. Worked a good many years as a government detective up in Canada. I'd be there still, but they shut down the service. It was the head of that whole operation who recommended me personal to the Pinkerton Agency."

"Which you was too good for."

"No. Other way around. Mr. Pinkerton cared more about hiring saints than men who produced results. He was more worried about looking respectable than getting the job done. Ran the agency like a Sunday school superintendent. Wouldn't handle divorce cases for fear it would soil his precious reputation. But divorce is a profitable business. That's a word you appreciate – profitable," Dunne says, pausing for a reaction to his observation. None comes. "That's why Tarr asked me to go to work with him, on account of he recognized my abilities. If he was alive you could ask him."

"He ain't. So you tell me."

"Chicago was booming those days. A lot of rich married men with money to keep mistresses. A lot of lawyers was of Allan Pinkerton's opinion, thought divorce was a shady business. Tarr didn't agree. Took every case he could lay hands on.

But grounds for divorce are slim. You got insanity and you got *flagrante delicto*. It was up to me to catch them *flagrante delicto*."

"Well, if it was such a damn tidy business, why didn't the two of you keep at it?"

"Because Tarr got greedy. Price of real estate was going up every day and he went to speculating in it. Then the Great Fire come along and all his property went up in smoke. Lawyer Tarr had borrowed a lot of money to buy them houses. So he done a flit to escape his creditors. Off he went owing everybody money – me included."

Harding eases back in his chair, laces his fingers over his round paunch. "Well, that was mighty inconsiderate of him to treat his peephole artist that way. But maybe the pleasure of playing peeping Tom was reward enough for you."

"I don't hold with defiling the marriage bed," says Dunne primly. "Marriage is a sacred thing to me. I was happy to see them adulterers get their just deserts."

"Who'd of thought it? A bachelor so eloquent in defence of married life. Another case of somebody not knowing what he's talking about."

"Well, I ain't going to be a bachelor long. And the woman that marries me will never have worries on that score." Dunne's declaration surprises him as much as it does Harding. His happiness seems to want to make itself known; it rises out of him, unwilled, unbidden.

There is Harding smirking at him, offensively. "I congratulate you. Who's the lucky virgin?"

Suddenly, for the first time since the interview began, Dunne feels all at sea. He has uttered his dearest hope, and now Harding is pawing it with his grimy hands, fondling it like one of his precious ore samples. Dunne is furious, but it is a fury he knows he must grind down. With an effort, he controls himself. "Never you mind who it is. Give me an answer. You want me or not?"

"You believe you can find him?"

"If I can't, nobody can."

"Then do it."

"Find him and then do what? Turn him over to the Choteau County sheriff to stand trial for his attempt on Tarr's life? That what you asking?"

"No, not that," Harding says quickly, dumping the ore sample back on the table as if it has gone hot in his hands. He seems to find it difficult to find the words for what he wants to say.

Dunne pulls his lips into a self-congratulatory smile. "No, I figure not. Because this time Gobbler Johnson might start blabbing about how his own lawyer, Tarr, was more interested in protecting your sweet interests in that disputed gold claim than he was in representing the client who hired him. And a jury might think old Gobbler had a right to take a shot at Lawyer Tarr, that it was deserved – whatever the law might say. And then he'd be loose again, with a bigger grievance against you."

Harding is looking longingly at the ore sample, as if he wishes he still had it in his hands, could feel its soothing weight. He clears his throat. "The case was decided on evidence. A contract signed by Johnson, witnessed. Proof from the bank that the purchase price for his claim was deposited in his name."

"I'm just thinking aloud here," says Dunne, "like a good lawyer might have done in court. The placer gold gives out on old Gobbler's claim, all the colour gone and went. At least what can be got with a pan, or sluice box, or rocker cradle. But a man who owns a stamp mill – you own a couple stamp mills, Mr. Harding, don't you?" Dunne pauses before placidly continuing. "That fellow figures there must be a quartz vein that fed the placer gold into Johnson's spot on the creek, and that fellow says to himself, I got the machinery to crack the meat out of the nut. So he makes Gobbler an offer on his played-out claim and Gobbler is happy to say yes. But then he gets to thinking, why's a smart fellow like Harding offering good money for nothing? So he reconsiders and refuses to carry through on the deal. Now, I'm just saying maybe and perhaps. If I was the fellow owned them stamp mills, I'd be mighty unhappy. I might be tempted to put Johnson's name to that contract and buy some witnesses to say they saw him sign it, then put the money in Gobbler's bank account and so on to cinch things tight. Me, I understand the position of the fellow with the stamp mill because a deal is a deal and I don't tolerate a welcher. But not everybody thinks like I do. I got a generous heart." Dunne waits for Harding to confirm his suppositions, but Harding only furrows his brows. "A shrewd lawyer might have said a thing or two about all this. He might have questioned that signature on the contract as a forgery. He might have examined the witnesses to it. He might have asked why Johnson never touched the money in the bank. But Tarr didn't. He just left that old fool prospector biting his lips while he waited for his lawyer to slip the knife in. But Tarr left the knife in the sheath. And that's mighty peculiar."

"All right, leave it alone," says Harding. "You made your god-damn point."

"So I take it you don't want Johnson brought in to have his say in court."

"There's that. And I got to think of my family. My wife and girls. Next time he might fire the house."

"So it's the other?"

Harding nods. Dunne leans over, takes a pencil, writes a figure on the back of an assay report, and shoves it towards Harding. "That's my price."

He squints at the number. "That's a pretty damn high price, you ask me."

"You got a lot of misery. The cure for what ails you don't come cheap."

"And how will I know you've taken care of it? I'm supposed to take your word?"

"I get half now, half when the corpse turns up."

"Nothing gets back to me. You got to guarantee that."

"Accident or suicide. Depending on the circumstances. Accidents and suicides don't point fingers."

Harding is busy lining up pieces of ore on the tabletop, fuss- ily shifting them about. "In the end, that damn claim ain't going to be worth half of what this is going to cost me."

"Don't cry over spilt milk," says Dunne. "Tarr was just the same as you. Both of you not satisfied until you got all the money there is to get. Gamblers who couldn't walk away from the table as long as there's one chip sitting in front of the other fellow. You didn't have Johnson's one chip and it was an aggravation to you. It's your nature, Mr. Harding. Don't apologize for it."

FIFTEEN

February 12, 1877

CAN ANYONE REALLY know himself? Father used to say every man is three people. You are the person you think you are, the person other people think you are, and the person you really are. On the other hand, I remember what my old professor of Greek, Sutherland, once said, that the ancient Hellenes believed that in the mists of time the gods had split us in two, and that our lives are nothing but a search for the missing half that will make us whole. How I want to believe that.

Three days ago Joe brought back news from his monthly saloon crawl. Ada Tarr is now Fort Benton's schoolmistress. The position fell suddenly vacant because the former holder of the post gave a Christmas orange to a little girl to let him put his hand up her dress. He has made an abrupt departure for places unknown. Joe says there is gossip that Tarr died leaving nothing for her support and a host of unpaid bills.

Since that unfortunate man's funeral, my head has been a muddle; I have not dared approach her. Write a letter of sympathy? But after having made such unseemly advances towards a married woman, how could I do that without appearing insincere, even cynical? Pay her a condolence call? Perhaps even worse.

The visit of any male – let alone a bachelor – would provoke a good deal of tongue-wagging.

But when I learned that she had taken up the duties of schoolmistress it felt to me as if things had somehow changed because she had set mourning aside to answer hard necessity. That she had elected to get on with life. And, somehow too, it struck me that paying a visit to the school would be different than paying a visit to her home where she would be surrounded by reminders of her husband. I told myself that going to the schoolhouse was no different than going to a place of business; it was a public not a private place. True, I had no plausible business to conduct there, but at least it was neutral ground.

Yesterday I waited in the street until I saw the children coming out of the building and heading for home. I crossed Front Street to the schoolhouse. Thick snow muffled the sound of my boots on the porch steps and the door opened noiselessly so she did not hear me enter. I saw her sitting at her desk, wiping slates with a rag. What a peaceful scene, late-afternoon winter sunshine lighting a few motes of chalk dust afloat in the air, the logs in the stove making small, cheerful noises as they crumbled to pieces in the flames.

She must have sensed my presence. Her eyes lifted from the slate on her lap. "Mr. Case?" she said. For a moment, I thought I saw distress in her face.

Suddenly, I realized I had rehearsed nothing to say. I had wanted to see her, so I had come. That was all the reason I had for being there. Making my way to her desk, I improvised on the move, hardly understanding what I was saying, spilling it out in a jumble. My heartfelt sympathies, my hope that she was bearing up, might I be of any service to her? And so forth and so on.

"Yes, thank you," she said. "Your kind words are very much appreciated." Then nothing more, she simply sat there, going on with her work.

I stumbled out, "I am sorry that circumstances have made it necessary for you to teach."

"It is good for me to be occupied. It gives me something else to think about," she said rather sharply.

I said surely she would have preferred some time to take stock, examine her choices.

"Would I?"

I blundered on, increasingly anxious. "I do not entirely know your circumstances," I said. "But if you require a loan to tide you over until your husband's affairs are settled, if that is the reason you took this position, I would be only too happy to help."

"Money?" she whispered. "What am I to make of that?"

I had put my foot wrong again. "A loan," I hurried to say, "but without obligation."

"The word loan implies obligation. I know of no other definition."

"Then let us call it a gesture. A gesture made by one friend to another. You once said you would like to call me friend."

"If you are expressing a wish to rescue me," she said, "I do not wish it. I have no interest in putting myself under your protection, or any other man's." Her face was flushed a bright pink; a vein was ticking in her neck.

"I think you have misunderstood me, Mrs. Tarr," I told her. "It appears no good deed goes unpunished."

"If I have misunderstood you then you must speak more plainly, Mr. Case."

I was growing as vexed as she. "Then I'll explain myself. Excuse me for thinking it, but I assumed there might be some relative you wished to go to and might be prevented from doing so by a lack of funds. Or that there were other steps you wished to take to escape your unfortunate situation."

"I do not find my situation unfortunate. Nor do I wish to be hurried out of it – no matter how convenient someone else might find it to see my back going down the road."

"I do not know what you mean, Mrs. Tarr," I said.

"I think you do. So let us let the matter drop."

"If I knew what this matter is you speak of – why, I would only be too ready to let it drop."

"Don't be coy, Mr. Case," she said.

"I think if anyone wants to see anyone's back it is you who wants to see mine. So I will oblige you. Good day." And I walked out, a hound with its tail tucked between its legs.

After Case had made his stony-faced exit from the Fort Benton school, Ada simply folded her hands on the desk and laid her cheek down on them. Behind the isinglass pane of the stove, she could see the embers slumping and settling in the grate, turbulent waves of heat shimmering like a mirage. In the stillness and quiet of the room, she felt her anger subside like them into a grey and bitter ash.

Everything Wesley Case could possibly say to belittle her, he had said. Everything he could do to demean her, he had done. New Year's Eve, how ready he had been to sham passion because a flirtation with a married woman carries no obligations. *Obligation*, there was a word that made him uneasy, which was why she had rubbed his nose in it. How impetuous and hot he had been then and how coolly scrupulous he had been to avoid her after that night, even going so far as to duck his face down at the funeral like a shamefaced boy. As if a crumb of kindness would compromise him. And then to make this mean-spirited assault on her feelings when she was at her lowest point, to demean the honest work she had taken up, talk to her as if she was nothing more than a red-kneed charwoman scrubbing spots from youngsters' slates, what was that but a ploy to remind her she was a pauper and give him the opportunity to dangle a bribe under her nose? Pocket my money, there's a good girl, make yourself scarce; throw yourself on the mercy and charity of relatives if you're lucky enough to have them. And all the while he had stood there, as good as jingling the coins in his pocket. And when she had chosen to tell him she needed nothing from him, he had seized upon that as a justification to act as if it were he who had been insulted, and retreat from her. All along, he had played her for a fool.

There were still a few sparks smouldering in the grey ash of her sadness. Ada Tarr sat up straight in her chair, grabbed the slate resting in her lap, and ferociously wiped it clean.

SIXTEEN

ÐUNNE BEGINS HIS search for Gobbler Johnson based on a simple proposition. He puts himself in the prospector's boots. If some undeserving son of a bitch had yanked pay dirt out of his hands, he wouldn't stray far from either the thief or what had been stolen from him. He'd keep a close eye on both. This is how he would operate, and he can't imagine anyone doing different. He is certain Gobbler is nearby Helena.

So he goes where the prospectors gather, loiters about in the saloons, where he finds sympathizers with Gobbler Johnson's plight, places where the name Harding is spat out like a curse. Patiently, he starts casual conversations that eventually meander their way to the topic of the disputed gold claim. The prospectors are all of the same opinion. Johnson has been cheated out of what is rightfully his. The problem is that nobody drops any hint where he may be. It has always been Dunne's experience that just as summer follows spring, somebody always talks, but in this instance, nobody does. They all hold that Johnson has pulled up stakes for parts unknown.

Dunne does what he always does when he runs into a dead end: he detours, shifts to new ground. No one has laid eyes on Gobbler since he took a shot at Tarr. The old man has been careful to cover his tracks, to make sure Harding gets no whiff of where he might be and settle matters with him once and for all.

Gobbler Johnson's success at doing just that suggests he must have someone helping him.

So Dunne begins to haunt the town's mercantiles. He plops himself down beside the stores' stoves where the men gather to talk politics and business, joke and spin tales. He shoots a little breeze himself. In particular, Dunne cultivates the shop assistants who, whenever they have a spare minute or two, drift over to where talk is flying thick and fast. Whenever he asks one of them to fetch him some hard candy, or a bottle of ginger beer, or to cut him a piece of cheese, he never forgets to press a small tip into their hands, wink, and say, "A young fellow requires a little walking-around money." He chats about their jobs, which gives them the opportunity to puff themselves up. All that paperwork, the bills of lading, the invoices, the accounts, the correspondence with suppliers, you can't imagine what a trial to the patience that is. They love to piss and moan about the biggest aggravation of all, the blamed customers, about having to listen to their complaints about high prices and shoddy quality, and, wouldn't you know it, the ones who bitch the most are the ones with bills long overdue.

It's the customers, their whims, fancies, and habits, that Dunne finds most interesting. The shop assistants are only too happy to enlarge on that subject. He will ask, Is it true that most men are creatures of habit when it comes to their stomachs? That when a regular crosses the threshold, you can pretty much fill his order from memory? And the clerks allow this is true. Why if the day comes that Amos Henderson don't ask for sardines, that'll be a sure sign the end times is just around the corner. And Kugler loves peppermints so much that if he lacks for cash, he'll short himself on flour to buy them.

Yes, Dunne will say, a favourite food is like an old friend, and old friends are the best, the ones you can trust and rely on. But surely there are some who like to kick over the traces and surprise you with some out of the wild blue yonder purchase? But no, the young fellows in the aprons can hardly think of such an instance. Maybe somebody might splurge on a more expensive brand of tobacco, or buy a better quality of canned beans now and then, but in a general way of speaking, a man knows what he likes and sticks to it. Humankind mostly resemble locomotives: they run on a track.

And then one day Dunne hears of an exception, a dumb Swede by name of Holstrom.

"Oh," says Dunne, "but foreigners is unpredictable."

The pimply clerk gives a hoot and says, "Well, he wasn't no ways unpredictable in the past. He's given us his custom for two years now and there was a time I wished he'd take it elsewhere. He'd come in every Saturday – and mind you now, he only knows about ten words of English – and he'd point to the shelves and a fellow never knew exactly what he wanted, or how much of it, and you'd reach for a article and he'd shake his head, and point again like a monkey. All the pulling down and putting back, it was more effort than it was worth. Because what he bought, it was all, you know, cheap goods, the very cheapest. Then one day about six, seven months ago he comes in with a list written out in English, and there was items on it he'd never bought before, and his order was about double the quantity, and the quality was pricier. So now he just hands me his order, goes off to the saloon while I fill it. When he's got a skin full of whiskey he collects his goods, pays cash on the barrelhead, and rides off. And all I got to say, whoever's drawing up that grocery list for Holstrom is making my life a good deal easier."

"Well, that's a mercy," says Dunne.

He resumes prowling the saloons, following a new angle. He's after Gobbler Johnson's origins. Dunne has assumed Johnson was an English name, but it could be something else, maybe one of those pickled-herring-eater names. So thoroughness being a point of pride with him, he goes right back at it.

One night he strikes up a conversation with a man called Tinker who knows Johnson well enough to be able to tell him something about his background. "Now," says Tinker, "Gobbler speaks American just as good as you or me, but his mother and father was some variety of Scandihoovian born in the old country, and he can talk that singsong lickety-split. I heard him do it once. Lord, how I laughed."

Finally, Dunne understands why nobody has talked. It's because Holstrom can't share his secret with anyone, at least in any lingo that can be comprehended by anyone but a hammerhead Swede. And the rest makes sense too; it's only natural that one Scandihoovian would stick to another like shit to a wool blanket. After that, all that is necessary to do is wait for Saturday to roll round, dawdle about the general store until Holstrom places his order, and then follow the man after he collects his supplies.

Where Holstrom leads him is to a small, secluded cabin back in the hills. From behind a screen of trees, Dunne watches Gobbler Johnson walk out of his cabin and greet his friend. The two men unpack the mule and carry the groceries into the cabin. He has to wait two hours to learn the last thing he needs to know. When Holstrom finally rides off, it is clear that the two men aren't sharing the cabin. Back in Helena, Dunne congratulates himself with the best supper that money can buy.

A month after Harding's pergola went up in flames, Gobbler has been found, but haste not only makes waste, it frequently makes a mess. So before he makes a move, Dunne spends a quiet Sabbath pondering every danger that may lurk ahead, every mishap that may be waiting to happen.

Now he stands in a clump of pines thirty yards from Johnson's cabin. He hobbled his horse a mile back, judging a stealthy approach by foot would be safest. Smoke trickles from the chimney, a flag signalling a warm, cozy berth, and the sight of it is a torment to Dunne. His toes are stinging in his boots; his cheeks and nose are dead to the touch. Still, this is no time for recklessness. He has carefully surveyed the old fellow's lair. Gobbler couldn't have situated his hideout better. The cabin is backed into a steep knoll covered in brush and pine that sweep down the slope to surround it on three sides. Its log front blends into the backdrop of timber, rendering it nearly invisible to the passerby. Of more concern is the small window in the front of the cabin that faces him across a patch of upland meadow naked of any cover except for a stand of bulrushes at the edge of a big slough. This is not favourable ground. Even if he were lucky enough to reach the cabin without Gobbler catching sight of him, he would be left with only two choices. Announce himself or burst through the door. Both are risky. It is impossible to predict Gobbler's state of mind, how edgy he might be. Dunne prefers to endure the bitter cold rather than a hot blast of shotgun pellets.

He bends over, blows his dripping nose, flicks snot from his fingers. When he glances up, there is Gobbler out on his doorstep, a skinny old man in a long, flapping coat, a bucket in one hand and an axe in the other. He's bareheaded, which means he doesn't intend to tarry outside for long. Dunne watches him start down a well-trodden path towards the slough. He doesn't stir until his quarry is well on his way and has his back turned to him. Then he draws his Schofield, slogs through thigh-deep snowdrifts until he gains the packed footing of the track that Gobbler has gone down. He's out on the slough, cutting a hole in the ice. Every blow of the axe rings sharply; it sounds as if he is striking metal, and this helps mask the clicking of Dunne's hobnailed boots on the ice-slick surface of the trail. The old man stoops to dip his pail in the water, and when he straightens up, Dunne is aiming a pistol in his face. Gobbler's shoulders jerk like a rabbit in the noose of a snare; his fingers go slack on the bail of the bucket. It drops with a clump. His goitre jiggles on his throat as he blinks furiously, the tip of his tongue running circles round his mouth.

"Easy now," says Dunne. "Take hold of yourself. Don't play up foolish."

"What you want, mister?"

"What I want is for you to pick up that axe – by the head, not the handle – and walk it over to me. Do it slow."

Gobbler does as he is told, shuffles towards Dunne, the axe handle wagging. Dunne eases the tool out of his hand. The sudden weight of it dangling in his grip drags an idea down out of his brain. It's a moment before Gobbler's whine bores through this thought.

"I say, do you hear me? If you're the law, I'll come peaceable. You can take that pistol off me."

"I ain't the law."

Gobbler offers a weak smile. "Well, if you got your mind set on collecting a bounty, there ain't no bounty on me. Choteau County ain't offered no reward for capturing Gobbler Johnson, no matter what you might have heared. No sir. Be fair warned, there ain't no profit in it for you to haul me back to Benton." He continues to jabber away, attempting to drive home his worthlessness. "Everybody knowed that shot I took at that bastard lawyer, it was fired high and wide. Plain as the nose on your face. I could have killed him dead if I wanted. But bloody assassination ain't in my nature. Just wanted for him to squirt in his drawers. That's all. That's the onliest revenge old Gobbler was after, to squeeze a squirt out of Lawyer Tarr." He kicks the snow with the toe of his boot, as if trying to scuff some response out of Dunne. Pleadingly, he asks, "That seem a crime merits bounty money, mister? Whoever said such a thing was wrong, mister, you been took."

"You best lie down in the snow now."

"What?"

"On your back."

"Why I got to lie down? What you mean to do?"

"I mean for you to do as I tell you. Get on your back, right there." Dunne shows him the axe. "Don't make me chop you down."

"I ain't agoing to. Not unless you give me a reason for it."

"It's all the same to me," Dunne says, holding the axe blade up to Gobbler's face.

Slowly, the old man sinks down on his haunches, begins to sob.

"Fall back, Gobbler. Hush now, hush now," says Dunne.

The old man's shoulders sink in the snow. He holds up his hands as if to grasp at the swollen, purple clouds overhead, to pull them down to cover himself, to hide himself under them. Dunne's boot comes down hard on his chest. "Jesus, Jesus, Jesus," Gobbler cries. "Why you treating me this way?"

"Won't be but a moment," says Dunne, pocketing the Schofield. "Quiet yourself, Gobbler. It ain't doing you no good." He rotates the axe in his hands until the blunt side is turned forward, marks a spot on Johnson's skinny thigh just above the knee. The blade rises high above his head, slashes down.

A crack of breaking bone. A shrill scream. Birds fling out of the trees, turn into mad whirring specks. The old prospector grunts his agony as if someone is rhythmically pounding his chest with a fist.

Dunne picks up the bucket, crosses to the hole in the ice, fills the pail with water, and walks back to Gobbler, who has rolled himself over on his stomach and is dragging himself up the path with his elbows, the broken leg flopping crookedly behind him. When Dunne approaches, Gobbler makes a snatch at his trousers, and Dunne recoils, slopping water on his own boots. He douses him with what remains in the bucket, and the shock of it coils Gobbler up like a worm. Plodding back to the slough, Dunne refills the bucket. When he gets back, Gobbler has gone absolutely still. Dunne locates an artery in his neck. A pulse throbs there. He has only fainted.

He waters the unconscious man like a garden, soaking every spot he missed in the first drenching. Finished, he looks down glumly at his own soggy boots. In weather like this, wet feet are a danger. Dunne puts down the bucket, picks up the axe, and marches to the cabin, where he finds that a good fire has been laid. He adds a few more sticks, adjusts the damper, takes off his socks and boots, and sets them to dry in the oven.

He's hungry. Padding around the cabin in his bare feet, he finds a skillet, a slab of bacon, and a can of Van Camp beans. He slices thick strips of meat into the pan and sets it on the stove. When the bacon is nearly done he adds the beans and gives them a few minutes to come to a bubbling simmer.

Dunne isn't sure how long it takes for someone to expire from cold, but he estimates it can't be any longer than it takes footwear to dry or a man to finish his breakfast. He eats without hurry; the room fills with the smell of hot wool and roasting leather. He finishes the last forkful of beans, pulls on his socks and boots; the warmth of them curls his toes with grateful pleasure.

Outside, he lops a bough from one of the pines near the cabin and strolls down to where the body lies, trailing the branch along behind him. Much to his surprise, he finds Gobbler has recovered consciousness, is stirring fitfully and mumbling like a man on a fever ward. The sparse hairs of his head are stiffened with ice. Gobbler bestirs himself, tries to creep away, but he's so far gone, so weak he is only capable of twitching and shuddering. These tics make his frozen clothes crackle faintly as if he were a bed of dry leaves some small animal was walking over.

Dunne sees it is true: a man can turn blue from cold. It is an interesting phenomenon. Gobbler's lips look as if he has been gulping ink. And those lips are moving, his teeth snapping out a harsh, scolding chatter. It takes a moment for Dunne to realize that the old man is actually trying to say something.

"How's that?" prompts Dunne. "What you want?"

He watches the old man make a great effort of will. "What *are* you?" he demands. "What *are* you?" His eyes are shrinking in their sockets. Maybe freezing isn't a peaceful death, akin to falling into a dreamless sleep. People have got that wrong.

Dunne squats down beside him. Gobbler's question doesn't make much sense to him, but he gives it thoughtful consideration before trying to answer it. "What am I?" says Dunne. "Well, I guess I'd say my profession is anticipating. That's my stock and trade. I look out for those who can't spot danger ahead. Most people can't put themselves in another man's feelings, but I can. So I asked myself, if you was treated like Gobbler Johnson was

254

treated by Lawyer Tarr and Harding, what would you do? No question I know what I'd do. I'd visit doom on them. I'd have their guts for gaiters. If God Himself stepped between us He couldn't turn me from my purpose. It's only human nature to brood on a wrong – a wrong festers and fills you up with poison. It don't let go. It don't give a man no rest, and sooner or later he's got to lance it, or die of the poison growing in him. And I give you credit where credit is due, Gobbler. You give them fair warning, sent that letter to Lawyer Tarr and burned down that piddling piece of Harding's property to remind them they weren't safe. You give them a chance to make amends. But that sort of people don't pay no mind to the right and wrong of things."

Dunne pauses, overcome with a queer feeling. He's crossed a line. It's happened to him once or twice before, confusing what really happened with what he was *sure* would happen. It was *you*, he reminds himself. And in a flash, he sees himself looking down at Michael Dunne cutting the words out of the *Fort Benton Record*, out of the books he stole from the school to write a warning to Tarr. It's difficult work for Michael Dunne's big hands, setting those tiny words down on the page like a typesetter, manipulating them into place and gumming them down. Such a delicate, finicky job that he can see how the effort of it worriedly hunches up his shoulders.

And then he is high above Harding's backyard, seeing Michael Dunne tramping through the snow to the gazebo, watching him laying the tinder and newspaper, watching the match bloom in the darkness, the fire swarming to announce to Harding that he isn't safe either.

II 5225 25II3231524255 1243353542. II 121II2 III3.

I am Michael Dunne. I did it.

"Now you might say," he whispers to Gobbler, "that you didn't intend Tarr no harm, that you only wanted to throw a fright into him by shooting into his office. But I don't believe that's the truth. You were meaning to kill him dead as Joe Cunt's dog, but you lost your nerve at the last second. But that don't mean that was the end of it, because losing your courage only made you brood all the harder. Ain't that so? Eating away at you until sooner or later you'd have had to come back at Tarr and Harding. Human nature has got to be satisfied. And you see, it was up to me to show those two they was in peril. I *anticipated* sooner or later you wouldn't be able to stop yourself from taking a crack at them. That's my gift, reading people. Now I ain't got much gratitude for it, very little thanks. So I settle for second best – I take money for it. Nobody never gave Michael Dunne nothing; I got to look out for myself. Otherwise, what'd I be?"

His legs are cramping. He stands to stretch them and when he does, he realizes the solemn quiet that blankets Johnson, a quiet he was deaf to because he has been listening so hard to himself explaining what kind of man he is. Giving Gobbler a nudge with his foot, he feels the weight that accumulates in a lifeless body.

There is nothing to do but tidy up. Dunne takes the pail and the axe and flings them out on the slough, near the hole in the ice. With the spruce bough, he sweeps away any traces of his own footprints near the body. When he starts back up the trail, a thought comes to him. There must be money, nuggets, or gold dust in Gobbler's shack. How else did he pay for his supplies? But then Dunne reminds himself to anticipate. Today is Monday. Holstrom will be back sometime this week to collect Johnson's grocery list. He will find him, assume his friend slipped on the ice, broke his leg, fell into the water, but managed to haul himself this far before he died of exposure. But Holstrom surely knows something about whatever Johnson used to buy his supplies. If it goes missing, Holstrom will wonder who took it. He'll start speculating. No, this is not the time to be greedy. Leave well enough alone.

Dunne returns to his task, carefully obliterating the footprints he left in the drifts. On the other side of the thicket where he had hidden, he does the same, working his way back in the direction of his horse. It's painstaking work, but he takes satisfaction in the care and attention required to erase his presence. Dunne is so intent on his job that when the first flakes of snow flutter down, he looks up in surprise. Above him hovers the dark cloud that Gobbler did his best to clutch. Greenish blue and purple as a bruise, it is leaking snow, faster and faster.

Dunne tosses the branch aside; it is no longer required, the snow will cover all signs he was ever here.

He lumbers through the white downfall, thinking of the future. He will need to remain in Helena for a little longer. It will be hard, but it must be done. For the sake of her reputation, he cannot tempt himself by being near to her. She will understand why he can't come to her just yet. Mrs. Tarr knows what is proper and what is not. She is the most understanding and knowing woman God ever made.

SEVENTEEN

A DREARY END TO February and an equally dismal beginning to March, and Case and McMullen find themselves still penned up in the ranch house most evenings, keeping constant company, and getting on each other's nerves. With every passing day, Case finds Joe's habits growing more and more irksome: clipping his moustache over the washbasin and leaving his whiskers in it, stubbing cigars on his dinner plate, and striking up conversations just as they are readying to turn in for the night. There's no escaping him then, the two of them cheek by jowl in the tiny bedroom, no more than a few feet separating their bunks, the small space brilliantly lit by the lantern on the washstand. Case sits on the edge of his bed yanking off his boots; Joe, naked from the waist up, faces him, his shirt balled up in his hands, wearing a look of rumination, always a warning sign.

"You know that beeve you and me butchered yesterday?"

"I am aware of it," Case says shortly.

"I was thinking, maybe tomorrow evening we might get ourselves spruced up and take a parcel of that meat to Mrs. Tarr."

"No."

Joe's eyebrows arch. "A schoolmarm's salary don't go far. She'd be glad of it."

"I assure you she would not."

"I think she would. Anyway, read your Bible. It says there we ought to be charitable to widows. Words to that effect."

"Ada Tarr is the kind of widow who will fling charity back in your face. Depend on it. We're not taking any meat to her."

"Well, maybe you ain't. But I have the intention. And I'll be a gentleman about it too. Tell her it's in return for that fine pound cake she give us. Then it don't smell like charity to her."

Joe's self-confident way of speaking causes Case to blaze with fury; he jabs a finger at McMullen, hears himself shouting, "Stay out of it! Nobody is going anywhere near her! Why in hell isn't it enough for you that I ask you to leave it alone!"

Joe's face has gone white, set itself in a plaster of Paris mask. "I don't know what put the burr under your foreskin, but I don't care to be talked to like that," he says, voice tight and quiet. Slowly, Case lowers his hand. "And you don't ask me to do something, you order me. And I ain't yours to order about. If you don't want me taking no little gifts to Ada Tarr, give me a reason why."

With a curt, contrite bob of the head, Case says, "I should not have raised my voice. But I don't need to explain myself. It's none of your business, Joe."

"Then it's none of your business if I do that poor woman a kindness. I guess what's good for the goose is good for the gander."

Case averts his gaze to the lantern burning on the washstand. "All right then, if you must know – she would presume I sent you – that you were my proxy." He hesitates. "Some weeks ago I offered her assistance. She rebuffed me – most unpleasantly. It was humiliating." He turns back to Joe. "Now do you understand?"

"What I understand is why you been growling at me like an old blind dog every time you hear my footfalls these past few weeks. She shooed you off and soured your mood."

Case bridles. "That's pretty glib reasoning. You have no idea what a galling man you can be. Do I question you about your personal and private matters the way you have insisted on investigating mine tonight?"

"No, you don't. But that's because you ain't got no curiosity about humankind."

"That is absurd. Of course I'm curious about others. I'm curious about you. I just exercise a little seemly reticence."

"You're no more curious about me than you are about Ada Tarr. Now if I'd got chased off by Ada Tarr I wouldn't have rested until I found out why she went so high-handed. At least high-handed according to your lights. But then your lights is most often directed at yourself, and that has a tendency to blind a man."

"My god," says Case, shaking his head, "if you could only hear yourself."

"Well, I do hear myself. But there ain't nobody else in this room listening."

"Maybe I'm not listening because you turn all the talk to me – a subject of which you are ignorant. So talk about yourself, talk about those," says Case impulsively, gesturing towards the scars on Joe's torso. "You say I have no curiosity – well, I've been curious about them for a long time. Only discretion prevented me from inquiring. But since you have given me leave, I pose the question."

"Do you want to know or are you talking like a book just to remind me I'm ignorant?" says Joe, brushing his hand gingerly over his scars as if mention of his wounds has set them throbbing with pain.

The simple question takes Case aback; the sight of Joe's hand moving over his body stirs remorse. "All right," he says carefully, "it's true. I do want to know."

Joe gets to his feet and, to Case's surprise, leaves the bedroom. When he returns, he is carrying a bottle of whiskey and two glasses. He pours them both a tot, lifts his glass, and squints at Case through the amber liquid. "Well," he says, "whiskey improves your complexion. You don't look near as white and angry." He lowers the glass, sits for a moment, thinking. "If I was to start with the name Tom Hardwick, I figure you'd recognize it?"

"Yes. There was a standing order for his arrest when I was with the Police."

"For killing all them Assiniboines in the Cypress Hills."

"Massacring them," corrects Case. "Men, women, and children."

Joe takes a quick, bird-like sip of his whiskey. "Once I left off my woodhawking days with Fancy Charles, I washed up in Benton. Prices was high here and I was short on scratch. Met Hardwick in a saloon. He was looking for men to go up north with him wolfing. He offered me a place in his outfit and I took it. At the time I agreed I was a little drunk," he confesses. "Set off in a pretty big party, nine in all. Five men, a half-breed boy of twelve, three Blackfoot gals Hardwick had collected as blanket warmers and cooks. Things went along fine until we reached the Little Bow River where we had a collision with some Assiniboines. Don't know whether they recognized Hardwick as the man tore through their people in the Cypress Hills or not. Any rate, there was a short, sharp fight. No casualties on our side, but we killed a buck." McMullen drapes a blanket over his shoulders; suddenly he looks older, smaller. "Hardwick went to damaging up the corpse, chopped all the fingers off its hands so the spirit couldn't pull a bowstring or trigger in the Mystery World. He said it would put a spook into them Indians. Teach them not to mess with us. I reckon it did the opposite."

"I take it they came at you again."

"You take it right, but that come later in September – when we was building a winter camp on the lower Belly River. The weather was hot that month, hot as summer. We was sleeping under canvas until we finished our cabin. Then one night – I'd just about peeled out of all my clothes but for my shirt – guns commenced to cracking all about us, a ball whipped through my tent, missed my pate by so much." Joe draws the tip of his thumb by his ear, looking as if he is hearing the hiss of the ball again. "I scampered out. A ridge to our left was all alight with muzzle flashes. The Blackfoot women was screaming and scattering and I could hear Tom Hardwick roaring like the Bull of Bashan. I run barefoot to the wagon where I'd stowed my carbine. But there was a campfire nearby that lit me up pretty plain." McMullen's expression changes, as if he is reliving the moment. "First bullet hit me here." His hand touches his thigh. "It took me down. Got hit seven more times, two bullets this arm, two in the shoulder, two this side, and one below the shoulder blade." His hand flits restlessly about his body, touching each wound. "Lay there on the ground howling for help. Only reply I got was the sound of hoofbeats. The whole lot of Hardwick's crew was doing a skedaddle. They was leaving me as entertainment for the Assiniboines.

"But the sound of them galloping horses directed every musket Hardwick's way. Indians didn't get no result from it. Hard-riding men ain't no piece of cake to hit in the dark. But the distraction give me a little space of time to drag myself into a thicket and hide. Presently, them Indians came whooping and hollering into our camp. I knew if them Assiniboines found me they wouldn't spare me no miseries because I was riding with their old foe Hardwick. I didn't count on drawing too many more breaths. When they went to ransacking the wagons I crawled through the brush to the river. Being it was fall, the water was low in the Belly. After a few tries I got my feet under me and crossed the stream, wading and sandbar hopping." McMullen studies the floor for a few moments. Then, as if he suddenly recalls where he is, his shoulders give a jerk. He rubs his face like a waking man and says, "Once I reached t'other side, I took stock of my condition. The musket ball to my leg had went clear through without striking bone. It could bear weight. My arm was in a similar state – two flesh wounds. The rest I couldn't judge. I tore my shirt up and bandaged myself as best I could. The rags left over, I wrapped my feet up in them. That left me jaybird naked.

"I meant to put as many leagues between me and them Indians as I could before the sun come up. I could hear them hoopty-doing in the distance and reckoned they had come across Hardwick's store of trade whiskey. That give me a chance. So off I turtled, dripping blood, beset by dizzy spells. I calculated to try and get myself to Fort Whoop-Up, a hike of a good many days, and I didn't think I had no more chance than a cat in hell without claws. But I had to give it a whirl. Come dawn, one of them spells got the better of me, and I fainted dead away. Didn't rouse until late afternoon. Laying there in the hot sun, I'd burned in locations a civilized man don't display to the light of day." All at once Joe says, "Mind if I ask you to turn that lantern down a tad? It's shining bright in my eyes."

"Not at all." Case goes to the washstand and lowers the lamp flame. In the diminished light, with the blanket hung on his shoulders, Joe is a grey moth fading into the shadows. Case resumes his place. "Go on," he urges.

"I got to my feet, stumbled on, stumbled on all night," Joe says. "That become my custom. By day, I laid up wheresoever's I could hide myself. When the sun went down, I moved on, Fort Whoop-Up filling up my mind. Cactus and sharp stones tore my feet to tatters. Sometimes I went delirious, but when my head turned sensible I kept telling myself, *All costs you got to keep moving. You don't, you die.*

"Food was mighty scanty. Mostly whatever dried, shrivelled-up berries the bears hadn't ate or the Indians picked. I couldn't find no berries, I dug roots with a stick. Sometimes I stuffed my belly with grass. When I couldn't walk no more, I crept like a baby. When I couldn't creep no more, I laid on my back and watched the hawks drifting about in the sky, dreamed I was a bird flying home to its nest."

Joe's face is a sobering sight. Case asks, "And you never thought to give up?"

"I did give up," Joe answers. "I come on a abandoned wolfer's cabin. When I seen that shelter, every particle of effort I still had left me. I says to myself, 'You got you a roof to keep the buzzards from lighting on your corpse.' I cried for the gladness of it. I went in, shut the door, and dropped down on a bunk." Joe wags his head quickly from side to side, as if he were trying to dislodge a fly from his ear. "I laid there a day and a night, waiting to give up the ghost, not a lick of hope left in me. Then a unexpected visitor arrived on the property and come upon me. A Blackfoot gentleman who saw some profit in hauling me to Fort Whoop-Up, believed the white folks there would reward him with whiskey and flour if he handed one of their own over to them. So he rigged up a travois and off we went. The whiskey-trading boys took me in, nursed me until they reckoned I was strong enough to survive the trip back to Fort Benton. Down I went with the next shipment of buffalo hides."

"Joe," says Case, "you astound me. That is a remarkable story."

McMullen suddenly assumes his customary jaunty air, but the bitterness in his eyes betrays it. "Hell, there ain't no interest in that tale. Matters didn't turn interesting until I got to Benton."

"I don't follow."

"Why, I arrived a hero, an example of the white man's grit. I'd took the worst them rascally savages could hand out and pulled through. Strange how taking a whipping from Indians can exalt a man. If them Indians had killed me, my name might have shone bright as Custer's. Citizens took up a collection, raised five hundred dollars, and made me a presentation. Doctor wouldn't take no fee for pincering the bullets out of me." A foolish smile hovers briefly on Joe's lips. "Took my money and set myself up in the Overland Hotel. I was still in a pretty bad way, but the town was dandling me in the lap of luxury. Had my meals delivered to my room. Entertained well-wishers in bed like I was King of England. Everything bright as a new penny. Then my visitors put a smudge on it. Said Hardwick was back in town telling anybody would listen that he was certain sure I was lifeless as a coffin nail when he and his friends made their escape. But a corpse don't holler for help like I done. Don't beg not to be left behind."

Case glances down at the floor. "Yes, to abandon a comrade –"

"Don't mistake me, I ain't looking for sympathy. Hell, a man panics, loses his head, I can see how it happens. If Hardwick had come by the Overland to check on how I was faring, if he'd said to me, 'Sorry we scooted on you, Joe. I feel bad for it,' I'd have shook his hand and said don't mention it. But he was lying to save face. Now I been known to brighten up a story to give somebody a laugh. I ain't talking about that. What Hardwick was doing was different. And worst, he was parading around town bragging he was going to take revenge on them Assiniboines for me. As if he knew my mind on that score. He didn't.

"All that went to work on me. I festered with it. It was pus no bread poultice could draw. So I decided to take the swagger and strut out of the bastard." Joe clamps his hands to his knees. "Next time the doctor come to see me, he warned me I better keep to my room on account of Hardwick was claiming I was playing invalid to avoid him, hiding under my blankets because I didn't have the guts to make no such scurvy accusation like I had spread about town to his face. Said he meant to finish the job them Indians botched, make me a corpse if I dared walk out among honest men."

Joe picks up the bottle and splashes a little more whiskey in their glasses. "Now I'm a easygoing fellow. Men like Tom Hardwick is liable to mistake that, take it for a invitation to walk all over you. But a amiable fellow when he turns, he's apt to grow dark and stormy. Hardwick put thunder in me. I was still mighty feeble, but I hobbled out and laid in the necessary. I asked a few questions in the right places and learned there was a bride of the multitude Hardwick favoured by name of Curly Josephine. He always visited her late afternoon because he wanted to be first ship in port, before anybody else discharged their cargo. Curly worked in a crib behind one of Baker's warehouses. I waited for Hardwick there. When he come round the corner the sun was low on the horizon. I threw a beam into his eyes with a little piece of mirror glass I held in my palm. It fair blinded him. I cut his legs out from under him with a pick handle

I was carrying, then set to beating him like a dusty rug, worked him over from shoulders to ankles. I'd have turned him over and done the front just like I done the back, but I was too winded.

"When I finished, he was whimpering like a new-weaned pup. I says to him, 'Think twice next time you threaten me, Tom Hardwick, because if it happens again I might come with a pistol instead of a pick handle.' And Hardwick, he lifts his face out of the dust and says, 'There won't be no warning next time, you cocksucker. You'll be six feet in the ground before you know it.' So I squats down beside him, gets my face close to his, and I says, 'You ever wonder how I took eight bullets and didn't die, Hardwick? When I was birthed, my granny read the bathwater in the basin they washed me in. She had the second sight and saw my life to come, and she says, "This boy ain't never going to die by no man's hand. God Himself means to take him of natural means, of a time and place of His ordering. Nobody else better try to meddle in the Almighty's plans."'"

McMullen looks up at Case as if he expects this statement to be disputed. He clears his throat. "I never believed my granny's prophecy until I come through what I did in the wilderness. And there in Hardwick's eyes, I seen he believed it too, and that he was dreadful afraid. He knew if he made to do me harm again I would kill him dead. Being under God's hand, I had the power. And from that day onwards, Hardwick give me a wide berth and never spread no more calumnies about Joe McMullen."

"I don't understand why the man threatened your life. You were hardly the guilty party."

McMullen's grimness evaporates. "Why," he says, "because I took some of my hero's money, went to the Fort Benton paper, had them print me up a bunch of posters. Them handbills give a warning to the citizens of Fort Benton not to make any sudden noises around Tom Hardwick after nightfall. Said the dark turned him cowardly, and he was likely to spook and stampede if startled. Said I didn't want no women, children, or small dogs trampled to death when he was affrighted and tried to make his escape. I put my name, Joe McMullen, Esq., at the bottom of my declaration, and tacked them posters up all over town."

"Well," says Case, "I guess that would do it."

"Yes sir," says Joe. "I needed to beat the bush to see which way the quail would fly. Would he shut his mouth or keep running it? Well, Hardwick kept on running it. I figure go public if you want to force somebody's hand."

In mid-March, calving begins. Each afternoon, Joe rides out and hazes into the corral any cows that show signs they are ready to deliver. The two men keep watch on them throughout the night, take turns every two hours to make sure none of the cattle are undergoing a difficult labour. Often they are greeted with wet snow or a chill rain that patters hat brims and shoulders. Case had expected these wretched vigils to increase the strain between him and his partner but all that is gone. Once again circumstances are forcing them to pull together.

With so much time to think as he tends to the cows, Case decides he had been wrong to approach Ada Tarr in the way he had. Sometimes only a hair separates timid earnestness and insincerity, they are so easily confused. Joe chooses to speak the truth insouciantly and with flair. Not everyone appreciates his style, but what he says cannot be ignored.

So in the first week of April, with the calving finished, Case pays a visit to the newspaper office. Three days later a notice appears in the *Fort Benton Record* among the advertisements tendered by harness makers, grocers, and gunsmiths.

> GENTLEMAN DESIRES TO KEEP
> company with an accomplished lady of fine character.
> The gentleman in question will present himself on
> the boardwalk outside McGibbon's Emporium
> directly across from Fort Benton School, Thursdays

between the hours of three and four o'clock p.m., to make himself known to interested parties. He may be identified in this wise: will have hat humbly in hand and a red handkerchief in his breast coat pocket.

The gentleman seeks a lady well conversant in the works of George Eliot, able to bake a fine pound cake, and proficient in the piano. A fine singing voice would be much appreciated but is not required. No triflers, please!

This announcement does not pass unremarked. The next Thursday, a number of inquisitive citizens make a point of shopping or hanging about in the vicinity of McGibbon's Emporium. Shortly before three o'clock, Wesley Case appears, red handkerchief in breast pocket, hat in hand, and takes up a spot on the boardwalk directly across the street from the school. Soon the pupils, dismissed for the day, come rushing out into a bright spring afternoon, shrieking with high spirits. The sun is melting the snow, wheeled traffic has churned the roadway into a morass, and pools of water are glinting on the icy crust of the Missouri. A stiff breeze blows, licking up tufts of hair on Case's head. Standing erect as a guardsman, he keeps his eyes fastened on the bluffs across the river, paying no mind to the amused glances thrown his way, to the whispers of the onlookers, to the rude comments and guffaws of the rougher elements. He waits patiently. A quarter of an hour goes by, and then another; the crowd begins to slowly disperse, to drift off shaking their heads in bemusement.

The door to the school remains shut fast. Case twirls his hat in his hand and blinks his eyes. At last, he draws out his pocket watch and consults the time. It is exactly one minute past four o'clock. Setting his hat squarely on his head, he removes the red handkerchief from his jacket, tucks it away, and retreats from his storefront post.

Ada Tarr is watching from the schoolhouse window. This is the second Thursday Wesley Case has trapped her indoors, kept her counting off the minutes until his appointed time of departure. A hard rain is pounding down, pocking the puddles in the road, making little silver spurs on the shingles of McGibbon's Emporium.

What was the meaning of that preposterous advertisement? Was it composed to mock her? But standing there in the midst of the downpour, hat clutched to his chest, hair plastered slickly to his skull, Wesley Case looks humble rather than sneering, the last woebegone seal left by its herd on a barren shore. Everyone else with a lick of sense has got off Front Street and under cover, but he still loiters about on the boardwalk, courting pneumonia.

A strong gust of wind swirls down the street, moulding his sodden trousers to his legs, streaking the rain sidelong, and rocking him on his feet. Ada wishes it would blow hard enough to tumble him over the horizon and out of view. The sight of him disturbs her frightfully because it elicits a pang of sympathy, and that she doesn't want to feel. She had never dreamed he would persist in making such a ridiculous spectacle of himself. And Case shows no signs of losing heart, of renouncing this absurd role he has chosen to play. Somehow, he must be *stopped*.

Case spots Ada Tarr plunging across the road, skirts hiked up in two white-knuckled fists to keep them clear of the puddles. What he's asking for he's about to get. Ada stops just short of the boardwalk and squints up at him, rain dashing on her face. The boardwalk provides him with an unfair advantage of height, so he steps down into the mud to bring them face to face.

"What is all this?" she says. "Explain yourself."

"I wished a hearing so I issued you an invitation, which I see you have accepted."

"It was not an invitation, but blackmail. Call it what it is. How dare you subject me to public humiliation. George Eliot, pound cake, pianos – those can only refer to me."

"They do. But I doubt very much the public is aware of your enthusiasm for the first two. I allow the mention of a piano may have given someone a second thought – but that is questionable. All in all, I believe you remain anonymous."

"I am not a plaything in your silly game." Ada's face is streaming rain. "What do you mean by this nonsense? What is behind it?"

"I thought it obvious."

"It is not obvious. I want you to explain yourself."

"Our last meeting was not successful. I acted very proudly. I have dispensed with pride. As you see."

"That tells me nothing."

"Very well. Do you remember New Year's Eve? You lectured me on the subject of Peregrine Hathaway's ardour. You approved of it. You thought his baying at Celeste's door spoke well of him. Well, here I am baying at your door in my own way, *sotto voce* perhaps, but I am an older man than he is. I cannot quite bring myself to howl as loudly as you might like. This is all I'm capable of."

Ada suddenly begins to shiver. "We are scarcely acquainted. What grounds do you have for making such a mad declaration? Do you imagine a few conversations sufficient to know me?"

"If you require more conversation, I will talk until kingdom come. I will keep talking just as long as you require. I intend to prove my sincerity to your satisfaction. Now, however, I must get you home. You're soaked and shaking. I'll hire a surrey at the livery. Return to the school and wait for me there."

And before she can protest, or demur, Case is striding away on his long legs, head bent and shoulders stooped under the slashing rain.

They scarcely speak during the drive back to Ada's house. Case's attention is fully occupied on keeping the surrey on the greasy track, which it threatens to slither off at every bend in the road. And the rain racketing on the leather top of the carriage creates such pandemonium anything less than a shout could not be heard. The wild, ragged noise is playing on Ada's nerves. When a ferocious burst of wind makes the surrey's top crack like a breaking board, she barely manages to stifle a cry. A quick, furtive glance tells her Case hasn't noticed; he is blind to everything but the rumps of the horses.

At her door, Case springs down from the buggy and helps her out.

"You said you wish to talk," Ada says, keeping her eyes lowered to the spots of mud on her skirt as if they are her chief concern. "I think now is as good a time as any. You best come in." Case follows her up the porch and into the hall. Her wet face gleams in the faint light of the curtained house. "I'm soaked to the skin," she says. "I must change my clothes."

"Yes. By all means."

Ada climbs the stairs, goes into the bedroom, and shrugs out of her wet garments. She dries her hair with a towel from the washstand, begins to dab her body dry with it. The rain pecks at the window, and her nerves.

She begins to scrub her body with the towel, rubs it punishingly with the rough cloth until her skin burns. Suddenly, from below stairs, she hears a mild tinkling. Case's fingers wandering over the keys of the spinet. Hugging her breasts tight, she paces back and forth until a glimpse of herself in the pier glass brings her up short. She stares at the stranger in the mirror, the naked body covered in red welts. Ada opens a drawer, takes out a fresh chemise and undergarments, puts them on. She stands listening. The spinet has gone quiet. She waits for him to go, for the front door to slam shut, but all she hears is the rain tapping maniacally on the window. Time passes, and then underneath the ticking of the rain, she hears Wesley Case's feet on the stairs. After three or four cautious steps, he pauses, takes three or four more, and pauses again. Listening to his footfall, she feels as if a shadow of herself is accompanying him to this room where she stands scandalously exposed in her chemise and drawers. The bedroom door stands open; she means to close it, ought to close it, but only lowers her head. She hears him stop at the doorway, wait a moment to be challenged or rebuked, then he enters.

EIGHTEEN

AT FOUR O'CLOCK IN the morning, lying abed, when the first intimations of light were turning the windowpane slate blue, Case proposed to Ada. It was not only the obligation of a gentleman in such a situation, it was also his heart's desire. But Ada demurred. "No," she said, "I will do nothing in a rush. I did it once. It was not a happy decision."

"You harbour doubts about me."

Alert to the hurt in his voice, she laid her hand on his rib cage and said, "Doubts about myself. All I ask is for a little time to resolve them."

Which compelled him to say that time was of the essence. Sooner or later, they would be found out, and the town scandalized. And she replied that they inhabited a small island here, far from prying eyes. And he said, had she forgotten that their small island had another inhabitant, Joe McMullen?

"Well," she said, "that is true. But Mr. McMullen is your friend."

"A very talkative friend."

Ada gave him a nudge with her knee. "As Miss Eliot says, 'Falsehood is easy, truth is difficult.' I advise you to take the difficult path. Confide in him. I am sure he wishes no harm to come to either of us. At any rate, we live in such close proximity, a lie cannot be sustained."

So Case had walked back to the ranch at dawn, received his scolding from Joe for the worry he had caused him, and after that tirade was finished he had confessed to him how matters stood, told him how he had offered Ada his hand, and how she had refused. Until she came to her senses, her reputation must be safeguarded at all costs. And Joe had nodded gravely and said, "Well, I ain't going to squawk. Sometimes ladies need protecting even from themselves."

In the weeks that followed, Ada and the ranch occupied all Case's thoughts. Trying to parse his new life with her was mystifying, but at least the ranch was nothing but straight ahead and go. Over the winter Case had ordered the latest agricultural manuals from Chicago, and now he was eager to put the ideas they advocated into practice. He talked to Joe about "progress in livestock breeding," and "scientific innovation and advance." McMullen didn't second these queer notions, believing that all this was nothing more than another way for smart operators to hoodwink you into buying downright useless novelties. When Case spoke of importing a purebred Hereford bull from the East to improve the bloodline of his herd, Joe told him meat was only meat. When it's on the plate nobody asks who sired it.

Of all Case's pet notions, Joe opposed most strenuously his plan to fence the property with barbed wire. He had no use for what he called the Devil's rope, which he said was good for nothing but tearing up horses that blundered into it. What's more, blocking people from crossing your land was damn unfriendly and unneighbourly. Case argued that a good fence would save them the hours they spent hunting strays and allow them to rotate cattle from pasture to pasture. It was *efficient*. Joe said that efficient was Lucifer's word; he wanted no part of it.

So Case went to work digging postholes on his own. In a sulk, Joe watched him from the doorstep for a morning and then, cursing and grumbling, came to lend a hand. Case made up for McMullen's grudging help with an excess of sweaty zeal. He felt life opening up before him, felt all things were possible. Around him the first, tender grass shoots were showing, and he could scarcely believe that a short month ago he and Joe were stumbling out of bed to play midwife to a heifer struggling to give birth, reaching into a cow to turn a calf, or tying a loop around a pair of protruding ankles to drag slippery, steaming life into the dark and cold. He could see the results of those efforts all around him as he worked, calves bunting their mothers' udders and fumbling for a teat. And after they had drunk their fill, they stood straddle-legged, dazed with contentment, until some mysterious spark sent them off bucking and snorting, their mothers trotting about in a panic if they lost sight of them, long yarns of slobber dangling from their jaws while they bawled plaintively for their young to return to their sides. It all stirred his spirits, sweetened his anticipation of the end of the day, which came punctually at five o'clock – McMullen scoffed that they were keeping banker's hours – when Case returned to the ranch house, washed, shaved, brushed his teeth with salt, and set off for Ada's.

Classes ended at four o'clock, but Ada seldom left the school until five, often later. She was conscientious about preparing lessons and spent a good deal of time copying out material for the next day on the blackboard since her pupils' parents and the school board saw no need to spend hard-earned money on textbooks. If children could learn things out of a book, they reasoned, what need was there of a teacher? There were assignments to correct, tidying and sweeping up to do before she could put on her bonnet and leave the still and silent schoolhouse.

Case had said he didn't like her walking about unaccompanied.

"And what's the solution?" she had said with a laugh. "If I were to be seen hanging on your arm every day, what would that do to the schoolmarm's reputation?"

And he had almost said, *If you would agree to marry me, your reputation would be secure.* But that was a touchy subject she dismissed or avoided whenever he raised it, so what he said was, "I don't like the idea of drunks taking liberties with you."

And she had nearly answered, *What? Take liberties with a woman carrying a pocket pistol?* But that would have required an explanation of something she couldn't explain herself. Gobbler Johnson was no more. Word had reached Fort Benton months ago that he was the victim of mishap and had been found frozen to death in an isolated spot near Helena. Yet she still carried the derringer in her reticule because setting it aside would be like breaking a comforting spell. So all she had said to Case was, "Schoolmarms are immune to liberties, don't you know?"

Most days, impatient to see her, he would arrive at her house before she did, take a seat in the parlour, flip through the pages of a book, drum his fingers on the arm of the sofa, jump up and part the curtains every five minutes in hope of catching a glimpse of her. At long last, there she would be, making her way briskly up the trail with a light, elastic step. He would go to the door, hover awkwardly there until she swept into the house and went up on tiptoe to brush her lips to his. Case would smell the sun and wind in her hair, feel the heat of her lightly perspiring body, see the flush of colour glowing on her cheekbones.

Immediately they would begin to talk. She would relate the miracle of the little chap who had suddenly mastered the multiplication tables, tell of the big boys whose attention she had captured with a spirited description of Caesar's Gallic campaigns. She told him that she had learned from her failure to teach the Harding girls; now she cut the cloth to the coat, not the other way around. She strove to teach her pupils what they could grasp and what would hold their interest. Her new approach was succeeding, and Case could see how her successes thrilled and energized her. "And do you know what happened today?" she would exclaim, leaning forward, eyes shining, her hand falling on Case's knee to capture his complete attention. "One of the little Slocum girl's older sisters told her there would be no school this summer. She hadn't realized. And the tiny mite came to me, wrapped her arms around my legs, and wept in my skirts, all because she would not see Mrs. Tarr *until September.*"

And Case, in his turn, narrated his day just as fervently, perhaps even a touch frantically, because he had a suspicion that Ada's refusal to marry him was because she believed he could not be constant to anything, and that perhaps included her. He would proudly enumerate how many posts he and Joe had sunk that day, how many yards of barbed wire they had strung. He explained in great detail how, by selling twenty steers to the Army for beef, the money got from them was going to be used to buy more heifers and increase his breeding stock. He told her he was well on his way to building a considerable herd, *responsibly and frugally.* All this was to convince her of his hardheaded acumen and ambition. One evening he went further to prove his worthiness, self-importantly divulged that he was engaged in confidential business here in Fort Benton, that he was acting as adviser and agent to one Major Walsh of the North-West Mounted Police. She had greeted this news a little dryly, a little deflatingly, saying only that she had never expected to entertain a member of the diplomatic corps in her very own parlour. But when she had seen how his face fell at that remark, she had given his hand a gentle squeeze and said that if he were going to keep company with her he would have to learn when she was teasing and when she was not.

Sometimes they got so carried away with sharing their days, with wrapping up ordinary, commonplace events in gift paper for one another, that they suddenly realized twilight was drawing in and they hadn't yet eaten. Ada would duck into the kitchen and hurry back with thick slices of bread and butter, cheese and apples, and they would keep on chattering as the room grew darker and darker. They would neglect to light a lamp just as they had neglected their supper, and would reach out and touch each other in the dim parlour, as if seeking proof that this new life they spoke about wasn't an illusion, that someone else was there to share and witness it.

But as spring gathered force, Case was also aware that anxious talk was circulating in Fort Benton. He heard it when he went into town to buy supplies. Everyone said that when the Sioux ponies had fattened on the new grass and recovered their strength, the warriors would ride out again, and there would be the devil to pay. On a trip to buy fence staples, Case dropped in on Major Ilges to receive a briefing on the situation. That night, he wrote to Walsh.

May 13, 1877
Fort Benton

My dear Walsh,

Significant developments here. Just when it was widely believed that the Sioux were likely to mount attacks in Montana and Dakota, Maj. Ilges has informed me that Crazy Horse has unexpectedly surrendered. He and his followers turned themselves in at Camp Robinson, Nebraska, on May 8. The Army took into custody 889 souls and some 12,000 ponies. Ilges was exultant. He predicts this will cause widespread demoralization among the Sioux. As a spiritual leader Crazy Horse is second only to Sitting Bull and he has no equal as a warrior. The Sioux believed that he would never lay down arms and now he has.

To add insult to injury, the day after Crazy Horse capitulated, Col. Miles attacked the village of the Miniconjou chief, Lame Deer, on Muddy Creek. Both Lame Deer and his best warrior, Iron Star, were killed, the camp burned, and most of the Miniconjou scattered into the hills.

Crazy Horse's people report Sitting Bull has suffered his own debilitating misfortunes this spring. In mid-March, a sudden breakup on the Missouri had sent a wall of water and ice floes racing through his camp, demolishing many of the Sioux tipis and sweeping away stores of food, clothing, and other necessities. Despite this disaster, he appears determined to continue to resist American power.

According to the Sioux who are now coming into the agencies in greater and greater numbers, in April Sitting Bull called a war council at Beaver Creek. Present were Pretty Bear and No Neck of the Hunkpapas, Flying By and Red Thunder of the Miniconjous, Turning Bear and Spotted Eagle of the Sans Arcs. Not much is clear what the outcome of this meeting was but it is said that Spotted Eagle and Sitting Bull argued adamantly for continuing to fight the Americans. The others, it is said, were more hesitant.

With Crazy Horse's example before them, Ilges believes that further defections of the Sioux will follow. He is of the opinion that that will leave Sitting Bull only two ways to keep the Sioux nation from unravelling: he needs a military victory, no matter how small, to put heart into his people, or he will have no choice but to lead an exodus into Canada.

With Crazy Horse now out of the picture, any likelihood of a Sioux triumph seems to be very slight. Ilges says it is reported that the surrendering Indians are in a dreadful state of privation due to Col. Miles's dogged prosecution of a winter campaign. His policy may have led to no significant or decisive battlefield triumphs, but by keeping on the Indians like a dog on a biscuit, he has made it impossible for them to provide food for their women and children, and by keeping them constantly on the move for fear of attack, has driven them into a state of starvation and exhaustion. Of all American officers, Miles is the most feared and hated by the Sioux. They have named him Bear Coat because of his favoured winter dress and for his ferocity.

According to Ilges, Col. Miles is no better liked by his fellow officers than he is by the Sioux. He has a reputation as a glory hound and is considered too ambitious by half. Like Custer, he was one of the "boy generals" of the Civil War, but a smaller peacetime army reduced his rank to that of a lowly colonel. He wants the star back on his epaulettes and knows nothing will get it sooner than defeating Custer's conqueror, Sitting Bull. But there is a fly in the ointment. If Bull escapes to Canada, that would put paid to this scheme.

Which brings me to an interesting rumour that Ilges related to me – gossip perhaps but if it is true, gossip of some import. He has heard from a number of officers passing through Benton that Miles has been actively lobbying his superiors for permission <u>to pursue Sitting Bull across the border</u> if he enters Canada, and attack him on our soil. It is held in some quarters that Miles has received a sympathetic hearing in the highest military echelons for this gross violation of international law. The Chicago papers that reach here by riverboat report that Gen. Sherman has already said publicly that he would regard any raid launched from Canadian territory by the Sioux to be an act of war perpetrated by Canada itself and justification enough for an incursion into our territory.

The dangers inherent in Miles's and Sherman's cavalier attitude to our national sovereignty are evident. It would be prudent for you to immediately inform Secretary of State Scott of Miles's propensity for recklessness so that the minister can move this matter into proper governmental channels and provide you with instructions as to what you are to do if Miles sallies over the border. <u>I advise you to request clear and unambiguous orders from Scott as to how you are to meet this eventuality; they are your only protection.</u>

Increasingly, I find it distasteful to counsel you to remain detached in the face of the misery of the Sioux. So let me say that, despite urging you to keep secret your distribution of ammunition to the Sioux, I personally applaud what you did. The action may have been impolitic, but it was generous. And I confess to you that I would prefer to see the remainder of the Sioux reach Canada than be obliterated by Miles, even though it is scarcely in our interests that they do so. One man's ambition to win a star hardly justifies the destruction of a people.

Having said that, I do not wish to be misunderstood. Sitting Bull is an enigma to the Americans; they cannot fathom his obstinacy. But if he arrives on your side of the line you will have to solve the puzzle. So far, he has given evidence of being as astute and formidable a leader as any American or Canadian politician. Like them, I have no doubt he will not hesitate to advance his interests by any means at his disposal. I urge you to deal with him as warily as you deal with Scott.

Yours truly,
Wesley Case

May 22, 1877
Fort Walsh

My dear Case,

You have got your wish. The long-expected visitor arrived before your last letter did.

First week of this month, I began to receive reports of a large body of Sioux approaching Canada from the Milk River country. So as to be on hand to greet them, left Fort Walsh with half-breeds Louis Léveillé and Gabe Solomon, three constables, and Sgt. McCutcheon. Rode hard until we reached the lower White Mud. Found evidence there of a recent Indian camp – a godawful big one – many tipi rings, fire pits, and dung dropped by a mighty horse herd. Discovered a burial scaffold nearby. Léveillé took a peek at the corpse and confirmed he was Sioux by beadwork on his clothing. Had died of bullet wounds, most likely the work of Bear Coat's boys.

Followed the Indians' trail the rest of the day. Next morning came under surveillance by Sioux lookouts on hilltops near Pinto Horse Butte. I ordered the men to proceed cucumber-cool, which produced general amazement when we entered their village. Had the boys dismount at the edge of the camp and bivouac. Wanted to leave the impression that riding unannounced into a large gathering of hostile Indians was an everyday occurrence for us – of no more consequence than our morning shave and shit. This created the impression I hoped for. The Sioux gathered in great numbers to gawk at us. Spotted Eagle, war chief of the Sans Arcs, passed the comment that he would never have believed that a handful of white men would dare to enter the encampment of Tatanka Yotanka in such a way. Hearing the name Sitting Bull, I took pains not to look any more surprised than as if I had been told John Smith was sitting in the lounge bar of the North American Hotel back in Prescott. Simply said if Tatanka Yotanka were available I wouldn't mind saying how d'you do.

Spotted Eagle returned, four individuals in tow. None of which looked as if he could be the Grand Panjandrum himself. One was as down-at-heels as the other. Then, instanter, a stocky fellow with a pronounced limp broke ranks, went directly for Sgt. McCutcheon, grabbed him by the hand, and commenced to give it a good shaking. The Sergeant looked as astonished as if a thousand of brick had fallen on his head. Bull had mistaken McCutcheon's sergeant's chevrons as indication he was the chief of the Old Woman's pony soldiers.

Spotted Eagle stepped in, sorted things out, and presented me to Bull, a man of about forty-five, sturdily built, and with a powerful hooked nose that looks like it could chop chain, but so shabbily dressed he resembled a doss-house inhabitant. After the flood on the Missouri impoverished his people, Bull apparently emptied his pockets for them. Among these Indians, it is charity that distinguishes a true leader, while our politicians begin to sharpen their shears to fleece their flock even before they get elected.

Met the new arrivals for a confab. Assure Ilges that I spoke to Bull and his people as I did with the Sioux who had come over previously. In effect, told them they were playing a new game of canasta and laid down the rules. Nobody, including Bull, objected to keeping the peace with the Yankees. But there was plenty talk of Bear Coat, who they said was hot on their trail. They all expressed fear the Long Knives would fall on them even in the Old Woman's country. To ease their worry, told them Miles's pony soldiers could not enter the Old Woman's land without her permission. Said that if Bear Coat tried to attack them, the Police would stand between him and the Sioux.

This promise to protect them from Miles <u>was given before</u> your letter of May 13 arrived warning me to do nothing concerning Miles without Scott's blessing, but I hasten to say I would give these Indians the same promise again. They are now my wards and I won't have strangers spanking them in my own parlour.

They are in a terrible state. Their lodges, patched together out of old hides, provide little shelter from the wind and rain. Children are saucer-eyed with hunger, old people are hungry, <u>everybody</u> is hungry. Now, it's as plain as day that the penny-pinchers in Parliament will never vote an outlay of money to supply these Indians with rations. They will have to hunt to feed themselves. Without ammunition they are condemned to starve. This is iron logic. Therefore, I have given leave to trader Légaré to trade them bullets, shot, and powder. Glad to hear you approve of my former actions in this regard, but I think it is also good <u>politics</u> vis-à-vis the Sioux. Black Moon and Four Horns got ammunition so how can I deny Sitting Bull the same? That would destroy any confidence they have in me as a square dealer. I'm not running for

Congress, I'm charged with keeping the peace <u>here</u>. If Sitting Bull is to be controlled, I must win his trust <u>and</u> his respect. That's not going to happen if he sees me dancing to "Yankee Doodle Dandy" every time they strike up that tune to the south. He's got to learn who is bandmaster in these parts. I believe I gave him proof of that the morning we departed his camp.

Just as we were saying our goodbyes, three South Assiniboines rode into the Sioux village driving five horses before them. One was White Dog from the Missouri country near Fort Buford, the war chief who Sitting Bull tried to make an alliance with before the Battle of Little Bighorn. White Dog must have been flattered by the Sioux grandee importuning him for his support, maybe thought Bull would do anything to win his friendship, which is why he didn't hesitate to flaunt stolen property under my very eyes. Was counting on Bull protecting him.

Right off, Léveillé recognized that the horses White Dog and his cronies had in their possession belonged to Father de Corby. He also overheard the Assiniboines boasting to the Sioux warriors that they had helped themselves to these fine buffalo runners on their way north. When Léveillé informed me of this, I sent Solomon, McCutcheon, and two constables to straightaway arrest the braggart. Immediately, he kicked up a fuss, appealed to the Sioux to help him. Were they going to let red coats take their friend? The Sioux appeared to be giving consideration to White Dog's pleas, so I laid hold of a set of leg irons and headed for him, trusty old Léveillé at my side. Shook those shackles in the horse thief's face and told him he'd better tell me where he'd got those horses from or I'd snap the ankle bracelets on him and haul his arse to the guardhouse in Fort Walsh. By now the Sioux seemed more interested in seeing how the game would play out than taking the Assiniboine's part. Sensing a change in the wind, White Dog lost his nerve and started to make excuses; he had found the horses loose on the prairie; he didn't know they belonged to a Black Robe. Bastard was clearly lying but when he volunteered to hand over the horses, I thought that was sufficient to make my point with the Sioux that I wasn't a man that topples over in a breeze.

But as I turned to go, White Dog passed a remark under his breath. I asked Léveillé what he had said and was told that the war chief had muttered he would "meet me again." I went hot, stuck my face in his, tore through him stem to stern. Informed him if he didn't withdraw his goddamn threat, I'd clap him in irons and give him a taste of convict's gruel. The worm turned then, claimed he hadn't uttered a menace, hadn't been heard right. Having made him eat his words, I decided to let the matter drop, since not one of the Sioux made a peep of protest. Confiscated the priest's horses and rode off at a leisurely pace to show we had no anxieties about retribution.

You might pass on to Ilges how I handled White Dog and emphasize that Sitting Bull has seen what he can expect from me if he kicks up a ruckus. Tell him I have my new wards well in hand. But enough said. I have not written so much since the days my old schoolmaster gave me lines to write because I laughed off his canings.

Yours truly,

Maj. James Morrow Walsh

P.S. Will keep in mind your warnings about Bull, but so far he doesn't strike me as bearing any resemblance to any hustings-huckster I ever laid eyes on.

Walsh's dispatch gave Case plenty to mull over. The Major had a habit of relying on snap judgments, and Sitting Bull had clearly made a favourable impression on him. The question was whether Walsh had arrived at a correct reading of the man. For Case, Sitting Bull was a fascinating puzzle, one that he and Ilges had often attempted to piece together from the scanty evidence available to them: the sketchy history of the chief's past relations with the whites, newspaper articles, the attitude to him expressed by members of other tribes, the observations made by the Sioux who had lately begun to turn themselves into reservation agents.

The journalists universally castigated Sitting Bull for his arrogance and reviled him as the mastermind behind the American defeat at Little Bighorn, a war chief deranged by blood lust, the man responsible for the slaughter of Custer's brave boys. The Sioux lately come into American custody presented a different picture, maintaining that on the day of the Little Bighorn, Sitting Bull had not joined the battle, but had remained in the camp to help protect the women and children. For them, what made Sitting Bull a great and revered man were the blessings the One Above had bestowed on him, great and powerful visions. He was foremost a holy man.

Ilges was inclined to attribute the extraordinary influence Sitting Bull exerted on his people to the gullibility of Indians all too willing to swallow medicine man hocus-pocus and mumbo-jumbo. Case didn't think this explained everything. In his days as a policeman he had visited enough Indian camps to see that the kind of consensus Sitting Bull appeared to have forged among his people was seldom achieved. In his experience, chiefs had little power or authority to order anyone to do anything. If they were respected, judged to be wise and upright men, then they were followed and deferred to. That Sitting Bull's people had been willing to endure so many hardships, to continue to resist the Americans for so long, and had now swallowed the ignominy of exile surely testified to a man endowed with a powerful personality.

But Case had a distrust of powerful personalities, which in his experience had a tendency to swell into alarming megalomania. What most stirred the rage of American editorialists against the chief was his serene refusal to concede that whites had any rightful claim to Sioux territory. Sitting Bull had presented them with a fact they could not refute, and it choked them with fury. But it appeared to Case that the chief, in his turn, was incapable of admitting another fact: that the struggle he had embarked on could not be won. The Little Bighorn was a pyrrhic victory that the Americans would revenge. As admirable as the chief's stubbornness was, however intelligent and clever he might be, God was always on the side of the big battalions. For the time being, Sitting Bull had escaped those battalions by crossing over into Canada. How long it would be before he resumed the fight against the white man it was impossible to say. If he yielded to that temptation, he would certainly heap more suffering and misfortune on the Sioux. And he would collide with Walsh; the consequences of that could be nothing but dire.

June arrives and Ada has still not changed her mind about matrimony, even though she speaks frequently and fondly of family life, of her beloved mother, father, and brother. The happy domestic scenes she paints move Case to dream of emulating her parents, of building just such a life, of having children and raising them on just such a pattern as she describes, in a home as harmonious and simple as his had been fraught with upset and complication.

Whenever Case begins to stalk the question of why she will not have him, Ada divines where he is heading and cuts him short. Not in a fashion that could be called abrupt or unkindly, but often with a wistful pleading smile as she says, "We must know each other's minds. We must see each other clearly."

Ada is happy; he knows she is happy. But she won't admit her happiness, or trust he has something to do with it. One night he thinks, What she wants me to do is explain my wasted years, to admit them, to assure her I will never abandon her as I abandoned so many things before.

So he does, confessing the aimless dilettantism, describing how he now realizes that his exile in the Police was both self-punishment and a flight from responsibility, details every sin except one. And excluding it from his confession is no better than a lie. Falsehood is easy, truth is difficult, according to Miss Eliot. In this instance, one is as hard as the other. He cannot bring himself to speak of Pudge, but keeping silent about him makes him feel again the pressure of his old friend's thumb, how it had squeezed him, left him feeling small, contemptible, humiliated.

Sitting in Ada's parlour, waiting for her to come home, Case will catch a whiff of the leather-bound books in her library and suddenly he is back in old Sutherland's study for a meeting of the university's Literary Society. One of six or seven young men sitting at Professor Sutherland's feet to listen to him expatiate on Truth and Beauty, to eat his cakes and to drink his tea, to hear him emotionally declaim Great Verse in a voice corroded by time. And when Sutherland was done, the young men would timidly read each other their poems, and while they did, Pudge would sigh, roll his eyes, and whisper asides to Case and only Case, his way of indicating they were the only two who were aware that they were in a stable of donkeys presided over by a senile, braying ass.

That is, until the afternoon that Sutherland called upon Case to read one of his own poems. In a trembling voice, a teacup and saucer balanced precariously on a shaking knee, he had read a sonnet. When he had finished, he glanced over at Pudge, seeking some sign of approbation, but Pudge was ostentatiously feigning sleep in one of Sutherland's tatty armchairs. Of course, later his friend had apologized with elaborate insincerity. "Orpheus himself, celebrated for his power to move inanimate things with the power of his sweet songs, could not have roused me from the coma that Perkins' ditty had induced. No reflection on you, Wesley. But give me your sonnet so I can savour it at leisure."

Even though he knew what was coming, it had been impossible to prevent Pudge prying the poem from his hands. It was returned by mail, punctuation and two misspellings corrected. At the bottom, Pudge had written, "Your rhymes tinkle like the dinner bell. And what a feast! So much meat! So well roasted!"

He was barely eighteen. Rereading his poem had left him feeling physically ill. This was the moment Pudge had made him his captive by rubbing his nose in his naïveté. Shortly afterwards, Sutherland remarked that the ancient Greeks had believed that human beings had been sundered in two by the gods, and all of life was a search for one's missing half, a yearning to merge with it. Pudge had sneered, "And what a merging it is, the monstrous Two-Backed Beast. And the outcome of all that grunting and snorting? As Augustine observed, we are born between excrement and urine."

And he had not dared to object to what Pudge said, only produced a cowardly, shamefaced snigger. *Poor Wesley clutching at straws. Clutching at Truth and Beauty, feeling them slip between his fingers.*

Harding was so well satisfied with the way Dunne had settled the business with Gobbler Johnson that he immediately proposed another job for him. In order to extract the gold from the supposedly played-out claims he had bought from panhandlers like Gobbler Johnson, Harding required experienced hardrock miners. The year before, he had begun to recruit "cousin Jacks," Cornishmen who had worked the tin mines of their native land. But the foreigners had proved to be stubborn complainers. They accused him of not supplying enough timber to shore up levels, and continually griped about dangerous work conditions. Now they were attempting to organize a labour union. Harding wanted Dunne to ferret out whoever was behind this disloyalty so they could be dealt with and the work run smoothly.

At first, Dunne had hesitated to accept this new assignment because he yearned to be united to Mrs. Tarr. However, he understood how too hasty a marriage could set tongues wagging since everybody knew how much time he and Mrs. Tarr had spent in each other's company while she was a married woman. It was difficult for him to calculate exactly how long to wait before he escorted her down the aisle, but a wedding two months after her husband's death did not strike him as being a respectful, decent interval. And making another substantial sum of money was not to be dismissed out of hand. It would demonstrate to Mrs. Tarr what a good provider Michael Dunne was.

So he went to work straightening matters out for Mr. Harding. But things did not go easily. The Cornishmen were a secretive and clannish bunch. They preferred to speak Cornish, a language every bit as baffling as the tongue of the heathen Chinee, which made it difficult to pick up anything by eavesdropping on them. They were difficult to befriend, or even strike up a simple conversation with; they seemed to want nothing to do with anyone but their own kind. And what a strange kind they were. Of this Dunne became convinced over the weeks he spent studying them as best he could, from a distance. On Sundays, the cousin Jacks raced their whippets and greyhounds – every man seemed to own a pair – and Dunne was there watching. When the races finished, the Cornishmen formed into choirs, stood in the very fields where they had run their dogs, and sang. Grown men mad for singing and cheering dogs. Dunne found these inexplicable enthusiasms, but they were evidence of passion, and passion was the weak underbelly, the soft spot that might yield to him.

One miner with a great mane of salt-and-pepper hair always won the Sunday races. He was known to feed his dogs more meat than he ate himself and he petted and fondled them more than most men did their children. He was the one Dunne turned to first to get the names Harding wanted. But the dog lover refused to give them up, even after he found his favourite bitch dead in her kennel of the strychnine sickness.

It was necessary to look elsewhere. When the miners finished their shifts, Dunne would see them as they walked home swinging their lamps, their voices raised in song. He paid particular attention to one young cousin Jack who often caused the rest to fall into a reverential silence so they could listen to him and him alone. The boy's face lit up whenever that happened. He was a runty, scrawny nobody who it was clear had nothing about him that anyone could ever possibly admire except his way with a tune.

Once Dunne had stuffed a kerosene-soaked rag in the lad's gob and told him if he didn't start singing the tune he wanted to hear, he'd fry the tongue right out of his head, burn his voice box to cinders, the boy gave him the names of the ringleaders. In a matter of days, Harding had fired them.

The problem was that the troublemakers didn't pack up their tools and look for work elsewhere; they stayed in Helena and kept agitating among the workers. Further steps needed to be taken. Harding ordered Dunne to do whatever was needed to rid him of these pests. Toughs were hired and Dunne led them on midnight visits to the recalcitrants' homes. Furniture and bones were broken, threats of worse to come were made. But the leaders of the cousin Jacks were a stubborn lot; they hung on grimly. Then gradually, one by one, they saw the wisdom of departing Helena. Still, it was almost six months after Randolph Tarr's demise that the last of them cleared out. With his work finished, Dunne decided enough time had passed to render a proposal to Mrs. Tarr seemly.

He had been anticipating this for a long time and had already taken steps to present himself in a fashion that Mrs. Tarr would find pleasing. Back in the days when he was her bodyguard, she had once teased him about his closely cropped hair, saying it looked like "a farmer had put a torch to the stubble." Dunne knew a hint when he heard one, and had grown his hair. He had also cultivated a moustache, believing it would lend him a dignified, substantial air entirely in keeping with a man soon destined to be head of a household.

He had often wondered what people meant when they said absence makes the heart grow fonder. Now he knew. With every passing week, his heart had grown fonder and fonder until some days he feared it might burst with fondness.

He imagined Mrs. Tarr pining for him as he pined for her.

In late June, Dunne returns to Fort Benton to reclaim his room above the Stubhorn, which he had paid Dink Dooley to hold for him. The quarters are hot as an oven, stuffy, and buzzing with flies. The dust lies thick and undisturbed. All this is evidence that nobody has been snooping.

Dunne had decided not to give Mrs. Tarr any warning of his return. He wants to be a romantic surprise. But it's she who surprises him. On his first tour of the town, he happens to see her outside the schoolhouse, whipping a handbell up and down, summoning a mob of scampering, squealing young pups into the school. Ducking into a shop, Dunne stands at the window and intently watches the scene. To see her bestowing sweet smiles on the children as they bustle past her into the school awakens a lurch of jealousy in him. He wonders how she could have suffered such a reverse, been condemned to minding the town's dirty little brats? But what he sees also pleases him. The thought of rescuing Mrs. Tarr from her awful situation causes him to experience a great upsurge of pride and purpose.

Still, there are things to be seen to before he takes the final step. He wants this to be an occasion Mrs. Tarr will never forget. He searches for the right words to tender his offer of marriage, scribbles away in his sweltering room, desperately scratching out phrases and adding others, fine-tuning his sentences until he is satisfied.

Next comes a new suit of clothes, something fashionable and festive, suitable for courting. The clerk presses what he says is "the latest English outfit" on him, a blue coat, white vest, lavender pantaloons, and lavender gloves, a style commended by *Harper's* to its gentlemen readers in 1868 but which has been languishing on the shelves for nearly a decade. He entices his customer to buy other gentleman's furnishings, cambric handkerchiefs, a linen shirt, and a ribbon-thin bowtie to complete his ensemble.

After that, Dunne pays a visit to Foster's Tonsorial Palace, has a thorough soak in a copper tub, a shave, and has the crop of unruly hair he has grown for Mrs. Tarr cut and styled. The black barber, Foster, carefully draws a part down the middle of his skull, creates two lavish wings of hair above his ears, and freezes them in place with pomade. Sprinkled with bay rum, newly trimmed and newly suited, his moustache oiled, Dunne pays a visit to Wetzel's mercantile and buys a tin of fancy biscuits with yellow roses painted on its lid. Tucking that under his arm, he sets off just before three o'clock for Mrs. Tarr's house; he wants to be waiting there for her when she arrives home from school.

As he trudges along, he addresses the sage and dusty tussocks of grass that border the trail, reciting the proposal he has committed to memory. "My dear Mrs. Tarr, I figure that you know the high regard in which I hold you, and I live in the dear hope you return my heartfelt sentiments, although I know I do not deserve such a blessing, you stand so high and I so low that I ain't worthy to touch the hem of your skirt. But let me say this, Mrs. Tarr, it may surprise you to hear it, but I am a man of property. Pardon for bragging on myself, but I have savings of seventy-five hundred dollars, and if you doubt it, I can show you the hard cash. Also, my health is sound. I vow there are plenty more good years in me, and I promise to use them years to work like a Trojan so as to keep you in comfort and style and see you don't want for nothing. So here it is, I have come today to ask you to do me the honour of becoming my wife. Please be so good as to smile on my request, won't you, dear lady?"

Dunne enters Mrs. Tarr's yard. He pauses under the searing sun and sweeps the property with an avid look. The chair he sat on for so many happy hours is on the porch waiting for him, near the window through which he so often peeked to catch a glimpse of Mrs. Tarr doing dainty, feminine things: reading books, drinking tea, looking pensive. He remembers the blissful sound of Mrs. Tarr's skirts rustling as she brings a tray out to him. He can taste it already, the glasses of lemonade, the cake he will eat in the days to come, all proffered with the most doting of smiles. Climbing the steps of the porch, claiming the familiar chair, he takes from his pocket the cambric handkerchief the clerk had prevailed upon him to buy and carefully wipes the dust from his shoes. He already feels as if he's the proprietor of all he surveys; it's a very pleasant, settled, domestic feeling.

He looks down at the tin on his lap. Are fancy biscuits a mistake? Or should he have brought flowers? There are lovely flowers painted on the lid of the biscuit box, but can mere paint convey warm thoughts and feelings? Dunne begins to pace the porch, swinging round and mechanically retracing his steps, until, beginning to sweat, he comes to a halt at the corner of the house where a bit of breeze can be felt. Standing there, leaning on the railing, his eyes wander out over the prairie. He spots Case coming down the path that passes Mrs. Tarr's house, headed for town.

The last thing in the world Dunne wants is for Case to see him on Mrs. Tarr's doorstep, looking so dapper, bearing a tin of fancy biscuits. He can think of only one hiding place, the privy. But it is around the back of the house, the side from which Case is approaching. It's a question of timing. When Case disappears behind a swell of rolling prairie, he must secrete himself in the outhouse.

Dunne waits; the moment comes when Case sinks from sight, and he breaks for the privy, scoots inside. A blade of sunlight streams through a knothole. Dunne screws his eye to the knothole as if it were a telescope. Case is drawing nearer, ambling along, hands stuffed in his pockets, another bastard born with a silver spoon stuck in his mouth. Look at him; so very pleased with himself, a man who had the good luck to pop out of the right cunt, otherwise he'd already be dead of hunger. He thinks he's a *gentleman*. But Dunne knows there's more gentleman in the arse of a pig than there is in Wesley Case. He knows things that should make the fellow weep with shame. He has the goods on him.

Then, unexpectedly, Case veers off the path and heads towards the privy. Has he been caught short by a call of nature? Case is almost there, so close that he could spit on him through the knothole, but then he passes by the outhouse, goes to the back door, doesn't knock, actually lets himself in with a key.

Dunne's breath locks in his chest. What's Case doing sashaying into the Tarr house, acting like he's the bloody lord of the manor? Dunne slumps down on the outhouse seat. He prides himself on solving puzzles. He examines this one from every angle, but every angle points him in the same direction, to the same conclusion. His eyes flit desperately about the dim interior of the privy and he sees, high above him, draped in a corner, a cloudy spider's web, a papery moth entangled in its strands.

Dunne bolts. He makes a stiff-legged dash through the yard and out onto the prairie. He has no destination in mind – all he wants is to get away from what he has just witnessed. Churning up a rise, shoulders heaving, then a sudden awkward plunge down the slope, gathering speed, a rolling boulder. The biscuit tin pressed to his chest in both hands, like a shield for his heart. Buckbrush, the thorns of buffalo berry bushes claw at his pant legs and snatch at his coat sleeves; the face of the sky twitches in his eyes. He runs on, weaving erratically.

A juniper root catches his toe and pitches him headlong to the ground, the biscuit tin punching his sternum. Dunne lies there, face down, panting, glaring at the dirt. When he finally sits up, he notices a rip in the knee of his trousers, a raw scrape slowly oozing blood, grains of soil embedded in his skin, peppering his flesh. Slowly Dunne pulls his knee up to his face and, like a cat, begins to lick the wound. A dry sob racks him. His beautiful new trousers are ruined. Everything is ruined. He is ruined.

NINETEEN

My dear Maj. Walsh,

I am sure that rumours of the present troubles with the Nez Perce have reached you. What appeared to be a situation of little consequence suddenly took an ominous turn. Yesterday I conferred with Maj. Ilges, who told me that the latest reports suggest that the tribe will soon arrive in Montana and that their ultimate destination is Canada. Maj. Ilges has kept in contact with all forts and military posts that have access to telegraph service so as to keep abreast of the Indians' progress eastwards, but reliable information is sketchy – although every indication is that they are moving quickly.

Ilges is extremely worried because the number of soldiers here at Fort Benton was recently reduced and he fears that he will not be able to offer protection to civilians outside the town if the Nez Perce appear in the vicinity. He vehemently denounces Gen. Howard for provoking a peaceable people into war. The Major calls the Nez Perce the palest Indians God ever fashioned out of red clay and lauds them for having taken up the raising of cattle and horses with great success, for accepting missionaries in their midst, and converting to Christianity in considerable numbers. Before now, they have always had excellent relations with whites. Ilges credits them with showing exemplary restraint when ordered to surrender their beloved Wallowa Valley to settlers and accept land on the Lapwai Reservation. The outbreak was precipitated, in his view, solely because Howard refused to permit the tribe enough time to round up their vast herds of cattle and horses so they could make a safe crossing of the Snake River, which was running very high as the deadline approached to evacuate their homeland. It appears that they reached their breaking point when settlers began to rustle the cattle the Indians had rounded up. Apparently even "praying Indians" are not immune to suffering depredation at the hands of their white Christian neighbours. The outraged young men retaliated for these thefts by killing several white men. After that, there was no stopping this whole sorry business. Panic swept Oregon and the Nez Perce fled under the leadership of Chief Joseph.

They are now believed to be on what they call the "buffalo road" that leads to their traditional summer hunting grounds in Montana. Chief Joseph has already fought several engagements with U.S. troops. Ilges has learned by wire that on or about June 17, the Indians drew Howard's forces into an ambush at White Bird Canyon, turned their flank, killed a third of his soldiers, and drove the rest into retreat. On the 27th, Howard, heavily reinforced, attempted to attack them again, but Chief Joseph and his people slipped through his fingers and made for Clearwater, where they hooked up with Chief Looking Glass's band. No one can be sure, but estimates suggest their combined force is something near 250 warriors, 450 women and children. It is said they have 2,000 of their renowned Appaloosa horses with them, which allows them to spell their mounts when they tire and keep distance from Howard's troops. All indications are that they are presently on the Lolo Trail, passing over the Bitterroot Mountains.

Ilges told me that his superiors are expressing anxiety over a wave of anger and disaffection that is sweeping through all the Plains tribes. It is said that Crazy Horse already regrets laying down his arms and is urging his people to leave their reservation and flee for Canada. There are signs of discontent among the Northern Cheyenne who were solemnly promised a reservation in their old lands, but are now told they will be transported to an Indian agency deep in the South. They, too, are said to be contemplating following Chief Joseph's example and making a run for British territory. What is even more disturbing, in Ilges's opinion, is that the Crow are said to be considering doing the same. The Major is greatly surprised that these faithful allies of the Americans in their Indian wars, who provided the Army with many scouts and fought alongside them in battle, are now talking openly of crossing the Medicine Line to the north. He remarked to me pessimistically that if the Americans cannot keep old friends like the Crow and Nez Perce from taking flight, what hope is there of restraining the rest of the tribes?

Which brings me to a delicate matter. There are rumours about here in Montana that Sitting Bull is making overtures to the Blackfoot in Canadian territory, holding out to them the prospect of a grand Indian alliance with the purpose of driving whites out of the West. What have you heard on that front? Ilges is most anxious for any light that you can shed on this matter.

Of course I do not know Sitting Bull as you do, but it seems to me that in the coming days he is likely to play a large role in whatever unfolds. The growing restiveness and disgruntlement among the Indians could lead them to set aside their traditional enmities in favour of forging a common front against the Americans. Bull, as you are well aware, would be the natural leader of such a league. His victory over Custer gives him enormous prestige; his staunch refusal to surrender makes him a potent symbol of Indian resistance. I believe it is his example that has turned the eyes of the Nez Perce, the Northern Cheyenne, the Crow, and the Sioux still remaining below the border, to the north.

Ilges says that all the Sioux on the agencies questioned by the Army testify that in the years before the Little Bighorn it was Sitting Bull who was responsible for strengthening the bonds between the bands and urging them to act as one people, not as Sans Arcs, Miniconjous, Hunkpapas, etc. The Northern Cheyenne were present in the Sioux camp when Custer attacked and helped overwhelm him. And as you yourself have testified to me, Bull tried to draw the Assiniboine into his war against the Americans. In my opinion, this points to a man of considerable diplomatic and <u>political</u> abilities. I have had experience of such men, having watched them at close hand conferring in my father's study. Whatever the wind, they make do with what it gives them. Sitting Bull is now becalmed, which makes him amenable to your wishes. But as Ilges said to me, it is beginning to appear that Sitting Bull is an Indian first and a Sioux second. If it is true he is courting his traditional enemies the Blackfoot, he has his reasons, and they need close examination. He may have felt the breeze freshening and is preparing to take advantage of it when it blows full force. Thousands upon thousands of indigent refugee Indians arriving in Canada with a grievance, against not only Americans but all white men, points to an approaching storm that may be very difficult to weather.

Yours sincerely,
Wesley Case

My dear Case,

Thank your for your communication of the 14th. Read with amusement your and Ilges's speculations about Bull's hand in creating a grand Indian alliance. True, Sitting Bull parleyed with Crowfoot of the Blackfoot this year, but his aim was to secure peace between the two tribes, an initiative I heartily encouraged. In fact, he has named one of his new twins Crow Foot to express admiration for his Blackfoot counterpart. I see nothing in any of this to suggest Bull was up to skulduggery or conspiracy. As you say, you see him from a distance but I think you need a better set of binoculars. Have talked at length with him, close up, and can read him a damn sight better than you can from where you sit. Break bread with a fellow before you judge him, that's what I advise. He gave me his word that he would not molest the Americans and so far he has kept it. That's good enough for me until I see evidence to the contrary.

If there is anybody to worry about stirring up a ruckus, it's that bastard half-breed Louis Riel. There are indications that he's been slipping over the border to sow sedition among the Wood Mountain half-breeds, claiming that the white man has stolen their country, etc. Apparently, he's been talking the same balderdash on the American side, telling both Indians and half-breeds that they have had their lands stolen and the time has come to clear all the whites out of the West from the Missouri up to the Saskatchewan. Needless to say, he proposes himself as high potentate of this imaginary Red Kingdom in the clouds. If I lay hands on him this side of the line, he'll cool his heels in the guardhouse and have plenty of time to dream his damn airy dreams. His five-year term of exile from Canada hasn't expired yet, so that cheap

Napoleon had better not put one of his grubby toes over the line anywhere in my neighbourhood.

So the next time you see Ilges do me a favour. Tell him on my behalf that he ought to send some soldiers to track that son of a bitch Riel down wherever he is in Montana and throw a scare into the gutless wonder. And tell him something else for me – if it's my responsibility to keep Sitting Bull on the straight and narrow then it's up to the Yanks to do the same with Riel. Tit for tat.

Yours sincerely,
James Morrow Walsh

No one had ever given Michael Dunne such a blow as Case had. His first impulse was revenge, to spit on his fingers, snuff Wesley Case out like a candle. But then, gradually, it came to him that the dirty cad might be made to pay for his crime twice.

Dunne began questioning Dink Dooley as to whether he knew anything about the whereabouts of General O'Neill's immigration agent, Patrick Collins. Fortunately, Collins had left an address with Dooley so that any of those he had attempted to recruit in Fort Benton could get in touch with him.

That address was all Dunne needed. Early one evening, two weeks later, he boosted himself out of an armchair in the lobby of the Franklin Hotel in Omaha, Nebraska, and buttonholed Collins as he was heading out for supper.

None too pleased at being accosted by a stranger when his mind was on his stomach, Collins waited impatiently while Dunne ponderously introduced himself, then he rudely said, "Well, what is it you want?"

"I want a meeting with General O'Neill."

"If it's information about our settlement you require, I'm in charge of that. I can see you three o'clock tomorrow." Collins waited for Dunne to confirm the appointment. "No? Well, then, I'll take my leave of you."

As Collins made a move to exit the hotel, Dunne called out, "The General needs money. I can get him bags of it. Money enough for a mountain howitzer if that's what he wants."

Collins swung back to him. "Shut your bloody mouth. Mad talk like that – in public – what do you think you're playing at?"

Dunne was unfazed by the rebuke, but he lowered his voice. "A mountain howitzer and enough stands of arms to supply a regiment. The General interested in that?"

"That's a very large claim, my friend. The General is beset with fantasists."

"I don't speak of what I can't deliver." Dunne put his hand in his pocket and drew out his memberships in the Hibernian Benevolent Society of Canada and the Toronto circle of the Fenian Brotherhood. He handed them to Collins, who glanced at the cards and gave a dismissive shrug before returning them.

"Congratulations. You paid dues. You are a sympathizer."

"More'n a sympathizer. A *soldier*. Soldier of the Irish Republic. Ask Joe Finnerty of Boston."

Collins smiled condescendingly. "Why would I waste a stamp?"

"Because I took care of the famous Peaches Malloy for Finnerty. Peaches, who sold himself to the British. Who was passing information to the enemy."

One of the hotel's employees had come to light the crystal candelabra under which they were standing. Collins took Dunne by the arm and directed him to a quiet corner of the lobby. "I heard about that," said Collins. "Somebody cut him another mouth." He laid the side of his hand to his throat as if it were a knife blade. "Here."

"Don't try to spring no traps on me," said Dunne, reaching up and putting a finger to the nape of his own neck. "It was a ice pick here."

Collins nodded slowly. "So you served under Finnerty in Boston."

"For a time. When Peaches joined the angels, I had to wave goodbye to Boston. After that, New York, Buffalo, Detroit. Wherever I was needed."

Collins took a notebook and pencil from his pocket. "Give me the names of your commanders in each of those centres." He noted them down as Dunne ran through the list. When he concluded, Collins said in a business-like way, "If you are the old hand you claim to be, then you know you must be vouched for before I can grant you an interview with the General. Luckily for you, Mr. Dunne, you have an appearance not easily forgotten. A description of your person should suffice to identify you. Now, where can I reach you if it is proved you are who you say you are?"

"Mrs. Henderson's Boarding House down in the Market."

"This money you promise – where is it coming from?"

"That's for the General's ears."

"I am the General's ears – as well as his eyes."

"Beg pardon for saying it, but I don't know that. The General broke with the Fenian leadership but it could be the old bosses encouraged a tattler to remain behind to keep an eye on him. Maybe you hew to the new line, believe freedom is better got with politics than the barrel of a gun. Me, I follow anybody who wants to spill English blood. That means General O'Neill."

"I fear I am in the presence of a dragon," said Collins.

"I got sufficient fire in my belly, if that's what you mean."

Collins pursed his lips thoughtfully. "We shall see, Mr. Dunne. We shall see."

Dunne remained caged up in Mrs. Henderson's boarding house awaiting a call from the colonization agent. He kept to his room, except when meals were served. On the seventh day of his wait, a hot wind began to blow out of the west. A madman playing patty cake, it wildly thumped the walls of the boarding house, shrieked and moaned, caused Dunne's window to shudder in its frame. Looking out of his second-storey room, he watched the sky turn nicotine brown above the roofs of Omaha, the sun turn smoky orange behind a screen of flying dust. The wind whipped the Missouri until chop bristled on its back like an old dog's white hackles.

The daylong, incessant howling fretted all the roomers' nerves raw, had them all on edge by the time they sat down to supper that night. Mrs. Henderson was particularly nervous and gloomy since several boarders had recently departed her establishment and she was down to three paying guests: Dunne, a young apprentice gunsmith, and Mr. Sumter, a drummer who travelled the Nebraskan countryside peddling cheap watches to dirt farmers. Mr. Sumter thought himself quite the card. Once, he had given Dunne a wink and told him that the timepieces he sold had a high rate of heart failure, that their tickers often stopped ticking and that he would soon have to leave Nebraska before the owners of those tin corpses caught up with him. It seemed Mr. Sumter believed cheating people a joke, but he didn't get a laugh from Michael Dunne.

That night, Sumter held forth on the gale, which he predicted would soon bring down a plague of Rocky Mountain locusts on Nebraska. "Same wind in '74," he said, helping himself to another grey chunk of Mrs. Henderson's sodden boiled beef, "and in on it sailed them devil insects. I was just outside Lincoln when they came. I took refuge from them at a farmer's place. The sky went black and I heard the roar of wings, and they started to drop down like hail, plop, plop, all around until they lay ankle deep on the ground, a crawling carpet of locusts, shivering and creeping."

"Oh, dreadful!" exclaimed Mrs. Henderson, holding up two red hands on either side of her face and wriggling her fingers in disgust.

"They consumed every blessed thing in their path, grass, corn, wheat, oats, the very leaves on the trees," said Sumter, evidently pleased with the effect he was having on his landlady. "And that weren't enough for the greedy beggars. Why next they went at the washing on the clothesline; sheets and shirts, pillow-cases and trousers – et every last thread of it. They et horse harnesses hanging on corral posts. They et the canvas and paint right off wagons. It was destruction like you never seen. The farmer's wife was out in her yard, swatting them with a shovel, and slipping around in the pulp of them like she was skating on ice. I stayed at the window wondering if they weren't going to gnaw her down to the bones too."

"Mr. Sumter, that's enough," said Mrs. Henderson, "we are dining!"

"I feared they'd chew the dirt right out from under the house," persisted Sumter. "I feared they'd eat a grave so big I'd just drop down in the hole, a house for a coffin. No, let the Almighty spare us that awesome affliction again. A man can't get ahead in this country. I believe we're facing ruination again. Pass the potatoes."

Unlike Sumter and his supper companions, Dunne wished the locusts would come, would accomplish the ruination of the country. When he returned to his room, he lay down on his bed and dreamily contemplated a cloud of destruction, millions upon millions of insects busy devouring everything in sight, busy getting to the bottom of things, revealing what the world was and always would be – a desert. He saw trees stripped bare, nothing left but skeletal branches and bony twigs outlined against a hot, clay-coloured sky. Spread under that sky, mile upon mile of dust clothed in a trembling shroud of insects. He stared at naked men and women, garments chewed from their bodies, starving horses and bawling cattle stumbling about dazed; he gazed at stray dogs coursing the ground, gobbling up the pests, jaws snapping as they gorged themselves, feasting on the locusts until their plague-swollen bellies dragged on the earth.

If that were the sight that greeted him in the morning, Dunne would be happy for it.

A little after midnight, sitting on the edge of his bed with a chair pulled close to serve as a desk, he wrote Mrs. Tarr a letter he hoped would bring her to her senses. It took him until dawn to finish it.

August 12, 1877

My dear Mrs. Tarr,

I write to you from Omaha, Nebraska, to tell you I am in decline. My good health has gone bad, my gums bleed continual and when I brush my hair it comes out in clumps. I went to the doctor and asked him why this might be. He give me a lookover and diagnosed it, said it is a common affliction of them who has had a great shock.

Now Mrs. Tarr I regret to tell you it was you who give me this great shock that led to my collapse. Accidental, I learned you have been keeping company with Wesley Case. I could not believe my eyes at first, but I kept watch on your place and saw it was true. On several occasions I seen him leaving the premises at times which point me to but one conclusion and that is that by trickery, lies, and low behaviour he has seduced you.

I have thought on this matter a good deal and I want you to know certain things. Here they are.

1. I left Fort Benton and did not make it clear I was coming back to you. This must've thrown you into deep bewilderment and despair. I know now it was most thoughtless of me to have destroyed your hope of happiness with me.

2. You was forced to mind brats to earn your daily bread, which must've been a great blow to you. I see how under such circumstances, a rich man like Wesley Case might've seemed to you the only way out since I was not at hand to rescue you from your pitiable circumstances.

I hold Wesley Case to blame. I will put you my reasons.

1. He broke the rules, which is to say he did not do as I done, which is not to pester you while you observed mourning for Mr. Tarr. Case barged in on you when you

was faint and weak of spirit because you thought I did not care.

2. He took advantage of your penniless condition by luring you with his fortune. I call that a despicable, nasty way for a man to operate.

3. Like all rich fellows, he thinks whatever he wishes for is his by right. The feelings of an honest fellow like me mean nothing to him. No matter I watched over you and would've laid down my life to keep you safe from Gobbler Johnson, as you saw evidence every waking hour of the day, which is a thing a man like him would never have done. I know his kind, Mrs. Tarr, they have used me all my life and tossed me aside with a laugh when they had sucked all they could from me. Beware, he will do the same to you. Men like him are deceivers not to be trusted.

I believe I have now proved him to be a villain, but there is more, and it is worse. Even before he played fast and loose with you, I knew him for a man of bad character. This goes back many years. I have proof of what I say but I won't put it down in black and white in a letter because him being around you so frequent the letter might fall into his hands. If I wrote down the things I know, he would sue me in a court of law, which is what a wealthy man always does because he knows the law looks on him favourable and scorns the ordinary man. He would hire himself some slick lawyer who makes a habit of proving that 2+2 makes 5, or that the sun comes up in the west. No matter the truth and right of a thing, men like Wesley Case always win in the end because they sit on bags of gold and buy the decisions they want with their filthy cash.

But if you want the truth and nothing but the truth about Wesley Case I will come to you direct and speak it to your face. All I will say here is that concerning him there was a MIGHTY SCANDAL THAT NEVER COME TO LIGHT BECAUSE STRINGS WAS PULLED. When you learn what he done you will see him for one of the most despicable beasts that ever walked the earth and you will be REVOLTED.

You can reach me at Mrs. Henderson's Boarding House, the Market, Omaha, Nebraska, by telegram, and I will come in a flash to reveal to you everything about that wolf in sheep's clothing, and the terrible deed he done that will raise the hair up on your head when you hear it. Then the veil will fall from your eyes and you will recognize you have only one true and constant admirer – Michael Dunne.

Yours truly,

Michael Dunne

Ada Tarr likes to think of the past few months as the summer of "Ada's wager." Her father had always scorned Pascal's wager as ignoble theology, but she substitutes the word *love* for *God*. If she puts her faith in love, lives as if it exists, isn't everything the better for it? And if it is real and she offers herself up to it, doesn't she have everything to gain? Though betting on love and refusing Wesley's offer of marriage seems to her at times a contradiction, she does not give in. She wants to draw out this summer of reckless happiness, give herself over to testing its strength, to seeing if it endures or snaps. She doesn't underestimate what is at stake. For one thing, she knows her job is at risk. Talk about the schoolmarm and Wesley Case is making the rounds, she is sure of it. There is a change in the townspeople; she sees arched eyebrows, a hard, critical glint in the eyes of the respectable, even store clerks turn aloof and superior when serving her. But until some fool man can be found to take her place and work for starvation wages, the Jezebel in their midst will have to be tolerated. The prospect of losing her pupils tears at her heart, but it also drives her to do the best she can for them while they are still under her tutelage.

Since she began teaching, she has been badgering the school board to supply books for her young scholars, but all the misers do is put her off. All summer, she has been copying out passages from books in her own library, compiling readers that can be printed on the press of the *Fort Benton Record* in inexpensive newsprint pamphlets. But her hope of presenting her students with their own "books" on the first day of school was dashed when she asked the school board for the little bit of money to pay to have them run off. Mr. Hooper, the chairman, had given her a disdainful smile and said insinuatingly, "I don't think that such a good idea, Missus. Aside from the expense, I'm not sure we'd approve of what you'd put into a youngster's book."

Slapped in the face for her efforts. All the work she had done. Some of it very close to an entire reworking of texts, rendering Grimm's fairy tales and Aesop's *Fables* in language even more bare and direct so they could be read and grasped by the smallest or most backward child, the hours spent compiling anthologies for the older children, searching out poems and editing selections of prose before copying them out in her finest copperplate for the printer, composing questions and commentaries to guide the children's reading and understanding – she was not going to meekly let all that thought and care go for naught.

So Ada turned to Wesley. Until that moment, she had asked nothing from him. Once, in a moment of thoughtless levity, she had made a joke about living like the impoverished heroine of a novel, under threat of summary eviction by a wicked stepdaughter. Wesley had immediately urged her to get in touch with Celeste's new husband; he would give her the money to buy the house from him. It had been nearly impossible to make him understand why she could not accept his handsome offer. Stubbornly, he had kept repeating, "What kind of man do you think I am? How many times must I repeat it? There is no *quid pro quo* attached." To say such a thing only demonstrated his naïveté.

But asking him to finance the pamphlets was another matter. That was for the children's good, not her own. Besides, he'd had a hand in the work from the very beginning. Ada had enlisted him to help her choose material for what she called the "big boys," the thirteen- and fourteen-year-olds who sprawled at the back of class. Surely he could make suggestions of what would appeal to them, excite their enthusiasm. Night after night, the two of them had sat in the parlour, books stacked at their feet, flipping through pages and madly scribbling, Wesley sometimes reading aloud passages so she could pass judgment on their usefulness and suitability. In these moments, she felt him to be her *spiritual husband*, flattering herself that they were just like George Eliot and Mr. Lewes, scandalizing society by living together without benefit of clergy but united in a perfect sympathy, working to achieve high aims.

Wesley had acceded to even her strangest requests. When she had asked him to translate some of La Rochefoucauld's *Maxims* for her students, he had jibbed a little, protested he was no scholar and joked about what would be made of any of that by shopkeepers' and farmers' sons? When she had answered that this was her homage to her father's memory, that he had taught her French from this little book, and that her attachment to it was very strong, Wesley had said, "Well then, I'll pay a visit to your girlhood," and gone directly to work. She had seen he wanted to *know her better* and she had had to turn aside to hide her tears from him.

She recalls Wesley on a feverishly hot summer night a month ago, sitting in a pool of lamplight, thumbing through an old French/English dictionary as he sat at the table half-naked, his shirt draped over the back of his chair. Wesley's face, his neck, his hands turned brown by the sun, the rest of his torso white as sized canvas, looking like an unfinished portrait. Over his shoulder he had commented, "Here is something that will have your big boys scratching their heads. It has me scratching mine. 'A man is sometimes as different from himself as he is from others,'" he said teasingly. "Explain that to me, if you can." And she had simply smiled and said, "I can't, but you illustrate it every day." And Wesley had grinned back at her, then lowered his head and returned to translating.

Ada wonders if "the perfect understanding" she had held up to Wesley as an ideal is the meaning found in moments such as this. *I do this thing because you ask it of me. I do this thing because I want to see you more clearly.* Perhaps there is nothing better than this, the sincerity of gestures, the willing slope of a shoulder turned to the task, the earnest curve of a back gleaming in the lamplight, love acting, the body as witness.

Ada has spent most of the morning sewing covers to her pupils' new readers. By eleven o'clock she realizes she will need more bristol board, which necessitates a trip to town to renew supplies. The work has left her feeling lighthearted. Every time she pulled a thread through those pages she had felt she was giving a pull to Mr. Hooper's nose. After making her purchase, she drops by the post office to see if a new circular from the Chicago bookseller she patronizes has arrived. It's a morning of angled late-summer sunshine that makes windows flash and gives a coppery glint to the street dust hovering in the air.

There is no circular but there is a letter. The writing on the envelope is unfamiliar. There is no return address and the postmark is smudged and difficult to read, but it looks like it might be Omaha. She knows no one in Nebraska. Perhaps it has something to do with the house, a communication from some lawyer whom Lieutenant Blanchard has hired to represent Celeste's interests. She thrusts the letter into her reticule.

Back at the house, she sits down, and beginning to feel some trepidation that the letter might contain a demand that she vacate the premises, she slits open the envelope and begins to read. The letter frightens and disturbs her; she has no inkling who might have written it until its author reminds her that he had kept her safe from Gobbler Johnson. She skips to the last page. The signature confirms that the author of the letter is indeed Mr. Dunne.

Michael Dunne, the faithful dog thumping his tail on her porch, begging someone to pat his head, the way he imagines stronger, deeper emotions underlying the insipid kindnesses she dealt him, how could he have imagined such things? She feels unbalanced, as if the ground has suddenly shifted. Just to think of the dreadful man turns her hands clammy with anxiety.

And that his insane delusions also concern Wesley – the claims that he has poached on Dunne's preserve; that he is a libertine; that he is a seducer; that a great cloud of scandal hangs over his head. It appears Dunne will stop at nothing. She is uncertain how to respond to this outrageous farrago of nonsense and slander. At first, she is tempted to do exactly what Dunne asks, send him a wire, a wire that will demand he *leave her alone*. Inform him in no uncertain terms that *she has no feelings for him whatsoever*. But, then again, any contact with this lunatic might be ill advised. What good could come from opening a conversation with a man suffering such bizarre delusions? Mightn't it encourage him to lay further charges of moral turpitude against Wesley? Perhaps lead to another declaration of love? The very thought of his doing such a thing is enough to make her heart skitter with fright.

Let Dunne hang fire in Omaha; complete silence may be the best and sternest refutation of his hallucinations.

Briefly, she considers showing the letter to Wesley, but then decides against it. He would surely read it as a call to somehow take action on her behalf, or as a demand on her part that he provide answers to the supposed revelations. Wesley has alluded to a scandal in his past that ended his engagement, but he clearly did not wish to speak further of it. She has always assumed another woman must have been at the bottom of that but never considered it any of her business to ask him to air youthful dirty laundry. No, she will not speak to Wesley about Dunne. Better to draw a curtain of privacy around this matter as one should do around a deathly ill patient.

Dunne had to wait until August 16 before he received the summons to the Franklin Hotel to meet with General O'Neill. At eight o'clock that night, Collins met him in the lobby and escorted him up to a suite of rooms on the third floor where the General, wearing a lavishly embroidered dressing gown, reclined on a chaise longue, one naked foot, with an engorged and inflamed big toe, propped on a pillow.

After Collins had made introductions, O'Neill said, "Excuse me for receiving you in such an informal fashion, Mr. Dunne, but I am temporarily *hors de combat*. I am losing a skirmish with the gout. But please, sir, draw up a chair beside me and let us talk about your proposal."

Dunne knew the General was tight as a tick. It wasn't that he slurred his words; rather, he spoke them so clearly and so deliberately it was obvious he was rehearsing everything he meant to say before he uttered it, and then merely reading it from the book of his mind. His face had a spongy look and his eyes didn't have much shine to them, as if somebody hadn't cleaned the chimney lamps for a long time and the buildup of smoke and grime was dimming whatever pitiful light his brain could still throw.

Collins picked up a chair, carried it over, and set it down near the General, signalled Dunne to sit, and went to stand behind the chaise longue as if he were providing himself as a pillar the General could lean on if the need arose.

"Now," said O'Neill, "Mr. Collins tells me you claim you can raise a large sum of money. You had better detail how you think that can be done."

Which Dunne did as if it were the old days and he was making a report to McMicken. There was a man by the name of Wesley Case who had a small ranch near Fort Benton. His father was a bigwig in Ottawa and had more money than Carter had liver pills. With O'Neill's help, he could snatch this Case and hold him for ransom. He guessed the father would cough up as much as twenty-five thousand dollars to get his golden boy back, maybe more. But as Dunne laid this out, he sensed the vague light that showed in the General's eyes was growing dimmer and ever more cloudy by the second.

When Dunne had finished, the General sat silent for a long time, stroking the lapels of his dressing gown with his fingertips. At last he said, "If the gentleman in question were a soldier, a policeman, a member of Parliament, I would consider him fair game. But he is a civilian. I wage war only on those who take a hand in oppressing Ireland."

"Well, so happens he did just that," said Dunne. "Take my word on it, he was one of the militia officers that fought you at the Battle of Ridgeway. He was in the North-West Mounted Police until a year ago. His old man pours money into that hound Macdonald's pockets. I ask you, do the Irish have a worse enemy than John A. Macdonald?"

Collins cleared his throat. "I can verify what Mr. Dunne says, sir. Case was in the Police. That was well known in Fort Benton. And what he says about Macdonald – he has a point." O'Neill craned his neck and looked up incredulously at his lieutenant. Then he turned back to Dunne.

"If this Case were on British soil, I would take him in the blink of an eye. It would give me joy to break the Englishman's law, which is the cudgel of a tyrant. He beats us to our knees with it and if we strike back, why then he cries to the world, 'Look, these Irishmen have no more respect for law than does a Hottentot. Patriots? No, they are nothing but common criminals.'" O'Neill fell silent; he appeared to have abandoned the thread of his thought in favour of staring at his gouty toe.

After a time, Dunne said, "That's a pretty speech. Here or there. What difference does it make?"

Dunne's challenge roused O'Neill. He pushed himself a little more upright on the chaise longue, wincing as his foot shifted on the pillow. "Mr. Dunne, I have no compunction about doing injury to Englishmen to gain our liberty. Americans are another matter."

"Who said anything about harm to Americans?"

"And if things go awry, if you are pursued by the law, what then? Do you surrender or do you fight to keep your prize?"

"That's an if."

"A big if. A bigger if is a dead peace officer. We have our friends in Congress. Public opinion supports our cause. I don't intend to jeopardize either by committing mayhem on American soil. It's not worth it."

"I'd say twenty-five thousand dollars is worth it. Your dirt farmers would have to sell a lot of sacks of potatoes, a lot of ears of corn, a lot of bushels of wheat to raise that kind of money."

"I see the *big picture. I paint it*," said O'Neill fiercely. "I juggle considerations you are incapable of appreciating. Get him out of here, Mr. Collins," he said. "I have nothing more to say to this dolt."

Collins stepped around the chaise longue. Dunne rose from his chair. The two men walked to the door. Collins paused and said to O'Neill, "I will see Mr. Dunne out, then go to my room. I have paperwork to do."

The General was attempting to fish a bottle from under the settee. He made a last precarious lunge at it, snatched it up, and nestled the whiskey in his lap. "Yes," he said without a trace of interest, "very good."

Dunne and Collins went out and down the hallway. They passed two doors and when they came to the third the General's aide stopped Dunne, lifted a finger to his lips, then unlocked the room and ushered him in. Dunne looked around him. The last light of a summer evening was on the walls. The room was hardly bigger than a broom closet. Squeezed into it was a roll-top desk piled high with papers. A cot was jammed tight under the window. Collins began to pace the last scrap of available floor space, head lowered, hands clenched behind his back. Dunne leaned a shoulder against the door and waited. Collins stopped, lifted his head, and said, "He was a great man. A very great man."

"Every dog has his day," said Dunne.

"*Most* days," said Collins emphatically, "he's drunk before breakfast. Too many hopes defeated. His will is gone. The Hero of Ridgeway they once called him. People who leaned on him, admired him, now they revile him. It's very sad." Collins shook his head. "I feared he would refuse. That this would happen."

"It don't need to happen," Dunne said implacably, face wiped clean of any emotion.

"What do you mean?"

"I got most of it already in place. I know where to hold Case. It's safe; nobody would find it. I been spending a good deal of time in Helena lately. There's a young fellow there, an old friend of Case's from their Police days by name of Peregrine Hathaway. I spotted him working in a bank there. He'll be of use."

"In what way?"

"He can be the one to contact Case's papa, act as a buffer. The money can be paid to Hathaway, then he hands it over to us."

"I'm not following. You mean to take on another confeder-ate? I'm not sure I like the sound of that."

"No, no, we *use* him. I know this boy's nature. He was moony over the daughter of a man I worked for. The girl's mother used to talk about how much this Hathaway admired Case – used to make me grind my teeth to hear it."

"And if he decides to go to the law?"

"He ain't going to the law. Not if he knows Case has a pistol to his head, knows we mean business. He ain't going to nobody. He's a weak sister – soft from the top of his head right down to his toes."

"You seem very sure."

"I'm sure. He'll be like butter in my hands." Dunne paused. "Something more. He's a high-toned Englishman, the sort that gets money dropped in their laps from the old country. Case's papa can arrange a bank draft through lawyers that looks like a inheritance from some relative of Hathaway's – father, maiden aunt – it don't signify who." Dunne smiled. "It gets better. Since he works in a bank, they know him, there won't be no questions about his identity. Once the money is got, he delivers it to us. That's all she wrote."

Collins nodded. "Your thoroughness is admirable, Mr. Dunne."

"All I need's a little expense money – and a few men."

Collins thought for a moment. "Contributions to the cause pass through my hands. A little of that might be skimmed with no one the wiser. As to the men . . . how many would you require?"

"I can make do with three if they're good. Hard men is necessary."

"That may take a little time. I can't recruit anyone from O'Neill City. Word would be sure to get back to the General. But I can think of three men who would suit. Two last known to be in Philadelphia. One in Baltimore. The Baltimore one, Halligan, is a holy terror." He considered for a moment. "But it may take time to get them here."

"How much time?"

"It's difficult to say. I must locate them first. As you can guess, they make it a habit not to be easily found. Maybe as long as a month. Perhaps longer. Then I must get them here."

"All right," said Dunne. "But I'm in charge. I don't want no misunderstanding on that score."

"Agreed." Collins put out his hand. Dunne shook it. "One other thing – if things go amiss, this cannot land on the General's doorstep," warned Collins. "His standing must be protected at all costs. For the good of the cause. You agree?"

"Yes."

"But if we succeed – that's another matter. The General won't refuse the money. He will see the light. He burns for another chance to redeem himself."

"Once we get the tin – Case and Hathaway go in the ground," said Dunne. "No loose ends."

"Of course." Collins smiled. "I met Case once. No love lost between us. I punched him in the face at a New Year's Eve celebration."

"Good for you." Dunne shifted his shoulder off the door-frame. "Once you get them men, send me a letter to the Helena Post Office. I'll need warning of their arrival." And with that, he departed.

As Dunne had waited for his interview with the General, he now waits for Mrs. Tarr's return telegram. If she sends it, too bad for Collins, too bad for O'Neill. If she doesn't, too bad for Case. He sits on the horsehair sofa in Mrs. Henderson's parlour, anticipating the knock of the telegraph delivery boy. At night he lies on his bed hoping to be solaced by a figure emerging from a multitude of white flecks, the shape of a skirt slowly taking form, Mrs. Tarr's face revealing itself as she joyfully hurries towards him.

Instead, all he sees is a vague shape swarmed by a dark cloud of locusts, hears the whir of their leathery wings, loud as a train rushing through a tunnel.

For ten days Dunne waits for Mrs. Tarr's reply. Finally, he realizes that Case somehow has dissuaded or prevented her from contacting him. He leaves for Helena. There, he moves into Gobbler Johnson's cabin, pulls up the floorboards, and begins digging the cellar that will hold his prisoner.

TWENTY

SEPTEMBER ARRIVES AND Ada is back in school, throwing herself into her teaching with even greater fervour. This may be, she thinks, her last chance to take her pupils by the hand and walk them out into the wider world, to awaken them to its possibilities and wonders. She thinks of them as her children. When she moves about the classroom, she cannot keep from touching them. She rests a hand on the shoulders of the older boys when she checks their calculations; she guides the hands of the smallest children as they form the letters of the alphabet on their slates; she smoothes down cowlicks and mends unravelling braids like a doting mother. When they need to be corrected she does so in a soft and gentle voice, and when she commends them she spreads the butter of praise thickly, without stint. They bask in her attention, wriggle and beam when she pays them compliments.

Ada has struck a pact with her pupils. If they are diligent, if they strive, if they learn as she knows they can learn, they will be rewarded during the last hour of the school day. When the weather is fine she turns them loose to play rounders, to skip, to toss quoits, to play hopscotch, or simply to wander about, drink the sunshine of the last warm days before cold weather descends while merchants look out their windows, shake their heads, and wonder what education is coming to.

On inclement days she encourages her students to decorate the covers of their readers however they like, or entertains them by describing the golden pagodas and clever elephants of Siam, the wandering life of the Bedouin of Arabia Deserta, recounts to them how the intrepid explorer Richard Burton penetrated Mecca disguised as a Mussulman, a city forbidden to infidels, on pain of death. She speaks of long-ago Byzantium, holding the big boys entranced with tales of plotters and traitors strangled by the Emperor's guard with bowstrings. The girls hear of Jenny Lind, the Swedish Nightingale, and the great actress Charlotte Cushman, whom Ada had once seen play Lady Macbeth, a glorious moment still alive in her mind. When her inspiration flags, she reads to them from *The Water-Babies* and *The Golden Key* and *Uncle Tom's Cabin*, her abolitionist mother's favourite novel. She wants to make them *feel* the world.

Walking home one afternoon, Ada senses autumn lodging wistfully in her, a sadness that looks back on the passing of things, the death of the very grass she walks on, the leaves withered on the bushes or tumbling along the ground in the breeze, all of it reminding her that the summer of Ada's wager is drawing to an end. But then she gives herself a shake and puts on a proper face, because Wesley is bringing Joe to supper that night.

McMullen is a frequent guest. On his visits, he plays feckless, older bachelor brother to Wesley, full of jokes and japes and outrageous stories, his way of conveying his affection for both of them. If one could choose a brother-in-law, one couldn't do better than McMullen, a man who would cut off his right hand for either one of them.

She pauses on the path. At her feet, clusters of scarlet mallow lie in the yellow dust like dying embers. Summer isn't done, she tells herself, not yet. Not for a while.

Three days later, Wesley leaves her house in the darkness of a Saturday morning. He explains he has work to finish on a horse corral, and wants to get started early. She luxuriates in bed until the sun rises and then goes downstairs to check on the weather, to see what kind of day she can expect. When she steps out the front door, there is evidence that a hard freeze occurred during the night; the planks of the porch are carpeted in rime, the grass is furred in frost. The entire prairie sparkles white except for one dark spot twenty-five yards in front of her house – Dunne in his black frock coat and derby.

She seizes the porch railing to steady herself; the cold sap of it climbs into her veins as he looks fixedly at her. Dunne doesn't move, doesn't speak. His face wears the expression of a blind man listening to a far-off sound.

Gathering herself, she calls out to him, "Mr. Dunne, there is nothing here for you! You have misunderstood! You must go away!"

He makes no answer.

"If I did anything to mislead you, I am most heartily sorry! But you need to go away and never come back!"

His queer silence, his queer look unnerves her. Ada backs away from the railing, her hand fumbling for the doorknob. She pushes open the door and eases herself over the threshold, then claps the door shut.

She stands, breath coming quick and short, then goes to the parlour window, parts the curtains, and looks out. Dunne is exactly where he was before, frozen in place like a block of black ice. But now his eyes are turned up the path that leads to Wesley's ranch.

That sight turns her cold. It is time Wesley was warned of the man's obsessions. Ada takes Dunne's letter from a drawer. She glances out the window once more; he is still in place. Clutching the letter in her hand, she slips out the kitchen door and starts for the ranch.

Case is nailing a plank to the corral when he sees Ada stride into the yard, halt by the well, and cast him an anxious look. Tossing down the hammer, he hurries over to her. "Ada," he says, "has something happened?"

"Yes, something has happened. Some time ago," she says, speaking urgently, "I should have mentioned it to you before but I did not. Just now I left Dunne standing outside my house. The man is mad. He has professed warm feelings for me and believes I return them. He is convinced you have stolen me away from him, and has gone to great lengths to attempt to discredit you in my eyes. He wrote me a letter some weeks ago." She thrusts an envelope at him. "Read it for yourself, but be prepared, you will not be pleased. I came as quickly as I could because I thought he may have intentions of coming here –" She hesitates. "You should be warned. He is full of malice towards you."

As Case dips his head to the letter, McMullen comes up leading a horse. "Hello, darling," he says. "What brings you out on such a cold morning?"

Ada holds up her hand to stop him.

Wesley has finished reading the letter. Jaws working, he crushes it in his hand and then flings it down the well. "That son of a bitch," he says.

"Who?" demands Joe.

"Dunne. He's been bothering Ada."

"Not bothering. Not really. Making a nuisance of himself perhaps – if that," she amends, hoping to mollify him. When he turns to go, she snatches at his arm. "Wesley, what do you mean to do?"

"I mean to have a word with him." He pulls away from her and starts down the path.

"Stop him," Ada says quietly to McMullen. "Bring him back." There's no mistaking it's an order.

McMullen knots his hand in the mane of the horse and springs up on it bareback. The horse gives a skittish dance of surprise, which Joe checks with a tug to the halter shank. "You believe Wesley means to tackle him?" Ada gives a curt nod,

sending Joe off at a trot, legs dangling and bouncing. He overtakes Case soon enough, but Case doesn't give him a glance;
he ploughs along holding his head as if he's afflicted with a stiff
neck and can't turn it either right or left to look at his friend.
Joe walks his horse alongside him. Considerable ground is covered without the two men exchanging a word.

Finally Joe says, "She asked me to bring you back."

"Not until I settle this," Case says, tight-lipped.

"You mean to fight him?"

Case is silent.

"I don't recommend it. That Dunne puts me in mind of one
of them tremendous big monkeys. I don't recollect the name."

"Gorilla."

"That's it. Gorilla. Wesley, you are a damned dictionary of
knowledge. Now me, I don't know much. I'm a practical man.
I got a different vantage point than you. Right now, that vantage
point is sitting up high on a horse and from where I sit I can see
farther than you down this trail, and I don't see no sign of Dunne.
I believe he's done a skedaddle. I'd say with Dunne gone, there's
no point to whatever you got in mind to do. We might just as
well turn back and put Ada's mind at ease."

"If he's skedaddled, he's skedaddled to town. I'll find him
there."

Soon Ada's place is in sight and McMullen is proved right.
Dunne is nowhere to be seen. Case insists they go inside and
search the premises. The house is empty. When they come out,
Case trudges stubbornly towards Fort Benton. Joe remounts his
horse, catches him up, and asks, "You ever consider that Dunne
might be carrying a pistol?"

"No."

"You carrying a pistol?"

"You know for a fact I'm not. Don't be ridiculous."

"Don't you be ridiculous. If Dunne don't have a pistol and
you fly at him, the size and looks of him, I prospect he'd tear

you up like soggy newspaper. If he does have a pistol he might just plink you like an empty can. Just a thought."

Case stops short. "I'm warning you, Joe! Make yourself scarce!"

McMullen's horse shies at the outburst. He turns it in a circle, pats it, makes soothing, clucking noises. Gradually, the horse quiets, but little shivers still run up and down its neck. Joe says sharply, "This here is a public thoroughfare. I reckon I have a right to pass down it."

"Not in my company," says Case and marches away.

Joe turns his horse in directly behind him, and this is the manner they enter Benton some time later, McMullen hard on Case's heels. Onlookers stop in their tracks to construe the strange scene, Case walking pell-mell, wrath written all over his face, a horse's nose at his back.

Joe sits his mount at the bottom of the stairs that lead to the one room that Dink Dooley rents above the Stubhorn. Case hammers up the steps to Dunne's door, bangs on it, and, getting no answer, storms back down them. When he barrels around to the front of the saloon and lunges through the doors, McMullen rides his horse up on the boardwalk, peers over the top of the batwing doors, and watches Case interrogate Dink Dooley.

In moments, Case is back outside, looking angrier than ever, so angry he forgets he had intended to maintain a chilly silence, and announces, "Dooley says Dunne isn't his lodger any longer. He cleared out weeks ago and took everything with him."

"Well, there's an end to it."

Case gives an obstinate shake of the head. "He's got to be somewhere here in town," he says, and pitches back into the street.

But no one can recall seeing Dunne that day, no one can recall seeing him for weeks. All inquiries about him prove fruitless.

TWENTY-ONE

EVER SINCE WESLEY read the letter, his behaviour had undergone a great change. At times he carried himself with a prickly pride and reserve, at others he had the guilty man's watchful, guarded manner, as if judgment would be levelled any minute. Ada felt herself kept at a painful distance. She said nothing for several days, thinking that he would soon speak about the incident, but when he didn't, she told him that she thought that whatever was bothering him needed an airing. "I take it Dunne was accusing you of some youthful peccadillo with a woman. There is no need to go about looking shamefaced. I am not an innocent. Young men are often imprudent." She hesitated. "But I do wonder what dealings you had with him in the past. I am curious how it is he claims to know so much about you."

"A word never passed between us until a year ago," Case said. "Whatever he claims to know about me he never learned from my lips. But he may have heard talk about me from others – nothing, I assure you, that could be construed as licentiousness."

"What sort of talk?"

"That I had been derelict in my duty as an officer." His brow furrowed. "There were whispers – no charge was ever brought."

"Derelict in your duty," she said. "That is a very vague term."

"That is the way the military prefers to frame things – with ample latitude."

"I see," said Ada carefully.

"No," he said with great finality, "I don't think you do."

His unwillingness to confide in her was exasperating. She presumed he dared not admit to her that at some time in the past his courage had failed him. If that failure had saved his life, she was glad of it. What was it about gentle men that made them disdain their gentleness? She had always believed that her brother Tom's desire to prove he wasn't a coward had led to the death of the mildest, sweetest boy God ever made. She didn't give a fig for Wesley's valour, or lack of it. It wounded her that he did not understand her better than that. She waited for him to come to his senses.

And as she did, events overtook them. The Nez Perce came down into Montana and apprehension and terror spread as it had the previous year in the days after the Little Bighorn. People began to evacuate farms and ranches to huddle in the towns. The citizens of Fort Benton could talk of nothing else. Wesley began to pay frequent visits to Major Ilges for updates on what the Nez Perce were up to. He often spoke admiringly of the Indians' pluck and daring, the speed with which they were covering ground in the race to Canada. The Army could not seem to keep pace with them. One day they were reported to be in the Yellowstone country; it was said they had relieved a party of English tourists of their elephant gun. What the Englishmen were doing with an elephant gun, Ada couldn't fathom, but Wesley had delighted in dwelling on that incongruous detail. And then in the next twenty-four hours there were contradictory claims. Wesley said the Major had received news of four different sightings separated by hundreds of miles. It was Wesley's opinion that either the Mongol Golden Horde had been mistaken for the Nez Perce, or the Indians could fly.

Then, late one afternoon, she returned from school and found Wesley's horse tethered to the porch rail, a blanket bundle across her haunches and a frying pan tied to the saddle horn. Lifting her skirts, she ran up the steps and into the house. Wesley was waiting for her in the parlour. When she saw his grave expression, when she saw the holster belt strapped to his waist, she dropped down on a chair and waited, mute and trembling.

Wesley delivered his news with curt urgency. "There is a pressing military emergency. Major Ilges sent me a message this morning. The Nez Perce are at Cow Island and have besieged it." He paused. "Ilges's garrison is badly undermanned. J.J. Donnelly has raised a force of volunteers to support the soldiers. Major Ilges believes that I might be useful in this situation given my experience in the Police and the militia."

"Think of how J.J. Donnelly and his friend treated you last New Year's Eve," she said, desperation in her voice. "A man insults you and now you make common cause with him?" She knew how weak that sounded, but a frail argument was better than none. She hurried on. "For weeks you have been expressing sympathy for these poor Indians, and now you mean to take part in slaughtering them?"

"I don't have to approve of Donnelly's politics to ride with him. And I hope not to have to fight these Indians at all. I fully expect the Nez Perce to retreat as soon as we reach Cow Island. The goal is to prevent the few souls there from being overrun. We are not intent on slaughtering Indians, only relieving the men trapped there."

His rectitude was unbearable. "Oh," she said, "you are playing soldier, spouting soldier talk. 'Pressing military emergency,' 'garrison is badly undermanned.' This is Major Ilges's problem. It is no business of yours." She threw him a despairing, angry look. "Won't you listen? I am begging you not to go. You have nothing to prove."

Ada saw she had startled him with that last statement, but then he composed his face as if he were on the parade ground. "It is not a matter of proving anything. But these men can't be abandoned. To turn one's back on them . . ." He faltered. She wanted to shout at him to save his breath. "There are lives to be saved," he said grimly. "I can think of nothing worse than to desert them."

327

"I can think of something worse. You brought home dead, draped over the back of your horse."

"There is little danger of that." Wesley moved across the room and went down on one knee before her chair and touched her hand. "Now hear me out. There is a possibility that if Cow Island is taken, the Nez Perce may proceed up the Missouri. The minute there is any inkling of that, you must immediately go into Fort Benton. They will not attack the town. Will you promise me? Joe is here to look after you if you need anything."

She nodded reluctantly.

"Good. I have not much more time left. We are to assemble and set off in less than half an hour. But I want to go knowing you understand that this is a matter of conviction. This is not a whim. I am –"

"Men and their honour," she said. "How much grief has that caused?"

He got to his feet, leaned in, and pressed his lips to her forehead, held them there for a moment. "Oh, Ada," he said, and then he was gone.

Standing at the window, she watched him mount, then urge the horse into a lope, followed him with disbelieving eyes until he disappeared from sight, taking from her the hope that he was going to relent and turn back.

As it turns out, Wesley is gone only five days, and when he returns, Ada embraces a pale and haggard man. It seems that in his absence Wesley has become a stranger to her, he talks feverishly about the coloured man, Edmund Bradley, killed at Cow Creek Canyon, his face running with sweat as he rambles on about him, voice low, hesitant, questioning. Wesley says that Bradley's wife is an Indian. She has a little baby. What possessed Bradley to turn against his woman's people? What possessed him to make common cause with the whites? And why did the black barber do the same? He had wept over Bradley's corpse as if he were weeping over the lifeless body of his own child.

And why, Ada asks herself, had Wesley been willing to risk everything as Bradley had done, why had he been willing to have her face a widow's sorrow?

Obsessively, he speaks of how Bradley died from a gunshot to the abdomen. The hours it took him to die, his fearful groans, his raging thirst, how he begged for water, and how they had had to deny him it because of the nature of his wound. "I have imagined such a death," he says, voice hushed. "But his agony was unimaginable. His face went grey with it. I did not think a black man's face could turn the colour of ashes."

"You must put your mind on other things. Do not let it fix itself there," she tells him gently, again and again.

And his reply is always the same. "I can't pluck it free," he says.

In sleep, he is plagued by nightmares she can't seem to rouse him from, it's as if he doesn't want to return to her, would rather face his gruesome dreams than look her in the face.

One afternoon when she came home from school, she surprised him reading some sort of dossier at the kitchen table, so absorbed in it that he was deaf to her footsteps. When he suddenly sensed her presence, he gave a mortified start, swiftly tucked the dirty bundle of foolscap down on his knees under the table, and sat waiting for her to dip herself a glass of water from the bucket on the counter and leave the room. She knew better than to ask him what he was up to.

Joe is as bewildered and worried by Wesley's peculiar behaviour as she is. She knows he is concerned that his partner seems to have lost all interest in the ranch, and that a year of work and sweat may be coming to naught. When he comes to visit, McMullen suppresses his usual jocularity; there are long, awkward pauses when they discuss the work that needs to be done before winter comes. On the last such occasion Wesley said, "The journey to Cow Island wore me down a little. But tomorrow I'll come by – we'll make a start on hauling grain."

But tomorrow nothing changes. Each morning when she leaves for school he is still in bed, staring up at the ceiling as if he were watching the progress of a comet overhead. Neither coaxing nor importuning can rouse him.

Then early one Saturday morning as she stands by the bed dressing, she gazes down on him, his arm flung over his eyes as if he is trying to blot out the world, and says, "I know how troubled you are, but I think you would do better, if instead of contemplating Mr. Bradley's horrid death, you did something to alleviate the misery of his wife and child. He cannot be helped. They can."

He takes his arm from his eyes, looks at her intently for a moment. "Let us go now," he says. "Yes, the sooner the better." Quickly he rises, goes to the dresser, jerks open a drawer. "I left a money pouch here – I meant to settle bills with it in Benton – but then the emergency arrived . . ."

It is perhaps too early to pay such a visit, the sun is scarcely up, but Ada decides not to point that out, fearing Wesley's sudden resolve might stall if a delay is suggested. "I will pack them a hamper," she says, "then make us some breakfast."

"No, no breakfast. We must go to them directly."

Standing in the pantry, Ada feels a lilt of relief. She stuffs a ham, jars of preserves, a loaf of bread into a wicker basket.

They set off a little after eight o'clock. A spell of warm weather has arrived. The morning holds the promise of a July day. When they reach town, none of the businesses along Front Street have opened yet; their shutters are down, their blinds drawn. Ada does not understand why Wesley is leading her this way. If he means to get them to the quarter of shanties and cabins where Fort Benton's Negroes live, this is a circuitous route. When she asks him where he is going, he says, "To the barbershop."

By then Foster's Tonsorial Palace is only a few steps away. Wesley stops before it, puts his face to the window, blinkers his eyes with his hands. He gives a peremptory rap to the glass.

Shortly, a lock can be heard turning. The door opens; Foster pokes out his head out and inquires tentatively, "Mr. Case?"

"If we may come in," says Wesley.

Foster nods and they enter the barbershop. It glitters with nickel finishings, bottles of bay rum, unguents, and face balm. Wesley stands in the middle of the floor, hands balled tightly at his sides.

With the utmost reserve Foster says, "I disbelieve you come for a trim, Mr. Case. Not with the lady with you. How can I do you, sir?"

"I wondered – as a close friend of Mr. Bradley's – would you be good enough to take his family a few things on our behalf?"

Foster moves behind the barber chair as if putting a barricade between himself and Wesley. He is a frail-looking man, extremely dapper in an immaculate striped shirt with red velvet garters at the elbows. His hands on the headrest of the chair make light, caressing passes on the leather. "Maybe you ought to deliver them things your ownself, Mr. Case," Foster suggests politely.

"I think not," says Case. "I am reluctant to face Mr. Bradley's child and widow." He hesitates. "Due to the circumstances of that day."

Foster's fingertips nervously skip about on the headrest of the chair. "Because we done left him behind? There was no help for it, Mr. Case."

Wesley stands there silent, shaking his head.

Foster turns to Ada. "That's the way Mr. Case put it at the time, Missus. Left behind. But you see, it was nothing but a body we left. Bradley's soul had already gone over. But Mr. Case, he was dead set against leaving him. He carried on something terrible. 'Can't leave nobody behind!' That's what he kept hollering at us. But Mr. Hale's horse was kilt dead, and he needed Bradley's horse to ride himself out of that mess. Mr. Hale dragged Bradley's poor corpse off his horse where Mr. Case had laid him, flung him to the ground and clumb up in the saddle. And then Mr. Case here, he said he'd pack the corpse out on his own horse, and he slung it up across his saddle, but Major Ilges wouldn't hear none of it. He said Mr. Case would get us all kilt, trying to pack that damn body out of there. And then Donnelly and one or two of the others laid hands to Mr. Case and held him tight, and Major Ilges pulled Bradley down once more and laid him out on the ground again and –"

"And I gave way," says Case. "I left him there."

"Had to, Mr. Case," says Foster. "The Major was right. If'n you hadn't agreed, you wouldn't be standing alive today before me. Them Indians would have catched you and snuffed the light out of you, too."

Case passes a hand over his brow. "If you would be so good as to express my condolences to the widow and see she gets these things, I would be much obliged to you, Mr. Foster." He sets the money pouch on the seat of the barber chair and gestures to Ada to place the basket down beside it.

Foster gives Ada a pleading look. "I wouldn't left Edmund neither, Missus, but I was thinking they meant for us to go back later, bury Edmund when them Indians was gone. But they was having no part of that. Wouldn't hear of it. But Mr. Case, he come with me, he come right along when the others wouldn't. Helped me bury poor Edmund Bradley right and proper."

"I recall your moving display of sorrow at his death," remarks Wesley. To Ada, it sounds a brusque, discordant thing to say.

Foster's face crumples. "Well, I had reason for it. I tole Edmund we coloured men needed to show the white folks we got some sand. I tole him we'd get credit by it if we rode with Mr. Donnelly. I says to him, 'Edmund, a natural man ought to get up on his hind legs from time to time.' I pestered and picked at him until I got him kilt." He appeals to Case. "But Edmund didn't get no blamed appreciation for riding out with Mr. Donnelly, did he? Them others thought so well of him they was ready to leave him out there in the sun to go high."

"A damnable business – all of it," says Wesley, "through and through damnable."

"Truer words never said."

In the silence that follows, it gives Ada a fright to catch Wesley staring into the barber's mirror as if it were a window, as if he cannot see himself there, as if his gaze was boring clear through the blindly staring man in the glass to some point hidden from her sight. A little panicked, she reaches out to touch his sleeve. Wesley's shoulders give a jerk; he gestures awkwardly to the money pouch and hamper posed on the barber chair. "If possible, I'd like to see his wife gets these things today."

"Yessir, Mr. Case. Before I take one customer."

"I thank you again."

When they step out into the street Ada laces her fingers into his. "Poor Mr. Foster," she says.

"Yes," he answers. Then, as an afterthought, he turns on her a hesitant, tortured smile that twists her heart. Wesley, it seems, is still trapped somewhere behind the surface of that glass. The attempt at a smile was the best he could do, an appeasing reflection of what he thinks she wants.

Sept. 28, 1877
Fort Benton

Dear Maj. Walsh,

Calico flapping in the breeze, tins of peaches and beans scattered over the hills, black, oily smoke – there's a picture of my mind right now. A mess and a muddle.

Have given up all pretense I can see anything clearly. Given the state of my head, I'm of no use to you or anyone else. You never wanted to be guided anyhow.

I've been drinking some. Maybe it shows.

Don't know why I bother to write since Nez Perce are said to be threatening the road between here and Fort Walsh, and this is unlikely to be delivered any time soon.

Not long ago, Maj. Ilges received intelligence that Chief Joseph was about to invest the freight station at Cow Island. His command being under strength, he prevailed upon John J. Donnelly to raise a body of citizen volunteers. I joined them. War makes strange bedfellows.

Covered the 120 miles to Cow Island Landing as fast as our horses could carry us. Clerks and soldiers there had withstood seven attacks by Nez Perce during night of 23rd. Indians had raided freight depot. What they could not carry off, they destroyed. Hills were littered with calico bolts, tin goods, etc. Hundreds of sacks of bacon were burning, heavy, black smoke everywhere. The men there told Ilges that a Farmer & Cooper wagon train was scheduled to arrive soon. The Major led us into Cow Creek Canyon to escort them in. Arrived too late. Their wagons were burning, one teamster dead. The rest had hid in a thick stand of willows. Attempted to drive Indians off, but ground not in our favour. They kept us pinned down for many hours under constant fire from hills above canyon. Were lucky to have suffered only one loss of life, Edmund Bradley, coloured man. Died of a gut wound – you know what that means. Long, painful death.

Yours sincerely,
Wesley Case

TWENTY-TWO

WITH A CONVULSIVE JERK of the legs, Case wakes in oppressive heat and silence. His first thought is, *But we are not moving. Why has the train stopped?* He searches for a carriage window, hoping to see a patch of lightening sky, but finds nothing. Gazing down the length of the railway carriage, he can make out nothing – no soldiers sleeping humped on the floor, listing in the seats, nothing but blackness thick as pitch. He hears an indistinct rumble. Another train transporting militiamen coming up behind them? A scout locomotive edging ahead to ascertain if the track has been sabotaged?

While he slept someone had wrapped him in a blanket. *In this insufferable heat? What was the fool thinking?* He kicks petulantly at the smothering, clinging warmth.

Ada murmurs a protest in her sleep and he realizes where he is. Lying absolutely still until her breathing once again grows regular and even, he carefully untangles his limbs from the sheets, swings his legs out of bed, and sits waiting for the waves of anxiety to abate, for his heart to slow. Finally he rises, goes to the window, and pulls back the curtains. What he mistook for a train is a low, thick-tongued stammer of thunder accompanied by tremors of sheet lightning. The freak October storm enters the room to keep him company; light blinks intermittently on the walls, and the heavy air is saturated with electricity. Case draws up a chair to the window and sits, elbow propped on the sash, listening to the drum roll of thunder, his mind marching in cadence to it, a brutal, jerky gait that carries him back to that June night eleven years ago, the streets of Toronto echoing with bugles calling out the militia, NCOs hammering fists to doors.

Shortly after midnight, he stumbles down his mother's staircase to the urgent clatter of a doorknocker and finds Sergeant Jimson on the doorstep. The Sergeant raps out his news in staccato bursts. "Reports that Fenians have crossed the border, Captain. Making for Fort Erie. Orders to muster at Front Street Drill Shed immediate. Colonel said to give you this." He runs his eyes over the note and learns he has been appointed temporary command of the 2nd Company. Major Lewis is incapacitated due to an ulcerated leg. There is a sudden clutch to the heart, he feels himself break a light sweat standing there barelegged in his nightshirt. Doing his best to sound calm, equal to the task, he inquires if all the other officers of the 2nd have been located and have received their orders to assemble.

"Corporal Phipps couldn't rouse Lieutenant Wilson, sir."

"Tell him to go back. Set fire to his house if you have to. We can't go short two officers."

The drill shed at Front Street is a confused melee. Sergeants bellowing at rankers, officers bellowing at noncoms, much milling about as scanty equipment and arms are dispensed. No food, canteens, blankets, or bandages available. Weapons that are older than the men, antique Enfield muzzle loaders, ball and powder for them in short supply. A few Spencer repeaters are on hand, just sufficient to arm the 5th Company of the Queen's Own, only forty cartridges to a man.

The first heat wave of the season and everyone is bundled up in winter uniforms because the commissariat has not yet authorized issue of summer kit. Tunics mapped with sweat, the drill shed hot enough to roast the Christmas goose. And into this bedlam, hours late, a nonchalant Lieutenant Pudge Wilson strolls, commandeers a chair, crosses his legs, and starts to trim his fingernails with a penknife.

But Case overlooks this studied insouciance, this tardiness, pretends not to notice Pudge neglecting his duties as he bustles about, ensuring that the 2nd receives its share of ammunition, as he worriedly checks and rechecks the company rolls.

At six-thirty that morning the Queen's Own Rifles, the 13th Battalion, the Caledonian and York Rifle Companies strike out for the harbour where the *City of Toronto* is waiting to transport them to Port Dalhousie. The streets are packed; astounding numbers have turned out to see them off, mothers, sisters, wives blotting tears with handkerchiefs, brothers, uncles, and fathers looking gravely proud. Politicians and newshounds who had sat up all night in newspaper offices receiving the latest reports telegraphed in have come down to the harbour to loyally applaud. Workmen on their way to jobs are pulling at sleeves and asking what the source of the trouble is, why the alarm? Soon there are patriotic outbursts, shaking of hats in the air, flapping of handkerchiefs, shouts of "Lay into them, boys!" "God Save the Queen" is sung, and like the miracle of the loaves and the fishes – where did they all come from? – a bounty of Union Jacks, tiny ones in the chubby fists of little children, big banners swaying on standards above the heads of the mob, flags the size of tablecloths draping lampposts.

Past the train station they tramp, arms swinging in unison, hobnailed boots cracking on the cobblestones, faces dripping sweat, heads steaming under shakos, the citizens of Toronto huzzahing until they're hoarse.

They board the steamer in good order and smartly set sail. Off starboard the sun is a bonfire on the horizon; the choppy waters of Lake Ontario stab bleary eyes with reflected sunlight. The troops crowd the ship's railings for a look at the smoke pluming Toronto, the shoreline slowly receding. A welcome breeze stirs. The sweat dries on their faces as the city dwindles, then is lost from sight. The men drift away from the bulwarks, settle down on deck, lost in thoughts of home and hunger.

No rations whatsoever had been stocked at the drill shed, so most knapsacks sag like empty socks. A lucky few have been provided by far-sighted mothers and wives with hard-boiled eggs, sardines, sandwiches, bread and cheese, which they share with comrades. A short-lived picnic breaks out on deck. The 8th and 9th Companies of the Queen's Own, fresh-faced students of Toronto's University and Trinity Colleges, improvise a game of cricket with a ball of twine and a barrel stave. Some throw their arms over one another's shoulders, sway side to side singing, "Tramp, tramp, tramp, our boys are marching, / Cheer up, let the Fenians come! / For beneath the Union Jack we'll drive the rabble back / And we'll fight for our beloved Canadian home."

He is scarcely twenty-three years old but these exuberant lads make him feel ancient. The rest of the Queen's Own are not much older than the university boys, a contingent of spotty-faced clerks, fledgling greengrocers, printers' devils, drapers' assistants, boys who have never fired a weapon at anything more menacing than a woodchuck. Looking at them, he experiences the sobering realization that these callow youths are now *his* responsibility. They are his to lead. And to do this to the best of his ability, he will need the support of Pudge, who is now his second-in-command. Some sort of understanding must be arrived at. After a short search, he find him enthroned on a coil of hawser, belly swelling out of his unbuttoned jacket like a batch of rising bread dough.

"A word, Lieutenant Wilson," he says, "before we arrive at Port Dalhousie."

"I trust a cold collation has been prepared to meet us there. If it hasn't, we must take turns spanking the quartermaster." Pudge sniffs conspicuously. "Nothing like the smell of marine air to give a man an appetite."

Gripping the rail, watching the spray breaking against the prow, casting tiny, shimmering rainbows, Case struggles to find the words to impress on him the gravity of the situation. "There is something that needs to be said. Troops take their lead from their officers –"

"Why then those poor dears are doomed, aren't they, Wesley? You and I – we're hardly made from heroic stuff."

"Talk sensibly for a moment, can you? These boys are green as grass. You and I, *we* are green as grass. The men we will face, the most of them, are Civil War veterans, have had a whiff of the grapeshot. With Major Lewis gone it is imperative that we pull together."

"Ah, Wesley, you talk as if we were a yoke of plodding oxen. You had a better sense of style in days past."

"In days past, yes. But I think you need reminding that this is not an outing of the Lilies of the Field."

"An interesting allusion – signifying what?"

"That you must not attempt to rule the roost here."

A nasty glint appears in Pudge's eyes. "One would think you had won a battlefield promotion – not ascended to your present heady heights simply because that old gasbag Major Lewis is out of action with a convenient sore on his leg."

The steamer begins to loose blasts from its whistle. Port Dalhousie is coming into sight. "Let us see to forming up the company for disembarkation," Case says. "And look to the state of your uniform, Lieutenant Wilson. Set a better example for the men."

"I am reproved." Deliberately, one by one, Pudge does up his buttons. The slowness with which he does it is a provocation. "There," he says, fastening the last of them, "now that I am spruce and tidy I am sure our men will be motivated to fight like demons."

From Port Dalhousie they move by rail to Port Colborne, where they cool their heels until midnight, awaiting orders. Then a courier arrives from Lieutenant Colonel Peacocke. Colonel Booker is to depart Port Colborne by train for Ridgeway no later than five o'clock next morning; from Ridgeway he is to march his men to Stevensville to join with Peacocke's troops. There they will confront the Fenians with their combined force.

But the long stall in Port Colborne has unravelled their army. It has been impossible to restrain hungry men from going foraging for food. The girls and taverns of the town have proved irresistible to others. After the long, sleepless night in the drill shed, many are dead to the world, asleep in barns and stables. Bugles trumpet, noncoms run through the streets baying like hounds. The roll is called on the train station platform. Indefatigable Sergeant Jimson has rounded up all of the 2nd; none are missing. But everywhere Case looks, he sees drunks feigning sobriety, others so exhausted they answer to their names as if they are talking in their sleep. Pudge has brandy on his breath and is in a black sulk.

They load the men on the train and wait. Hundreds of militiamen packed cheek by jowl in the stifling carriages. The men complain of thirst; he silences them, assures them they will soon be under way. One hour creeps by and then another. He feels the atmosphere curdle with resentment because he has refused them leave to fetch water. In truth, what he fears is that if they escape the carriage, there'll be no getting them back. Someone retches out a window. Men doze fitfully in their seats.

At five o'clock the train gives a jolt and almost throws him to the floor. Sleep had overtaken him. The locomotive advances at a walking pace, a pilot engine preceding it to ensure Irish sympathizers have not done damage to the tracks. All around him, soldiers are knuckling their eyes, coughing, peering out the windows at a smoky red dawn. It takes an hour before the train wheezes and gasps its way into Ridgeway, where they stumble off the train.

Colonel Booker orders assembly to be called in the village square. He has brought a horse by private railway car and does not wish to deprive himself or the citizens of Ridgeway of a mounted review of the troops. The thermometer on the wall of the post office already shows 85 degrees; the men stand numbly in formation while Booker's horse is saddled. Then another delay. A delegation from the village council hustles a man forward to the Colonel. He claims he has seen soldiers of the Fenian Irish Republican Army flitting through his apple orchard. Booker tells him he is mistaken; the latest intelligence received by wire puts the Fenians in an encampment near Stevensville. Or thereabouts. However, to dispel any concerns the population may have for its safety and the security of its property, Booker orders bugles to sound and the locomotive whistle to be blown to announce the arrival of Her Majesty's forces and reassure the loyal inhabitants of the village.

After that, Booker squanders an hour inspecting the troops on his prancing horse and subjecting them to a patriotic address. He emphasizes repeatedly that haste is imperative if they are to reach Stevensville by ten o'clock and keep their appointment with Colonel Peacocke. No time must be lost; the pace of march must never slacken.

They set off in column. The morning sunshine bakes their shoulders; their boots raise a chalky dust from the roadway that turns into paste on their sweaty skin; they itch in their wool winter-issue uniforms. The fields are greening, showing the first shoots of wheat, oats, and corn. The branches of the maples and oaks hold an emerald fog of new leaves. It all shimmers vibrantly, eerie as a mirage.

Within a mile, the first men begin to flag. He turns back from the head of the company to encourage stragglers not to lose contact with the rest of the troops. Some are squatting, drinking water from ditches. When he orders them to leave that muck alone, it will make them sick, someone impertinently replies they must fill their bellies since they have no canteens to fill. Several pay him absolutely no mind, keep lapping up water like dogs. Not quite open mutiny, but on the brink of it. At last, with curses and threats, he gets them on their feet and moving again.

Then he spots Pudge, sitting on an oak stump at the side of the road.

"Lieutenant Wilson," he says, "why have you halted?"

Pudge croons, "The grand old Captain Case, he had ten thousand men, he marched them up to the top of the hill –"

"Damn you!" he says. "Get to your feet!"

Pudge doesn't move. "You know, Wesley, at this moment you put me in mind of my father. It was Pater's idea I join the militia. Threatened to cut off my allowance if I didn't. He believed a dose of discipline would do me a world of good. But I do not care to be done a world of good. And if you persist in trying to order me about, you will find you have bitten off more than you can chew. I won't be corrected. Not by the likes of you."

Just then the advance shivers to a halt. At the top of a ridge, two hundred yards ahead, shakos are bobbing up and down on the ends of musket muzzles, the agreed-upon signal to indicate the enemy is in view. The dancing shakos do what he can't – they bring his recalcitrant lieutenant to his feet. "It must be a mistake," Pudge says. "Booker said the Irish were at Stevensville."

With the halt, the green dream they have been tramping through vanishes like the dust they have been raising. Everything falls into hard, sharp focus. He leaves Pudge contemplating the jigging shakos and runs to the head of the column to receive the company's battle orders. Colonel Booker dispatches scouts to estimate the enemy's strength, then gives company commanders their assignments. Armed with the best weapons, Spencer carbines, 5th Company will take the centre and lead the advance, while 1st Company is deployed to the left and 2nd to the right, to form skirmish lines. The rest of the Queen's Own are placed in supporting, flanking, and reserve roles. The advance is sounded.

He moves the 2nd off the road, takes out his telescope and searches for the enemy. In the far distance, at the top of Lime Ridge, he can just make out the banners of the Irish Republican Army, gold harps, gold sunbursts on an emerald field, a swarm of green-uniformed men throwing up defensive earthworks.

He fans the 2nd out in skirmishing order across a pasture dotted with thickets, Pudge anchoring one end of the line, young Ensign Hardisty the other, he the middle. Grazing sheep are scattered everywhere in front of them, white as remnants of snow in spring. But this is no spring sun the 2nd is advancing under. Its white blaze crimps his eyes into a defensive squint as he leads his men forward, doing his best to feign confidence and authority as his heart thuds dully and the blood roars in his ears like a windstorm.

It's open meadow for five or six hundred yards ahead of him – but Pudge's wing of the line has a clump of maples on its right and is wandering off course, nearer and nearer to it. Pudge is doing nothing to keep his men in formation; he simply toddles along behind them, looking aggrieved and put upon as he decapitates thistles with his sword. He shouts a warning to him. "Lieutenant Wilson, take care! Keep an eye on the wood! Look sharp!"

Pudge gives a cavalier wave of his sabre, and as he does the thicket of maples sparks as if it were a flint struck with steel. Pudge's shako flutters off his head. His hand touches his hair in disbelief. The next instant, he dives down behind a tussock of grass. His troops drop to one knee and fire at will, Enfields booming, stringing blue ribbons of smoke.

Case orders a volley from the centre. Down the skirmishing line, Ensign Hardisty's men raise their muskets and open fire. Muskets emptied, the 2nd freezes as clipped leaves lazily spin down from their target. A ewe is bucking and bleating on the grass, a bright spreading stain of red on its wool, the rest of the flock bounding away in a terror that could be mistaken for high spirits. In that instant, he imagines his own death in a sun-soaked meadow, his blood soaking the sweet grass, the wild ox-eye daisies.

The 2nd provides a stunned audience for three Fenian snipers who burst from the maple bush and hotfoot it back for their own lines. Nobody touches a ramrod. Nobody fumbles for powder or ball. Then somebody begins a hip, hip, hooray. All the company joins in, brandishing their muskets, tossing their shakos in the air. The cheering lifts Pudge up from his patch of grass.

Faces shine with relief and pride. His untried, exhausted boys have stood their ground, held their own. "Well done!" he shouts. "Reload! Stand to while I confer with Lieutenant Wilson!" Passing down the skirmishing line, he hands a word of encouragement here and there to the grinning militiamen. When he reaches Pudge, he takes him by the elbow and draws him out of earshot of the ranks.

"Granted the skirmish line is a loose order of advance," he says. "But not so loose that an officer skulks along behind the formation. You *lead* the line, Lieutenant Wilson. That is your place. And you keep a watchful eye on the terrain."

Pudge's forefinger is worrying away at the hole in his shako; his eyes are turned to the centre where the battle is heating up. The snapping reports of the Spencers are like bursts from a string of firecrackers. A drum throbs insistently.

His second-in-command does not seem to have heard a word he has addressed to him. "I would advise you to tuck us in behind the 5th," Pudge says quietly. "Well behind them."

"Tuck us in behind the 5th? Are you mad? We are to guard their flank, see to it that the enemy doesn't turn them, roll them up."

"The 5th have the repeaters," Pudge says, as if that is reason enough to ignore the order.

"And you are suggesting we hide behind them? Keep well clear of the action?"

"In the confusion of battle – how should I put it – orders are often misunderstood, often difficult to execute." Pudge gives him a knowing look. "Consider this my personal appeal to you to take advantage of this well-known military phenomenon."

"You and your personal appeal can go to hell," he says, voice shaking with anger.

He knows Pudge is furious as well, recognizes it from the calculated fashion with which he draws a brandy flask from his pocket and sips it, from the evenhanded coolness with which he speaks. "You know, last year when you fell enamoured with the lady from New Orleans and decided to no longer keep company with your old friends, they used to lament your disloyalty. I consoled them as best I could by pointing out the impossibility of turning a pig's ear into a silk purse." He caps his flask. "I take it that this display of high ideals, of high purpose, is an attempt to forget who you are. But Wesley, the son of a vulgar woodcutter, of a man whose trouser cuffs leak sawdust on the floor of every drawing room he enters, remains what he is despite all attempts to mimic his betters. Lord knows, I made a valiant try to make a gentleman of you, but it was like trying to clean the Augean stables."

Despite the calmness with which Pudge speaks, he can feel a sour, violent hatred emanating from him. It is a struggle for Case to collect himself, keep his voice level. "So I am a poser? And what of you? The *beau sabreur* with the Code Duello in his pocket." He taps Pudge's sword scabbard with his finger. "Lieutenant Wilson, I know how you have longed to test your steel. The moment has arrived."

He strides away from Pudge to where his men wait, raises a telescope to study the progress of the 5th. There are tremors in his hands; he has trouble bringing the glass to bear. But at last he steadies it. The 5th are stalled for the moment behind a rail fence, facing a pocket of stubborn Irish resistance. He sweeps the telescope over what lies before the 2nd, a stretch of low ground covered in marsh grass, backed by a fieldstone wall. Beyond the wall is a copse. From that copse a puff of smoke emerges, briefly hangs in the air. It cannot be a single sniper. A sniper would not make that mistake. There must be a body of Irish in that wood, and one of them, unable to restrain himself, has fired too early. When the 5th dislodge the Irish before them and resume their advance, they will pass very near that wood where an ambuscade has apparently been laid.

He feels a moment of panic, indecision, then orders his men to go into a crouch, advance as swiftly as possible under cover of the tall marsh grass, and rendezvous behind the fieldstone wall. And they do, without being detected by the Irish, whose attention seems to be focused on the 5th. Panting, trying to catch his breath with his back propped to the wall, he realizes he has committed the gravest of errors. In his rush to protect the flank of the 5th, he neglected to send a messenger to warn them of a possible ambush. And at this very moment, he can see the Queen's Own spilling over the rail fence, beginning to move forward. Even if he dispatched a runner now, how would a messenger locate the commanding officer in that ragged wave of men?

There is no choice; the 2nd must immediately attack the wood, root out any Fenians hiding here. He issues his orders. His most junior officer, boyish Ensign Hardisty, is to remain behind the wall, the position of greatest security and safety. Pudge will lead his platoon to the right and take cover behind a cord of wood curing on a small rise. As company commander, he will take the left, place himself directly between the Irish in the thicket and the 5th.

His plan is simple and desperate. On a signal from him, Hardisty will loose a volley on the copse, poke a stick in the Irish nest of hornets, prompting them to return fire. When they do, he and Pudge will attack from the left and right with bayonets fixed, catch the Irish with their muskets emptied.

Turning to Hardisty, he inquires urgently, "Do you understand, Ensign? You are not to fire until you receive my signal."

"Yes, sir."

"And you, Lieutenant Wilson, do you have your orders clear? Go quickly to the rise, wait until you see the Irish return Ensign Hardisty's fire, and then fall on them."

Pudge's crisp, firm response surprises him. "By God, I shall. With a will."

"If you wish, I can lend you Sergeant Jimson for the attack. The man is solid as oak."

"Sergeant Jimson is not required. I would prefer not to have him."

"Five minutes to reach the hillock, and not a second more."

"Good as done."

While he and his men crawl through the marsh grass, the stalks rustling and brushing their faces, they disturb a crowd of butterflies, small scraps of brightness that flutter above their heads; one lights on his sleeve, rests there, opening and closing its frail orangey-copper wings. He looks down at it, hears the angry gavel of gunfire from the 5th slamming repeatedly, over and over, trying to calm his fear by drawing air into his lungs in time to the serene movements of those wings. His breathing needs steadying. He feels an urgent need to urinate. Then, suddenly, the butterfly takes flight from his forearm, flutters, soars like a kite that has jerked free from his fingers.

They reach their objective, a trench dug to drain the field of spring runoff, slide down into it, squat in stagnant water spotted with little islets of green scum. This time when the men drink, he does nothing to stop them. Instead, he too gulps handfuls of warm, fetid water, splashes it on his burning face and neck. Fear has sucked every drop of moisture from his mouth. It is all he can do to restrain himself until the men are finished drinking. Hidden to the waist by the water, he pisses in his trousers.

Bobbing his head above the lip of the ditch, he looks towards the stack of wood on the hillock. No sign of Pudge yet. The crackle of the Spencers is skulking closer and closer. There is not much time left to act. He counts to a hundred and raises his head above the embankment again. Still no Pudge. Ensign Hardisty is waiting expectantly for the order to loose a volley on the Fenians.

Striking his thigh with his fist, Case swears under his breath.

"Sir?" says phlegmatic Sergeant Jimson, a man perplexed by any sign of emotion in a superior.

"Fix bayonets," he says. There is a click of steel as the men lock sword bayonets to the barrels of their Enfields. "Boys," he says, "when I go, follow hard. Do not hesitate." He flags an arm at Hardisty, whose troops rise up behind the wall, level their muskets, and discharge them with a heavy thump. Smoke billows, writhes, twists down the wall in tendrils of black ivy.

The Irish return the favour; muzzle flame spatters the shadowy thicket.

Pistol in right hand, he paws at the greasy side of the trench with his left, struggling to pull his boots clear of the grip of the mud. He hears himself screaming, "Charge! Charge!" All around him bayonets spring from the earth, a wicked bristle and glitter of light. Up over the embankment they scramble. He is running hard, the dark wood heaving before him, jouncing in a crazed dance, the burning sky listing and yawing, raining glassy shards of light into his eyes. He feels his knee twist, stumbles. Private Jones tears by him, shrieking as if his bayonet was dragging him towards the Irish against his will.

The wood barks gunfire. A body strikes the ground beside him, rolls and skids. He storms into the trees, branches slapping his face, twigs jabbing at his eyes. Dim shapes whirl and stagger, the green of the Irish uniforms blending with the green of the foliage. Shrill shouts, the din of muskets, some Irishman shouting "Mary, Mother of God! Mary, Mother of God!" He shoots at any figure that doesn't wear a shako, swinging his revolver from right to left.

Dazzling shafts of sunlight slice through the canopy, flash lightning on contorted faces, lick fire from bayonet blades. Bodies blunder over deadfalls, collide with tree trunks. Guttural oaths, animal grunts, the crackle of frantic flight, acrid smoke stinging his nostrils, flooding his eyes with water. The final kick of the revolver in his hand followed by the click of a hammer striking empty chambers as he sights a fleeing back down the barrel of the pistol.

As suddenly as it began, it is over. The 2nd has taken the wood. Owners and occupiers of stillness, a silence broken only by the scraping pant of breathless men, the sound of someone biting back sobs. The momentum of the charge has carried

them into a clearing. Militiamen cling to branches or prop themselves against trees, sit slumped, heads between their knees,
shoulders heaving. He fingers a scratch on his forehead. Sharp,
nagging pain is pure rapture; it proves he is alive.

His legs feel cottony and feeble; he sinks to the ground just
as Ensign Hardisty's detachment slowly edges through the
brush, their bayonets moving like tentative, inquisitive antennae. "Well done, sir. Well done, indeed," he hears Hardisty say,
a voice reaching him from a far-off room.

He croaks when he answers, tongue fumbling in his mouth.
"They ran," he says. "I don't know why. They just broke and
ran." He hauls himself off the ground. "I saw one of our men
go down as we charged. Back there," he explains vaguely. "Send
someone to check on him." He doesn't trust his legs; the ground
under him is shifting sand. "Casualties?" he calls to the 2nd.
"Dead? Wounded?"

A corporal, rendered speechless by shock, holds up a hand
shattered by a Fenian minié ball. Dripping blood braids the
sleeve of his tunic. He orders a tourniquet applied, delegates a
man to lead him back to the rear.

A cluster of men gathered at the edge of the clearing, staring down at something at their feet, attracts his notice. "What is
it? What have you got there?" he calls to them.

"A Fenian, sir. Dead." The answer sounds oddly apologetic.

He crosses to where they are. An Irishman lies sprawled on
his back near a single birch marooned in the clearing. The dye
he used to colour his surplus U.S. Army tunic green has not been
a success. He looks to be covered in splotchy green mould.
Already bluebottles are raising a buzz around him.

He stoops to examine the body. A youngster, scarcely more
than sixteen or seventeen. His flesh is fading to a spectral white;
a few wispy strands of penny-coloured hair are scribbled below
his earlobes, a boy's vain try at sideburns. A ball has smashed his
right cheekbone; his broken skull lies on a smear of brains and
coagulating blood. The damage to the cheek gives a mocking

squint to his eye, as if he is looking askance at those who have robbed him of life. A sheaf of yellow paper protrudes from his tunic pocket.

Reaching down, pulling it free, he directs his attention to the paper to avoid the scornful, accusing face. It is a Fenian proclamation addressed to the population of Canada West under authority of T.W. Sweeny who bears the majestic, grandiloquent title of Major-General Commanding the Armies of Ireland. Here and there phrases wriggle into his consciousness. *We are here neither as murderers, nor robbers, for plunder and spoliation. We are an army of liberation . . . We appeal in the name of seven centuries of British iniquity and Irish misery and suffering, in the name of murdered sires, our desolate homes, our desecrated altars, our million of famine graves . . .*

He hears a familiar voice behind him. "*Veni, vidi, vici*, so said Caesar. So says Captain Case." Pudge and his platoon have finally appeared. Lieutenant Wilson strolls over to the corpse, fumbles a pocketknife out of his trouser pocket; as he does the men crowd round, curious to see what he is up to. Now Pudge is kneeling beside the body, using his knife on it. He straightens up, displays a button, passes it tantalizingly before their eyes. It is brass, lovingly polished. The initials IRA are stamped on it, wreathed with a garland.

"Here, gentlemen," says Pudge, "is a watch fob for a hero. I present it to our Captain. Every time he fingers his watch chain, he will be warmed by the memory of his triumph." Pudge holds it out to him. It is spurned with a shake of the head. Lieutenant Wilson shrugs. "No? You are too modest. There will be nothing to show the grandchildren when they climb up on your lap on a winter evening, nothing to give credence to your war stories. Ah well, then I will keep it." He glances down at the corpse. "And you, you Irish bastard," he says, "this is for the hole your friends put in my shako." And Pudge kicks the corpse so hard he shifts it.

His first impulse is to strike him, knock him flat, but he checks himself, simulates an icy reserve. "The dead will not be subjected to any indignity by a soldier of the 2nd. Their personal possessions will not be touched. Do I make myself clear?"

The men shuffle back from the corpse. Pudge, however, makes a great show of tucking the plundered button away in the pocket of his tunic.

"Ensign Hardisty, assemble the men outside the wood. Sergeant Jimson and Lieutenant Wilson, remain here with me."

The 2nd beat a hangdog retreat from the thicket. Burly Sergeant Jimson clasps his huge hands behind his back and sucks a moustache tip, looking puzzled.

"Lieutenant Wilson, I want an explanation for your failure to press the attack as ordered."

Pudge gives his captain a tiny, patronizing smile. "Spying a conveyance in the distance that appeared to be an artillery carriage, I moved my men to intercept it before it could be trained on Hardisty at the wall. Alas, it proved to be a farmer's wagon. He had stripped his home of articles of value, fearing Irish marauders would pillage his property. I had mistaken a roll of carpet extending from the back of the buckboard for a cannon barrel. You can well imagine my chagrin at such a mistake."

"And that is all you have to say for yourself? The best you can offer?"

"I think it sufficient. I would not expect you to question a brother officer's statement." He indicates Jimson by a nod of the head. "Especially in the presence of one of the rank and file. It is hardly good form."

"And you, you put all our lives in danger, for the sake of your precious skin."

"Frankly, my men seemed pleased with the initiative I showed in intercepting that farmer's wagon. Of course, I did not canvass them on their feelings, but I think it fair to say I read in their faces a proper gratitude towards me. It is not me but you who plays fast and loose with lives." He shrugs. "You are too much a striver after glory, Wesley. You must have a regard for the welfare of those under you."

He has to wait several moments to be sure of his voice; his throat is choked with rage. "Sergeant Jimson, bind Lieutenant Wilson to this tree," he says, indicating the birch near the dead Irish boy.

Pudge gives a snort of laughter. Jimson's eyes shift uneasily.

He repeats the order. "Tie him to that tree and be quick about it, Sergeant."

"Tie him with what, sir?"

"Use his revolver lanyard. And make sure it's tight."

When Jimson makes the first move towards him, Pudge cries out, "I'm warning you! If you put a hand to me, you'll regret it!"

Befuddled, Jimson throws a questioning glance. "Captain Case?"

"I have given you an order, Sergeant. If Lieutenant Wilson resists, use whatever force is required to subdue him."

Pudge offers no resistance. He allows Jimson to gently manoeuvre him to the tree, turn his back to it, and bind him. The task completed, Sergeant Jimson steps away. Pudge's chin hangs on his breastbone; his eyes are fastened on the ground. "You have made your point, Wesley. I have been humiliated," he says so quietly he can scarcely be heard. He lifts his eyes. "I concede. Whatever lesson this was supposed to teach me, I have learned it. Now cut me loose."

"No, Lieutenant, that cannot be done. Your concern for your own safety places us all in great jeopardy. You cannot be trusted. The men need to be protected from your influence. I am holding you in quarantine."

Pudge struggles in his bonds. "Let me loose, damn you!"

"If I free you, you'll scamper for the rear – desertion in the face of the enemy. A thing difficult to explain away. Now your father's cuffs don't leak sawdust like mine, he is a very fine gentleman. I merely wish to save that *very fine gentleman* from disgrace."

Once again, Pudge lunges forward, this time so hard that the tree shakes.

"Sergeant, please go and inform Ensign Hardisty that Lieutenant Wilson's strange behaviour is attributable to heat-stroke," he says. "Tell him that as soon as I have made the Lieutenant comfortable in a spot of shade, I'll join the men and we will proceed. Give this explanation loudly so the men can hear it."

"Very good, sir." Sergeant Jimson's face betrays neither approval nor disapproval. He goes off smartly.

"I beg you – don't leave me alone here," says Pudge. For the first time, his plea sounds genuine.

"You have company." He points to the dead Fenian. "Tell him your troubles." Reaching into Pudge's tunic pocket, he fishes out the button, moves to the corpse, and lays it on the dead boy's chest.

Behind him, he hears Pudge say, "How like you, Wesley, to fall prey to sentimentality, to ice the cake with sickly sweetness. Cheap flamboyance changes nothing. He's still dead." Case leaves him and walks out into the fierce white heat. The body of the militiaman who had fallen beside him during the charge is laid out on the ground, hands folded on his breast, a handkerchief covering his face. The sounds of battle swell and subside, sudden jolts of musketry followed by a desultory popping, then another furious discharge. Rolling on, waxing and waning.

The incident with the button has left the 2nd crestfallen; they seem to believe his criticism of Lieutenant Wilson pertains to them, too. "Keep your heads, and peg away at them, boys!" he cries, offering them a cheerful front. "Peg away at them and by nightfall we shall have those beggars back to the United States or in hell!"

They answer him with a throaty hurrah. And peg away is what they do for the next hour, sometimes stymied, sometimes sending the Irish into flight. They are lying prone on a pebbly ridge, shot sprinkling them with dirt and stone chips, when bugles sound the call to retire. Assuming it to be a mistake, he sends a runner post-haste to the commander of the 5th to verify the withdrawal. In minutes, the courier is back with news that the 5th is running low on ammunition for their Spencers. Colonel Booker has decided to relieve all front-line troops and send up the reserves to replace the Queen's Own with the 13th Battalion, the York Rifles, and the Highland Company. He is confident fresh troops will deliver the blow that breaks the Irish back. The Queen's Own is to retreat to Garrison Road and await Colonel Peacocke and his reinforcements, which are expected shortly. They will assist Peacocke in mopping-up operations, if such operations are required.

The rest of the companies of the Queen's Own are heading back to the crossroads, ignorant of the reasons for the retreat. Rumours of a disaster are spreading. To the right, he hears cries of "Cavalry! Cavalry! Look out for cavalry! Irish cavalry on the way!" The infantryman's terror of horsemen falling on them when they are on open ground sweeps through the ranks. They flee as fast as their legs can carry them. Meeting white-faced boys breaking for the rear, the reserves moving up to the front assume the worst has occurred and take to their heels too. In minutes, what was meant to be an orderly withdrawal turns into a panicked rout.

And the Irish, seeing them in flight, seize the initiative and follow in hot pursuit. A breaker of green uniforms plunges down the slope of Lime Ridge, curls around sugar bushes and thickets, cascades over stone walls and snake fences, as the Fenians come howling down on them, rifles snapping.

Looking about him, he sees that exhaustion, hunger, heat, and sleeplessness have sapped his company of their last reserves of will to fight. Only the success of the advance had kept up their spirits. There are several whose faces are purple-ashen, they no longer sweat – victims of heatstroke. A number of wounded are using their muskets for crutches. Another warning cry of "Cavalry! Fenian cavalry!" and the 2nd too goes pelting, limping, staggering down the hill for Garrison Road.

At the crossroads, the buglers peal the "Call to Prepare for Cavalry." There is a confused scramble to form a tight square, to turn the milling crowd of troops into four walls of extended bayonets to repulse the expected cavalry charge. Colonel Booker is clinging to the back of his wild-eyed horse, which has caught the contagion of fear from its rider. The Colonel is pointing with his sword and screaming, "There! There! To the west! The west!"

Three horsemen canter into view, study the havoc on the crossroads, and lope off.

The ranks tensely stand shoulder to shoulder, breath held, waiting for the Irish Republican cavalry to whirl down on them. The officers who occupy the centre of the square move about, reassuring the men. "All will be well. Stand firm and they will turn. Cavalry cannot break a square. *Cavalry cannot break a square.*" Some shake uncontrollably; one boy faints, drops face first into the dust. Snatches of the Lord's Prayer and the Rosary are stammered.

A cloud of dust rises above a ridge. Out of it appears not cavalry but a Fenian regiment of infantry. Booker has made a serious misjudgment in preparing for a cavalry attack. Before the order to form square can be countermanded, the inviting target dispersed, the Irish deliver a concentrated volley into the mob of tightly packed bodies. It is like shooting rats in a barrel.

Around him, the square collapses, smashes with a cacophony of shrieks and groans, reeling bodies. The mighty walls of Jericho crumble to dust and a fearful wind sends the dust flying down Garrison Road. Booker's horse spins like a top, squealing, blood spurting from its haunch, the Colonel bellowing for the halt to be sounded. But when the bugler blows, it sounds like a wail of grief. For those dazed few still stuck to the road in shock, that plaintive, mournful sound tears loose their boots and they join the stampede.

He and a handful of other officers do their best to stop the fleeing troops. But the men rush by them, frantically casting aside muskets, ammunition pouches, knapsacks. In the blink of an eye, Garrison Road looks as if a military supply wagon had overturned and spilled its goods. Booker gallops by, bucketing from side to side in the saddle, shouting his final order. "Port Colborne! Port Colborne. Make for Colborne!" His staff takes after him on foot.

Rooted in the powdery dust of the country road, he stares back over the ground so hard won and then so easily lost, sees the Fenians moving to the right to harass the Highlanders who had been sent up to relieve the Queen's Own and who are making a fighting retreat, kilts swinging, bagpipes dolefully droning. Elsewhere, the Irish are driving militiamen through the fields, their retreat marked in the newly sprouted crops.

The debacle is complete. His company is gone, blown away like leaves in a November wind. Dependable Hardisty is gone. Stoical Jimson is gone. Except for the wounded tottering by, he is alone. A militiaman hops along on one leg, dragging the other behind him. Four brave souls hitched to a farmer's buggy loaded with seriously wounded rattle by. One of them shouts a warning. "You best fly, sir. In twenty minutes the bogtrotters will be down on you when they're finished with the Highlanders."

He swings around to face Port Colborne and the comet-tail of the rout, determined to retire with dignity, at a walking pace. But once the enemy is at his back, his stride proves to have a mind of its own. It lengthens. Then it becomes a trot; next he is running, pounding the turnpike like he had pounded the cinders of the racetrack of his old school in the days he had won ribbons for his turn of speed. He overtakes the men hauling the buggy of gravely wounded, races by those sitting numbly in the road, legs collapsed under them, past those retching and shuddering in the ditches, done in by heat prostration.

The heat throbs in his temples, stitches his side, burns his lungs and mouth. The road begins to slither in his eyes and he falls, lies grinding his cheekbone ferociously into the clay.

When he sits up he notes a narrow country lane intersecting the road on his right, bordered by two rows of elms that meet above it in an arch of leaves. It has to lead to some farmstead, to water. He staggers down it, the sound of birdsong trickling down on his head. At the end of the lane stands a small house of yellow brick, surrounded by outbuildings, chicken coops, and a pigsty. Walking into the yard, he shouts a salute to the house. There is no reply. A flock of hens pecking a pile of horse dung by a well squawk and scatter when he approaches. A dented tin cup sits on the well cover. He pumps himself six cupfuls of icy water, gulps them down one after another until his forehead and teeth ache. Ducking his head under the spout, he sends a gush of water over his hair and neck, flicks his head back and forth trying to clear the havoc and confusion of the past hour from his head.

He sees Pudge lashed to the birch.

The farmhouse radiates emptiness and abandonment. Still, a family might be cowering inside, fearful of Irish pillagers. He gently taps on the door. Again, no response. He lifts the latch, calls a diffident hello into a mudroom reeking of sour milk and cow manure. Nothing. He eases into the kitchen.

The family has bolted. The breakfast dishes are still on the table, bacon rinds and congealed egg yolk on plates, cold coffee in mugs, a jar of strawberry jam unsealed, several flies trapped in its stickiness, a heel of brown bread lying on the table. He spoons the jar clean of jam, and swallows the bread so quickly he chokes several times.

Going back to the mudroom, he rifles through the work clothes hanging there, trousers spattered with cow shit, thread-bare shirts laundered so often their red-and-blue plaids have faded to pale remnants of colour.

His mind is focused on Pudge. To reach him, he will have to pass through the enemy lines. That attempt would best be made in the guise of a civilian. Exchanging his uniform for farmer's clothing, he lays out tunic, trousers, and shako on the kitchen table, and places his sword alongside them, his pledge the farmer's clothes will be returned. He tucks his revolver into the waistband of his pants and leaves his shirttails hanging out to keep it con-cealed. But if he requires a disguise, so does Pudge. He finds a pair of coveralls, stuffs them into a milk pail, and covers them with chickenfeed from a sack in the corner of the mudroom.

This time he keeps to the countryside, hoping to avoid the Irish troops moving up the road. Then a half mile into his journey he encounters a platoon of Irish soldiers, coursing the fields like hunting dogs. Caught in the open, he simply stops dead in his tracks and gapes, his impression of a rustic stunned by the sight of invaders. They are a tough-looking crew, broad shouldered and barrel chested, men who look like they'd been swinging picks since infancy.

When they question him as to what he is doing and where he is going, he shows them the pail and whines out, "All the ruckus scared off my milk cow. She ain't been milked this morning, her bag will be about to burst. I got to lure her to me with these here oats."

One of them says, "Yours isn't the only cow we scared this morning. A whole herd of them took one look at us, bawled, and took fright. There wasn't a bull in the whole lot of them. Nothing but steers and heifers."

There are guffaws and whoops. They wait belligerently for a response. He grins sheepishly, awkwardly, rubs his chin as if struck dumb. It is the tribute they demand. Satisfied, they slope off with a final warning. Take yourself home. The Irish army is mopping up and you might catch yourself a minié ball.

He trudges on until he comes parallel to the crossroads on Garrison Road where Booker had met disaster. The Irish army appears to have turned it into a mustering point; it is plugged with soldiers. Amidst all this bustle, a civilian in their midst will likely be assumed somebody else's problem or responsibility; with any luck he should be able to pass unmolested through the crowd, reach the other side of the road, and head for the spot where he left Pudge.

Many of the Irish are cooking; a haze of smoke floats in the air. Patrols are herding new captives to join those already sitting morosely under guard. Three men drive a herd of plough horses pried from the hands of local farmers into a rope corral. There is singing and laughter. A green-uniformed soldier trundles a cask of beer on a wheelbarrow, plunder from some roadside tavern.

Screwing up his courage, he moves down among the enemy troops. Soldiers bake bread dough twisted around ramrods, bacon spits in frying pans, potatoes roast in hot ashes. Men play cards on blankets spread on the ground. The atmosphere is curiously peaceful and domestic. No one gives him a second look. He spies a group of Irish officers astraddle the road, conferring on horseback. Dipping his head, he tries to sidle by them, unnoticed. Then behind him he hears someone call out, "You there! Halt!"

Slowly, he turns and faces the officers. One wears a good deal more gold braid on his uniform than the others, a fine figure of a man with a full auburn moustache that gives proof of careful cultivation and grooming. "You there, suffering Jesus, what are you doing traipsing your arse around here!"

"Looking for my milk cow. The commotion scared it off," he says, working up a humble, conciliatory smile.

His questioner crosses his wrists on the pommel of his saddle. "The man is looking for his cow, Captain Maloney," he says disdainfully. "Here, gentlemen, is a stellar example of the Anglo-Saxon character. They care for nothing but property, property, and, once again, property. They are a people devoid of spiritual feelings or exalted sentiments. They swallow defeat like a cup of warm milk and go looking for their cow." Then he adds, "But perhaps I must correct myself. This one must think he is under the special care of the angels to go cow-hunting on a day such as this."

There is a burst of laughter from the Irish officers. "Well put, General O'Neill," says one of them.

O'Neill demands to know where he has come from.

"Back up the road."

"And *up the road* where you come from – are the Canadians regrouping there?"

"No."

"And if they were, would you tell me?"

"Not in a month of Sundays."

The General smiles down at him patronizingly, eases back in his saddle, stretches his legs against the stirrups. "An honest man at least." He gestures to his officers. "Has anyone of you anything with which to write?"

One of them passes him a notebook and pencil. O'Neill lays the notebook on his thigh, swiftly scribbles something, rips off the page, and hands it to him. "There," he says, "I've written you a pass. If anyone interferes with you, show him that. The Irish Republican Army demonstrates the utmost solicitude towards civilians. It is a point of pride with us to conduct ourselves at all times in such a fashion as to shame those mercenaries who serve the Queen of England for pay." He waits for thanks. "Do you understand what I am saying to you?"

"Yes, I can look for my cow."

O'Neill scornfully waves him off. "Yes, yes, go look for your cow. Be quick about it. Do not clutter the premises."

Case veers off Garrison Road and makes for the copse where he had imprisoned Pudge, a blurry green smudge in the early-afternoon heat. The ground it had taken the Queen's Own hours to win he navigates in ten minutes. Outside the wood he listens for any sound that would suggest the enemy's presence, but all is quiet and still. He slips into the trees, proceeding gingerly, careful not to disturb any deadfall, stopping to cock an ear for voices or movement ahead. All he hears are bird cries, the faint rustling of leaves. On the edge of the glade, he crouches behind a bush, puts his hand to the revolver butt, and studies the scene. The sun glares in the clearing. And there is Pudge Wilson, his back to him, still bound.

One thing is not as he remembers it. The body of the Irishman is gone; a whorl of matted grass marks where it had lain. His breath snags in his throat. He rises, steals forward, addressing the bowed shoulders in a loud whisper, "Pudge? Pudge?"

His eyes run round the circumference of the glade, flick over the black trunks, the dark scramble of underbrush, catch the glint of the Irish soldier's button, nested in the grass where the body had lain. Turning back to Pudge, seeing how the lanyard has sawed deep into the flesh of his wrists, Case hurries forward.

What greets him is impossible to absorb. First, the slaughterhouse stench of blood, shit, and tallow. Then the swarm of yellow jackets that the smell has attracted. They bead Pudge's bloody lips and form a quivering, chaotic halo above his head. A cloudy film floats on his blank eyes. His jaws are cracked wide as if he is still screaming. A drapery of intestines falls to his knees, spilling from a belly ripped from crotch to breastbone, and yellow jackets, drunk on the odour of freshly butchered meat, are parading there.

His attempts to compose the body, to close Pudge's jaws, to scoop his vitals back into the yawning cavity, enrage the insects. They settle on every inch of his exposed skin, stinging him, lighting him up with darts of pain. He does not flinch from their attacks. He does not flinch when he frees Pudge from his bonds and the weight of his lifeless embrace sags them both to the ground. He does not flinch when a cupful of blood empties from Pudge's mouth and baptizes him with a slick caul. All he wants is to walk the two of them away from this, back to the moment when a petulant, rash decision was made so he can undo it. But despite his best efforts, Pudge will not walk, cannot be made to walk. He is extinguished.

Case watches as the storm advances. Sheet lightning convulses the horizon. Paroxysms of greenish-yellow light flicker in his eyes; there is a laboured, hollow groaning from the belly of the sky.

There is no shaking the one he left behind. He is sure that is the message of the thunder.

TWENTY-THREE

FOR SEVERAL DAYS IN Fort Benton, the subject of most casual street-corner talk is the strange thunderstorm that had broken unexpectedly over the town so late in the season. But then another distraction rumbles down Front Street, an impressive convoy of Murphy wagons, flanked by a contingent of cavalry. In a matter of hours, the news is all over town that one General Alfred Terry is in command of the wagon train and he is headed for Fort Walsh to open peace negotiations with Sitting Bull.

When Case hears of this, it does not come as a complete surprise. Two months before, Ilges had informed him that vague rumours were circulating among the officer class that the United States government was about to form a commission to open talks with the Sioux. Immediately, Case had contacted Walsh to find out what he knew of this, and received a short, testy reply from the Major. "Nothing. But I have been ordered to stand ready to round up the Sioux and bring them in to talk – if this goddamn thing ever materializes." For many weeks, Case heard nothing more concerning this. The flight of Chief Joseph and the Nez Perce from Oregon, the anxiety and fear aroused by their presence in Montana was the chief preoccupation of everyone on the frontier.

Now, however, the notion of an overture to the Sioux has been resuscitated. What Ilges refers to as the Terry Commission has been given the responsibility of treating with Sitting Bull. What exactly the commission's mandate is, Ilges does not know, but he presumes that Terry has been asked to extend the olive branch to the Sioux.

Case has his suspicions, however. Months of intricate diplomatic manoeuvring on the part of the United States, Canada, and Britain have to have prompted this step. A meeting between Terry and Sitting Bull could not have been engineered without the blessing and cooperation of all three governments. What he cannot see is how any outcome can please all three parties concerned. In his opinion, it is highly likely that the Americans will settle for nothing short of total submission on the part of Sitting Bull. Only the return of the Sioux to American territory will satisfy British and Canadian expectations. As for the Indians, he is certain that the best they can hope for is to gather a few paltry crumbs swept off the negotiating table.

News of the Nez Perce presence in the vicinity of the Bear Paw Mountains, which lie very near the freight road that connects Fort Benton and Fort Walsh, has, for the present, stalled the commission here in town. It is clear that Terry is not ready to run the sort of risk that Custer did – one eminent general slaughtered by Indians is humiliation enough for the United States. He is waiting for Colonel Miles to clear the path for him.

Bear Coat Miles is pursuing Chief Joseph just as he hounded Sitting Bull. Case surmises that if Chief Joseph and his people do cross the Medicine Line, that will be the end of any chance of Terry's holding peace talks with Bull. On the face of it, outwitting and outrunning Miles would be a small triumph for Chief Joseph, but Sitting Bull would take heart from it, seize every advantage he could from the situation. In the past, the Sioux chief has been diligent in attempting to forge alliances with other tribes. If the Nez Perce reach Canadian soil, it can be presumed Sitting Bull will pursue the same policy with Chief Joseph and his people. Two renowned Indian leaders, united in their stalwart resistance to American authority, might prove an irresistible attraction to many other Indians, draw more and more of the tribes over the border and into the Grandmother's country, disrupting the entire frontier.

For many months, Case and Ilges have been circling the enigma of Sitting Bull, speculating on his character, trying to predict his next move. Their discussions have been a sort of parlour game, but nevertheless a serious one. Now the Sioux chief has taken a step that astonishes Case, something as surprising as Crazy Horse's unexpected surrender six months before. Apparently, the most prominent of the Sioux chiefs has agreed to sit down with Terry and discuss terms. Case is skeptical that Bull, even if he has realized the hopelessness of his situation, would be ready to yield as Crazy Horse did. He would like nothing better than to witness the forthcoming proceedings between the Americans and the Sioux.

His thoughts turn to Walsh. Case assumes that the Major will not accept the mission of bringing the Sioux to the negotiating table with good grace; he will find it beneath his dignity to be cast in the role of delivery boy to General Terry, and that may create its own complications.

So Case goes to Ilges. During the course of their various conversations, he has talked about having dabbled in this and that in his former life, and he now informs Ilges that he has received a telegram from the Toronto paper where he once was employed, asking if he would consider covering the upcoming talks for it. Would Ilges consider intervening with Terry on his behalf, lobby the General to grant permission for him to accompany the commission when it departs for Fort Walsh? Ilges agrees to assist him, and Case's claim to be a special correspondent to the Toronto *Leader* soon produces results. General Terry accedes to his request. Terry, who has two other men of the press accompanying him, Jerome Stillson of the *New York Herald* and Charles Diehl of the *Chicago Times*, can hardly deny a Canadian journalist the right to cover an affair of such importance to his nation. Case has no qualms about using his former connection to the

Leader and to the editor who had summarily dismissed him more than ten years ago to get him what he wants.

Two days after that, word arrives that Chief Joseph has finally surrendered to Colonel Miles in the Bear Paws. The way now cleared, the Terry Commission sets off for Fort Walsh, and Case goes with it.

Ada remains at school until six o'clock, preparing lessons and marking assignments. In the past few days she has made it a habit not to bring her work home with her so that she can keep Wesley company in the evenings. His spirits have improved; she thinks the cause for it is the Terry Commission and the hope it brings of settling the troubles with the Sioux, a topic that is frequently on his lips. He seems steadier, but she thinks any further diversion she can provide will help keep him from sinking into the black state that had so alarmed her after his return from Cow Island.

The house that greets her is forbiddingly dark and quiet. She calls up the stairs and gets no reply. Dreading he might have had a relapse – is lying up there with an arm flung across his eyes as if he is barring the light from his mind – she goes up to check on him. But the room is empty, the bed neatly made, the counterpane so tight and smooth it looks as if it has been pressed flat with a hot iron. The sight of it turns her hands cold and clammy. This is how a punctilious houseguest would leave his quarters when he departs.

Ada hurries downstairs. On the kitchen table she discovers the sheaf of soiled and tattered foolscap she had come upon him reading once, and which he had so quickly hidden from her sight. But now here it is, centred on the table as precisely as the bed had been made. Beside it are several pages of writing paper covered in Wesley's minuscule script. It is some time before she dares to pick up the letter, but then she does, and begins to read.

My dearest Ada,

By the time you read this I shall be well on my way to Fort Walsh to attend the talks between General Terry and Sitting Bull. I regret not to have given you warning of my intention to make this journey, but I feared if I did you would attempt to dissuade me and succeed. I have an opportunity to witness something significant and to see the Sioux chief at close quarters as he and General Terry face each other across the negotiating table. Perhaps I may be of use to Major Walsh as these events unfold.

And there is something else, far more important to me, which I must say. Late one night, a little more than a week ago, I resolved to reveal something to you from my past. I thought it only right and fitting that you should see me more clearly – even if it means running the risk of you showing me your back, the thing I most dread. You have always demanded that we make ourselves known to each other, and you are entitled to the truth.

But each time I tried to find the moment to speak, I lost my will.

Instead, I have decided to leave you a written account, one that will explain an event from my past. I believe that my absence will give you the time and the solitude to come to a quiet and reasoned decision about my nature. I realize that if I were there to see your face when you learned the truth, I might beg you to take pity on me. That would hardly be fair. Perhaps all this strikes you as craven equivocation but if it is, my heart is not aware of it.

Beside this letter, there is a document, an honest record of my conduct in a battle that occurred more than ten years ago. I wrote it shortly after the incident to which I allude. I have kept this statement near me all these years as a reminder that I was responsible for ending a man's life. My father asked me to write it out to assist his lawyers in preparing my defence. At the time, there was talk of a court martial to examine my role in the death of a fellow officer, one Lieutenant Wilson. Lieutenant Wilson's father, a Church of England bishop, was claiming that as the commanding officer of a company I had been negligent in not seeing to it that his son – whom Bishop Wilson had been told suffered heatstroke during the course of battle – had been evacuated behind the lines. The bishop claimed that due to my disregard for his son's safety, Lieutenant Wilson had lost his life at the enemy's hands.

When my father urged me to write a statement of fact, that is exactly what I gave him. It detailed all my actions, revealing that I had done far worse than Bishop Wilson presumed. Dismayed by what he read, Father judged my statement the product of hysteria or an unsound mind and never submitted it to the lawyers. What I had written did, however, supply him with one bit of useful information. Father learned that only one other man, a Sergeant Jimson, knew the whole truth of the matter. Sergeant Jimson disappeared from Toronto before any questions could be put to him. I have no doubts my father suborned him.

Everything else you need to know is contained in the manuscript I have left you.

Do not take offence when I tell you that you are not only the love of my life, but my dearest comrade. Comrade, I admit, is not a romantic word. But it best describes how I have come to think of you, as the one person I can bring myself to bare my soul to. Unjudged, I have been left to judge myself. I killed a man I once thought a friend. He will always be a shadow at my side. Once you read these papers, you will surely see him standing there too, and perhaps that will be the end of us.

I expect to return from Fort Walsh within two weeks. There is nothing more to say except that I hold you in my heart and always shall.

Yours,

Wesley

Ada sits, her right hand resting on the foolscap, and decides she does not have the strength to begin to read the document Wesley has left her. Not just now. She rises and goes to the window, looks out at an evening autumn sky, slowly filling with faint and tiny stars.

As a putative journalist, Case has been assigned a berth in a Murphy wagon outfitted with writing tables, pigeonhole cabinets, and filing cabinets to accommodate Stillson and Diehl. But those two gentlemen clearly resent him as a tagalong, an interloper who has wriggled his way into a story they considered theirs alone. So Case elects to spend most of his time trudging alongside the lumbering column of wagons. Long hours on his feet provide several benefits. Exhaustion helps him sleep reasonably soundly at the end of the day, and putting one foot in front of the other helps him register in his body the distance opening up between Ada and himself, a way of preparing himself to accept how remote and estranged from him she will likely be by the time he makes his return to Fort Benton.

For two days, Case tramps along beside the four-mule hitches bouncing their loads and passengers over the rut-strewn trail, chewing dust as he chews his thoughts, his ears filled with the rattles and shrieks of wooden wagon boxes, the jangle of enamel cookware, the elaborate curses of the cavalrymen, the cries of the civilian freighters as they snake their teams over the canvas-coloured landscape, a cold October wind slapping tears into his eyes.

And then on the third day of the journey, he hears the cries of drivers running down the length of the train, "Whoa, mules! Whoa!" and lifts his eyes from his boots to see the wagons come to a shuddering stop. A lieutenant makes for the head of the procession at a gallop. Freighters rise from their seats and strain to catch sight of whatever has brought about this sudden halt. The possibility that Sitting Bull's agreeing to meet with General Terry was only a trick to draw the commission into an ambush, which has been argued nightly around the campfires, is now in every man's mind.

But word soon passes down the column that it isn't Sioux who have halted the march. It is only a delegation of Mounties come to escort them into Fort Walsh. The cavalry troopers relax, sit easy in the saddle, teamsters casually loop reins around brake handles, light pipes and cigars. Diehl and Stillson poke their heads out of their lair, descend with notebooks in hand, and trot off. Case hangs back for a few moments before following them.

Facing the head of the wagon train is a line of scarlet tunics, spaced like fine stitching on the hem of the khaki landscape. In the watery autumn sunshine, the Police helmets gleam like alabaster. General Terry, all six feet and more of him, walks out to meet them, accompanied by his aides and staff.

Colonel Macleod, Commissioner of the NWMP, has come from headquarters on the Oldman River to welcome the Americans. His aquiline nose and luxurious mutton chop whiskers are as impressive as the American general's towering height. The two of them shake hands before a backdrop of irreproachably spit-polished and pipe-clayed Police. Brass buttons and buckles flash, steel-pointed bamboo lances glint, pennants flicker their snake tongues in the wind. Sergeant Major Francis, chin tucked down on his neck, sits his horse plumbline correct. There is a pugnacious look on his face that suggests he'd like nothing better than to charge these damn upstart Yankees the way he charged the Ivans at Sebastopol. Case knows many of the guard of honour, old barrack mates such as Constables Jolly, Atkinson, Foster, and Dewar, as well as others he once paraded and patrolled with. But they remain rock-solid still when he gives them a friendly wave. There is no sign of Walsh, which Case finds strange. The Major is not a man to miss a ceremony.

Notebooks poised, the journalists Diehl and Stillson wait to record some apposite, historically memorable exchange between Macleod and Terry. But after passing a few anodyne pleasantries, the two men separate to rejoin their commands. Wheeling smartly, the Police form a column of twos, and lead the caravan off towards the Cypress Hills.

At twilight, the wagons buck and bang their way up to the walls of Fort Walsh. Sioux warriors gather before their small travelling lodges to watch the Americans' arrival from a wary distance and in a hostile silence. Soon the soldiers are putting up tents and firing portable cookstoves in the shadows of the palisades. Curious Police come drifting out of their barracks to mingle with the newcomers, to shake hands and strike up conversations. Seeing that, the Sioux withdraw inside their tipis as if the scene is something too shameful to be witnessed.

After a quick supper and a cursory wash, Case immediately goes looking for the Major, only to learn that Walsh is unavailable, that he and Colonel Macleod are hosting a dinner for Terry and his staff. When he asks if a message could be delivered to the Major while he dines, the duty officer cautiously allows that he thinks that is possible. Case writes a note that announces his arrival and asks if Walsh and he might meet. He waits a time for a reply, and soon his note is returned to him, the Major's answer scrawled below his own request. "Here's a surprise, the bad penny turns up! Eight o'clock tomorrow morning outside the gates of the fort. Macleod has given Terry my quarters for his stay. I am homeless. I have nowhere to entertain notable visitors such as yourself."

The next morning, Case watches Walsh come striding energetically through the gates. The sun is making a slow ascent, shimmering on the frosted grass. A short way off, the Americans are clustered around their cookstoves, which send up a powerful aroma of brewing coffee, johnnycakes, and frying side pork.

The Major greets Case with a broad grin and brisk handshake. "I'll be damned, Wesley. Last night at supper Terry had his chest puffed out like a pouter pigeon while he cooed about the distinguished journalists he was trailing in his wake. And then he names you as one of the ink-stained wretches. You could have bowled me over with a feather."

Seeing nothing but complications in attempting to correct Walsh's belief that he really is a bona fide reporter, Case merely says, "Well, I tried my hand at the profession years ago. And temporarily resuming that occupation presented me with a chance to see you again."

"And very glad you seized it. Here, let's have a proper jaw. And a stroll as we do. I need a breath of fresh air after last night," he says, his face suddenly darkening.

They set off across the parade ground. Case senses that something has lit the Major's fuse and the spark is perilously near the black powder. It becomes clear he has taken a dislike to General Terry and soon begins to enumerate his faults – he was a lawyer before he became a soldier and he still acts like one. He keeps house with two spinster sisters in Chicago, probably crochets in the parlour with them of an evening – after he's done the washing up.

The Major says, "Terry's certainly not the man to handle Sitting Bull, the Sioux bear him a terrible grudge. They know full well that he was the commander who set Custer loose on them. They aren't fools. I don't know what the Americans were thinking, choosing him as their chief negotiator."

Case says, "Perhaps they decided he was exactly the man for the job. That is, if this mission is merely a pro forma exercise, a charade."

"Damn expensive charade. Think of the cost of it, the men involved. This expedition is not cheap." The Major sounds as if he is trying to convince himself and not quite succeeding.

"It's cheap enough if the Americans want to keep Bull exactly where he is – here in Canada."

"Well, I would have no objections to Bull staying put," says Walsh. "He's better off where he is. Not that anybody has asked my opinion. The Yankees are in charge of this show. The rest of us are stage dressing."

And with that, Walsh launches into a list of his most recent complaints and grievances. He speaks of how he had had to fortify himself, overcome a natural, proper disgust for what Macleod instructed him to do. Persuading Bull to meet with a man who had sought to have him and his people killed was not to the Major's taste. But he had followed the Colonel's orders, to the letter, and managed, against all odds, to eventually coax the Sioux chief to go to Fort Walsh. And had he received any praise or gratitude for his efforts? Not a bit. No one appreciated the difficulties he had had to surmount to bring the chief around. And what was most distasteful about the whole business was that Bull had been in mourning for a young son who had been kicked in the head by a horse and had died shortly before Walsh arrived in the Sioux camp. Pestering and plaguing a grieving father at a time like that – it wasn't something he was proud of. And on top of that, while he was pleading with Sitting Bull to treat with the Americans, Colonel Miles was attacking Chief Joseph and the Nez Perce, just fifty miles from where the Sioux were camped at Pinto Horse Butte. Daily, Bull had been receiving messages from Chief Joseph begging him to throw the weight of his people into the Nez Perce's battle with the Long

Knives. And this wasn't the only source of pressure coming to bear on the Sioux chief. All his young warriors, encouraged by their relatives, were asking to be unleashed on the hated Bear Coat and his men.

"All the young bucks dancing, chanting their death songs," Walsh says, "hanging their saddles with medicine bundles, painting themselves, dressing in their best so as to leave a pretty corpse if they met their death fighting Bear Coat Miles – it was a dicey proposition. A nod, one word from Bull, and they would have been off like a canister of grapeshot."

It was a moment, according the Major, when everything hung in the balance, and it had fallen to him to put his finger in and tip that balance in the right direction. One night, as a fierce autumn blizzard shook the walls of Bull's tipi, Walsh had sat with him, threatening, cajoling, haranguing, and entreating him not to go to war with the hated Bear Coat and his troopers. When dawn came, Bull was still wavering. Then, out of the storm, rode a gravely wounded Nez Perce messenger. He told the Sioux that Chief Joseph had laid down arms, but that White Bird, a war chief of the Nez Perce, had refused to comply with the terms of surrender. During the night, he had slipped a hundred warriors and a hundred women and children through Miles's lines. They were now just short of the border, soldiers hard after them. All their ammunition was gone; they had no food or winter clothing; the women and children were perishing in the cold and snow. If the Sioux did not come now to help them, Bear Coat and his soldiers would overtake and slaughter them all.

When they heard this, Walsh says, Sitting Bull's people shouted that they must go and rescue their strong-hearted Nez Perce friends. Just as the excitement reached its peak, scouts galloped into the village shouting a warning that a large body of white men was approaching. There was no stopping the Sioux then. Two hundred warriors sprang onto their ponies and heeled them out into the flying snow. Walsh had ridden with them. "I had no choice," he says. "If I could not restrain the Sioux from confronting the Americans, it was my duty to play the part of intermediary, to attempt to prevent violence from breaking out, to try to convince Colonel Miles to turn back."

But it wasn't American soldiers they met on the snowy plain. The scouts had been mistaken. It was White Bird and a pitiful remnant of the Nez Perce who they saw stumbling towards them through the blizzard.

Walsh and Case reach the foot of the cemetery hill, which overlooks the fort. The Major halts and lifts his eyes to its crest, where a few spindly wooden crosses stand stark against the brightening sky. "I tell you," the Major says softly, "hell is cold, not hot. I caught a glimpse of it that night. The snow coming down hard, blanketing those poor wretches, turning them white as ghosts. There were many badly wounded warriors, others so dog-tired they were listing in their saddles. The most of them, even the worst off, were leading ponies with a couple of young-sters clinging to their backs, little tots of two and three. There were children with broken arms and legs, who had taken tumbles getting out of the Bear Paw Mountains in the dark of night. The women were shot up as badly as the men, blood frozen on their robes. One young lass had taken a bullet to the breast. It had run up her chest and out the side of her head. She was still riding, riding with a newborn strapped to her back. If I live to be as old as Methuselah, I'll never see a sight to equal that."

Walsh's jaw clenches as if he is afraid to continue, fears he will surrender to an unmanly display of emotion. Case suddenly senses the large soul of the man, something easily obscured when the Major has an outbreak of petulance or vanity. Before he can offer him a sympathetic word, Walsh abruptly swings around from the foot of the hill and starts back towards the fort. Silently the two men follow the footprints they have left in the frostbitten grass until, finally, Walsh resumes his story.

"The Sioux took the Nez Perce into their lodges, nursed the sick and injured, fed them their choicest bits of boss ribs, buffalo hump, and tongue. Handed out robes and blankets and warm clothing to people whose bone marrow had turned to ice. They paid honour to the dead left up in the Bear Paws, strangers they didn't know. Sang mourning songs until their throats gave out. And here was I, supposed to tell Sitting Bull, with such sights fresh in his mind, to pack up directly, sit down and talk to an American commander, and General Terry at that. Well," he says with barely contained fury, "my bosses ought to be proud of me because, by the living Christ, I did just that, did as I was told. And it wasn't the easiest, sweetest thing I ever done. Bull was hopping mad. All the headmen were. 'Look,' they said to me, 'look at what the Long Knives do. And you ask us to go to Fort Walsh and shake hands with them? To hear them say, You come back to the other side of the Medicine Line with us and we will be good to you, like fathers? We do not believe it. Bear Coat is a day's ride away. What if our leaders and best fighters go to parley with One Star Terry and it is a trick? What if Bear Coat comes down on our villages in the night when the people are sleeping in their beds, kills the children, the women, the sick, the old, tramples down our lodges, shoots our horses as he has done to the Sioux before? What will we be then? Broken, snapped over Bear Coat's knee like small, dry sticks. No, we will not go with you. We will not listen to the Americans make their promises. They promised us the Black Hills forever just like they promised the Oregon country to the Nez Perce forever. They talk of forever until they have a hunger for a piece of land, or the yellow stones they are so greedy for, and then forever trails out of their head like smoke. Then they shout, "Get out of here! Go instead to this place or that place." And the places they try to push us to are always bad, worthless places.'"

Walsh pauses. "But I kept wheedling away at Bull. He was suspicious and wary, afraid that the Americans would seize him at the fort and take him back to Montana in chains, and if they didn't do that, that they'd ambush and kill him on the way to the big parley. I swore to him on the head of my little daughter Cora that I would not let that happen. And in the end he agreed to come to

Fort Walsh because he trusts me. *I* shook him out of the bed-clothes and got him moving. *I* kept him and those other Sioux headmen on the straight and narrow for a hundred and fifty god-damn miles. They would go docile as lambs for a piece and then they'd have a fit of second thoughts, plunk down on the trail to smoke a pipe and speculate about what kind of trouble the Americans had in wait for them. No, they'd say, we are turning round, going back to Pinto Horse Butte. And I'd placate them. I'd persuade them. I'd chivvy them back up on their ponies. It was *me* who got them here well before Terry himself thought it safe to poke his cowardly nose out of Fort Benton. For what? So the Sioux can be humiliated by sitting down with General Terry?"

"You followed your orders and delivered Sitting Bull," says Case. "Your part is over. It's in the Americans' hands now, as you yourself said. There's nothing more for you to do."

This does nothing to ease Walsh's uneasiness. "You know what kept Bull on the move coming here?" he says. "I told him the Grandmother said he must speak to Terry." Walsh hesitates. "I said if he did her this favour, surely she would do him one in return." The Major shakes his head. "I believed it when I said it. But now I wonder if I wasn't deluding myself because it was convenient to do so." He moodily considers the horizon.

"No one can look at this business," Case says, "without won-dering the best way to navigate it. That is always a concern in matters like this, it comes with the territory. But you must remind yourself that Sitting Bull, in his turn, will always put the welfare of his people first. That is his primary concern and, by any reckoning, one cannot expect him to do anything else. He will do what he needs to do. Just as you have done." Quietly Case says, "You cannot assume he came here purely out of trust in you. And you should be careful not to count on friendship as any kind of constant."

"Why would he have made this long journey except for friendship and trust?" Walsh demands. "And if it wasn't for that, then what do these things count for in the end?"

Looking at Walsh's troubled face, it strikes Case that the Major's earlier indignation at not receiving his due for bringing Sitting Bull into parley is merely a reflection of his anger at having compromised his own principles. Case says, "I think you hold yourself to too high a standard, and Bull as well. A man in your position needs to be realistic and keep his sympathies in check. Sitting Bull will choose his friends to suit the situation. There is plenty of talk in Montana that he's trying to form alliances right now – with the Blackfoot, the Assiniboine, wherever he can make them."

"I've heard the same things and questioned him carefully about it. He gave me his word this isn't true, and I believe him."

"You know very well that alliances are kept in secret and only announced when the time is fortuitous. If he is content to sit in your pocket now it is because it affords him some benefit and protection. But I suspect the time will come when he won't find it so comfortable there. When it does, he will have no scruples about doing whatever he needs to do to advance his cause."

Walsh's answer is sharp. "Not at my expense. He would never do anything to harm me personally. I'm not as bad a judge of character as you seem to think. I've had plenty of time to take the measure of the man. I've eaten with him, slept in his lodge. And I'll tell you this, I've never met a straighter, more upright fellow." The Major hesitates. "And I'm the one who has put him squarely in my pocket, in spite of what the costs may be to him."

Case feels a surge of impatience. "It's the way of the world. If it became a choice between survival and friendship, which do you think Sitting Bull would choose? Which would you choose?"

The Major snaps, "Way of the world? Don't patronize me, my boy. And what business do you have, pronouncing on the character of a man you haven't met?"

Case says, "Then rectify my ignorance. Introduce us. I'd like to meet him." As an afterthought he adds, "And interview him for my paper."

Walsh stands, pulling at his bottom lip. "You know that might be a worthwhile thing. Canadians ought to have a chance to see matters from Bull's side of the fence. The government is in such a damned fever to pitch him out the door. It's all Colonel Macleod and his henchmen can think of, earning credit with Ottawa for evicting Bull from the property. How happy they would be to see him plunked down on some American reservation to grow potatoes and polish a missionary's pew with his arse for the rest of his days." He gives Case a sidelong glance. "Somebody ought to tell the truth about how things stand here at present, set the record straight for the public."

Feeling a twinge of conscience, Case hastily says, "There's no assurance an interview that presents the truth *would* be published. I can make no promises on that score."

Walsh turns a deaf ear to Case's qualification. "I'll get Louis Léveillé to translate for us. Terry has asked the Sioux to dance for the commission tonight. He thinks that gesture will please them, set a good atmosphere for the talks tomorrow. Maybe we can meet after the Sioux perform." He stands a moment, thinking, then says, "I must be off now. I have an appointment with Colonel Macleod. I'll get a message to you when I have the interview arranged. Give careful thought to your questions for Bull. You have a lot to learn about the man."

Case watches as Walsh crosses the parade ground, his gait tentative, his eyes contemplating the ground. Case has never seen the man in this light before. The lion is limping because he believes he has betrayed a man whose loyalty he owns. That is the thorn in his paw and it needs to be drawn.

The air is filled with the shriek of eagle-bone whistles, the heartbeat of rawhide hand drums, the shrill, quavering voices of the Indian singers. A huge bonfire roars in the fort's square, pine knots crack, greasy billows of smoke churn and spit sparks, the whitewashed palisades of the fort are smeared with the violent red and yellow brushstrokes of the fire.

The night is crisp and clear; a blue moon stares down on the dancers. The breath of the Police and Americans, bundled up in heavy coats, smokes as they gaze at the breech-clouted warriors weaving and stamping, sweat steaming from their naked skin. Bodies are slashed, blazed, dotted, and zigzagged with paint. A yellow face, a vermilion mouth. One eye, rimmed in white, stares out of a coal-black countenance. A blue mask spotted with white raindrops pecks at onlookers. Heavy braids whip and jerk as warriors stalk and lunge, re-enacting old war deeds, their moccasins kicking up clouds of dust that shimmer and glow in the light of the flames.

Rain in the Face wears an eagle-feather bonnet capped with curved and menacing buffalo horns. His body is completely covered in charcoal, except for his ribs, which are marked with bone-white streaks of paint. The skeleton gyrates, singing his battle exploits to Macleod and Terry. An interpreter leans down between their chairs, mumbling Rain in the Face's words in their ears.

The dance, intended as a conciliatory gesture before the opening of negotiations, has taken an unfortunate turn. It is known that Terry is well aware there is no greater hater of the Custer family among the Sioux than Rain in the Face. Once arrested by Tom Custer, the General's brother, the Sioux warrior spent three months in the Fort Lincoln jail before he made his escape. Now he describes to General Terry how he revenged himself on the Custer brothers at Little Bighorn. Shaking a scalp-decorated coup stick in Terry's face, he points out which of his trophies he peeled from Long Knives' heads, demonstrates how he rode among the soldiers at Little Bighorn, caving in their skulls with his stone hammer. Terry sits, lockjawed, one hand pulling at his beard while Rain in the Face taunts him with the carnage he wreaked.

Leaning against a palisade wall, Case fastens his eyes on a figure huddled up in a blanket in a dark corner of the fort. Earlier that evening, Louis Léveillé had pointed him out to Case and identified him as Sitting Bull. Seemingly oblivious to the proceedings, the chieftain keeps to his corner, praying, mourning the recent death of his little son.

Case turns his gaze to Walsh, positioned directly behind Terry and Macleod, standing with his arms folded across his chest. The Major may have been relegated to the second rank of luminaries, but he is not a man to let himself pass unnoticed. He has exchanged his uniform for a fringed buckskin jacket and a slouch hat decorated with an eagle feather and long silk scarf. Has Terry remarked that Walsh shares Custer's taste for strutting about in fancy dress? Has he noted the scarcely disguised amusement with which the Major is watching Rain in the Face's performance?

Earlier that afternoon, when Léveillé had brought news from Walsh confirming that an appointment had been set with Sitting Bull, Case had seized the opportunity to enlist the Métis scout's services, have him introduce him to some of the chief's lieutenants and translate certain questions he had concerning their leader. The answers he received had been most informative. But as the hours passed, and the interrogation of Sitting Bull grew nearer, Case had felt a growing trepidation that soon turned into a bad-tempered disquiet. Perhaps Walsh was right. What business did he have judging the Sioux chief, or anyone else for that matter? What was he risking, proceeding with this interview? What had he risked by leaving Ada and coming here at all?

All afternoon, agitated thoughts had raced through his mind until he sought to banish them with a bottle. The whiskey hasn't smoothed him out as he thought it would; it has done the opposite. Now he is full of Dutch courage, and ready to let the cards fall where they may.

The dancing ends a little before ten o'clock. Case lingers outside the gate of the fort, wondering why it is taking Walsh so long to scare up Léveillé. A short distance away, soldiers and

Police are fraternizing in the American camp. The tents are tinted powder blue by the moonlight. Coffee pots are on the boil and a brisk trade in souvenirs is under way between Police and soldiers: insignia, badges, uniform buttons, even the odd lance pennant and regimental guidon change hands. Loud raconteurs hold forth, a game of craps is being played on a blanket spread on the grass, a policeman and a soldier arm-wrestle on a packing case, strain mightily for the honour of their respective nations as their compatriots lay wagers and cheer them on.

As he watches all this, Case takes an occasional pull from a hip flask, reinforcing his resolve. Walsh finally appears, Léveillé in tow. Louis is looking chastised and penitent, and Case wonders if the scout hasn't been dressed down by Walsh for taking him to meet the Sioux headmen. The Major likes to run things his way.

"Case," says Walsh abruptly, "are you ready? I don't see you carrying a notebook."

"What is writ in my impeccable memory is never lost."

Walsh must have caught a whiff of his breath. He gives him a suspicious look. "Are you drunk?"

"No. But I have had a few drops."

Walsh frowns. "Well, come along then."

Sitting Bull's travelling lodge is set apart from the rest of the Sioux tipis to afford the grieving father privacy. A fire burning inside plays on the skins and flickers in the doorway. The entry flap is pinned open; Bull is expecting them.

Léveillé calls out a greeting; the trio stoops and enters. Walsh presents the chief a rope of tobacco wrapped in red flannel. Hands are shaken all around. Léveillé introduces Case at length, which leads Case to surmise that the guide has been given instructions by Walsh to inflate his stature and importance. Sitting Bull solemnly nods, regarding him with a shrewd eye throughout Léveillé's peroration.

This is the first time Case has seen the famous chief at close range. He is a formidable-looking man, barrel chested, the head monumental, face broad, deeply creased, thin lipped. But it is Bull's sharp, penetrating black eyes that rivet his attention, so much so that when Léveillé finally concludes his lengthy introduction, and Bull gestures to his guests to seat themselves on the mountain sheep fleeces he has spread for them, Case hovers awkwardly on his feet for several seconds before sinking down next to Walsh.

Bull lights a pipe, a polished red stone bowl with a stem sheathed in bird skins and hung with eagle feathers. He prays before passing it round. When the pipe is finished and reverently cleaned, Bull leans back against a willow backrest under a medicine bundle suspended from a lodge pole, and begins to knead one of his legs with big sinewy hands.

Suddenly, Case says, "I am sorry to see that your leg troubles you."

Sitting Bull gives Léveillé a questioning glance and Louis interprets what Case has said. The chief nods slowly and then, in a sonorous bass, begins to speak, Léveillé's translation singing accompaniment. "Many years ago when I was a young warrior a Crow challenged me to fight him, man to man. I put on my Strong Heart bonnet and sash and went out to face him. I killed that Crow but I took a ball from his musket in my foot. It has troubled me for a long time, but it is a small trouble." He pauses, perhaps to lend weight to the implication that he now faces larger concerns. Then he says, "But let us speak of why you have come to me." Pointing to Walsh and using the name the Sioux have given him, Bull says, "Long Lance told me you were once one of the Old Woman's pony soldiers, but that now you cry the news all over her country. He says that is why we must talk. That you can speak the truth about Sitting Bull and his people so that all of the Old Woman's white children will understand how the Americans made us suffer. Then they will have pity on us." Sitting Bull smiles. "And Long Lance tells me you are a great friend of his. I am a friend of Long Lance too, and I would like his friend to be mine also."

"Yes," says Case, "Walsh and I are very good friends. Such good friends that when he is puzzled he comes to me for counsel and I point the way to him."

Walsh remarks, "That's pretty damn thick, Case."

Léveillé's eyes flit uncomfortably from Walsh to Case, uncertain whether he should translate what has been said. There is a moment of silence. The Major gives a grudging bob of the head. "All right, Louis, get on with it."

The Métis passes on Case's claim to be Walsh's adviser. The chief studies Case for a moment, then leans forward and taps him on the knee with his forefinger. "What you say surprises me. Why does Long Lance need your wisdom? Why does the Old Woman give him her pony soldiers to lead if he does not know the way to go?"

"Sometimes the horse with the biggest lungs, the biggest heart, gallops so fast he cannot see the holes that lie ahead that will break his legs. He needs someone to warn him of them."

"And Long Lance is such a horse?"

"Yes. He is the kind of strong horse that runs as if nothing can bring him down."

Walsh interjects. "Bull isn't interested in your half-baked ruminations about my temperament."

Case ignores him. He sees that the chief is pensively fondling something dangling on his chest. When he looks more closely, he sees it is a crucifix.

"The way you look at me," Sitting Bull says, "I see you think that I am a horse like Walsh too."

"Not entirely the same, no. But like Walsh, I believe that once you have decided on the direction you wish to run, you will not quit it."

"And what is it I should quit? That I do not understand."

"I believe you would be wise to quit the Old Woman's country and go back over the Medicine Line."

Walsh hisses, "Know your place, man. This is not your affair to meddle in."

"And why should I do that?" says Bull. "I am happy in the Old Woman's country."

Case ponders his answer, trying to frame how he will express what he has been turning over in his mind since arriving at Fort Walsh. "You will not like the words I am about to say to you, but I think them to be true. Once I wrote to Long Lance that it was better for you to be here. But now I think it would be better if you and your people went back over the Medicine Line."

"And why has your heart changed?"

"Because I lived a long time in the place where the Grandmother's counsellors have their meeting house. My father was a friend to many of them. I tell you they are not men who think like Walsh. I have a strong feeling that they have already decided that the Sioux will never be British Indians. One day they will send you back over the Medicine Line to the country of the Long Knives. When that day comes you will be in a weaker position than you are now to bargain with the Americans. You have never touched the treaty pen with the Long Knives before. If you do so now, maybe they will be grateful, a little kinder to you." Case shrugs. "Perhaps this does not please you, but this is what I think now." He glances at Walsh, who wears a severe and disapproving look.

"No," says Bull thoughtfully, "this is my country. I was born in the Red River country among these kind of people." He points to Léveillé. "The half-breeds, the Slotas, taught me to shoot. I was born in the Old Woman's country."

"I spoke to some of your people today. They tell me that you were born down on the Missouri, not up here. Why is it you claim to be a British Indian?"

Bull fishes something out of a pouch hanging around his waist. He passes it to Case, who turns it over in his hands. It is a medal with the effigy of George III stamped on it. "Many years ago," says Sitting Bull, "this Grandfather came to my people and said to us, 'Let us fight the Americans together.' And we fought them as he asked. When that war was over, this Grandfather who you hold in your hand gave away our land to the Americans, but we knew nothing of this. For many years we lived free before the Americans came and said to us this land is ours; the red coats gave it to us. Now," says Bull, "if we were not British Indians, how could the Grandfather give away anything of ours? But he did. So he must have believed we were his Indians, British Indians. Now we have come to the Old Woman's country and she must make a place for us here. In return for the land her relative gave to the Americans."

Walsh greets this rebuttal jubilantly. "Bloody well done! The man belongs in Parliament!"

Case turns to the Major. "That is exactly the point I have been trying to impress on you. He will make his case in any way he can."

Bull murmurs something to Léveillé. The translator says, "Sitting Bull wants to know what you and the Major are talking about."

"Tell him," says Case, "that I have told the Major that Sitting Bull makes a clever argument. That he is wily like a fox."

"Have a care, my boy," the Major warns him. "You go too far."

Smiling at Case as if he is a wilful child, Bull says, "You call me a fox, but you do not know me. I will tell you who I am. I am a *wichasha wakan*, a holy man. Since I was very young I have understood the talk of birds – I do not know the language of foxes. I have dreamed the thunderbird dream, which is a fearful dream, a gift that Wakan Tanka gives to very few of his children. That dream gave me the right to paint my face with lightning, which is a great honour.

"Wakan Tanka sends me visions. In the time of the choke-cherries, the time of the Sun Dance – the summer that Custer came – I made sacrifice." Sitting Bull pushes up both his sleeves and displays pale scars that spot his forearms like drops of melted wax. "Jumping Bull dug fifty pieces of flesh from each of my arms with an awl. I prayed and cried out to Wakan Tanka while he did it. Then I danced around the Sun Dance pole, praying, taking neither food nor water for a long time. I do not remember this, but the people say that suddenly I went still as stone. I stared up at the sun. The people came and laid me on the ground, sprinkled me with water until I came back to this world. That was when I told my good friend Black Moon what I had seen in the place I had gone to.

"A voice had told me to fix my eyes just below the rim of the sun. There I saw, thick as grasshoppers, pony soldiers riding hard and fast towards one of our villages. But the horses and men were upside down, their heads to the earth. The Long Knives' hats were falling from their heads. The voice said to me, 'These soldiers have no ears. They are to die, but those who kill them must take nothing of theirs.'" Bull has a distant look, as if hearing the voice again. "I saw Custer's coming in this vision. When Black Moon told the people what I had seen, they were very happy because they knew that if the pony soldiers rode against us we would kill them all."

"That is a powerful vision," says Case. "I am sure the people were happy to hear it. But the Sioux did not obey the voice, did they? They took many of the things that belonged to the dead soldiers."

Case can hear the sorrow in Bull's voice even before Léveillé translates his words. "That is a thing that troubles me. The people should not have taken the white man's weapons, clothes, horses, and mules. It was forbidden. I think Wakan Tanka wanted to teach us not to envy the white men's goods."

Case says, "On the other side of the Medicine Line the Americans say there will be more soldiers falling from the sky. But you do not dream this vision, you work and plan for it."

"No. I will stay here in the Old Mother's country. Just as Long Lance asks, I will not make war against the Long Knives."

"Here is what the Americans say, that just as you brought the Oglala, the Brulé, the Miniconjou, the Two Kettles, the Sans Arc, the Hunkpapa, the Blackfeet Sioux, and the Northern Cheyenne together to rub out Custer, you work now to bring all the tribes together. The Americans say you have sent messengers to the

Assiniboine, even to the Sioux's old enemies, the Blackfeet, the Cree, the Slotas, and you say to them, 'Let us kill all the whites no matter where they live, whether they wear red coats or blue coats. Let us remove them from the face of the earth and live free as we did before.'"

"I am tired of war," says Sitting Bull. "I do everything that Long Lance asks me to do."

Case glances at Walsh, whose head is lowered, his fingers twisted in the fleece he is seated on. It is as if he wilfully refuses to entertain any possibility that the Sioux chief's responses may be half-truths. And Sitting Bull's unflappability, his calm, repeated assertions that he is guided by no one but Long Lance, are provoking Case's head to throb. Spurred on by whiskey and frustration, he says testily, "Yes, you do what Walsh asks now because the uniting of the tribes has not yet come to pass. But I think if you grow strong, you will do as you please."

"I am at peace with everyone now."

In a harsh whisper, without raising his head, the Major says to Case, "You've had your answer. Stop persecuting him."

Pointing to the crucifix, Case says, "I am curious why a Sioux holy man would hang the white man's God around his neck. I wonder what it means."

"The Black Robe De Smet gave this sacred bundle to me when he came to the Hunkpapa camp to ask me to touch the treaty pen years ago at Fort Laramie. I liked this Black Robe. He was very brave and went everywhere among the Indians, lived with them without fear. Even when I said I would not touch the pen, he gave me this sacred thing. The Black Robe said the Man on the Sticks' power would protect me." Sitting Bull gazes down at the cross on his chest. "I think this man hung himself on the sticks just as the Sioux hang themselves from the Sun Dance pole to suffer and win the favour of Wakan Tanka. That is a good thing to do."

"No, Jesus was nailed on the sticks by others."

Sitting Bull tips his head. "Who were the others? Why did they do this to him?"

"Where the hell is this going?" says Walsh. "You are supposed to be interviewing him, not giving him a Bible lesson." The Major addresses Sitting Bull. "A friend betrayed the Man on the Sticks to his enemies for money. Thirty pieces of silver."

"Ah," says Bull mischievously, a shadow of a smile hovering on his lips. "Then his friend was a white man. The white men love the coloured metal."

"That is what is often said," Case declares, "that it was done for money. But I believe there was another reason."

"I would like you to tell me the reason he did such a wicked thing."

Case glances at Léveillé, warning him with his eyes that what is coming next will be difficult to translate. "There were two men," Case begins, "one called Judas, and the Man on the Sticks, who was called Jesus. For a long time Judas listened to Jesus' words and did everything he was told to. As you do with Walsh." For a moment, Case looks steadily at Sitting Bull, who smiles back at him serenely. "Everything that Jesus said, Judas agreed with, saying, 'Yes, this is true. This is wise. I must listen to this man.' But I think as time went on, Judas began to feel small and weak. He said to himself, 'Why must I do as this Jesus says? Am I not as strong and wise a man as he is?' And he could not get this out of his mind. This is what happens when one man's will struggles with another's man's will – there will be a falling out. I have seen this come true in my own life. The question – which is the stronger man? – must be settled. I think it will be the same between you and Major Walsh."

"That's enough," Walsh barks. "I won't have any more of this. This bloody farce is over. Stand up and leave *now!*" He swings to Léveillé. "You have no need to translate what I've just said."

Bull is startled by Walsh's sudden fury; his eyes dart back and forth between the two men. When Case begins to get to his feet, Bull reaches out a hand and restrains him from rising. The deep voice begins to roll, but when the Métis follows Walsh's directive and remains silent, Bull speaks to him in a tone of command.

Léveillé says, "Sitting Bull wants to know why I no longer speak his words. He says he has something to say to Mr. Case."

"Christ, all right, proceed if that's what Bull desires."

Sitting Bull says, "I smell whiskey on your breath. Whiskey makes a fool even more foolish. All this time you have been trying to turn Long Lance away from me. This is how it is with discontented men who cannot find their own way. They are blind, yet they tell others what path to turn down. But turn yourself," says Bull softly, "turn yourself, and leave others to do as they think right."

Case feels his face colour and he stumbles to his feet. "I bid you goodnight. I have nothing more to say." He hesitates, and adds, "Except to say I am very sorry for the death of your son. That is a hard thing to bear."

"On your way," says Walsh, voice clipped and bitter.

He goes out of the lodge and into the night. For a moment, he regards the shadows of policemen and soldiers mingling on the ground lit by the campfires, and considers how he has bungled this encounter. He had meant to reveal Bull to Walsh, but instead has been revealed himself. Prosecuting his case the way he had only ensured it would be lost. Most likely, he has only succeeded in pushing Walsh a little closer to the Sioux chief.

TWENTY-FOUR

AT THREE O'CLOCK SHARP the next afternoon, Walsh, resplendent in his dress uniform, leads Sitting Bull and some twenty-odd lesser Sioux chiefs into the officers' mess to commence talks with the Americans. Before the Sioux settle on the buffalo robes, which are spread on the floor in front of the table where the Terry Commission is seated, Sitting Bull insists on shaking hands with Walsh and Commissioner Macleod. The Major notes that he refuses General Terry and his boys the same courtesy, simply gives them a small, disdainful smile. Bull has blood in his eye.

The room is crammed with Police, soldiers, and anyone else who has been able to finagle admittance to the grand occasion. They are stacked three deep along the walls. The members of the press have been provided with ringside seats and a table so they can make notes on the proceedings. Walsh feels his mouth tighten when he sees Case, thinks how he'd like to put a boot so far up his arse that he'd taste shoe leather. His little speech about Judas last night had been enlightening. Case is a man well acquainted with the ins and outs of treachery.

Glancing over to the wife of the Bear That Scatters, he wonders if the Americans realize that the Sioux are thumbing their noses at them by including a member of the weaker sex in their delegation. A woman attending a council is unthinkable to the

Sioux, a mockery. And she isn't the only insult being offered to the Yankees; Spotted Eagle has come to the peace parley armed. He is cradling a huge war club studded with three knife blades, and wearing a scowl that suggests he would like nothing better than to start swinging it.

Sitting Bull has donned his Sunday best, a dark navy blue shirt spotted with white dots of paint, black leggings with wide red flannel stripes, ornately beaded moccasins, and a fox-fur cap hung with a badger tail. He has not braided his hair, but left it hanging loose, fanned out over the blanket draping his shoulders. Walsh has never seen him so splendidly dressed.

The discussions get off to a rancorous start. Sitting Bull demands that the Americans join him on the buffalo robes, claiming he cannot see those in the Terry Commission behind their table, and accusing them of trying to hide their faces from him. Terry retorts that it is not the habit of white men to sit on floors; they prefer chairs. But Bull refuses to relent and is satisfied only when the members of the Terry party finally haul their chairs to the front of the offending piece of furniture and drop down on them peevishly.

The Sioux insist that there be no pipe ceremony. They want it known that their only reason for coming to this meeting is because Long Lance had asked them to; they have no intention of solemnizing or sanctifying any part of it by smoking sacred tobacco with enemies who have never told them anything but lies. This puts Terry in a bind, forcing him to state his terms without benefit of the professions of good faith and eloquent speechifying that always characterize such meetings.

He commences by telling the Sioux that they can return to American soil without fear of any retribution or punishment being exacted for the massacre of Custer and his men. While he is saying this, Spotted Eagle keeps broadly winking at Walsh, as if to say, You can fool some of the people all of the time, all of the people some of the time, but you can't fool all of the people all of the time.

Next, Terry informs the Sioux that in return for not being punished for their misdeeds, they must agree to go to a reservation and hand over their horses and guns. The government will sell this surrendered property and use the proceeds to buy cattle for the Sioux so they can begin a new life as ranchers and farmers. The minute he hears this proposal, Walsh knows Terry's goose is cooked. These warriors will no more turn over their horses and guns for sale than they would put their women and children up on the auction block.

The chiefs say nothing, only light their pipes and puff away, faces stony. Minutes pass, the anxious silence occasionally broken by a cough, the scrape of a boot on the floorboards. Out of the corner of his eye, Walsh can see Macleod's troubled look. The room grows warmer, begins to reek of musty long johns, tanned hides, and black shag tobacco.

At last, Bull gathers his blanket around his shoulders and rises to address the commission in a booming voice. Although this is Bull's voice Walsh is hearing, the words don't seem to belong to the man he knows. The Americans' translator is making him sound like a pouty, incoherent child. The fellow is clearly incompetent.

Spotting Léveillé, Walsh beckons him over and asks him to interpret what Bull is saying. The Métis scout stands beside the Major, murmuring into his ear.

"Ever since we fought on the side of the British sixty-four winters ago, you have treated my people cruelly," Bull says. "All we asked was to be left alone. But you kept stealing what was ours. You are responsible for all the troubles between the Sioux and the Americans. In the end we had nowhere to get away from you except the Old Woman's country. I know this country well. It was on this side of the Medicine Line I learned to shoot a gun, and that was a good thing because if the Sioux had not learned that lesson, we would all be dead today. You would have killed every one of us. Now I have come back to this country and I am happy to be here. Someday soon I will visit the Red River country and thank the Slotas for teaching me how to defend myself from you."

And then Bull breaks off his speech, approaches Macleod, shakes his hand, turns to Walsh, smiles, grips his hand hard and holds it for several moments, looking into his eyes. Then he faces the Terry Commission and announces, "I am a friend to every person on this side of the Medicine Line. You see how these men treat me with friendship? They gladly take a hand when it is offered to them. Use your eyes and your ears to learn that I live in peace with them. And why is that? Because they keep their promises to me. Today, the Old Woman lends us this house to use as a medicine house. Only the truth should be spoken here. But you come here to tell lies in her house. You dishonour her and you dishonour yourselves. The Sioux have let you speak because Long Lance said it was the Old Woman's wish that we listen to you. But do not say two more words to us. Go back to where you came from. I intend to stay in the Old Woman's land. All the Sioux think as I do. We will fill this country with the children we raise here, strong men and women."

He stops his speech again and goes about the room, shaking hands with every Mounted Police officer he encounters. Walsh glances over to Case sitting at the table with Stillson and Diehl, pencil in his hand but writing nothing. The fool is not making a record of what is occurring here.

Sitting Bull halts beside a Santee chief, the One Who Runs the Roe, points to him, and says, "You drove the Santees out of their land over ten winters ago. Those of their leaders you did not drive away you put ropes around their necks and hung them. Now the Santees call this place home. Let this man make plain to you how you treated his people."

Walsh listens to the Santee repeat Bull's accusations that the Americans have stolen land, lied, and provoked war. A succession of other Sioux headmen say the same things. Finally, the wife of Bear That Scatters takes the floor. She whispers a few barely audible words. Walsh asks Léveillé what the woman has said, but his translator only shrugs, he too having been unable to catch her words. The Americans' interpreter tells her to speak more loudly. She does. The interpreter calls out to Terry, "She says over there on the other side of the Medicine Line you don't give her time to breed." There is scattered laughter. The prim bachelor General flushes crimson.

A few more complaints are directed at Terry and then the Sioux rise and begin to make for the door. The General halts them, demanding to know if they are absolutely refusing the President's amnesty.

Sitting Bull says contemptuously, "If we told you more, you would have paid no attention. That is all I have to say. This part of the country does not belong to your people. You belong on the other side. We are British Indians. This is where we belong."

Once more he leads the headmen over to Macleod and Walsh and there is another round of handshaking. Bull takes the Major's hand last. He holds it pressed between both of his, nodding his head slowly. The look on Bull's face needs no translation. Walsh has no doubts that it gives the lie to every damn thing Case had said the night before.

October 20, 1877

I've tried to speak to Walsh, apologize for my behaviour, but each time I approach him he quickly busies himself with another task or conversation. Once he cut me off short by saying that a reporter who took no notes could scarcely be trusted to write anything that would portray a proper picture of Sitting Bull to the public or the government, and that I had been nothing but a waste of his goddamn time. He then stalked off in high dudgeon. Perhaps I ought to tell him that he can add deceit to the list of my misdemeanours, and inform him that although my posing as a journalist may have been inexcusable, I intended no harm to him by it. Quite the contrary.

With any luck, his frostiness may thaw and he may come to realize that despite the way I conducted myself with Sitting Bull, I felt I was acting as his faithful agent, just as I did in my communications to him from Fort Benton. I have always striven to serve his best interests, and never strayed from the desire to see to it that his recklessness does not set him on a wrong course.

At present, Walsh is busy trying to recruit Stillson and Diehl to assist him in improving Bull's standing with the white man. So far, the Major has only managed to persuade the chief to let Stillson make a sketch of him, but both correspondents told me – rather smugly and triumphantly – that Walsh promises interviews will be granted in the next few days before Sitting Bull heads back to Pinto Horse Butte.

Of course, the Major has his own reasons for cultivating these gentlemen of the fourth estate. He knows the power of the press to buff a man's reputation, has seen how it picks its darlings and displays them to advantage. They did it for Custer in the days before the Little Bighorn and, if they could do it for Long Hair, they can do it for Long Lance. Walsh wants to be regarded as the only fellow who can hold Bull in check, the one man who can preserve peace on the frontier. If he can be seen as indispensable, he believes no government, fearing a public outcry, will dare dismiss him.

But there are signs that Walsh's superiors, who know of his penchant for saying things he oughtn't, are angling to get him away from Stillson and Diehl just as quickly as they can. Colonel Macleod has ordered him to return to Pinto Horse Butte with the Sioux when they depart from Fort Walsh. I'll wager Walsh is doing all he can to see that the Indians don't leave here too soon. He wants more time to make an impression on the American journalists.

The meeting that occurred between Terry and Bull three days ago was quite the instructive spectacle, confirmation of my earlier suspicions that the United States never had any intention of treating seriously with the Sioux. The terms they offered Bull were ones he could never accept and keep the loyalty of his people. Terry obviously knew that.

The Americans are happy to see the Sioux remain here, and happy to saddle Canada with the responsibility for them. The United States could not avoid making some response to British pressure to negotiate with Sitting Bull. Now that they have sat down with him, it would be difficult to accuse them of bad faith. They will be able to argue, "We made an offer. It was refused. What more do you expect us to do?" It is clear what they wished to achieve from the very beginning.

If the Americans got what they wanted, so did Sitting Bull – for the time being. Given the situation he faced, a choice between remaining in Canada without assurances that his right to stay was recognized by our government, or returning to the United States under Terry's terms, it appears Bull has decided to gamble on Canada. It was a masterstroke the way he managed to enter into the record his claim to be a British Indian. None of the Police, not even Colonel Macleod, disputed this assertion. How could they, after his effusive display of affection and loyalty towards the Old Woman's pony soldiers, his flattering portrayal of British upright-ness as opposed to American deviousness? I did not see a single red coat who did not take his depiction of us as anything but the truth. I could almost hear them thinking, "Yes, British fair dealing has tamed the savage." But as yet, fair dealing has come without a price tag. It has cost us nothing. Let us see how we do when the time comes to put our hands in our pockets and provide material support for these people, as that day will surely come.

The Sioux, as yet, show no signs of being eager to set out for Pinto Horse Butte. They are making the rounds of the Police barracks, socializing with their new chums who enjoy playing host to them, enjoy basking in the esteem the Indians show them, and rewarding that esteem with dainties and delicacies unfamiliar to their guests: tinned sardines and saltine crackers, gingersnaps, and hot chocolate. After overindulging in rich plum pudding yesterday, Bear's Cap was stricken with a stomach malady that left him groaning and in fear for his life. Surgeon Kittson ruthlessly dosed him with both an emetic and an enema. Kill or cure, I suppose. Bear's Cap's friends, who insisted on beholding the white man's way of healing, found the results spectacular beyond expression.

There is no prospect yet of getting out of Fort Walsh. While the Sioux remain here, so does the Terry Commission, seemingly eager to maintain the pretense that if Sitting Bull would only relent in his hostility and obstinacy, they in turn would be more than willing to resume negotiations.

Walsh's ostentatious shunning of me has spread a chill among all the Police; former acquaintances are barely civil to me. Stillson and Diehl, whom I am forced to bunk with in the wagon, are no friendlier. The Major has obviously not refrained from sharing his opinion of me with them.

Turn yourself, Bull had said. Right now, if I could go in any direction, it would be back to Benton, although I can scarcely expect my reception there will be any less wintry than it is here. I do not deserve a warmer one, having unconscionably loaded every responsibility for the ranch on Joe's back ever since riding out with Ilges for Cow Island. I would not be surprised to find him long gone, and my cattle bawling from hunger.

And Ada. God knows I have no right to hope. God knows I still do.

A brief spell of warming, followed by a cold snap, glazes the snow that had fallen on the Nez Perce as they had fled Colonel Miles weeks before, lending it a bone china lustre. It crackles and shatters under the hooves of the Sioux ponies as they gallop the last mile to Pinto Horse Butte. The wolves, the Sioux scouts, are braiding their ponies among the tipis, crying the good news that Bull brings from Fort Walsh, announcing that the holy man has scolded and humiliated One Star Terry and claimed the Old Woman's country for his own. He returns unharmed and brings his good friend Long Lance to celebrate with them.

People spill excitedly from the lodges, the women carrying little ones in their arms and on their backs. Children rush to the outskirts of the village and scale the highest icy drifts to be the first to welcome home the riders. The village's warriors, bundled up in Hudson's Bay blankets and buffalo robes, keep a more sedate, more dignified pace, although their poise is ruffled when they plunge through the crust of the snow and have to flounder and flail their way out of the banks.

Everyone gathers in the evening light, the sun tiny and orange on the horizon, the moon already up and showing the blue scars on its face. The horsemen are spotted riding hard in a jagged, zigzag gallop. The people hear them shouting encouragement to their ponies, which are throwing up rooster tails of white flakes as high as their haunches, a joyous wave of bounding ponies and flying snow, buoyed by the honour songs the village begins to sing.

Gall, broad and solid as an ancient cottonwood, waits to meet his old friend Sitting Bull. Gall would not go to Fort Walsh to talk with the Americans. His heart is too bitter. Ten years ago soldiers had tried to arrest him; when he fought back they thrust their bayonets into his body many times and left him for dead on the ground. At the Little Bighorn, two of his wives and three of his children had perished at the hands of the Long Knives. But now he lifts his voice in thanks for the news that Bull is bringing, that Wakan Tanka has given them this country, a land where there are still herds of buffalo to shake the earth, a place where the Long Knives are forbidden to disturb the winter sleep of the Sioux with the noise of bugles, the crack of Spencer carbines.

The riders end their wild dash in a spray of snow and milling ponies. Wives and children, brothers and sisters, cousins, and grey-headed parents crowd in to greet the horsemen. Sitting

Bull looks weary. He salutes Gall but does not halt his pony, simply heads it towards his lodge.

Walsh is hemmed in tight on all sides; many hands are held up to him to shake. Everyone has an invitation for him. Sleep in my lodge. Eat in my lodge. A troop of children scampers along beside the Major's horse as he wends his way through the camp. They pat his boots, tug at the skirts of his buffalo coat, begging to be noticed. At last, he pulls a funny face, the one his daughter Cora loves, and they scream with laughter, feign fear and run away.

Preparations for feasting are under way. Fires bloom in the swiftly falling night. Women butcher game, set cook kettles on the boil, put sticks strung with meat over fires. Drums throb and singers break into song. Walsh and Léveillé have agreed to dine with Gall tonight. He ushers them into his lodge where they are served the choicest delicacies: marrow soup, buffalo tongue, antelope steaks, hump, grilled venison. They wash down the rich meat with black tea thick and sweet with sugar. Each time a new dish is offered Walsh protests he cannot swallow another bite, but Gall forces more on him, and the Major tucks in with feigned gusto. Only when the last pipe is smoked, the last gobbet of meat eaten, the last cup of tea drunk, does Gall heed Walsh's protestations of weariness, and lets him go to claim the bed the old blind Santee chieftain Inkapaduta offered him for the night. The Major says goodbye to all his host's kin and to Léveillé, who will sleep in Gall's lodge.

Outside, Walsh pauses. All around him, the tipis glow like overturned funnels, their skins bright as lampshades, the fires inside sending up thin fingers of smoke to stroke the black belly of the sky. Each warrior's best buffalo runner is tethered outside his entrance, snuffling and pawing the ground. People pass from lodge to lodge, paying visits, their shadows flitting here and there. A dog trots up to Walsh, sniffs the grease and fat on his fingers, licks them, gives a cough of pleasure.

He thinks that if he had been born fifty years ago, it would have been a good thing to be born a Sioux. Jimmy Walsh wouldn't have been a square peg in a round hole here, by no means. A bellyful of fresh-killed meat, a skirmish now and then to keep the blood from going mouldy, a life on the back of a horse. Go off to some spot in the wilderness and dream up your own religion. Each man his own parson. Each man his own boss. That's what he was meant to be – Jimmy Each Man for Himself. And instead, son of a bitch, here stands old Jimmy Everyman.

Sitting Bull does not feast, does not sing, pays no visits but one. He limps a half mile through the snow to the burial scaffold of his dead son. The skeletal frame leans its shoulders against a wall of stars, holds up to the sky the tiny bundle he so carefully wrapped in his best blankets and robes against the cold teeth of winter, the lightest of burdens resting in the arms of thin poplar poles.

Bull stares up at it, feeling in his own skull the power of the hoof that left its mark on his little boy's head as if it were soft as dust, or snow, or mud, hears the child's breath growing slower and fainter in his ears.

He mourns the flesh that will never live under his hand again. Above all, he grieves that his son will never taste the sweetness of the gift his father has brought back to the people, a place here in the Old Woman's country where they can live in the way Wakan Tanka asks of them.

At Fort Walsh he had pushed down his grief with two palms, left it to struggle like a dog when a raccoon mounts its head to drown it in a stream. But now he takes his hands away and his sorrow lifts its head, gulps for breath, and howls in the night.

TWENTY-FIVE

CHILLED TO THE BONE, tired and wrung out, Case approaches Ada's house. Feeling like an old man, he stiffly mounts the steps, knees creaking, hips grinding rawly in their sockets. Rattling around for three days in the back of a Murphy wagon has taken a toll on him.

He knocks softly at the front door rather than entering the house as he would have in days past when he felt he owned that right. There's a faint stirring inside, the sound of footsteps. The door opens and there is Ada, eyes widening in surprise. "Oh," she says, "I presumed it was Joe." She takes two steps backwards, as if in faltering retreat. "You're shivering. Come in. There's hot coffee on the stove." Then, without another word, she makes for the parlour, leaving him to divest himself of his garments. Case clicks his heels together, contritely knocking the snow from his boots, pulls off his coat, and hangs it on a hook in the vestibule.

He goes to the kitchen and pours himself some coffee. The welcome was as he had supposed it would be, guarded and distant. She appears to require a moment alone to gather herself to deliver her sentence. But when he enters the parlour, Ada is on the sofa with a pile of student papers on her lap, brow furrowed to illustrate her concentration. Her pencil flies furiously over one of them. He eases himself carefully down in a chair as if it were made of glass.

"Well," she says, glancing up at him, "Odysseus returns." She makes a gesture to the papers. "And finds Penelope busy at her loom. I did not expect you so soon. How was Major Walsh? Sitting Bull?" There is a brittle brightness to her voice.

"Both tolerable," he says, his voice hedged with circumspection.

"I am glad to hear it."

"You are angry. You have every right."

Ada thinks for a moment as if weighing the correctness of his observation. "It seems I am. Joe and I have been debating whether this time you had not taken permanent leave of us."

"Ada, I promised you to return."

"Yes, you did promise. After the fact, wouldn't you say? But when a man takes flight with the frequency you do – twice in the space of six weeks – one begins to wonder if he will not finally make good his escape."

He fidgets with the cup, staring down at it, lifts his eyes to the mantel clock, watches the second hand complete a circuit. Finally, he says, "I gambled everything when I left that document with you. I need to know the outcome."

When he turns back to Ada, he sees two red spots printed on her cheekbones as if someone had brutally pressed their thumbs against them. "And what exactly did you imagine were the stakes in that wager?"

"Your regard, your affection."

"How careful you are. What very moderate words you choose – regard, affection," she whispers.

"And did you ever give me reason to presume you felt more? My every profession of love has been met with one response – you would not marry me. I don't deny you were correct to have reservations. No doubt you sensed something amiss, a shadow about me."

She considers that. "No. You give too much credit to woman's intuition. I sensed nothing in the beginning. It was only recently . . . when you fell prey to melancholy that I wondered what was at the root of it."

"And now you know," he says, with a hopeless shrug of the shoulders.

"Lieutenant Wilson."

"Yes. I may as well have killed him with my own hands."

"That you feel guilt – that is understandable. But do not overstate the case. You seriously misjudged a situation. There were terrible consequences. But could you have foreseen exactly what would happen?"

His throat is dry. He takes a sip from his coffee to revive his voice. "For years," he says, "I've wondered if deep inside me I did not want it to happen. I know I wished Pudge Wilson ill. I seized the moment and indulged my spite."

"So a wish is as good as a deed?" He sits mute. "Am I nothing to you but a judge? Well, I won't pass sentence. It's not my business to convict or exonerate you." With some heat, she adds, "You drop that confession – that so-called *statement of fact* – in my lap and go out the door. As if you wanted no part in what consequences it might have for us, wanted to blithely wash your hands of any part in deciding our future."

"I did not want any hand in influencing your decision, which I would not have been able to restrain myself from attempting to do if I had stayed. I feared I would beg you not to leave me."

"That sounds a very hollow excuse."

"I was too much of a coward to sit and watch you read that confession. The prospect of it frightened me. Just as the look on your face frightens me now."

Ada says softly, "You were not the only one, Wesley. I was most terribly frightened too."

"Of what?"

"I feared you would be too ashamed to keep your promise to return, that you would not be able to face me. You are a prouder man than you think. And so I went to the school board –"

"And offered your resignation. Say no more. You wish to remove yourself from Fort Benton. That is perfectly understandable."

"No. I requested a week's leave of absence before Thanksgiving so we could be married in Helena. I had the idea that by making this gesture – giving you what you had always asked for – I could bring you back to me. I have a superstitious streak . . ." Ada falls silent for a moment, then shrugs. "And if this silly charm did not return you, I was willing to suffer the chagrin of a besotted woman who foolishly announces a wedding that will never come to pass. But that is neither here nor there," she says resolutely, straightening her back. "You wanted a decision from me. There it is. For you to accept or not."

"Are you in earnest?"

"Deadly earnest. And if you are in earnest," she says, "you could signal it by putting a proper notice in the Benton paper." She gives him a timid, wry smile. "Nothing frivolous, nothing along the lines of seeking a woman familiar with the works of George Eliot. Just an honest declaration. If you wish to do this, do it right."

"Of course I will." He rises, feeling unsteady on his feet. "I don't know what to say."

Suddenly there are tears in her eyes. "You might promise not to leave me again. That would be a beginning."

He moves across the room, sits down beside her, takes her hand. It is cold. "Of course I will promise," he murmurs. "I swear it. But what changed your mind? After all this time?"

"After Cow Island, I thought you would never do such a thing again. And then you did, without a word of warning. And I knew your history of turning your back on things, of your failure to remain constant. Despite your promise to return I could not convince myself you would."

"I may have changed my work many times. I plead guilty to fleeing my father. But I would never desert you, Ada. How could you think that?"

She sounds as if she is speaking to herself and is surprised by what she is hearing. "A loneliness I had never felt descended on me when you were gone. A loneliness like grief. The strength of it surprised me. The truth is, I couldn't think clearly. Everything was a muddle."

Case puts his arm around her, tries to draw her to him. Momentarily, she resists, but then permits her head to fall on his shoulder. She smells of limewater perfume, both astringent and sweet. "I think you thought very well," he says. "Splendidly well. You are a champion thinker."

"I was mad with worry. My weakness astounded me." The cloth of his jacket muffles her voice. "Do you know how far behind I've fallen in my work because of you?" She pulls away from him and takes hold of one of her pupil's papers. It trembles in her hand. "Multiplication of fractions," she says. "I was in such a state – I made a botch of the lesson when I taught it. Every exercise is dreadful."

"Give all the little buggers alpha plus. I have been rewarded beyond all expectations. Why shouldn't they as well?" he says, and finally Ada smiles.

TWENTY-SIX

THE MEN FROM the East whom Collins had promised Dunne
finally arrived in Helena at the end of October: Declan Figgis,
Conor Toomey, and Joseph Halligan – the one the other two call
Priest. They all are American born. This is the only thing about
them that universally pleases Dunne. An Irish accent might be
noticed and remembered.

Figgis is short, wiry, red haired, sprinkled with freckles, and
looks to be in his twenties. Dunne would prefer an older man with
a little seasoning. Toomey is middle aged, lantern jawed, and
meaty. His knuckles are conspicuously scarred from collisions
with other people's teeth. Priest, as his nickname implies, has an
ecclesiastical appearance and a floury complexion. Figgis, the
most garrulous of the three, has volunteered that Halligan was
once a priest but was defrocked for unspecified sins. Toomey, in his
plodding way, corrected Figgis, saying that Halligan was never a
real priest; he only did a short stint in a seminary. But ever since he
was judged unsuitable for the church, Priest has been convinced
that he is damned, which is a good thing. Feeling he has nothing
to lose, he will stop at nothing. Both Toomey and Figgis are clearly
terrified of Priest and defer to him, which annoys Dunne. After all,
he, Michael Dunne, is the man Collins put in charge.

In the close quarters of Gobbler Johnson's cabin, Dunne has
noted the strengths and weaknesses of each man, meditated on

how the tools he has in hand can best be used. Figgis is a gabbler, enthusiastic to get on with the job, maybe too enthusiastic. Since Dunne insists they are not yet ready to act, Figgis argues there is no reason why they can't visit the saloons and cathouses of Helena, chafes at being marooned in the wilderness and denied all amusements.

Compared to Figgis, Toomey does what he is told without complaint. Of course, this may be because he is stupid and has no mind of his own. Dunne suspects if he wasn't there to see that Toomey behaves, Figgis would twist him around his little finger.

Priest, on the other hand, is everything Dunne can ask for. When they first sat down to plan how to snatch Case, Priest's first remark was, *Leave no witnesses*. For Dunne this poses a problem, not in principle, but because of Mrs. Tarr. If she were to see something, he's not sure that the terrible Priest could be restrained. This means Case cannot be taken at Mrs. Tarr's house, or anywhere near it, on the off chance she stumbles into a situation. She may have betrayed him, but Dunne can't bear the idea of any harm coming to her. So Case needs to be seized on his ranch, which brings Joe McMullen into play, and Dunne knows of his reputation – push him at your peril. He can be a desperate customer. Things could go awry, shots be fired, a ruckus kicked up, which would bring unwanted attention down on them. Maybe even involve Mrs. Tarr, who lives so near to Case's ranch.

Figgis refused to entertain the possibility of anything going wrong; he put all his faith in the luck of the Irish to bring the thing off. "Let's just do it!" he kept repeating impatiently.

Finally Priest, who had sat silent and thoughtful while Dunne and Figgis quarrelled, stepped in. "No, Figgis, Mr. Dunne has identified a difficulty. That difficulty is McMullen. I will solve him."

"What do you mean, solve him?" said Toomey, who constantly needed to have everything explained to him.

"I will execute him," Priest answered with a serene tuck of his chin.

Dunne marvelled at Halligan's choice of words. Execution sounded so apt, so efficient. But he needed to be sure. "It must be done quietly," he said.

"Yes," Priest said, "that goes without saying." He got up, went to his bed, removed a carpet bag from under it, took an article from the bag, and brought it to the table. Reverentially, he unclasped a fine rosewood case. It held two large knives, one with a wicked curve to it, the other, long and straight as a bayonet. "Surgical knives for amputations," Priest explained. "Plenty of weight to them but no loss of keenness. Sharp as scalpels. German manufacture. Look at the craftsmanship." He stroked the scimitar-shaped instrument as if it were a woman's thigh. "With this you can remove a limb, presto. This," he said, touching the other blade, "is the style now preferred in Europe. The handle, you see, is metal. The knife can be boiled or placed in a carbolic bath after use. It is a much more hygienic item than the other." He lowered the lid on his beauties. "One in each hand, I shall carve him to pieces instantaneous while he sleeps." Priest raised his eyebrows to his listeners. No one said anything. "Now that matters are set-tled to everyone's satisfaction, I think I will take a nap."

And that is what he did, stretched himself out on his cot and went to sleep. Priest spends many hours dead to the world. Then the tranquil man he is during waking hours becomes another. He twitches, shivers, and groans in his sleep like a dog. Dunne half expects that one of these days he will bark and howl.

As far as Dunne is concerned, if a solution to McMullen has been found, it doesn't mean the plan is watertight. Their ship could still take on water and sink. Figgis, Toomey, and Priest are city men who can't ride worth a damn. They will need a wagon to transport them to Fort Benton and to get them and Case back to the cabin. Something unanticipated might happen – in mat-ters like this it frequently does – and Dunne doesn't fancy the idea of trying to escape pursuit in a slow, cumbersome buck-board. The wagon is a fly in the ointment. It worries him, and worry leads him to ask himself if there aren't other things that he has overlooked. After a day of stewing, he tells the others he must go to Fort Benton to scout the situation one last time, to examine it for hitherto unforeseen dangers. He wants to *look for himself one last time. Just to be sure.* Figgis mutters something about an old woman, but Priest does not raise objections. So the small spark of mutiny goes out.

Fortunately, Dunne's old room in the Stubhorn has not been let to a new tenant since he vacated it two months ago. He pays for three nights and receives a promise from Dooley that he and three friends can rent it for the following week; they don't mind bunking on the floor. Those arrangements made, Dunne consults his pocket watch and notes it is now two-thirty; shortly, Mrs. Tarr's pupils will be dismissed for the day. He does his best to suppress an urgent desire to catch a glimpse of her, but it overmasters him, sends him hurrying off to the mercantile that faces the school, where he takes up a post at the storefront window.

The children spill out the schoolhouse door at three o'clock sharp. A few minutes later, Mrs. Tarr emerges, wearing a grey redingote and a bright red tam-o'-shanter. The sight of her stops his breath, drives a nail in his heart. He watches her make her way across the road, gain the boardwalk. Dunne is so rapt that he doesn't realize a store clerk has come up behind him with an armful of canned goods to display in the window. "Beg pardon, I got to stack these peaches," the clerk says, but Dunne doesn't budge. Mrs. Tarr passes by so near to where he stands that, if a pane of glass didn't intervene, he might brush her cheek with his fingertips. Then she is gone. The clerk says insinuatingly, "But I see you prefer a different kind of peach. She's the talk of the town, that one."

Dunne asks him what he means.

"Was in this week's paper. Our schoolmarm is off soon to Helena to get hitched to that fellow Case."

Seconds ago, Dunne had felt so close to her that he could have sworn the breath of their two souls were fogging this very windowpane. The clerk has to nudge him repeatedly to get him to shift from the spot.

Dunne goes to the office of the *Record* and buys the newspaper containing the wedding announcement. There it is in black and white, the date of the upcoming marriage, November 26. Several things become clear to him as he reads and rereads the announcement. The difficulties with the wagon are solved. They can take Case when he makes his wedding journey. Grab him a few miles outside Helena where there will be no one to raise an alarm or give chase. Then it is only a hop, skip, and jump to Gobbler's cabin, a safe and easy trip by buckboard.

Dunne senses an unseen hand in all this, a hand offering Case up to him before that scoundrel can make Mrs. Tarr his wife. All is not lost. Michael Dunne can see to it that that dear lady is not forever taken from him.

After a long but jubilant ride, Dunne arrives in Helena, and when he gets back to the cabin discovers a girl there, a cock-eyed, straddle-legged slut of fourteen. It seems that the minute he left to make his investigations in Fort Benton, Figgis and Toomey had disregarded his order to stay put and gone on a spree in Helena, went cavorting about in public with this rancid little whore blossom. If that weren't bad enough, they had brought her home with them and have been sharing her favours. While the girl sobs on the bed, inconsolable because he has told her she's going back to Helena *"immediate and direct,"* Dunne berates Priest.

"And you, why didn't you stop these two addle-brains from going to town and making a goddamn spectacle of themselves?" he demands. "We ain't advertising a circus. *We don't want to be noticed.*" He stops himself there, remembering the girl. Little pitchers have big ears. But when he glances over, he sees she is too wrapped up in her weeping to have heard a word he said.

All Priest has to say is, "I spoke to the young Jezebel. I did my best to convince her she was dicing with damnation. But she refused to listen."

Figgis cries, "You diddled her too!"

"Only when I saw how incorrigible she was," says Priest. "There was nothing to spoil."

So Dunne takes the rotten fruit back to Helena, to get her out of earshot before he divulges the change in plans to Figgis, Toomey, and Priest, to give them the good news that all that's needed is to wait for Case to come traipsing down Mullan Road and topple directly into their laps.

With the wedding a little more than three weeks off, Case throws himself into the ranch work that Joe had not been able to do on his own. McMullen offers no recriminations, simply turns a willing hand to whatever needs to be done. The cold sets in early and the long days they keep are often accompanied by wind and rain, sleet and snow. Case develops a dry, persistent cough, which concerns Ada, but he claims it is a result of shovelling barley, comes from the chaff and grain dust he is constantly breathing.

When Ada suggests that it might be better if they not make the trip to Helena, that they can just as easily be married in Fort Benton, he laughs and says, "Remember that you said you had no intention of being married in Fort Benton and being subjected to a shivaree, have a hundred drunks singing, beating pots, and snickering outside our door. I mean to see that doesn't happen."

Case knew what she had really been saying when they had had that conversation. If she could glide into the married state without drawing any more attention to herself, she might not have her job and pupils taken from her.

The day that Joe, Case, and Ada set out for Helena, the temperature hovers a few degrees below freezing. The sun is glassy-bright; the cutter carrying Ada and Case spanks briskly down Mullan Road, Joe behind it on his prettiest mount, a red roan that he calls "a horse fit to decorate a wedding party." The journey passes pleasantly, with frequent stops at way stations so that the travellers can warm themselves, get a meal – or in Joe's case, because he's in a highly celebratory mood, have a dram. McMullen keeps urging Case to take a little "cough killer" with him, but Case only grins and says, "Marriage is a sober business, Joe."

At the last stopping place before their destination, Joe bumps into three waddies laid off for the winter from a ranch in the Sun River country. They are headed to Helena to hibernate for the winter. One of them is an old acquaintance of McMullen's, a man known as Vinegar Rufus. Joe joins Rufus and his friends up at the plank bar and they are soon all happy with who-hit-John. McMullen confides that the lady and gentleman eating steak and eggs by the stove are friends of his who are bound for Helena to get wed. The ranch hands immediately volunteer to accompany them, to usher the happy couple into town.

So Ada and Case embark on the last stage of their journey, ribald jokes and bawdy songs showering down on them like wedding rice.

Case slaps the reins to the rumps of the horses and grimly says, "Well, I guess we couldn't dodge a shivaree. Thanks to Joe. Look at him leering at me like a Barbary ape."

And Ada laughs and taps him on the cheek with a gloved finger. "My boy's cheeks must be red with the cold," she says. "Because he's too old to blush."

The buckboard waits, hidden by a stand of pines beside Mullan Road. Figgis is on the driver's seat; Priest and Toomey sit hunched in the back of the wagon, double-barrels on the floor beside them. Every man has a flour sack in his pocket to mask his face when the moment comes to apprehend Case. Dunne is on horseback nearby, eyes fixed on the point where the trail curves behind a clump of trees. When Case appears, the buckboard will block the trail; they'll seize the villain, cut the team loose, and drive it off, stranding Mrs. Tarr. Dunne wishes it could be otherwise, but someone will find her soon enough, take her into town.

The men are growing more and more disgruntled the longer they wait, are beginning to doubt his assurances that *this* is the day. But what groom would risk a honeymoon without a bed? Dunne has made the rounds of the hotels in Helena, asking whether a Mr. Case had made a reservation for a date on or around the twenty-fifth. He told all the deskmen the same story. The gentleman in question is an old friend and business associate of his, he explained. He wants to throw a welcome party for him, but he needs to know when his friend will arrive. The Franklin House helpfully informed him that Mr. Case had made a booking by wire and was expected on the twenty-third.

The men's lack of confidence in his leadership annoys Dunne. But before dark descends they will learn that he knows what he knows.

Then they hear a tune, feeble in the distance, and cock their heads, listening intently. Dunne strains in the saddle, striving for a first glimpse of the travellers. Suddenly, four men canter into view around the turn in the road, scarves cinched over their ears, hats tugged down tight against the cold, boisterously singing. The words waft up to the watchers in the trees. "Cotton-eyed Joe, Cotton-eyed Joe, / What did make you treat me so? / I'd a been married forty years ago / If it hadn't a been for Cotton-eyed Joe." Dunne recognizes Joe McMullen among them. A cutter follows, harness bells tinkling. Ada and Case are in it.

"Dunne?" says Figgis.

Dunne holds up his hand. "Wait. There's too damn many." He watches the procession until Mrs. Tarr's red tam-o'-shanter, bright as a drop of blood, loses itself in a tangle of trees.

Priest clambers out of the wagon. Dunne feels a hand on his thigh, hears him say, "You have miscalculated."

"It's only a matter of time. We'll get him." But Dunne is not so certain that in this instance he is indubitably correct.

TWENTY-SEVEN

THE DAY BEFORE Wesley and Ada are to take their vows before a justice of the peace, Joe McMullen sallies out of Helena's finest haberdashery with a parcel of smart new wedding clothes tucked under his arm. He has given Ada fair warning, told her if she doesn't take care to swan herself up in her finest, he is going to pull every eye off the bride.

Ada had said, "Well, Joe, that won't be many eyes to attract. We're going to have to drag another witness off the street to make it legal."

Joe finds this a sad state of affairs. The way these two are getting married is like a Baptist housewarming, all solemnity and seriousness, no whoop and joy. Another face or two more would do no harm to the occasion. At least he'd have somebody to kick his heels up with.

Just then, much to his surprise, McMullen spies Peregrine Hathaway coming out of a bank. Wesley had mentioned that the young deserter had been bound for Helena when he had left Fort Benton by stagecoach, but Case hadn't been able to say if that was Hathaway's ultimate destination or whether it was simply a way station on a longer journey. Like a boy licking his lips over a tasty pudding, Joe bustles over to catch his victim unawares. "Hello," he says, "they must've emptied the jails and asylums. What the hell are you doing here prancing the streets like you owned them?"

Hathaway's shoulders give a startled hitch. His face is pale as paper; Joe notes that he's lost the brick-red colouring life in the outdoors had given him in his days as a policeman. He must be working under a roof now. "I am employed in Helena," says Peregrine, doing his best to cover his discomposure and muster a full supply of dignity. He jerks his thumb in the direction of the bank. "There."

"I might have guessed it from the look of you," says Joe. "Ain't you the very vision of bankerdom. Celluloid collar and all. I knew you was going to pull yourself high in the world, but I never thought you'd go so lofty as to sit atop a mountain of gold."

"It's a very humble position," says Hathaway defensively. "I'm being schooled in the business."

"It's a tough trade," concedes Joe, "taking the widow's mite and turning it into a dollar for the boss. But harden your heart – you'll make a success of it yet."

"Well, yes . . ." Hathaway casts his eyes from side to side as if seeking an escape route, but McMullen seizes his arm and begins to propel him down the road, saying, "But all work and no play make the banker a dull boy. Come along and take supper with some old friends at the Franklin House. If Ada and Wesley was to learn I didn't bring you to say howdy-do, they'd beat me like a rented mule."

"Mr. Case and Mrs. Tarr? Here?"

"Mrs. Tarr's her name for today." Joe winks. "Tomorrow she changes it to Case."

"You don't say!"

"I do say. And they're short a witness for the wedding. So far there's only me to stand up with them. How's your spelling?"

"Beg pardon?"

"They need someone who can write his own name without

chewing his tongue off when he does it. Let me put you to the test. Spell me Peregrine."

"Mr. McMullen, surely you aren't serious."

"Hathaway, you are the sweetest, most innocent thing. Being a banker ain't changed you a bit, has it?"

When supper begins, Hathaway is blanched white with mortification. Surely Mr. Case views him with contempt for the irresponsible way he evaded his obligations to the Police. He is embarrassed for his drunken display the last time he saw Mrs. Tarr. But when not the slightest hint is made of how shamefully he had behaved, and when both she and Mr. Case question him with genuine interest about his prospects at the bank, little by little he grows more at ease and expands on his new life. Several times during the course of the meal Mrs. Tarr actually leans over, smiles, and pats him fondly on the knee as if to say, Well done. You've sailed through a dark patch. We are proud of you.

Hathaway is so pleased with his reception that when he notices that Mr. Case is looking a little listless, appearing to flag, he orders two more bottles of wine to keep the party going. But no sooner is the first bottle uncorked than the groom-to-be is rocked with a spasm of coughing, and, once it has ended, begs to be excused. "I'm feeling a little out of sorts. But please, don't let me spoil the occasion. Carry on, enjoy yourselves."

"Wesley," says Mrs. Tarr, beginning to stand.

"I just feel a little tired and very warm," he says, motioning her to keep her place. "They overheat this dining room. Truly, it's nothing. Stay and have another glass of wine with our friends, my dear."

But when Case is gone, she cannot conceal her anxiety, and this puts a pall on the general mood.

"Go on up to him," McMullen finally urges her. "No need to hang about here."

"I'm sure he's fine, but if you don't mind –" Ada swallows the last of her wine, rises with napkin clutched in her hand, and carries it away with her in a state of worried abstraction.

By midnight, Case is shaking with chills. No matter how Ada piles the blankets on him, he complains of being cold, says that every breath he takes slides a painful blade between his ribs. Both of his cheeks are flushed a hectic red, and he is racked with fits of coughing. By morning, he is burning with fever. Ada summons Joe and sends him to find a doctor. By the time McMullen returns with a physician, Case is delirious.

The diagnosis is pneumonia. "I will apply a linseed poultice to the affected side," the doctor informs Ada. "And it is imperative his temperature be lowered. See to it Mr. Case is sponged hourly. A little Dover's powder should help him sleep. When he wakes, dose him with brandy in milk. That will stimulate the action of the heart."

Ada merely nods. She does not inquire what Wesley's chances are. She is terrified what the answer might be.

Dunne senses things slipping out of his grip. Since the fiasco on Mullan Road, Figgis has grown ever more saucy and disrespectful. He hands Dunne the same looks his father used to, as Mr. Hind used to, as Mr. McMicken used to – the face you show to a soft-brain. Worse, Figgis encourages Toomey and Priest to treat him likewise. When Dunne asks how could he be expected to know that Case would fall in with other travellers, Figgis retorts that's not the point. And he doesn't say it to him, but directs his comment to Priest and Toomey. "Some carpenters measure twice and cut once, but Mr. Dunne is a carpenter who measures and measures and measures and measures. A board is safe with him. It ain't never going to feel the saw's teeth" is what that scoffing bastard says. And Toomey giggles. And Priest contemplates his white hands and long, shapely fingernails as if he were admiring a string of pearls.

"There's time yet," Dunne replies.

Of course Figgis jumps on that. "Same answer you give Priest on the Mullan Road. I suppose there's time according to your calendar. One thing is sure. I ain't going to need to tell my grandchildren about this exploit. They'll be here to see it."

Dunne lies awake all night, reheating Figgis's insults, seeing again the scum of derision on his face. He knows he must assert himself, regain control. He must *general* them. Generals search the terrain for opportunities. They construct a strategy from *facts*. This is what he will do.

Next morning, he saddles his horse and heads off to Helena to survey the ground. These are the facts he winnows after he pays a visit to the Franklin House and takes a prowl about the premises. Case is quartered in room number 208, at the end of the hallway near a door that gives access to a fire escape. The door is secured from the inside by a flimsy hook. The fire escape descends to a narrow alley. The alley is shadowy and dark. Only by peering directly into its mouth could anyone make out a wagon parked there.

Better still, when he asks the man on the desk if Case is in, he is told, "Yes, but he's not to be disturbed. We don't even clean his room. He's caught some ailment or other." This is cheering news. With Case an invalid, it seems that they will have only one able-bodied man to deal with, in the person of Joe McMullen.

When Dunne gets back to the cabin he states his plans with the authority and confidence of a true commander. This is the situation. This is what we will do.

But when he finishes, he sees the dunderheads haven't understood. No one congratulates him, no one even asks a question. Toomey gently stirs his coffee as if it were a cup of blasting oil. Priest looks up at the ceiling as if he expects to see the sun shining down on him from there.

Abruptly, Figgis says, "We took a vote. We ain't taking orders from you no more. You dilly and dally like an old woman. When we snatch Case, Priest's in charge."

To no one in particular Priest says, "'Let this cup pass from me.' I do not want it, but I bow to the wishes of the majority."

"Oh no you don't," says Dunne. "This is my show. From the start. I give Collins the idea. Collins put me over you."

"Collins ain't here," says Figgis. "He don't know you for the muddler we know you for."

Priest says, "No need to humiliate Mr. Dunne, Figgis. Tomorrow we will accomplish this thing and we will all be friends again. Won't we, Mr. Dunne?"

Dunne says, "Nobody is running this but me."

Priest gives him a cleric's understanding smile. "Mr. Dunne, you do not have the temperament of a man of action. Certainly, once we get this Case fellow, you can take care of the other arrangements – set things up with the young gentleman at the bank to approach Case's father, see to details concerning the delivery of the money. We all appreciate your acuity in such matters, but in matters where physical risk is involved you have proven most hesitant."

The general has been deposed, his insignia ripped off him. He has been broken to the ranks. His eyes sting with the shame of it.

For thirty-six hours Ada has hovered by Case's bedside. Joe has volunteered to share the nursing, urged her to catch a little shut-eye, eat a scrap of food now and then, but she won't listen, not to a word of sense. When he scolds her, she says there's no point in eating, food sticks in her throat. There's no point trying to sleep. As soon as she drops off, the silence jolts her awake. If she can't hear the creak and whistle of Case's breathing, she fears the worst.

For the past twelve hours, Case has been hacking up rusty-red phlegm. The doctor won't commit to whether this is a dire sign or not. All he will say is, "It is not unusual." Ada sponges Case diligently, but the fever still rages. The doctor says, "It is not unexpected." Nothing is surprising or significant to him. Ada says to Joe that if Wesley were to levitate and fly about the room, the quack would purse his lips and sagely observe, "It is not unheard of."

Joe feels almost as much apprehension about Ada's state as he does about Case's. Several times he has seen her teeter from dizziness, snatch a piece of furniture to keep upright. Morbid thoughts possess her. Holding Case's hand while he mutters delirium-scrambled words, Ada says bleakly, "I knew it would all go wrong if I married him. And now it has."

"Maybe you ain't noticed, but you ain't married to him yet. So what you said don't follow. And don't say it again because I don't care to hear hopeless talk coming out your mouth. He ain't going to die. If the angel of death wants Wesley Case, he's going to have to wrassle you for him. I put my money on Ada Tarr. Why, you'd chew the feathers off that angel's wings and spit them in his face, wouldn't you?"

Ada rewards him by forcing a weak smile to her lips. "I suppose I would."

"But angel-wrasslers got to keep their strength up. So why don't you go downstairs, have a bowl of soup, a piece of bread and butter? Sit quiet for an hour," he coaxes.

"Perhaps," she says, uncertainly. For the first time, Joe sees her tempted to follow his instructions.

"Not perhaps," says Joe. "Do it." He takes her to the door and gives her a gentle shove into the corridor.

Ada drifts off down it, one hand trailing along the wall, feeling her way to the stairway like a blind woman. She calls back to him, "Don't forget to give Wesley his Dover's powder! At five o'clock! Ten grams in warm water! Make sure the water's warm, Joe!"

But when Joe examines the vial of powder, there's nothing left in it but a skim of dust. That she has overlooked how low she was running on medicine testifies to how dazed she is by exhaustion. McMullen glances at Case, who, for the moment, seems to be passing a tranquil spell. Knowing how Ada would upbraid herself for her negligence, he decides to dash out and get more medicine. A ten-minute errand, and Ada will be none the wiser.

Dunne, Toomey, Figgis, and Priest are headed for the Franklin House crouched in the buckboard like refugees fleeing the sack of a city. Dunne is grateful the soft grey light of late afternoon is guttering out and that there is so little traffic on the roadways.

Saloon and shop lamps are already lit against the encroaching darkness. Condensation on the windows diffuses the light cast on the street in a jaundiced blur. A man Dunne recognizes steps into one of these yellow pools. He gives a tap to Priest's shoulder and points him out. "McMullen," he says. "There's some luck. We move fast, we can carry off Case while he's out."

All Priest says is, "Whatever arises, we will manage."

But Toomey, who has been assigned to drive, has trouble manoeuvring the wagon into the tight confines of the alley. Precious time is lost while he clumsily gees and haws the horses into place. Dunne is halfway up the fire escape before Figgis and Priest even clear the wagon box. With a stiff jerk of a crowbar he pops open the door just as they join him on the landing. The three men pause to pull on their hoods. Dunne squints through the eyeholes of his, peers into a corridor stained with snuff-coloured shadows. No one is in sight. Priest gestures to Figgis, who has the role of lookout, and he tiptoes to the end of the hallway, positions himself at the top of the stairs that lead down to the lobby. Priest and Dunne move to the door of Case's room. Priest's arms are crossed at the small of his back. Each fist grips a surgical knife.

"No harm to the woman. Whatever happens," Dunne insists, voice muffled by the sacking covering his face.

Priest gives a little hitch to his shoulders and says, "If you would open the door, Mr. Dunne. My hands are occupied."

Dunne slowly turns the knob. His right hand is inside his jacket, resting on the grip of his Schofield. Priest's eyes gleam hungrily in the holes of his hood. If Priest menaces Mrs. Tarr in any fashion, Dunne is prepared to blast his brains to smithereens.

Dunne can breathe again. There is only one occupant, Case, lying insensible, barely conscious on the bed.

Holding up the knives as if he were lifting steel candles to light the room, Priest intones, "Dress him."

That's easier said than done, but Dunne gets Case's clothes on him, his feet stuffed into boots, his arms through coat sleeves. For seconds at a time, Case is aware of being manhandled, mumbles fitful protests. At last, Dunne slings the sick man's arm over his shoulder, steers him out of the room, and begins to drag him down the stairs, Case's boot toes clattering on the steps. Priest follows, knives once more tucked behind his back.

The instant the victim is bundled through the fire escape door and Dunne and Priest are clear of the scene, Figgis strides quickly down the corridor, ducks into Case's room, and starts rifling drawers. It will take Dunne some time to get their unwieldy prize down the stairs and stow him in the buckboard. He suspects a man like Case has something of value lying about, money, maybe a gold watch.

Figgis has his head buried in the wardrobe when McMullen steps into the room. Joe is baffled. What is Case doing out of bed? Why is he rooting around looking for clothes? "Wesley?" he calls out. The shoulders flinch, the head snaps around. He is confronted by two black eyes staring out of a white sack, sees a hand creeping to a pocket.

Joe drives at the man. Figgis's revolver barely clears his pocket before McMullen clamps down on the wrist, pins it to the wall, and sinks his teeth into the arm. Figgis gives a groan, shudders, the revolver falls to the floor. Joe heels it away, sends it skittering under the bed. With his other hand, he claws at the hood; a finger hooks in an eyehole, he gives it a wrench, feels the cloth rip. Figgis is flailing at him with a water pitcher. Battering him with desperate blows to his spine, trying to pop open the jaws locked on his arm. Each time one thuds into his body, Joe's nostrils whistle pain. But he stays clamped on the muscle, grinds it in his teeth, tries to burrow his hand between the trespasser's legs, latch on to his privates, give them a good mauling. But the intruder keeps switching his hips from side to side, dodging the attack.

The pitcher cracks hard into the side of Joe's head and shatters in a shower of crockery; his legs turn to aspic and sag. Figgis bucks them both off the wall, sends them reeling across the room, banging into furniture, ricocheting off walls. They trip on the threshold of the doorway and crash heavily to the floor in the hallway. The impact bounces Joe's teeth off their hold on the arm and he discovers himself lying face to face with a carrot-top son of a bitch whose skin is covered in fly-shit freckles.

Figgis lurches to his feet, injured arm dangling, pitcher handle still clutched in one hand. He eyes the fire escape. But Joe is blocking the way, still on his hands and knees, crouched, bristling, one foot weakly pawing the floor for a purchase to help him rise. Suddenly, he makes a scuttling crab-like rush at the interloper, swipes at his ankles, and Figgis turns tail, flees for the lobby.

Joe shouts after him, "Where's Case? What you done with him?"

If there's anyone in any of the rooms lining the corridor, they don't dare stick a head out to investigate the commotion. Joe's ears are still ringing from the blow to the head. He crawls to the door of Case's room, pulls himself up on it, but his legs sag under him. He waits a few moments and then he staggers to his own room, buckles on his pistol belt, shuffles down the hallway, and, clinging to the banister, eases himself down the staircase, step by step, to the lobby.

The deskman shrinks a little when he sees the livid, swelling knot on McMullen's head, and faces a blunt question. "Mr. Case been down today? You seen him?"

"I have not. You mean to say he's recovered?"

Joe ignores the inquiry. "A red-haired fellow came through here just now. Which way did he go?"

The deskman is severe and disapproving. "I can't say. But he was going like blazes. This is a respectable hotel. We don't tolerate rows. We had to put that fellow out of here once before. If he's an acquaintance of yours, I'd ask you to entertain him elsewhere."

Past the desk, Joe can see Ada at a table in the dining room. She has fallen asleep in her chair. Without removing his eyes from her, Joe says, "He's a stranger to me, but you seem to know him. What's his name?"

"I don't know his name," the deskman snaps. "All I know of him is that he and another stranger brought a local girl in here for supper one night – a girl who don't belong in the Franklin – and we had to ask them to leave."

"What's the girl's name? Where can I find her?"

"There's no welcome for girls like her here. So don't get any ideas about bringing her into this establishment for a frolic because –"

When McMullen swings his furious eyes back on the deskman, they stopper his words like a cork smacked into the mouth of a bottle. "You talk a lot but you don't talk what I want to hear," says Joe. "I said, what's the girl's name? Where do I find her?"

"Betsy Eberhardt. She's touched in the head. Came in here with those two fellows and had about a dozen different-coloured ribbons in her hair and was wearing men's galoshes –"

"I ain't interested how she bedecks herself. What I want to know is where do I find her."

425

"Lives with her granddad," the deskman says primly. "They got a shack behind the blacksmith's shop on this very street, eight, nine doors down to the right."

Joe glances back to Ada, still nodding in her chair. She'll stir soon. He consults the clock on the lobby wall. Ten minutes short of five. "If Mrs. Tarr comes out the dining room before I'm back, try to delay her from going up to the room. I need to get somebody to keep her company."

"It's not in my place to interfere with a guest," says the deskman.

"Do what I tell you," says Joe, "or I'll be interfering with you."

He goes out of the Franklin; his legs are still shaky as he crosses the street to the bank. Peregrine is behind his teller's cage, counting cash. When he sees Joe moving unsteadily towards him, his fingers rise from the bills and flutter about his waist. "Mr. McMullen, whatever is wrong? Don't tell me that Mr. Case –"

"No he ain't dead. But you're needed. Now."

Peregrine doesn't hesitate, quickly gathers his coat and hat. The other tellers look up from their work; the manager rises from behind his desk to protest, but before a word clears his throat, the two are out the door.

Walking quickly towards Franklin House, McMullen sketches for Peregrine what has happened, gives him instructions to break the news to Ada and to afford her all the comfort he is able to give. He has business to attend to regarding the red-haired man, but will be back as soon as he can.

The shack behind the smithy looks like an apple crate. It doesn't even have a window, but the chinks between the rough planks ooze a little light. Joe raps on a door hinged with old boot soles. The girl who answers is a little mite of a thing with a rat's nest of sandy hair and eyelashes so pale at first he thought she had none at all. Despite the time of year, she is bare legged and wears a thin cotton dress. But she's bright and cheery enough. "Hello there, mister!" she cries.

"Miss Eberhardt, I'd like a word."

"Do come in," she says. "In the dark, I get lonely."

The shack is a dismal place, reeking of a slop can in the corner, and so cold that Joe can see his breath. There's a rusty unlit stove and a coal scuttle holding a few tiny chips of coal hardly bigger than his thumb. Betsy Eberhardt apologizes for the chill. "I don't light a fire till Grandpa gets home. The black-smith lets me pick through the scraps of coal that fall by his forge." She displays two small grimy paws and laughs heartily. "See! I just done harvesting!"

"Well," says Joe, "I'm lucky to find you home then."

"Let's visit," says Betsy, as if he's some old family friend.

"I met your red-haired gentleman today," says Joe.

"Was Mr. Figgis in town?" she says, giving a delighted clap of her hands. "Why ever didn't that blamed rascal come see me?"

"I reckon he would have liked to but he was occupied."

"Was Mr. Toomey with him?"

"I didn't see Mr. Toomey."

"They're rivals," Betsy confides. "First Mr. Figgis wanted to marry me and then Mr. Toomey did. I say, let them fight it out between them."

"That's a good policy," Joe concedes.

"It's how I operate," Betsy says, doing her best to look coy and fetching.

"You was surprised Mr. Figgis was in town. I guess that means he hangs his hat elsewhere."

"He got a nice little cabin up in the hills. About five miles from here. Well, it ain't all his – he shares it with the other three fellows. They invited me to visit."

"Four men, you say?"

"Yes, Mr. Figgis, Mr. Toomey, and a man they call Priest. I think he's sweet on me too, but I don't think priests is allowed to marry. And then the one who shooed me out of there, that blasted Mr. Dunne." She wrinkles her nose. "Him I wouldn't marry for love nor money."

McMullen asks, "Could I take a chair, Miss Eberhardt?"

"Yes. But we only got two. When Grandpa comes home, you got to give it up."

Betsy busies herself dragging the second chair out of a corner and up to the table. He lets the name Dunne sink in his mind, settles his breathing as she watches him with naked curiosity. "I'd like to pay your friends a visit too," he says once he has recovered his coolness. "I wonder, could you tell me how to get to their cabin?"

Betsy launches into directions, but they're so haphazard and mingled with chatter about how smitten the men in the cabin are with her, how jealous they are of each other, that by the time she's finished Joe has only the vaguest idea of where they're roosting.

"Miss Eberhardt, do you think you could make me a map?"

"I could, but there ain't no paper nor writing things here."

Joe considers for a moment, then takes out one of the handkerchiefs he bought for the wedding. "Maybe you could take a bit of coal and draw on this."

"Oh, that's too fine and pretty a article to dirty up!" Betsy exclaims.

"I got another in my pocket," he says. "Picture me a map and the other's yours."

Delighted by the promise of a gift, she works away, twisting a lock of hair around her finger, giving him directions as she draws. "Right here is the roofs of Helena. You follow Mullan Road out of town about half a mile to this here stream," she tells him, scribbling a wavy line on the cloth, "cross over it – it ain't deep enough to get your feet wet – and move thisaways into the hills," she says, making peaks and then laying down an arrow over top them. "Keep headed this direction maybe three more mile and soon enough, there you are, you've found it!" she cries triumphantly, slapping down an X on the cloth to mark the cabin. Finished, the map is a crude reference, but together with the information she's supplied, Joe thinks he has a chance of finding the cabin.

McMullen places the other handkerchief on the table under Betsy's admiring eyes and tells her he best be on his way.

"When you visit them boys you tell them they better come round and see Betsy soon. Tell them they ain't the only fish in the ocean!"

"I'll do that."

Betsy follows him to the door. "Mister, how old are you?"

"Me?" says Joe, taken aback. "I'm fifty-four next birthday."

Betsy thinks long and hard. "You're nice, but I guess you're too old. I reckon Figgis is a better age for me."

"Yes," says Joe, tips his hat to her and departs, feeling the throb in his bruised back and head. Maybe I am too old, he thinks, there's a time I wouldn't have felt a beating so. Taking the vial of Dover's powder out of his pocket, he shakes a little into the palm of his hand and licks it up. He needs the opium to help his body do what is required of it now.

It's a sorry, lamentable sight that greets Joe at the Franklin House. Hathaway is pacing the room in a frenzy. Ada sits on the bed, back bowed, face slumped in misery. She throws him an accusing look. "Why did you leave him, Joe? What were you thinking?"

McMullen wants to keep her from heaping blame and recrimination on her own head for running short on Dover's powder. "I had to answer a call of nature," he lies. "Gone but a few ticks. But I seen one of them."

She shakes her head in disbelief. "Whoever are they? Whatever can this be about?"

"I ain't certain. But there seems to be four involved. Dunne is one of them."

For a moment Ada sits motionless, a little bit of a sparrow frozen to a winter branch. Then she stirs, passes her hand over her forehead slowly. "Yes. Dunne," she says in a feeble voice. "I see it."

"We must go to the sheriff," announces Hathaway, aglow with resolve. "These fellows must be made to feel the full weight of the law."

"No," says Joe, "I don't want no posse made up of saloon scourings and halfwits blundering about in this. No sheriff calling out to Dunne to surrender his prisoner and give himself up. There ain't no predicting what he'd do faced with that."

Ada speaks with quiet desperation. "You're saying his intention is to murder Wesley. Is that it, Joe? Is it?"

"I ain't about to try to read his mind. But if all he wanted was Wesley dead, he could have attended to that directly, right here in this room. Instead, Dunne hauled him off. And I'm going to get him back."

"Yes," says Hathaway, "I see what you're thinking. Fall upon them as they fell upon Mr. Case, without warning – effect a swift citizen's arrest. I agree. Give me a moment to collect my revolver, Mr. McMullen, and we'll be off."

"You ain't going. You're staying here to look after Mrs. Tarr."

Peregrine bridles. "If you doubt my courage, Mr. McMullen, I assure you it will not fail. I would give my life for Mr. Case."

"I don't doubt that. But I'm better suited to what needs doing. I got no scruples," says McMullen. "You're a good boy, Peregrine, and scruples might get underfoot and bring us down." He passes the handkerchief-map to Hathaway. "This is where they're supposed to be at. Give me three hours. If I ain't returned by then, fall back on the law. Tell them there's four of them."

Suddenly, Ada says, "There's another way, Joe. The two of us could go in the cutter. If I were there, I might be able to reason with Dunne."

"Never. Get that out your head."

"I know him. If I came with you, if I appealed·to him – I think it might stay his hand."

"He ain't the only one, Ada. There's three more. I ain't walking you into that. Understand?" He attempts an encouraging
smile. "I'll be fine. My granny foretold I was going to die in a bed.
I walk out of here right as rain and that's how I'll come back."
McMullen hesitates, then declares, "And when I do I'll have Wesley
with me. I swear it." He stands looking at her, willing his words
to sink in. But there's no change in her stricken face, no sign she
believes him. So Joe quickly sidles through the door, feeling the
weight of a vow he's not sure it's in his power to keep.

TWENTY-EIGHT

DUNNE HAS CONSIDERED IT from all sides. There's no gain-saying it; Collins, as his contribution to the enterprise, has hung three millstones around his neck. Figgis, the lookout, bungled his job, made a dog's breakfast of it. He brags he smashed McMullen's brains to jelly, left him as good as dead, but Dunne knows a lie when he hears it. Figgis lost his hood and was *seen*. And he won't admit the damage he has done to the undertaking. He just frets and whimpers over his chewed-up arm. "A dog bite ain't noth-ing to a man bite," he says. "They infect up terrible. I got to see a doctor right quick or I'll lose it." Dunne knows Figgis. Sooner or later he'll take himself off to Helena seeking medical atten-tion. That can't happen.

Case is chuffing like a steam locomotive, is hot as a tin stove-pipe, his lips are turning blue, and it all falls on Michael Dunne's shoulders to preserve this valuable property. Nobody else will lift a finger to help. He asked Priest to take a turn caring for the unconscious man. All he said was, "Oh, Mr. Dunne, I'm not like you. I lack the motherly touch." Then he laid himself out on his bunk and dove down into sleep, began mumbling. Dunne catches a word here and there dropping from his lips. Priest is dreaming the Rosary.

Toomey is outside keeping watch. He's lit a roaring fire that is shooting up sparks like Bangalore rockets and flapping flames sky high, a beacon to attract any passerby. Dunne went out and told him to extinguish it, but Toomey said, "It's cold enough to freeze the balls off a brass monkey out here. If you think I'm putting this out, give it another think, Dunne."

He has given it another think. That fire will soon be out.

If people won't listen to common sense he must do what he must do.

The scrape of chair legs on the floor interrupts Dunne's glum thoughts. Figgis is headed to the door, arm dangling like a wounded wing, face full of self-pity.

"Where you off to?" Dunne asks.

"To take a crap, if it's any of your business."

The door closes behind Figgis, and Dunne glances over to Priest, Hail Marying away, oblivious to the world. Dunne fetches a cool compress for Case's forehead, smoothes and pats it down in place. Then he collects his tools.

Outside, he throws his eyes to the sky. There's a breeze trundling sacks of cloud westward. The moon is full, a brimming basin of the purest, whitest milk. For an instant, a passing cloud curdles its surface, blighting the land in shadows, but then the moon reappears and fills the snowy clearing with a shimmering blue radiance. It sketches the trees against the sky in inky scratches. Padding along, Dunne sniffs the air. It smells of new snow.

When he jerks open the privy door, the moonlight swarms into the cramped space, turning Figgis's surprised eyes greener than grass, causing the smouldering red of his hair to suddenly blaze. Dunne sweeps away the fire with a single stroke of the curved surgical knife, uncapping the skull. Figgis topples over on his side, soundlessly, ankles shackled in his lowered trousers. Dunne chops at the fallen body until it disintegrates, falls to pieces smoking in the cold air.

Breath gone, Dunne backs out of the charnel house of butchered meat. *That*, he thinks, *got out of hand.* The trees crowding the cabin rub their branches together in a low, soft moan. He wipes the sweat from his neck, spelling out in numbers the word for

Figgis's new condition. There's an appealing, steadying balance, a shapeliness to the integers. Each ends in a 2. Each is divisible by 2. "12, 42, 52, 12," Dunne says softly to himself. *Dead.*

Toomey's great bonfire flares in his eyes. A hundred yards off, he can see it besieging the night, trying to scale its black walls with bright ladders. Toomey is standing before it in a grateful trance, arms extended, holding his palms to the crackling, snapping heat.

They have all lost their minds, thinks Dunne. *Every last mother's son of them.*

Priest is awake in his bunk when Dunne trudges heavily into the cabin. Seeing him, Priest scoots his back hard against the wall, draws his knees up tight to his chest, pulls the blanket up under his chin, and goggles at him, dumbstruck. Dunne realizes there must be something amiss in his appearance. Inspecting himself, he finds suspicious matter speckling his shirtfront, sees his cuffs are soaked in gore, his hands gloved in scarlet, that his boots squelch blood.

Priest is shrinking himself up smaller and smaller and beginning to mewl like a famished cat. "Shush," says Dunne, "shush now."

When Dunne lays a hand to his shoulder, Priest springs up on the bed. He seems to be attempting to scramble up the log wall, hand over hand. Dunne plucks him back down on the mattress. Over and over, Priest hoarsely jerks out three words through clicking teeth, "I adjure you . . . I adjure you . . . I adjure you –" Dunne clamps a hand to his mouth, stopping the incantation. For a moment, the well shafts of Priest's eyes transfix him; he stares down into them searching for their bottom, but all he can see are tiny reflections of his own face on their surfaces. Two Michael Dunnes, divisible by two. Then Priest begins to struggle violently, to flop and jerk, and his contortions cause Dunne momentarily to lose sight of himself.

The long-bladed knife makes its first pass through Priest as if he were made of feathers and air. His back arches; he wildly paws the handle of the surgical instrument in the same way he had frantically groped the log wall for an escape. Slowly, he slides down the blade and falls flat on the mattress. Dunne passes the knife through him four more times, measured, deliberate thrusts so he doesn't lose control of himself the way he did with Figgis. Each one, he notes, causes the Michael Dunnes reflected in Priest's eyes to fade a little. With the last thrust, they disappear entirely.

He shifts off the bed to prevent the blood creeping into the mattress from soaking his trousers, and stares woodenly at Case, wondering if his rest has been disturbed by Priest's death throes. It doesn't appear to have been. Dunne takes the corpse by the hair, drags it outside, and pitches it onto a snowbank.

He realizes the time has rolled round to change his patient's cold compress. Before he does that, he fastidiously wipes his sticky fingers on his trouser seat. When he touches the forehead with the moist cloth, Case's eyes flicker open, and recognize him for the first time.

"You," he says.

"Yes," says Dunne soothingly. "No need for worry. I'll get you through this." The look he gives him is almost fond. Dunne is remembering when Bishop Wilson had come to Stipendiary Magistrate McMicken and asked his old friend to investigate the gossip surrounding the death of his son, gossip that claimed Wesley Case should be held responsible for it. McMicken had obliged him by sending his best bloodhound, Michael Dunne, to nose around, find out what he could. And he had turned up a soldier, Sergeant Jimson, who had been witness to Captain Case's villainy. But then, suddenly, McMicken had told him to let the matter drop. Despite the stench of wrongdoing, the bloodhound had been asked to pretend that he smelled nothing and to leave the dead cat lying under the floorboards.

Dunne had had no doubts that Case's father, a man with close connections to the government, must have whispered a little something in the Stipendiary Magistrate's ear. A bagman tipped the political scales more easily than a bishop. At the time he had resented Mr. Edwin Case's interference, but now he's grateful for it. Without it, this man wouldn't be his to profit from.

Case's eyelids flutter, close. His chest resumes a tortured rasping, the sound of a file being drawn against metal. *Steam*, Dunne thinks. *That'll help.* He puts a kettle to boil on the stove.

He would prefer not to go and put out Toomey's fire. There are other things he'd rather do. Scrub the filth off him. See to the health of this man who is worth twenty-five thousand dollars. Collins deserves none of the loot. He lost any claim to it by recruiting idiots unfit for the task. The money belongs to Michael Dunne now. He feels a little dazed, a little tired, but the thought of the ransom heartens him, bolsters his will as he waits a little for his strength to return before he steps back into the moonlight to remove the last obstacle to his peace of mind.

No matter whether he finds Wesley dead or alive, Joe means to see Dunne dead before the night is over, to close those pale, shallow eyes that have no more life in them than two saucers of stale water. Dunne is careful and cautious but maybe the same can't be said of the other three. Men who get themselves involved in a crazy man's plots are likely to be reckless and loose in all their habits. Maybe he'll find them drunk, celebrating the capture, or careless in some other way that can be turned to advantage. He can't count on it, but right now he needs a hopeful thought.

When Joe reaches the stream Betsy Eberhardt had wriggled down on his handkerchief, he casts about for signs of the captors' passage, and discovers wagon tracks on the bank. Before going on, he cuts pine branches and lays them out on the ground in an arrow. If he doesn't succeed in freeing Case and it happens to snow, as it looks it might, he doesn't want a posse to give up the pursuit with the lame excuse that the trail had been blotted out. He will lead the lawmen by their noses so they do not shirk their duty; Case must have a second chance to be rescued if he fails in the attempt.

And this is how he continues to proceed, dismounting at intervals to mark the way at unexpected twists and turns. It slows his progress but he wants to leave no room for any confusion as to where to find Dunne and his crew.

After a long period of sitting silent, Ada asks Hathaway to see the map drawn on the handkerchief. She spreads it out on her lap, her forefinger hovering above the cloth, repeatedly tracing the lines and symbols of the crude drawing. Uncomfortably, Peregrine watches her do this, not daring to speak, wondering if this is a prelude to a case of hysterics. At last, Ada looks up at him, her face set. "McMullen is wrong," she says. "We need the law." She thrusts the handkerchief into his hand. "Take this to the sheriff. Tell him what has happened. Give him every detail. And see to it he gets moving."

This is not what he had expected, this sudden show of decision. "But Mr. McMullen said to wait three hours before going to the sheriff. He was most definite on that point," says Hathaway. "He must have his reasons."

"He was mistaken in his reasons. This needs to be rectified. There's no more time to waste. Don't delay. Go!"

And Hathaway does as he is told.

Left alone, Ada's mind whirls even faster, her apprehension mounting. She paces the room, thinking of how it is like a man to run so straight at a problem that he blindly runs by other considerations. Joe would not let her accompany him, but if he succeeds in rescuing Wesley, how is he going to get him back to Helena without a conveyance? Pack him out on the back of his horse? Without blankets? It would be a death sentence. And if she had not been in such a jangled state of mind she could have prevailed on him to take the cutter, which would make a service-able ambulance.

She finds herself at the window looking up at a huge wall-eyed moon, imagines it staring down into the narrow chasm that holds the town of Helena captive within its steep sides, searching her out.

Go on, she urges herself. *Go on. Plunge.*

And plunge she does, goes flying about the room, tearing blankets from the bed, rolling them into a bundle, tossing a small bottle of brandy into her purse to warm and invigorate Wesley. The bottle makes an ominous chink. Fearing it has broken, she fumbles her hand inside the reticule and finds the bottle is still intact, encounters the small hard object it had struck. The chilly, slippery feel of the nickel causes her to pull back her hand. Grabbing the bedding, she hurries to the stable, has the liveryman hitch the team and light the lamps on the cutter. Soon she is away, guided by the map she has burned into her mind.

It has taken Dunne longer than he supposed to gather himself. He is not sure, but he thinks he may have even dozed off for a brief time. Now the night air feels colder than it did before, gives him a feverish shiver. As he closes in on Toomey's fire, he composes his face to look friendly and agreeable. But then he recalls Priest's horror when he saw him. He must not make that mistake again. He must not reveal himself in the light. He must coax Toomey to come to him, to come into the dark. Dunne's arms are crossed behind him, the knives clutched in his hands; his chest angles forward like an old man walking into a strong wind. A procession of broken cloud troops across the face of the moon. Intermittently, the clearing lightens and darkens with its movement. Ahead of him, the bonfire is twisting up a whirlwind of white smoke beaded with flying embers. Toomey's back is to him, the crackle of the fire, the pop and sizzle of resin filling his ears. Dunne stops a few yards short of where the light of the fire madly quavers on the snow. "You!" he shouts.

Toomey starts like a hare. "What the hell you doing, creeping up on me like that!"

"Come here. I want to talk to you."

"If you want to talk to me, come here yourself. I ain't yours to order about."

Dunne makes out Toomey's Henry repeater slanted over a log, five or six steps away from its owner. A pack of cloud closes on the moon, the light fails, and Toomey cranes his neck to better see the target of his belligerence.

An image flashes into his mind of a boy sitting on a chair, facing him. *Take his picture*, he thinks.

He lets the surgical knives fall soundlessly into the snow behind his back, draws the long-barrelled Schofield out of his coat pocket. In the dim light of the cloud-shadowed clearing, he finds it no easy job to set the bead at the end of the barrel on his target.

"What are you doing, Dunne?" says Toomey.

Just as an eddy of wind folds Toomey in smoke, obscuring him, Dunne fires. Like a corpse bursting the bounds of its shroud, Toomey comes tearing out of the smoky billows. "Figgis!" he screams. "Figgis! Priest! Priest!"

Dunne is between him and the cabin, so Toomey veers to the right, heading for cover in the bulrushes that hem the slough. Dunne follows without haste. The moon has slid out from behind the clouds. Now when he lifts his pistol and aims it, the bead on the end of the barrel glistens in the moonlight bright as a candlewick. Dunne walks ten paces and fires, walks another ten and fires again. The second bullet catches Toomey just at the edge of the bulrushes, sends him floundering into them, his passage marked by thrashing cattails. Dunne fires into the agitation until the bulrushes go still. Cautiously, he steps over the trampled stalks and finds the wounded man lying flat on his back. Dunne stands looking down at what he has accomplished.

All at once, it begins to snow; flakes briefly hover above Toomey's face. Dunne watches them drift and settle on his brow; their cold touch seems to prompt him to stir. "You cocksucker," Toomey spits. "You traitor. You Judas."

Dunne wrinkles his forehead as if the accusation is incomprehensible to him. "Remember, it was you fellows threw me out. I only got one vote. What else you expect me to do?" But the stupidity stamped on Toomey's face tells him there's no reasoning with the man. So he thumbs back the hammer of his revolver and proceeds to conclude his argument.

Although Ada had committed the map to memory, when she picked up the first of McMullen's trail markers in the bouncing light of the cutter's lanterns, she felt as if she could hear Joe giving her a kind and encouraging word. The arrow directed her across the stream like a pointing finger. Without a moment's hesitation, she urged the team into the low water, the runners of the cutter scraping on the gravel bottom, the sound of hooves splashing, and then the sleigh was bucking and jolting up the opposite bank. She paused a moment for her heart to still, watched the steam lifting off the legs of the team, and then gave them a slap with the reins, sent them into a brisk trot.

All along the way, at every moment of hesitation or indecision as to which way she must take, Ada discovers more signposts revealed in the light of the swaying lamps. On she goes, the cutter rocking and slithering along the trail, the snow thrown up by the horses' hooves pelting the dashboard with soft thumps, as she hunts for another of dear Joe's messages written on the snow.

Rounding a thicket, McMullen is greeted by a strange light flickering above the brow of a hill. The location roughly corresponds to where the girl had marked the cabin on her map. It puzzles him. Such a big fire don't fit with nobody who wants to keep his whereabouts quiet, he thinks. A lure for a ambush, a snare of some description? And then another possibility hits him. Has that bastard Dunne put a torch to the cabin to burn it down around the body inside?

The thought is like a kick to the gut. A hot rush of acid climbs his gullet, scorches his throat, and settles in his mouth. He leans over and spits the sourness out. His head hanging, his back bowed, he feels the soreness and stiffness from the beating he took lodged in his muscles. "Too blamed creaky for this," he says aloud, and then the squeak of runners, the faint jingle of trace chains, the muffled thud of hooves pushes that thought out of his head. Backing his horse into the trees, he draws his revolver and waits for whatever is coming.

A sleigh sweeps round the bend, the team's heads swinging. Joe heels his roan to block the path. The horses shy, the cutter slides to a stop. Faced with a pistol, Ada cries, "Joe! It's me!"

McMullen peers hard into the glare of the cutter's lamps, then lowers the barrel of his gun to the ground. "Goddamn that young fool! Why didn't he stop you! I'll break him to pieces!"

Ada keeps her voice reasonable and level. "How did you imagine you would transport Wesley? We will need the cutter to get him back to Helena. Don't you see?"

"No, I don't. Not at all."

"The law is on their way by now. Let us sit tight."

"Waiting ain't a help – it's a hindrance. Look," he says, pointing to the glow in the sky. "You see that? It's those that took Wesley. Hard by, where I have a chance to strike them. But what the hell am I supposed to do with you?"

There is a snap in the distance. Then more, one after another, quick cracks like the flick of a bullwhip. The sound of a pistol firing.

Joe wheels his mount, goes pounding up the slope where the fire beckons with a palsied forefinger of light. Ada spills out of the cutter, chases after him, reticule clutched in her hand.

A steady, insistent whistling causes Case to open his eyes in a place he does not recognize. He has been abandoned; the chair in which Ada should be sitting is empty. Pulling himself up, he looks for the source of that annoying, high-pitched whine, and finds it, a kettle jetting steam on the stove. Then his eyes fall on bloody footprints tracked across the floor.

He remembers a hand stroking his brow with a cool cloth. Not Ada but Michael Dunne. Collecting his breath, his wits, the little vigour he has, he swings his legs out of bed and fumbles for the floor with his feet. When he stands he sees another bed, the sheets stained scarlet.

Dunne is moving delicately, gingerly through the bulrushes, careful not to brush up against them and excite their whispering. The hushed, insinuating voices of stalks and dry leaves say the same scornful, dismissive things that have been said about him all his life. Is the day coming when the birds will sing against him? When he lies in the coffin, will the earth rub its salt in his wounds?

Stepping out of the bulrushes, he sees a horse and rider circling the fire. The screen of gauzy snow obscures the horseman's features but he surmises it can be nobody else but McMullen. Indignation swells up in Dunne. They come at you from all sides, like a pack of dogs. Turn one over on its back with your boot and here is another one snarling and snapping at you.

McMullen's gaze is fixed on the cabin. Dunne starts shucking empty cartridge cases from the long-barrelled Schofield, replacing them with new rounds. The revolver loaded, he draws his Wells Fargo Schofield detective special from its silk sleeve sewn inside his coat. A piece in both hands, he marches forward.

Out of the corner of his eye, McMullen detects movement on his left, a dark blob moving through the light snow that has begun to fall, and he shifts his red roan around to face it. There's no mistaking Dunne, a tub on legs, trundling towards him like an outraged landowner ready to run a trespasser off his property. Joe sidesteps his horse out of the light of the fire and spurs it at Dunne. The roan makes two skittish jumps before she breaks into a gallop. McMullen means to turn Dunne, put him to flight, run him down. It's a cool man who'll stand firm against a horse bearing down on him full speed. But Dunne is holding his ground, his arms up at shoulder height as if he means to embrace the charge. There's nothing to do but go directly at him, knock him over, trample him, kill him on the ground.

Four flashes, four reports. Joe feels his horse plunge downward as if she has gone headlong over a cliff. The sky jerks out of sight and a smear of white rushes up and smashes into him; something breaks loose deep inside him, filling his mouth with blood. The weight of the dying horse pins him to the ground. He can see its head rising and falling, hears a bubbling snort coming from its nostrils.

"Get your feet under you, girl. Come on, come on," Joe encourages her. If he can get her to try to rise he might be able to tug his leg loose. A broken bone is grinding in his thigh, flashing pain up his spine. Jarred out of his hand by the fall, his revolver glistens several feet out of reach. The horse makes an effort to rise, then quivers like a plucked string and goes absolutely still. Suddenly Dunne is looming over him, wearing the hazy, perplexed look of a man with too many things on his mind.

McMullen says to him, "I reckon this is better than dying behind a plough. I only wish if someone has to send me over it would be a better man than you, you black-hearted son of a bitch."

"Every time I turn around, people coming at me, meaning to do me harm. If it ain't that, they're pestering me, Do this for me, Mr. Dunne, do that. Why's everybody want something from me?" He looks to be directing his words towards the cabin.

443

"Sick people ought to have more sense than to leave their beds," Dunne says petulantly. "Now I got to put him back where he belongs." He trudges away from McMullen.

Joe raises himself up on an elbow to see Wesley clinging to the doorframe of the cabin, Dunne headed towards him.

Breathless from the long run up the hill, the sound of the four shots stammering panic in her ears, Ada halts by the fire. The first thing her eyes fall upon is a dark hump resembling earth heaped on a newly dug grave; she sees it is Joe's horse, and rushes over, drops down by McMullen's side. With strangled vehemence he says, "Go for the cutter, girl. Fast as your legs can carry you."

"Joe –"

He gestures. "Dunne. He'll be back. Get out of here."

She lifts her eyes and sees square shoulders moving towards a stick figure teetering in a golden doorway, Wesley so feeble he can scarcely stand. Plunging her hand in her purse, she rises and starts numbly after Dunne, hears Joe calling out to her, "No, Ada! No!"

"Mr. Dunne! Mr. Dunne, wait!" she cries.

Dunne stops dead in his tracks. His head swivels back over a shoulder and peers intently at her. Ada sees Wesley waving to her, hears him calling out in a hoarse, choked voice, "Go back! Go back!" Joe is yelling to her too. Their warnings gusting about in her head, she lowers her eyes, walks on, watching the clean white snow that passes under her feet.

At first Dunne doesn't trust the sound of Mrs. Tarr's voice coming out of the ether, calling his name. But then he sees her head and shoulders surrounded by a multitude of bright white flecks, swarming, the swirl and billow of her skirts. The glow on a silvered plate, an image captured in an instant, is turned to flesh and blood. And it *is* Mrs. Tarr's voice that has asked him to wait, not the flat, characterless voice that haunted him before, a voice without qualities; there is no doubting it is her voice, coloured with kindness and goodness.

Frantically, he scoops up snow, scouring his hands, scrubbing his face to make himself presentable for her, washing himself clean. *I must offer her my best self*, he thinks. *My very best self.*

He hears Case begging her to go back but she doesn't heed him. And McMullen is shouting the same to her from behind the swaying curtain of snow she is parting, but Mrs. Tarr is not listening to anything but her own heart. She does not hesitate. She is coming to him.

She is very near now, her face gleaming wet with snow, gleaming with resolution. How he wishes that he could offer her his arm and parade her before everyone who thought him worthless, lead her into his father's house, escort her into Mr. Hind's parlour, stroll with her before Mr. McMicken's wondering eyes, walk her through all the days of his life before he was loved.

She is extending a hand to him now; some small glinting gift closed in her little fist. He is humbled by her consideration, ashamed that he has nothing for her. But then love is not a balance, one thing piled against another; he knows that now.

As he reaches out for Mrs. Tarr's hand he sees a flame leap between them; it sears him with joy; it topples him.

And Ada falls to her knees beside Dunne's body, trying to pat out the fire that is wicking the threads of the hole scorched in his shirtfront by her derringer. "Look what you have made me do, Mr. Dunne," she whispers. "Oh, look what you have made me do."

TWENTY-NINE

FOR MONTHS HIS daughter had been besieging him with letters. "Please come home and pay me a visit. I am lonely for you and your stories." So, shortly after the failure of the Terry Commission to persuade the Sioux to return to the United States, Walsh requested and was granted a long leave to visit his family. The Major was as eager to see his little Cora as she was to see him. The few letters he had received from his wife were nothing like his daughter's; they exuded nothing but chilly resentment.

As he travelled east through the United States by train, news of his journey preceded him, and Walsh found himself beset by newspapermen at every stop. They swarmed him at stations where he waited for his next connection, clambered into his car when the locomotive halted to take on coal and water. In the articles they wrote, they admiringly dubbed him "Sitting Bull's Boss," characterizing James Morrow Walsh as the white man who had single-handedly brought the bloodthirsty red scoundrel Sitting Bull to heel, contrasting his success with the American failures to control the chief. Reporters pressed the same question on the Major: Who or what was responsible for the recent troubles with the Plains tribes? Walsh pulled no punches with his answers; he laid bare knuckles to politicians' faces. The blame, he said, rested with the U.S. government's habit of breaking treaties with the Indians, and with the sticky-fingered reservation agents who stole the provisions destined for the people in their care, then sold them for their own profit. These remarks plucked many sensitive nerves in Washington, and when they twanged with outrage, the reverberations were felt all the way to Ottawa. A discomfiture to both governments, he was given a good dressing-down and told to clamp his jaws shut.

But soon, Sir John A. Macdonald was once more in power. With the Liberals sent packing, Walsh believed things were looking up. Macdonald, Old Tomorrow, had created the NWMP; surely, he would take a paternal interest in his offspring. When the Prime Minister decided to place the direction and oversight of the Police within his own portfolio, everything pointed to better days for the force, better days for Walsh. He felt his star was on the rise.

But Old Tomorrow had noted the Major's peccadilloes, how he had spoken without reserve while on leave. He saw how, with a little coaxing, penny-a-line scribblers had tempted the Major to say intemperate, undiplomatic things. Walsh was cheeky, overconfident, impulsive, and naive, dangerous qualities for a man in his position.

But, for the present, there was no denying the Major's value. He did have influence with Sitting Bull. In uncertain times, this was useful. And the times were uncertain. When spring came, the Americans set ablaze the prairie wool that sustained the buffalo. By day, smoke blackened the sky. By night, raging fires danced lividly on the horizon. That summer, corralled by flame, the buffalo did not come north. The tribes above the Medicine Line converged on the last oasis of game, the Cypress Hills, threatening a bloody collision with the Sioux. The Blackfoot, Cree, Assiniboine, and Saulteaux all complained that their old enemies were stealing food from the mouths of their children. An outbreak of tribal warfare and the price of putting it down was not a cost a frugal government cared to contemplate.

Hunger also drove the Sioux to undertake forays into their old hunting grounds in Montana where a few small herds of buffalo were still to be found. On these expeditions young men occasionally helped themselves to ranchers' horses and skirmished with their traditional enemies, the Crow. A group of buffalo hunters led by Sitting Bull exchanged shots with two companies of Bear Coat's soldiers. Such incidents prompted anger on the part of the United States. Why did Canada not restrain the hostiles? If the Canadians would not or could not control Sitting Bull and his warriors, the Americans would be forced to take steps to protect themselves. So Walsh was moved to Wood Mountain, the doorstep of the Sioux. Let the braggart demonstrate he could do what the newspapermen claimed, exert a salutary influence over his bosom chum Sitting Bull. Let him stop the depredations. The transfer was a demotion in everything but name. A lonely, isolated post, a handful of men to put fingers in a dam ready to crack in a hundred places.

The following winter, famine haunted the Sioux. The children's swollen bellies were filled with nothing but wind. The women grew gaunt and haggard, the men hollow-eyed with hunger. The babies sucked their fingers and wailed. Old people wrapped themselves in their blankets, lay down to stare into the fire and die. The desperate Sioux began to slaughter their prized horses for meat. The blood of buffalo runners streaked the white plains. Nights, the wolves howled and gulped the crimson snow.

Walsh gave out all the food he could spare from the Police stores, but it was not enough. At mealtimes, women and children huddled in the cold outside the barracks, waiting for the constables to pass out leftovers. Like dogs, the Sioux fell on the scraps, licked the tin plates clean of bacon grease. When spring arrived they were reduced to snaring gophers, robbing eggs from birds' nests, and boiling soup from the hooves of the butchered horses that littered the earth when the snow melted.

Old Tomorrow knew an opportunity when it showed itself. He had no intention of loosening purse strings to feed the Indians that the Americans had foisted on him, Indians that continually aggravated relations with a testy, powerful neighbour.

He would take the starvation stick in his hand and beat them back across the border with it. The Sioux needed to understand two things very clearly: the Canadian government would never provide them with rations and it would never grant them a reservation.

Walsh was not the man to carry out this hard-faced, hard-fisted policy. After all, he had taken it upon himself to hand out food to the Sioux without government authorization. In a report submitted to Macdonald, he had the temerity to praise the stoicism and restraint the Indians had displayed during the winter of famine. The Major was far too sympathetic to the Indians' plight. Some whispered he was going native. It was no secret he had fathered a child with a Blackfoot woman. There was talk of a harem of Sioux concubines; the most notable and beautiful, White Tooth, was a niece of the Sioux chief Little Saulteaux. Walsh, it was said, had more in common with a Turkish pasha than he did with a married officer and gentleman.

Some NWMP officers, such as Lief Crozier and Acheson Irvine, complained that Walsh was asserting a monopoly on Sitting Bull so he could prance and preen in the public eye. Fame had gone to his head. By the next year a story was making the rounds that he planned to exhibit Sitting Bull in fairs and carnivals all over Eastern Canada, to line his own pockets by parading his pet Indian.

Eventually, Macdonald decided it was time to sever the umbilical cord between Walsh and Sitting Bull. The Major was ordered to the Fort Qu'Appelle detachment, two hundred miles east of Wood Mountain, far enough, it was hoped, to make it impossible for him to exert any influence on the chief. But before leaving Wood Mountain, Walsh pledged to Sitting Bull that he would request permission from Ottawa to speak to the President of the United States on behalf of the Sioux people. He would bargain for better terms. If the President would not give them, Walsh said he would petition the Grandmother to give the Sioux a reservation in Canada. He gave one last caution to Sitting Bull before departing. He told his friend he must make no decision about returning to the United States before he heard from him.

When Police visitors to the Sioux camps reported to Ottawa that Walsh had made promises to assist the Indians, Old Tomorrow concluded the Major's behaviour was incorrigible. Once again the loose cannon was careering around the deck, wreaking havoc, smashing carefully laid plans to splinters, cutting the legs out from under the captain of the ship. It was time to lash Walsh in place. He was recalled East where he could do no more damage, plunked down in his own parlour to stare out the window at a sleepy town.

With Walsh exiled, the newly appointed commissioner of the NWMP, Lieutenant Colonel Irvine, and the man who had taken over the Major's command at Fort Walsh, Lief Crozier, went to work. They paid Sitting Bull no deference or respect. Instead, they turned their attention to lesser chiefs, hammering home the point that if the Sioux wanted food and land they would get them only by returning to the States. Their children would waste away to nothing in Canada if their fathers did not take them south.

One by one, hunger gnawed loose the chiefs' allegiances to Sitting Bull. The exodus to the States began. Spotted Eagle was the first to go. Rain in the Face, who had painted himself as a skeleton and danced so defiantly before General Terry, saw the flesh melting off his people's bones and took them across the Medicine Line. The ferocious Gall, who had lost two wives and three children at the Little Bighorn, and bitterly hated the Long Knives, crossed the Milk River with Crow King to surrender to the Americans. At the last minute, when they had second thoughts about laying down their arms, Major Ilges, newly transferred to Fort Keogh, turned artillery on their village and shelled them into submission.

The only chief Crozier and Irvine could make no headway with was Sitting Bull. He still placed all his faith and hope in Long Lance; he was waiting for his friend to come back from his parley with the President. The Americans sent Fish Allison, an Army scout fluent in Lakota, to try to cajole Sitting Bull into striking his colours. But Bull would not listen. Over and over, he repeated he could do nothing until he talked to Major Walsh; he needed to open his heart to Long Lance. Then, on April 28, 1881, Bull suddenly struck out from where the Sioux were camped at Willow Bunch, bound for Fort Qu'Appelle. With him went thirty-eight lodges of his poverty-stricken people.

But Long Lance was not at Fort Qu'Appelle as Bull had thought. The chief was stunned. No one could tell him when the Major was returning or even if he would ever return. The Sioux made camp there where a pitifully few ducks and fish taken from the lake scarcely dulled their hunger. The mission priest accepted a couple of skinny, played-out nags as payment for flour. Each dawn, Sitting Bull stood on the shore of the lake, praying to the One Above, and peering into the mist as if he expected Long Lance to emerge from the grey vapours rising from the cold waters.

At last, the Sioux turned wearily back, retraced the two-hundred-mile journey to Willow Bunch. When he arrived at his encampment, Sitting Bull received another hard blow. Many more of his band had gone over the Medicine Line, among them his dearest daughter, Many Horses. Of the thousands of Sioux who had come to Canada, all that remained loyal to him now were a few hundred, many of them old and ailing.

By July, all hope was exhausted. Sitting Bull led his people over the Medicine Line and turned himself in at Fort Buford. He handed his fine Winchester carbine to his five-year-old son, Crow Foot, to surrender to Major Brotherton because he could not bear to do it himself.

The ring was finally snapped in the bull's nose. Nine days after the surrender, the Sioux chieftain and his people were loaded on a river steamer and sent off down the Missouri.

The arrival of the *General Sherman* in the growing, newly prospering town of Bismarck could not have been better timed. July 31 was a Sunday. Church services had ended, affording the godly the same opportunity to line the bank of the Missouri as the waddies, the saloon-haunters, the bummers, the wharf rats, and the paisley-vested bottom dealers of the gaming rooms. They stood squinting into the blazing sunshine as the steamer's paddles churned the silty water, its stubby prow laying a creamy furrow down the river, its funnels scattering smoke and cinders into a pale blue sky.

As the river steamer drew nearer the levee, loosing shrill blasts from its whistle, anticipation mounted. Reporters licked pencil points and passed around a flask of brandy, priming the journalistic pump; a welcoming committee of dignitaries adjusted their hats, pulled cuffs, fingered watch fobs, and prepared sober, official faces. The rowdies began to roil, prompting mothers to gather their chicks to their skirts to keep them from being sucked down into a whirlpool of swirling riffraff.

The steamer edged to the dock; mooring lines were cast and secured, a gangplank rattled into place. Ashore, hats were lifted and waved. The deckhands surged to the gunwales and returned the salute. There was much neck-craning and bobbing on tiptoes, a bit of sporadic cheering and a smattering of hand-clapping, as if the audience was urging Sitting Bull to bound on stage and commence the afternoon's entertainment.

In a few minutes, captive Indians began to appear on deck and the restive crowd quieted. In the hush, Sioux began to shuffle down the gangplank, throwing worried glances at the mob. Every onlooker was speculating on which of them was Sitting Bull. The Indians had put on their best articles of clothing, buckskin leggings with richly quill-worked and beaded cloth strips, war shirts, eagle-bone breastplates, plumed head-dresses; some had draped themselves in the Hudson's Bay blankets they had acquired in Canada. All the spectators were eager for their first glimpse of Sitting Bull, but they had no way of identifying him; no photograph of the Sioux chieftain had ever been taken. Everyone assumed that Bull, given his position, would cut the most impressive figure. But in the midst of this display of finery, it was difficult to decide exactly who was the most dazzling.

A member of the fourth estate cried out, "Which of those beauties is the Slightly Recumbent Gentleman Cow?"

A boatman leaned out over the railing and pointed. "There!"

Towards the tail of the retinue, a stocky man came limping down the gangplank in an old white shirt, blue pantaloons, and worn moccasins sprinkled with a few seed beads. His braids were wound with strips of red flannel, his shirt was streaked with scarlet, so too was his face, neck, and the part in his hair. Red was the colour of life and charity. A red border painted on the bottom of a Sioux lodge announced that all who visited there would be fed. In the hard times, the hunger times, Sitting Bull had opened his hands to his people and given away most of his worldly possessions to feed and comfort them. His generosity had made him poor. Now he had become the object of charity. The captain of the boat had given him a gift, a pair of smoked goggles, which lent him the black, blank stare of an insect. His gaze unsettled everyone it fell upon; it seemed so terrible, so inhuman that they found themselves averting their eyes from it.

Nervously, some wag yelled, "I reckon he can't take the sun shining off all these white faces!"

The boatman called back, "No, that ain't it! Old Bull got hisself a bad eye infection! He can't bear light no more'n a mole can!"

Once disembarked, the Sioux gathered in a defensive huddle as Bismarck's first citizens converged on Sitting Bull for a closer inspection. Their interpreter was the Army scout Fish Allison. B.D. Vermilye, personal secretary to the general manager of the Northern Pacific Railway, offered to transport Sitting Bull up from the levee and into the town in the manager's own private railway car. The Northern Pacific was eager to get as many inches of newspaper coverage as it could milk from the occasion. But Bull's first encounter with a steam locomotive was not a success. He did not like the hissing sound it made, and opted to ride in an army ambulance to the reception and dinner for officers, principal headmen of the Sioux, and selected invitees from Bismarck that awaited them in town.

Already, Sitting Bull's fearsome reputation was waning. He was descending into celebrityhood. At the sumptuous Sheridan House, Allison happened to mention that Sitting Bull could sign his name, a Canadian trader had taught him the trick. As the Sioux sat on the carpeted floor of the hotel lobby, smoking their pipes, Bull was surrounded by men requesting his signature. Paper was waved in his face and pens thrust at him. Stolidly, he signed for all.

When the autograph session was finished, the Sioux were marshalled and herded to the Merchants Hotel, where a lavish dinner had been prepared with a specially printed menu that guests could carry off as souvenirs. The doorway to the dining room was crammed with gawkers; every window that gave on to the street was filled with faces that peered at the Sioux as they ate their way through a five-course meal. Bull was particularly taken by something that was as novel to him as a steam locomotive – ice cream. He enjoyed it a great deal more than the great black engine, and worked his way through several bowls of it, questioning his dinner companions as to how this food could be prepared on such a hot day.

Three hours later the dinner party trooped out into the street and stood blinking owlishly in the yellow glare while the mob that had watched them dine milled around them, trying to purchase trinkets from the Indians. Fish Allison lit a cigar and shot a few contented smoke rings into the air. As he watched them unravel, a bare-headed man in a grey ditto suit emerged from the crowd, came up and spoke to him. After a few minutes' conversation, the two men shook hands. The Army officers started to shepherd their prisoners back to the steamer. Allison followed at the rear. Wesley Case stood in the street and watched them proceed to the levee.

The *General Sherman* was due to depart at seven that evening. It took Fish Allison until five-thirty to persuade the officer in charge of the Sioux to agree to permit a gentleman who had once met Sitting Bull to pay the chief a courtesy call. By the time Allison collected Case, it was nearly six. They went to a small, stiflingly hot portside cabin where Bull was sitting cross-legged on the floor with his young son, Crow Foot. The little boy studied the intruders with childish hostility. Bull did not lift his eyes, but said a few words quietly, tamping tobacco into his pipe.

Allison translated. "No more autographs."

Case moved to a bunk, sat down, leaned forward to dip his head level with Bull's. Allison shut the door and remained standing, one shoulder propped against it, ready to interpret. Case said to Bull, "Do you remember me?"

The dark lenses of Bull's goggles slowly rose and turned a glassy, unreadable stare on Case. Very carefully, he removed them and laid them in his lap, revealing hot red eyes, crusted with mucus. "I remember you. You are Long Lance's counsellor." He smiled to himself, a sad, mysterious twist of the lips. "So you have come to see the horse you said should quit running. I have stopped. The Long Knives have put hobbles on my legs. I hope it pleases you."

There was no sign of self-pity in the man's face, just a resigned, half-mocking acceptance of what had befallen him. Case wished that he could speak the Sioux language so he could better convey sincerity when he spoke. He had nothing to rely on but the hope that Sitting Bull would hear conviction in his voice. "No, it does not please me to see how you are treated," he said.

Bull received this with a skeptical look. "Then you must have come to make me admit what a wise a man you are. You said that a day would come when Long Lance and I would part

455

ways. That one of us would turn his back on the other. And you were right."

Case said, "I have come here for one reason only. To deliver a message to you from Major Walsh."

Bull's eyebrows gave a twitch. He struck a lucifer and sucked the flame into the bowl of his pipe. When the pipe was drawing steadily, he let a long wisp of smoke escape his mouth. He seemed to be readying himself to maintain an implacable silence.

Case lowered his eyes to the floor and thought of the letter he had received from Walsh. It had taken him utterly by surprise. The day he departed Fort Walsh with the Terry Commission, the Major did not exchange a single word with him. Case had believed that time would give things a chance to blow over, permit Walsh to forgive him for how he had harried Sitting Bull, and to excuse him for the wilful, self-righteous way he had behaved. He had clung to the slim hope that perhaps the Major might come to realize his interests had always been uppermost in Case's mind. But months passed and he heard nothing from him. At last, he wrote a letter of apology. It was returned with one line scrawled on the envelope: *Major Walsh still on leave.*

And when the Major did return from the East, news soon made the rounds in Fort Benton that he had been removed from command at Fort Walsh and placed in charge of a handful of men at Wood Mountain. Could anything have been a more bitter humiliation to Walsh than losing his beloved B Troop to another officer? The star of the man who had showed such brilliant promise at the Kingston School of Cavalry, who had been one of the most admired and gallant officers of the NWMP, was apparently on the wane. Those he had offended by speaking the truth about how the Sioux had been treated punished him by shunting him off to a dreary backwater. Case had no doubt how Walsh would respond to this attempt to teach him a lesson. It was not in the Major's nature to yield, or even bend.

Viewing Walsh's plight from a distance, relieved of the task of trying to temper his belligerent recklessness and prickly pride, Case was forced to concede that, intemperate as the Major was, intemperance fuelled his fierce convictions. Whatever else might be said of him, once he decided his course of action was just, he would not swerve from it, and his failure to swerve kept him mouldering at Wood Mountain, year after year. Then came the final indignity. Case heard that Walsh had been sent to Fort Qu'Appelle, a piddling, insignificant post.

Not long after that, following years of silence, Case received a letter from the Major. It arrived just days before Sitting Bull formally surrendered to the Americans. In it, Walsh detailed everything that had happened to him in the last few months, excoriating with unbridled fury the stupidity and callousness of his superiors. There was an undertone of sorrow to this anger, the grieving rage of a man impotently beating his head against the bars of a cell. Case found this moving, but also profoundly disturbing. Clearly, Walsh understood that his career in the Police was finished, but could not bring himself to make the admission on the page.

There was a downcast, humble, self-effacing quality to the letter's conclusion. Walsh pleaded with Case to go to Sitting Bull and explain that Long Lance had never abandoned him, to say he hoped his friend would believe that he had done all he could to keep his word. Case knew he would do as Walsh asked. He wished to make amends. Years ago he had tried to separate the two men. If a breach had opened between them, now he felt he must attempt a reconciliation.

Case lifted his face to Sitting Bull. "I hope you will hear what I have come to say," he said.

Sitting Bull's reply was dignified and firm. "Long Lance told me not to give up my pony and my gun to the Long Knives until I got word from him. While I waited, the rest of the Old Woman's red coats told me, 'Go. No one wants you here.' But I shut my ears to them and waited. I waited for Long Lance until I could wait no more. Then I rode to Fort Qu'Appelle to speak with him – but he was not there."

"Major Walsh was not at Fort Qu'Appelle because the counsellors of the Grandmother ordered him to travel east. He had no choice but to do as he was told. They are very disappointed in Walsh."

A wary intelligence glimmered in Sitting Bull's eyes. "And what is the reason for this disappointment?"

"Major Walsh believed he could make the Grandmother's counsellors understand that they were treating your people harshly. Even when it was clear they would not listen to the truth, Walsh would not relent. He would not leave them alone. Then they told him they would never let him talk to the President for you, nor would they allow him to ask the Grandmother to give you a reservation. These things would never be permitted. They told Walsh he must do only what he was told and nothing more." Case paused, trying to discern if what he was relating was being taken in by Bull, but the deeply lined face remained impassive. "So you see," he said, "those above Walsh tell him everything he did was wrong. But he will not agree with them. He says he did only what was right."

Bull nodded and gravely said, "So the strong-hearted horse gallops as he chooses. I am pleased to hear that. It is not just that any man should be harnessed to the wagon."

"And because he will not quietly pull the wagon where they want it to go, soon they will drive him out of the Grandmother's police. It is only a matter of time before they do that."

Sitting Bull sat quietly for some moments. Whatever his thoughts were it was evident they disturbed him. The little boy shifted nearer to his side and scowled at Case, as if issuing a warning to stop troubling his father.

At last Bull said, "Because he was my friend they do not trust him."

"Yes. The Grandmother's counsellors have long memories. There is nothing they dislike more than proud, stubborn people who will not bow their heads to them and agree with everything they say. Those who don't, pay the price. So will Walsh."

"Perhaps you believe Long Lance had to sacrifice too much for the sake of friendship."

Case thought of Joe, his crushed leg. How he struggled to mount a horse now, of the agonized hitch to his gait. He thought of Ada waking in a slippery nightmare-sweat, how she cried out, terrified just as he was terrified when he dreamed of Pudge. Ada said it was Dunne's face in the blue moonlight, the joyful look that filled it even as the life drained out of him, the strange ecstasy written there that haunted her, troubled her more than any reproachful, condemning gaze ever could. Case knew the steep price that Joe and Ada had paid to save him, was reminded of it every day when he saw Joe crossing the yard in the morning, leaning on a stick because his leg stiffened in the night, or when he walked into the parlour and discovered his wife sitting with a dazed, murky expression on her face, reliving that snowy night almost four years ago when she and Joe had come to deliver him from his captor.

Case said, "It is not for me to say whether Walsh sacrificed too much for you. There was a time I thought that when two people were on different sides of a dangerous river, they should not try to cross it. I advised him to consider his actions very carefully, not to put himself at risk. It was wrong of me to ask him to go against his nature. But now the Grandmother's counsellors have sent him to a little room in a little town. That is no place for a man like Walsh. He is very angry with the men that put him there."

"I would not like to be those men. I have seen Long Lance angry. Sometimes he was angry with me." Sitting Bull smiled at Case with gentle irony. "That is sometimes how it is with strong-willed men. They knock heads." He tapped out the ashes of his pipe on the floorboards. "I remember how in the first hungry spring in the Grandmother's country, Black Moon, Four Horns, and I went to Long Lance at the post in Willow Bunch. All the children had empty bellies. I said the Grandmother was rich and we were poor. I asked him, 'What Grandmother does not reach into her pot and give her children food when her pot is full of meat?' I spoke to him impolitely because I thought of the children crying for food in our tipis." Bull rested his hand on his boy's shoulder and fell silent for a moment. "I believe that day Long Lance was sick with the sweating sickness," he said.

"St. Anthony's fire," Case offered.

When Allison translated for Case, Bull nodded. "Yes, the Fire Sickness. One time when he visited my camp I saw how it came on him and how his body burned. It gnawed his bones. He had fever one moment and shook with cold the next. I think that day at Willow Bunch he suffered from it and it put him in a fierce mood. He answered me rudely. He said I gave him nothing but trouble. My young men stole horses from the Americans and then he had to spend weeks in the saddle looking for them. He said if I was not careful of the way I spoke to him, he would put me in irons and lock me up in jail. I did not like to be threatened that way. Before I knew it, I drew my pistol and waved it in his face. But he caught my wrist, pushed me out the door, and threw me down in the dust outside. My mouth was full of dirt and that was a bad, bitter taste to me. I had eaten too much of the white man's dirt. I started to get up, ready to kill him, but he kicked me down again. Then Four Horns and Black Moon took hold of my arms so I could not shoot Long Lance. I struggled with them against the wall of his cabin and we broke a window. I lost my heart fighting my friends and I sank to the ground. Long Lance stood over me, trembling with the Fire Sickness, shouting at me.

"I got to my feet and went away without speaking a word to him. Back at my camp, all the young men cried out that Long Lance should be punished for what he had done to me. My blood was still very strong and wild so we got our weapons and ponies and went back to show Long Lance that he must not deal with us in such a way. He and twelve of his men were standing before their post. Long Lance had laid corral rails on the ground. He shouted to me that if we crossed over those rails, he would shoot us down like dogs. That was a foolish thing to say because there were many more of us than twelve, and if he fired on us I would not be able to stop the young men from killing all the Old Woman's pony soldiers. I could see how afraid Long Lance's men were. They were ready to run.

"I told the young men to let me go alone. I had a good horse. I rode at a hard gallop right at the poles, but at the last moment I jerked my pony up, stopped just before the place Long Lance said I must not go beyond." He shook his head as if trying to dislodge that memory. "I stopped because I knew he would not have hesitated to shoot me. He would have thought it weak not to do as he had sworn to do. But at the last moment, I saw what would come of riding past the poles he had put on the ground. We could have killed them all that day, but once that was done, my people would be caught between wolves. The Americans on one side, the British on the other. And who would suffer the most? The women, the children, the old people. They would be torn to pieces by the wolves. That is why I stopped my horse." A look of sorrow settled on Bull's face. "Sometimes, I think that is when my people began to lose faith in me. They thought I did not kill Long Lance because I had lost my courage. Is that why Rain in the Face, Gall, even my own daughter decided to leave me? Did they think I was too weak, and because I was weak there was no hope for us?"

Bull's expression pleaded with Case for an answer to his questions. Even the child beside him seemed to be intently awaiting his reply.

"No," said Case, "it is because they could not bear to starve and suffer any longer. But it is also true that it is hard to see the difference between wisdom and weakness. To stop before you reached those poles, that was a strong thing to do. You checked yourself for the sake of your people."

"In the old days I would not have done it," said Bull, sounding a little doubtful, a little regretful.

"Perhaps you do not remember something you said to me that night we first met. You told me not to try to turn Walsh away from you, but instead to turn myself – seek the way I should go. That is what you did when you faced Walsh across the poles. You turned yourself away from a foolish thing and took a better path."

Before Bull could reply there was a rap at the door. Allison opened it. A sergeant poked his head inside. "Captain says all visitors off the boat directly. We set off soon."

"All right," said Case, rising from the bunk. "I will write to Walsh and tell him everything that has passed between us here. Is there anything you wish to say to him?"

Bull clipped the goggles back on and lifted himself up off the floor. His son stood too, as if he were the tiny shadow of his father. Bull stretched out two hands and clasped Case's hand between them. "If you see Long Lance shake his hand like this. Tell him this is the way I wish to say goodbye to him. His hand between both of mine."

"Yes," said Case, "if Walsh and I ever meet again, I will shake his hand exactly as you have shown me."

Bull said, "I will come with you a little ways." He and his son followed Case and Allison up on deck. All four stood at the railing, feeling the breeze, a pleasant relief from the oppressive heat of the cabin. Case looked down, watching the river insistently tugging at the sides of the vessel. Bull said, "The Long Knives are taking me down the river. No one has told me where it is I am going."

Case drifted into a reverie. He was remembering those teas at the Literary Society presided over by old Sutherland, professor of Greek. Sutherland had liked nothing better than to talk about tragedy, to define it for them, to hold forth on the different varieties of it, Greek and Shakespearean. He could fill an afternoon piling up subtle distinctions. One day, Pudge Wilson had suddenly roused himself and said, "Courage in the face of certain defeat – that's what tragedy is." It was Case's best memory of his old friend.

He contemplated Bull, who had no idea where he was being taken. A man in the grip of the river and in the hands of the men steering him down it. Next spring, maybe the spring after, Case meant to drive his cattle north over the border, to good grazing. There he, his family, and Joe would settle in a land from which Walsh and Bull had been banished. He knew that, in some way, he would never be able to shake the feeling that that country would always be theirs, not his.

Suddenly Crow Foot gave a cry, breaking into his thoughts. His finger was pointing to the sky. Case followed it and saw a red kite swooping, swinging like a demented pendulum across the blue expanse. He turned his eyes to a level stretch of bank a hundred yards off where Ada was running, skirts fluttering as she clung to the kite string; their son was stumbling after her, his hands held high as if he were straining to seize the bright red piece of darting paper. Joe, with his halting gait, was following them, shouting with glee, brandishing a stick above his head.

When Case learned that Sitting Bull was to be displayed at Bismarck, he decided that his family should accompany him there. A change of scene, an outing to a town with so many civilized amenities would do them all good. This morning he had spied the kite in a shop window and bought it for his son, Edwin. All day the boy had been waiting impatiently to see it fly, his mother counselling patience. "We need a breeze. We need a breeze," she had murmured to the boy.

Now at the end of day the breeze had come; it was wrinkling the Missouri, herding the clouds before it. Case leaned his elbows on the gunwales and watched the trio chase the wind, chase the kite, chase whatever it was they were pursuing.

Bull lifted up his little son above the gunwales so he could see everything better. The antics he was witnessing seemed to baffle the boy's father. He turned to Case and asked, "What are those people doing? What is the purpose of that thing?"

Case heard Crow Foot laugh. He saw the boy's hands were raised high above his head, that he was reaching upward, just as his own son was doing.

"The purpose of that thing?" said Case. "Joy. Nothing but pure joy."

ACKNOWLEDGEMENTS

It is impossible for me to acknowledge all of the works consulted during the writing of this novel, but I would like to make mention of a few in particular: Robert M. Utley's *The Lance and the Shield: The Life and Times of Sitting Bull* (Ballantine Books, 1993); Ian Anderson's *Sitting Bull's Boss: Above the Medicine Line with James Morrow Walsh* (Heritage House, 2000); Captain John A. Macdonald's *Troublous Times in Canada: A History of the Fenian Raids of 1866 and 1870* (W.S. Johnson and Co., 1910); J.A. Cole's *Prince of Spies: Henri Le Caron* (Faber and Faber, 1984); Hereward Senior's *The Fenians and Canada* (Macmillan of Canada, 1978) as well as his *The Last Invasion of Canada: The Fenian Raids, 1866–1870* (Dundurn Press, 1991); editor Jerome A. Greene's *Battles and Skirmishes of the Great Sioux War, 1876–1877: The Military View* (University of Oklahoma Press, 1993); Hugh A. Dempsey's *Firewater: The Impact of the Whisky Trade on the Blackfoot Nation* (Fifth House, 2002); and Evan S. Connell's *Son of the Morning Star: Custer and the Little Bighorn* (Harper Perennial, 1991).

I would like to especially thank my editor, Ellen Seligman, and my agent, Dean Cooke, for the generous advice and encouragement they have provided me over many years. I also wish to thank the Pierre Elliott Trudeau Foundation for the Fellowship which they granted me and which was of great assistance while I finished this book.

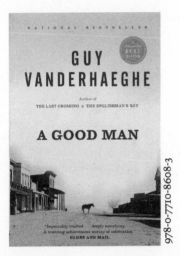
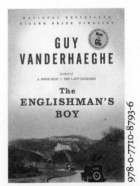
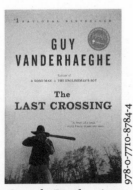

GUY VANDERHAEGHE's most recent highly acclaimed novels are *A Good Man* (2011), *The Last Crossing* (2002), and *The Englishman's Boy* (1996), which have come to be thought of as his frontier trilogy. His previous fiction is *Things As They Are* (1992), *Homesick* (1989), *My Present Age* (1984), *The Trouble With Heroes* (1983), and *Man Descending* (1982). Among the many prizes and honours Vanderhaeghe has received are the Canada Reads award, the Governor General's Award (twice), the Writers' Trust Timothy Findley Award, multiple Saskatchewan Book Awards, and the Harbourfront Festival Prize. He has been a finalist for The Giller Prize, the International IMPAC Dublin Literary Award, and the Regional Commonwealth Writers' Prize. *The Englishman's Boy* appeared on CBC as a television miniseries. Guy Vanderhaeghe lives in Saskatchewan.